MW00914022

BLOOD
AND
PARCELS

T. Q. BERNIER

Copyright © 2013 Theresa Bernier.
www.tqbernier.com

All rights reserved. No part of this book may be reproduced, stored, or
transmitted by any means—whether auditory, graphic, mechanical, or
electronic—without written permission of both publisher and author, except
in the case of brief excerpts used in critical articles and reviews. Unauthorized
reproduction of any part of this work is illegal and is punishable by law.

This is a work of fiction. All of the characters, names, incidents, organizations, and dialogue
in this novel are either the products of the author's imagination or are used fictitiously.

ISBN: 978-1-4834-0438-7 (sc)
ISBN: 978-1-4834-0440-0 (hc)
ISBN: 978-1-4834-0439-4 (e)

Library of Congress Control Number: 2013918563

Because of the dynamic nature of the Internet, any web addresses or links contained in
this book may have changed since publication and may no longer be valid. The views
expressed in this work are solely those of the author and do not necessarily reflect the
views of the publisher, and the publisher hereby disclaims any responsibility for them.

Any people depicted in stock imagery provided by Thinkstock are models,
and such images are being used for illustrative purposes only.
Certain stock imagery © Thinkstock.

Lulu Publishing Services rev. date: 11/15/2013

For my children: James Jr., Tina, and Tiffany
There is no accomplishment in this world greater
than being your mother. I am so proud of you.

*

For my husband, James
Thank you for always encouraging me to dream
and for loving me beyond measure.

*

Foremost, I give thanks to God.

PREFACE

Dear Reader,

Words have always fascinated me. They are powerful. Once spoken or written, they become immortal. They often echo through time, setting events in motion. When I was a child, my mother use to say that my head was always in a book, and she was right. Long after the lights were out, and I was supposed to be asleep, I was under the covers with flashlights, spellbound in the pages of places and people far away. When she would demand that I put away the book, the stories would continue in my head. I would conjure up my own exotic and mysterious tales until sleep overcame me.

Blood and Parcels is inspired by two past events in which I was moved by written words. The first occurred after my father's passing. I found letters from the 1930s in his files, written to him from his relatives in France. Those old letters intrigued me. These people were a part of my ancestry, yet I knew very little about them or their lives. So, I set out to learn about them and developed a deep appreciation for their journey.

The second incidence happened on a Saturday morning. I was dusting a shelf when my old high-school yearbook fell on the floor. It fell wide open to a page where one of my classmates had written about me, "One of these days I will go into a bookstore to buy a book, and guest who the author will be?" Coincidence? Maybe. Yet that occurrence touched me like no other. It stirred me into remembering my dream of writing a full-length novel, and the next day, *Blood and Parcels* was started.

While the characters and events are fictitious, the journey is real. Most of us are immigrants to this great land of America. In each of our histories, someone somewhere was inspired to blaze the trail.

I hope you enjoy reading *Blood and Parcels* as much as I enjoyed weaving the tale. Each of the characters took on a life and told their own story. Regardless of how I tried to mold them into who I wanted them to be, I never knew for sure what antics they would pull on the next page.

-T.Q. Bernier

PROLOGUE

The August heat in Marseille was relentless. Beads of sweat dotted Nicole's skin as she made her way to the Saint Pierre Cemetery, and she yearned for the cool trade winds of home. It was hot there too, but there was always a refreshing breeze. She passed Fort Saint Nicholas and Fort Saint Jean, the two massive structures at the entrance of the Old Port and the Quai des Belges, the fish market at the end of the harbor. Turning a corner, she found herself on a side street populated with outdoor cafes. Colorful umbrellas adorned the sidewalk. Beneath them people carried on lively conversations, seemingly oblivious to the stifling temperature.

She smiled wistfully. It had always amused her, this habit of French people, to have dogs snoozing at their feet while they dined. Here was no exception. As she passed the cafes, she counted at least seven dogs lying comfortably under the tables. Her mind drifted back to a tiny, French island with its flavor much like this. On that particularly moonlit evening, she had been having dinner with her husband. They were enjoying the ambiance of the fragranced, tropical night when suddenly a big, black dog had appeared from under her chair. Looking down at the dog, she'd mouthed a loud ohoooooo, which had surprised her husband. They'd drunk too much French wine. He had started to laugh, and his cackle had been infectious, consuming them both in laughter.

A group of middle school children crossed in front of her. Their animated chatter, resonant of its own French melody, efficiently halted her musing, and she again focused on her mission.

When she spotted the cemetery, her pulse quickened. Reverently she approached the enormous iron gates, and they groaned noisily in protest when she pushed them open.

It had taken days to find the location, but now, as she neared the tombstone, her thoughts were on the woman who rested there. She wondered just how many of her ancestors were buried here. Plenty, she knew. In time she would research it, but today her mission was based on only one.

She'd always known she would come. She had known, since finding the photos in her father's files, that she would eventually make this pilgrimage.

She passed several large trees, the sizes of the trunks indicating they were old enough to have been there when they had buried her. Most of the tombs and marble stones seemed centuries old.

As she walked between the tightly spaced graves, the sudden movement of a flock of birds in the branches startled her, and she paused in reflection. It was solemn yet so peaceful here.

Up ahead on a gentle slope she spotted it, and she approached with much reverence. She knelt on the grass and ran her fingers over the marble stone, tracing each letter in the name. Even in this sweltering heat the marble was cool under her fingertips. Catherine Bellemare Dusant, 1850-1933, her great-grandmother.

At last, Nicole had come full circle. She had crossed the continent and come to Marseille, the second largest and oldest city in France, to pay homage to a proud and passionate family. A family that had overshadowed her and had set the course of her own life; a family into whose fabric she is so intricately woven that to tell her story, she is compelled to tell theirs.

PART I

CHAPTER 1

"Why is it moving so slowly?"

Grumbling, Catherine lifted her skirt and ran back up the steep path between her small house and the sprawling Mediterranean Sea. The sunbeams reflected multicolor hues of brown dancing in her hair as it flowed melodiously, like the soothing waves behind her. Perspiration trickled down her back, and she wiped the drops that formed on her forehead to prevent them from falling into her eyes.

Jonah was coming home!

She had barely slept the night before, finally drifting off in the wee hours of the morning only to be up again at first light. She had bathed, washed her hair, and changed her dress three times. Repeatedly, she had inspected herself, spinning around and around in front of the vanity mirror and smoothing her hands over the cascading curls that reached her waist. Satisfied with her appearance, she'd still been fidgety. Using her father's telescope, she'd moved from window to window. When she had spotted the vessel as a tiny speck in the distance sea, her shouts of joy had resounded throughout the house. She had impatiently trekked up and down the path, willing the vessel to hurry its journey to shore.

Now cresting the top of the hill for the fourth time, she dolefully entered the kitchen. The smell of simmering onions assailed her, making her stomach growl. Her mother, Suzanne, was standing at the stove, and her sister, Marie, was sitting at the table kneading dough.

"Catherine, you will wear out your shoes if you keep running back and forth like that. It will not make the vessel sail any faster. He will be here soon. Sit down and eat something. Have patience."

"Mama, Catherine will not need patience," Marie snorted. "Soon she will have so many servants and nothing to do but to make love and babies."

"And you are so jealous," Catherine retorted, yanking Marie's ponytail.

"Owww!" Marie yelled. "You're going to pay for that, you louse! I'm going to tell Jonah how you snore."

"I do not snore!"

"Oh yes, you do," Marie taunted, making snoring sounds. "You're going to wake up the whole Dusant household with that dreadful noise."

"I am not eating that bread, Mama! Marie's slobbering all over the dough."

"Your father will be home soon. Let's not talk about the Dusants. It upsets him," Suzanne replied, stilling her quibbling daughters.

Catherine turned and faced her mother, "Mama, why does Papa still dislike Jonah?"

"Oh, he likes Jonah," Suzanne replied a little too brightly. Then haltingly she continued, "It's just that Jonah's family is rich and known for being dishonest. He worries about you."

"Well, I am not marrying Jonah's family. I am marrying Jonah."

"Oh, Catherine, if only that were true," Suzanne said wistfully.

Just a short distance away, Catherine's father, Charles, anchored his fishing boat. He had been out to sea all morning, and his back ached from lifting the heavily laden nets, but he was pleased with the results. His customers would be as well. He too had seen the vessel way out on the horizon. As he had looked up and seen it, he had fervently hoped that it would be swallowed by the sea. Immediately, he'd felt remorse.

Charles did not dislike Jonah Dusant. He just did not feel that Jonah was the right man to marry his firstborn daughter. Catherine was high-spirited and stubborn, but she was also trusting. She was no match for Jonah's passionate and underhanded family.

He finished securing his boat and hoisted the heavy, gray canvas bag to his shoulder. He had wanted a son to help him with his fishing business, but God had seen fit to give him two daughters. He was thankful.

As he started up the incline, the thought occurred to him that Jonah could eventually assist him. The deep lines on his forehead intensified. "Never," he muttered. "I do not want to entangle myself in business with a Dusant."

They were not all bad people, but there were certainly a few with whom he wanted nothing to do. They had a reputation for being ruthless, going after what they wanted and acquiring it at any cost. Jonah's father, Ivan, and Ivan's cousin, Edward, operated a fleet of fishing and trading vessels, and they traveled far and wide exporting and importing goods. They ran the business out of their estate in Toulon.

In his presence, Jonah was always a gentleman. There was just this undercurrent that Charles detected in him, even though Jonah tried to hide it. It was a feeling that, if he was pushed too far, he could become just as vicious as his relatives. That is why Charles feared for his daughter. Living among the Dusants would not be easy.

He entered the kitchen where the three women in his life were conversing. He kissed his wife and sat at the table while she fixed his breakfast. From the corner of his eye, he looked at Catherine. She was radiant. How could he refuse her this happiness? He would quell his feelings and carry on with this wedding, but with God as his witness, he would kill any Dusant who brought her harm.

A scowl creased Jonah Dusant's brow as he stood at the bow of his vessel. The shoreline loomed ahead, and the sails were full mast, but they depended on the wind which was not cooperating.

The *Louise Catherine* was the newest vessel in the company's fleet. It was a clipper ship with long, slim hulls and tall masts, and it was designed to move with speed, thanks to its enormous sails. The ship had been purchased from America by his father as a means to further increase the company's profitability. It was bigger and faster, and this meant that they could export and import more cargo in shorter periods.

Jonah had christened the vessel *Louise Catherine* in favor of the two women he loved most, his mother and his fiancée.

He lovingly caressed the portrait he held of Catherine—her warm amber eyes the color of sherry stared back at him, and the impish smile he adored played at the corners of her mouth. The vision of her was what had carried him through these past months, and now he was impatient. He wanted to hold her, and this damn vessel was taking its sweet time.

Jonah's life as a mariner was not easy. The nights were black and lonely, and the days were endless. Bad weather was swift and treacherous, and piracy was a constant threat. He and his crew were seasoned sailors, but they had gone through times when they thought they would not survive. In the past, he hadn't minded so much because there was always a willing woman in the ports he visited. That had all changed once he met Catherine. She was the missing link to his soul, and all other women failed in comparison.

He remembered the first time he had seen her. On a whim, he and his cousin, Clifford, had gone down to the local market in Marseille, something they rarely did. As they'd walked among the stalls of merchants, they'd spotted her.

"What a fine little morsel," Clifford had remarked.

Mesmerized, they'd stopped to watch her as she completed a purchase at a produce stall, smiling brightly at the elderly merchant when he handed her a brown sack. She had been wearing a yellow dress that clung lovingly to the curve of her small waist, and she'd radiated an air of confidence.

"Wait here. I am going to introduce myself."

Being his usual roguish self, Clifford had sauntered over to her and said something inappropriate. Her smile instantly faded. She reached up and slapped him hard, and then she'd quickly stalked off among the throngs of people.

Clifford's hand had instinctively reached up to touch his cheek, and, for once, he had been speechless.

Jonah had laughed at the expression on his cousin's face, but he too had been captivated. He had known many women, but none had ever triggered such a reaction. He had not even spoken to her, yet he knew he had to get to know her.

While Clifford fretted about being publicly embarrassed, Jonah had walked over to the produce stall where she had been and asked the merchant about her. The old man had been reluctant to tell him anything, only relenting when he swore that he meant her no harm. When he found her, he pursued her until he wore down her resistance. It had not been easy. She was a little spitfire. He smiled at the memory. *I believe I fell in love with her on that very first day.*

He had met resistance from both families. His family had strenuously disapproved when he told them that he wanted marry her. He had listened angrily as they said, "She's a peasant. Find a woman of your own status to marry."

He had tried to convince her father that he loved her more than life, that he would always protect her. Because of their love for their daughter, Charles and Suzanne had given in to the marriage, but Jonah knew they would never trust him.

"The whole lot of them be damned," he grumbled. One thing he knew without doubt: Catherine was his. He would marry her. She would bear his children, and he would make her happy, even if it took everything he had.

From the starboard side of the vessel, Jonah's his first mate, Raphael Greaux, quietly studied him. He had known Jonah since the day he was born. Raphael had never married. His wife was the sea, and his skin, browned and leathered from too many voyages, attested to it. He had worked for the Dusant family for more years than he could count. He had no relatives, but he considered Jonah and Jonah's father, Ivan, his family. It was in Raphael's arms that the young Jonah had cried when his mother, Louise, had died unexpectedly, his father being too crushed with his own misery to console the boy. Raphael knew Jonah trusted him more than anyone.

He had sailed with Ivan long before Jonah was born. He had sometimes sailed with Ivan's cousin, Edward, too, but his preference had always been Ivan. When the older men had turned over the voyages to their sons, he had requested to sail primarily with Jonah.

Raphael ran his fingers through his long, white beard. He might be an old ruffian, but he was not a thief. He'd had enough experience with Jonah to consider him an honest man. Clifford Dusant was not honest. On the few voyages that he had taken with Clifford, he had witnessed him practice his wiliness. He often shortchanged the traders by giving them less merchandise than was stated on the bill of lading. His charming smile belied a hardened thief. Rafael knew that Clifford sold the stolen goods and pocketed the money. He would never say anything to Jonah because he didn't wanted to cause strife between the cousins, but he saw everything, including the jealousy in Clifford's eyes when he looked at Jonah.

There were many women who wanted to be Jonah's wife, but only one hung around like a worthless fly on freshly caught fish. Lucinda Perou had her fancy on marrying Jonah, and Raphael was certain she had not given up. A scowl creased his already lined, sun-parched face. He disliked her as much as he disliked Clifford.

He had watched a change come over Jonah after he met the Bellemare girl. Jonah was both handsome and rich. Women threw themselves at him, and mostly Jonah accepted what they offered. On this voyage, he had hardly left the vessel. Even when the ladies made their way to the docks in search of him, Raphael knew that Jonah had not responded. He was pining only for Catherine.

Raphael smiled wistfully. Once, a long time ago, he had known how it felt to love a woman like that. He was young then, but the feelings of that love still stirred in his groins. He had lost her to a bout of tuberculosis the year Jonah was born, and he had sworn never to love again. It was then that he had married the sea, an unfeeling wench that would never break his heart.

He glanced again at the bow of the ship and chuckled loudly. The boy had not moved. He was cranky and moody. Yes indeed, Jonah had been hooked and barreled by Catherine.

Catherine ate a ham sandwich while keeping her eyes steady on the window. The *Louise Catherine* was definitely making progress. The vessel was clearer now, her tremendous white sails bellowing in the wind that had picked up considerably. She had to get back down to the shore! She stood up quickly, almost overturning the table.

Marie exclaimed. "Mama, she's going to break her neck running like that."

Suzanne wiped her hands on the white cloth next to the stove. She walked over to her husband and massaged his shoulders. "It will be okay, Charles. He is not a bad man. Our Catherine will be fine."

When Jonah saw Catherine, his exhilaration increased. The crew was busy anchoring and securing the vessel, and still he stood immobile, mesmerized by the sight of her. He barely felt Raphael's sharp jab on his shoulder.

"You're so damned love sick that I can knock you right off this vessel and you wouldn't feel it. The rowboats are ready. Go before you break your fool's neck craning it like that."

Muttering a barely audible thank you, Jonah bolted for the rowboats. As he approached the shore, he saw Catherine lift her skirt and run into the water. Still, he was unprepared when she flung herself at him. He lost his balance, capsizing the rowboat and throwing them both into the sea.

They were soaking wet when his lips found hers. The sweet taste of her mouth coupled with the salty taste of the sea made him delirious, and he pulled her firmly against him.

He was nuzzling her neck when he heard Raphael clear his throat behind him. "Jonah, you two are creating a spectacle. This is not becoming for a young lady. Control yourselves."

Raphael's softly spoken words were like an effective splash of ice water. Jonah pulled away from Catherine, and embarrassment colored Catherine's cheeks. She rested her forehead on Jonah's wet chest.

He kissed the top of her head. His voice was gruff with emotions when he said, "Go change your clothes. I am going back to the vessel to change mine. I will come to your house in a few minutes."

When Catherine entered the house, she walked quickly, hoping to make it up the stairs unseen to the bedroom she shared with Marie. She should have known Marie would be on the lookout for her. As she tiptoed pass the parlor, she heard her exclaimed, "Catherine, what happened to you? You're dripping wet! "

Catherine groaned. She knew Marie had willfully said it to attract their parents' attention, and sure enough they came out of the kitchen.

"Catherine, what happened? Did you fall? Are you hurt?"

"Only my pride, Mama. I got a little too excited when I saw Jonah, and I capsized the rowboat."

"But I do not understand. How could you capsize the rowboat?"

"Yes, Catherine," Marie said, "tell us how you capsized the rowboat."

Catherine looked at her younger sister. Mischief was written all over the girl's face. It was clear she was thoroughly enjoying Catherine's discomfort.

"I ran into the sea to meet Jonah, and when I hugged him, he lost his balance. We both fell into the water when the rowboat capsized."

"You did what?" her father roared. "You could not wait onshore like a respectable young lady? You had to put on a show for the whole seashore? Everyone must think I raised a hussy."

Catherine looked apologetically at her parents. "I am so sorry, Papa, but Jonah will be here any minute. I have to change my clothes." Turning to her sister, she mouthed, "I will get you later." Then she turned and walked up the stairs.

Jonah openly admired Catherine when she walked into the parlor. Aside from the damp curls framing her face, there was no sign of her topple into the sea. Freshly groomed, she looked radiant.

He was seated uncomfortably on the small sofa, his long legs stretched out at an awkward angle. He beckoned for her to sit beside him, but she sat in the matching arm chair. He smiled when he thought of how she had practically attacked him by the seashore in her eagerness to touch him. Now she sat chastely using the arm chair to separate them.

Moving to the end of the sofa closest to her, he reached over to touch her face. "I had to see you one more time before I head home to

Toulon." Then he leaned in closer. "That was quite a welcome home. I must be the envy of every man who saw it."

"Shush, I don't want Mama and Papa to know the whole story."

"They're bound to find out. We had a lot of gawkers."

"They're going to have spasms when they hear about it."

"It's not so bad. We're going to be married in a matter of weeks. Besides, if that is a taste of what's to come, I cannot wait."

He stood up and pulled her up into his arms. She buried her face in his neck. Tilting her chin, he whispered huskily, "I know I am not supposed to do this in your father's house, but I need just one kiss to sustain me on my way home." He bent his head and hungrily explored her mouth. Feebly he tried to pull away, but she continued to cling, planting enticing, little kisses along his neck and jaw line. "Catherine." Jonah's voice was thick with passion. "The crew is waiting for me. I have to compose myself before I say good-bye to your parents."

Pouting, she released him, and he kissed the top of her head. Quieting his raving body, he gave her one last yearning look before moving toward the kitchen to look for Charles and Suzanne.

Below the high cliffs of Toulon, the *Louise Catherine* made her way home. The Dusant estate stood high above the steep cliffs overlooking the sea like a proud eagle surveying its domain. The property covered quite an expanse of real estate, with the main house at its center. A number of smaller cottages housed numerous cousins and employees. The families of Ivan and Edward Dusant resided in the main house. It was a massive, white structure made of thick, stone walls replete with wraparound galleries. A steep walking path from the estate through the cliffs led to a spacious boatyard.

Lucinda Perou watched from one of the windows high above as the *Louise Catherine* docked at the boatyard. She had bathed, perfumed herself, and styled her long, black hair. Jonah was coming home. She wanted to look her best. She would never accept that he had chosen a peasant when he could have her. If he wanted a wife, she was the better choice. She just needed the right chance to prove it to him.

"You're wasting your time, Lu. He doesn't want you. You were just a distraction, one of his many toys," Clifford whispered in her ear as he twirled a lock of her hair around his index finger. She had been so engrossed in her thoughts that she had not heard him walk up behind her.

"I am the better man for you. I know what you need, and I am willing to give it you, just like all the sweet times before. We're so good together. What do I need to do to convince you?' He moved aside the heavy curtain of hair from her shoulders and kissed her neck.

"Stop it, Clifford." Lucinda slapped his hand away. "Why don't you go practice your charms on the peasant? Make her forget about Jonah. That's what I need from you."

"I tried. In fact, I saw her first. I made the first move on her, but the golden boy had to beat me at that too. He always has to have what I want, including you." He abruptly dropped her hair and turned away in anger. "I am going to put a stop to it, I swear."

Lucinda had been born and raised on the estate. Her father was the captain of one of the fishing vessels, and her mother was the head cook. She and her parents lived in one of the cottages, but she roamed the main house at will. She'd grown up with Jonah and Clifford. She knew they were romantically inclined toward her, and through the years she'd played them both to her advantage. She could get whatever she wanted from either one, but it was Jonah she desired. She knew there were other women in the ports he sailed. That never bothered her because he'd said he had no real interest in them. Then he had met that peasant, and everything had changed. Lucinda slyly smiled as she moved away from the window. He was home now, and she would be joining him in bed tonight.

CHAPTER 2

Ivan Dusant had watched the *Louise Catherine*'s progress since she had first appeared on the horizon. He missed Jonah when he was on a voyage, and he worried about his safety on the seas. Jonah was all he had left of Louise. He would not survive losing him too. Each time he looked at his son he saw the woman he would always love. Jonah had his mother's sense of humor, her quick smile, and her lovely, green eyes.

In the beginning he had not been pleased with Jonah's choice for a wife, but he had seen the positive changes that Catherine had brought his son. Jonah was happy, and that was all that mattered. He wanted him to have a woman he would love with his very soul, as Ivan had loved Louise.

His kindhearted wife had disliked seeing anyone in distress, and in the end, her desire to take care of everyone had been her demise. He frowned as he remembered that day. A group of Jews had settled at the mouth of the harbor, in the exact location where the company's boatyard was now. Fleeing the developing war in Germany, they had set up a makeshift camp in the protective haven of the bay surrounded by the cliffs where they could fish, but they were destitute. Louise had taken up the habit of bringing food and clothing to them twice a month. She'd said there were a lot of young children in the camp, and it made her feel awful seeing them in that condition. She would secure the packages on the back of her horse and ride down through the cliffs to the settlement.

She loved that horse, a big, gentle, brown mare, and she was an experienced rider. Ivan never could understand what had happened to spook the horse. When she had not returned by late afternoon, he and Edward had gone down the path in search of her. They found her lifeless body on the side of the road, her head at a strange angle. Her neck had been broken. A little farther down the path they found the horse, its hind legs broken.

The pain had been so intense that Ivan had wanted to die, and had it not been for his son, he might have ended his own life. He never fully recovered from her loss.

Ivan greeted Jonah with a warm hug. "I see you stopped in Marseille before coming home."

"Yes, I had to see Catherine. I was going insane with my desire to hold her."

Ivan chuckled. "How is her family coming along with the wedding plans?"

"As far as I know, things are moving forward. You know Catherine and I would have preferred a smaller affair."

"Nonsense; you are my only son. I want to celebrate your wedding in grand style. I am glad Charles understands this and did not argue when I insisted the wedding be held here in Toulon."

"Charles would not have argued with you, Father. He cannot afford the amount of people you want to invite. Just promise me that you will not take over the entire planning. Charles and Susanne are proud people. Please protect their dignity by allowing them some control over their daughter's wedding."

"I will bend as much as possible to their wishes." He changed the subject. "Edward is waiting in the library. Let's go talk to him about another successful voyage."

Edward Dusant was seated behind a big oak desk. The library was a large room with comfortable chairs and sofas. The walls were lined with bookshelves that held a myriad of books, from Shakespeare to Edgar Allan Poe. Volumes of law books and tons of books on maritime trading adorned the shelves.

Edward moved around the desk to greet Jonah, giving him a firm handshake. "Welcome home. Was your voyage to Algeria and South Africa profitable?"

"Yes, our shipment of wheat, barley, and spices were well received by both countries, and we successfully brought back the precious metals and gunpowder ordered by the French navy. I have already made preparation for the shipment to be delivered to the naval yard early next week."

"Very good. I heard there was some rough weather off of the coast of Africa. Did it present you with any problems?"

"We had some days of rough sailing, but the *Louise Catherine* handled it well. She glided above the waves with hardly a problem. May I suggest that we purchase another clipper ship? Clifford and his crew would benefit greatly from a vessel like the *Louise Catherine.*"

"Point well taken. Your father and I will look into it at our first opportunity."

Edward sat at the edge of the big desk while Ivan stood leaning against the window that opened to the spectacular view of the sea. Jonah sat in one of the chairs.

"Now," Edward continued, "the wedding date is soon approaching. How is the groom? Are you having second thoughts yet? There is still time to change your mind. This is indeed a big step you are taking."

"I have never been so sure of anything in my life, Edward. I love Catherine, and I cannot wait to bring her here to Toulon and make her my wife. Now, if you both will excuse me, I would like to go to my chambers and unpack. I will see you at dinner this evening. Good afternoon, Father, Edward."

As Jonah went down the corridor to his section of the house, he passed Lucinda in the hallway. "Hello, Lu." He smiled and continued on his way.

Lucinda returned a halfhearted smile when Jonah walked past her. She'd known that he was in the library meeting with Ivan and Edward, and she'd purposed lingered in the corridor in hopes of gaining his attention. A frown replaced the fake smile on her face as she watched him stride down the hall.

That's it? She thought. *I went to all that trouble to look beautiful for him, and he passes me like a common servant? We will see about that later tonight when he is rested. He will not treat me like a servant then.*

#

"I am sorry, Cathy, about today. I really shouldn't have done that." Marie genially rubbed Catherine's arm. They were lying on the bed they shared, their heads close together.

"You shouldn't have, but that's okay cause I am going to tickle you until you're really sorry." Catherine tickled her sister until they were both laughing.

When they had settled down, Marie whispered, "Pierre has asked me to marry him. He plans to speak with Papa next week."

Catherine looked at her little sister. She was five years older than Marie, but they looked like twins. Pierre Gelfand was a good boy. He was steady and strong and had a good trade as a carpenter. Catherine liked him and admired his work. He had made the banister on the stairwell of their house. He was short and well built, with sandy-blond hair.

"Marie, that's wonderful! I like Pierre, and so do Mama and Papa. I noticed he had been hanging around here a lot recently. I thought he was just looking for work from Papa. I had no idea the two of you were that serious. Do you plan to marry this year?"

"Yes, Pierre is building a house next to his parents. It should be finished by November. We plan to marry by the end of the year."

Catherine reached up and ruffled the brown hair that was so much like her own. "You're my baby sister. I guess I was too busy seeing you as a little girl and not as the beautiful woman you were becoming. Papa and Mama will have two weddings to plan in one year." She sighed. "At least Papa will be happy with Pierre. They are already comfortable together. It is not like that with my Jonah. He becomes nervous whenever Jonah comes around."

"Give Papa time, Cathy. He is still adjusting to having a rich son-in-law."

After unloading her secret, Marie fell promptly asleep, but Catherine remained awake, her mind drifting back to the time when she had first seen Jonah at the marketplace. He and his cousin, Clifford, had been wondering around the produce stalls, and she remembered thinking how out of place they looked, so well dressed. People of their status rarely came to the market.

She had just paid for her purchase when Clifford walked up to her and whispered in her ear, "You look so sweet. I would love to take you to my bed and ravish you."

She reacted instantly. She raised her hand and slapped him hard across the face and then quickly left, giving him no time to follow.

That was why she was so surprised later that afternoon when there was a knock on the door. Her parents were visiting the neighbors, so Marie answered. Marie's expression was full of questions when she announced to Catherine that Jonah Dusant was at the door requesting to speak with her.

Catherine's heart started thumping. She had been sure he was there to have her arrested for slapping his cousin. She decided she was not going without a fight. She mustered up her courage and marched to the door. Marie followed.

She didn't give him an opportunity to speak. Intrepidly she exclaimed, "I don't care if you are here to arrest me. I would slap him again for his rudeness. So go ahead, get the gendarmes! I will tell them to their faces how rude Clifford Dusant was to me. Being rich does not give you the right to insult and intimate people. I will not tolerate his rudeness—or yours, for that matter."

At the mention of the gendarmes, Marie hurriedly slipped out the back door to get their parents.

Jonah reached out to touch her, and his action only made her more defensive. Stepping backward into the house, she reached for a cast-iron skillet. "I swear you will have further need for the gendarmes if you touch me one more time," she said, waving the skillet in front of his face.

When her parents arrived, her father demanded to know what was happening. Jonah explained that he was there to apologize for his cousin's bad behavior at the market. He said he was doubly sorry for upsetting Catherine a second time, and then he hurriedly left

When she was sure he was a safe distance away, she explained to her family her version of what had transpired at the marketplace. Her mother said Jonah had done the noble thing by coming and apologizing, but it had not stopped there. He kept coming back. He brought cheese, wine, and flowers. He invited her to all sorts of outings. But she refused his efforts to court her.

Then one night a particularly strong storm swept across Marseille. The wind howled all night, destroying a good portion of the roof. Catherine had woken to the sound of hammering and the smell of eggs frying.

When she walked into the kitchen, her mother handed her a tray with two sandwiches and two coffee mugs and asked her to carry it outside to her father. Still in her nightgown and in a dreamy state from sleep, she walked outside with the tray, vaguely wondering why there were two coffee mugs.

Squinting up at the roof against the early morning sun, she saw Jonah. Mortified, she tried to duck back into the house, but it was too late. He had seen her. He climbed down the ladder and took the tray from her. She felt unkempt, and the amused look on his face made it all the worse.

"What are you doing here?" she snapped at him.

"I am helping your father fixed the roof," he answered earnestly, playfully touching her nose. "I love your freckles. They make you even more appealing to me."

She'd marched back into the house, angry at her mother for setting her up. He'd stayed for lunch, and before long, he had succeeded in getting her to agree to go to the opera on an official date.

The rest is history. Catherine yawned and finally drifted off to sleep.

#

Lucinda tiptoed into the kitchen and opened the drawer where she knew her mother kept the keys to the big house. She slipped them into her pocket and eased out the door.

In the blackness of night she ran undetected across the yard to the back door used by the servants. She fit the key into the lock and silently climbed the stairs that led to the long corridor on the second floor. Then softly she opened the door to Jonah's private parlor and slinked into his bedroom.

He was sound asleep on his back, naked. She felt the heat between her legs intensify as she admired his toned physique. She slipped off her nightgown and eased herself into the bed. Lightly she ran her hand over his chest, her fingers exploring the fine scattering of brown hair. Then she bent her head and licked each nipple. They hardened. Smiling with satisfaction, she continued kissing the length of his body, moving down to the nest of dark, curly hair at his middle. The moan he gave encouraged her. Climbing on top of him, she nibbled and kissed her way back up his body. He encircled his arms around her, pulling her head down for a kiss, and she whispered his name.

His eyes flew open. "What the hell!" He struggled to get up, throwing her off. She tumbled to the floor. "Lucinda, what are you doing?"

"Loving you, Jonah." She got up off the floor and came to him again, wrapping her arms around his waist.

He firmly took her by both arms and pushed her away. "I do not want to hurt you, Lu, but you know I am getting married in a matter of weeks. I love Catherine. Now go home and do not come back here again. Not like this."

Lucinda stumbled out into the main corridor. She was a woman scorned. She was hurting and needed to be comforted. She made her way to the only door where she knew she would be welcomed. Again she took off her nightgown and crawled into a man's bed. He too was naked, but he was always welcoming. Her eyes were wet with tears when she whispered, "Love me, Clifford."

Clifford gladly obliged her, and in the throes of passion, Lucinda cried out the name she knew Clifford hated most, Jonah.

#

Catherine, her parents, and Marie arrived in Toulon three days before the wedding. Ivan welcomed them warmly, and Edward's wife,

Rose, saw to their every need. Catherine liked Rose, though she thought Rose and Edward were an odd couple. He was standoffish and aloof. She was warm and welcoming. He was tall and lean. She was round and plump.

One morning Catherine decided to take a peek at Jonah's chambers. He had told her that it had been completely remodeled, and she was pleasantly surprised at the tastefulness of the decor. Pretty, white curtains with blue trimmed borders adorned the windows in the parlor and bedroom. A generously sized, blue sofa sat invitingly in one corner of the parlor, and in the far corner was a big, mahogany desk with neatly stacked piles of papers. A huge four-poster bed dwarfed the bedroom. An oak dresser stood next to the bed and sported a smiling portrait of Catherine. Multicolored, braided rugs were scattered on the hardwood floors in both rooms.

Wearily she sat on the blue sofa. She had to admit that she was nervous about moving into the house. She had not seen much of Clifford since the marketplace episode, and he had been cold and unfriendly the few times she had seen him. She wanted so badly to extend him an olive branch. He was Jonah's cousin. They had grown up more like brothers. She never wanted to be a cause of contention between them, but he was showing no interest in meeting her halfway.

He had been seated across from her at the dinner table last evening. He had engaged in lively conversation with everyone but her, and each time she had tried to take part in the topics being discussed, he had purposely excluded her. After a while she gave up trying to join in the conversation, opting to silently observe him.

I am going to have to be careful. She thought. *He's nothing like Jonah. He's filled with jealousy and anger.*

He was a good-looking man, tall and slender with dirty–blond, unruly hair that seemed to stick out in every direction regardless of how much scented pomade he placed in it. His facial features resembled his mother's, but he possessed an arrogance she assumed was his own.

"You seem so deep in thought." Jonah's voice startled her out of her reverie. "Are you already homesick for Marseille, or is it wedding jitters that have you so serious?"

Catherine made room on the sofa and motioned for him to join her. "A little of both. I am nervous about moving in here with your family. I want very much to fit in, but it's going to take time. I am almost sorry now that I slapped Clifford that day at the market. He hasn't forgiven me; I can tell."

"I don't want you worrying about Clifford. He will come around. You just hurt his pride, that's all. He's not used to beautiful women rejecting his advances. You, my darling, are a novelty, so he doesn't know how to react to you."

He pulled her into his arms and drizzled kisses over her nose, eyes, and mouth. Catherine shivered when she felt him nip and lick the soft flesh of her neck while his hands caressed her legs under her skirt. His voice sounded raspy when he said, "I am going to have to get up from here, or I will not be responsible for my actions."

Giving her one more lingering kiss, he eased himself up. "I have a meeting with Father and Edward in a few minutes. See you soon."

Jonah detoured through the kitchen, hoping to find Lucinda. He had not seen her since the night he had thrown her out of his chambers. He wanted to tell her he had no hard feelings and that they were still friends, but his ultimate reason was to make certain she posed no difficulties for Catherine.

Clifford was going to present enough of a problem. Jonah had picked up on Clifford's snobbishness toward Catherine at dinner last evening. He planned to speak with Clifford about it if his attitude toward her did not improve. In the meanwhile, Jonah wanted to smooth things out with Lucinda.

She was not in the kitchen with her mother as he had hoped, so he walked the short distance across the yard to the cottage. He knocked several times before she opened the door. She was still wearing her nightgown, and she was pale and disheveled.

"Hi, Lu. Can I come again?"

"Sure, Jonah." Lucinda moved aside for Jonah to enter the small parlor. Inside, the house was neat and clean. "I won't throw you out the way you did me. Why are you here anyway? Did the peasant tire of you already, or are you here for a little diversion before the wedding?"

Ignoring her comment, Jonah reached out and touched her forehead. "Are you feeling okay?"

She brushed his hand away. "I just have a headache. What do you want, Jonah? I know you are not here because you are concerned about me."

"I came to tell you there are no bad feelings. We've been friends since we were children. I'll always consider you my friend. Let's forget about what happened the other night, okay?" He touched her cheek. "Are we good?"

"You and I will always be good, Jonah. Just remember that when you get tired of her. I will be waiting." She opened the door. "Now go back to her."

"I will not tolerate your giving Catherine a hard time. You know that, Lu." Jonah looked at Lucinda sternly and then turned and walked away.

Clifford, Ivan, and Edward were already seated when Jonah walked into the library. The jalousies were opened wide, and a cool breeze was blowing, lifting the white curtains on the opposite side of the room.

"Aha, there he is," Edward said. "We were beginning to think your bride-to-be was keeping you too occupied to join us. Have she and her family settled in okay? Rose has been doing her best to make them all comfortable."

"Yes, everyone is fine, and Rose is doing a remarkable job. I am sorry to have kept you waiting," Jonah said as he took a seat beside his father.

"Good," Ivan replied. "Now that we're all here, let's go directly to the business at hand." He clasped his hands as if deep in thought and then leaned forward in his chair. "I know this is the week of your wedding, Jonah, and I would have preferred not to have to discuss business at such a momentous time, but I do not have a choice. I received word yesterday that we have been commissioned by the French government to carry a cargo to St. Barthelemy, also known as St. Barth, a small island in the Antilles. The cargo will consist of food supplies and ammunitions."

Ivan looked at Jonah and Clifford. "I want to tell you a little about the island since neither of you is familiar with it. It's under French control, but suffering from bouts with violent gales, droughts, and fires. Because of this, the colonists have been sailing to neighboring islands looking for work and better living conditions. In an attempt to keep the remaining colonist from leaving, our government is trying to stir new life into the colony. We have citizens living there from Normandy, Nice, Marseille, Bordeaux, Brittany, and many other French provinces, including Toulon."

Looking pointedly at the two younger men again, he continued. "This is why the island is so important to our government and this voyage crucial to us. I have been advised that the cargo is already being prepared and will be ready by the end of June, so we will sail by the first week of July. It will take a minimum of four months depending on the weather and the wind. That will place us in the treacherous gale season."

Ivan stood up and paced the room. "It's very tiny, just a speck on the map, and it's a haven for pirates. I sailed there many years ago when it was under Swedish rule. I delivered a cargo of gold coins and ammunitions. I saw it as an island with great future potentials. It is in a strategic location, perfect for the French military to maneuver. You will need to be careful when entering the harbor, though. The island is volcanic in nature and is encircled by shallow reefs."

Edward took over. "The biggest dilemma Ivan and I are faced with is which one of you to send. Jonah will be newly married. It would not be fair to take him away from his bride so soon after the nuptials." He hesitantly looked at his son. "That means you and your crew will make the voyage, Clifford."

"So I am your second choice as usual. I know you both prefer Jonah, but bear in mind that I am equally qualified and experienced. For that matter, I will welcome the opportunity to be away from this place. All this wedding hoopla is making me crazy."

"Your father and I do not doubt either of your qualifications," Ivan interjected. "You are both skillful captains. We are concerned, as always, for your safety and that of your crew. The *Louise Catherine* is a more modern and faster vessel. We would prefer to have her make the voyage. Between the two of you, it does not matter who is her captain."

Jonah leaned forward. Addressing Clifford, he said, "Please take the *Louise Catherine*. She is indeed more equipped for such a voyage. I have no claim on her. She belongs to the fleet, and you have yet to take her out to sea."

"I will sail the *Marie Rose,*" Clifford replied spartanly. "She can handle anything the sea throws at her. It is not open for discussion. I will go and speak with Simon and have him prepare our crew. If that is all, Ivan and Father, I will bid my leave now." Clearly irate, he got up and headed for the door.

"Ah, one moment, son," Edward said as Clifford put his hand on the doorknob. "I would much appreciate if you said nothing to your mother about the voyage. She is busy with the wedding, and I do not want to upset her with your leaving."

Clifford rolled his eyes heavenward and said sarcastically, "Of course, Father. The wedding must take first place above everything. Everyone in this house knows that!" He slammed the door shut behind him.

"I don't know what is bothering him lately," Edward said. "Maybe the voyage will be good for him. There's nothing like the sea to clear one's mind and soul."

Clifford left the house and started down the steep path that led through the cliffs to the boatyard to find Simon Vante, his first mate. He was furious. His father trusted Jonah more than he did his own son, and his mother was running around frantically planning Jonah's wedding.

"Where the hell are you, Simon?" Clifford bellowed when he arrived at the boatyard. Angrily, he kicked the side of a fishing boat.

Men like Simon and Raphael had the salt of the sea in their veins. They thrived around the boats. They could always be found cleaning and maintaining the vessels, fishing off the white cliffs, or dozing under the cool shade of a partially overturned fishing boat.

Simon was to Clifford what Raphael was to Jonah. They were both rough characters who used colorful language. Although Simon was younger than Raphael, the two were good friends and enjoyed each other's company when they were at the boatyard. They refrained from discussing Jonah or Clifford because they knew their opinions of both men largely deferred, and they would probably end up in a fistfight should either make a derogatory remark about the other's captain.

Clifford found them both on the high cliffs above the sea, each with a fishing line dangling from his hand. They were so engrossed in their conversation that it took Clifford several shouts amid the high sea breeze before Simon finally heard him and climbed down the rocks.

Simon's excitement was evident at the mention of the upcoming voyage. He gladly promised Clifford he would start contacting the crew since many of them worked other jobs between voyages and would need adequate time to get their affairs in order. He also promised to make sure the *Marie Rose* was ready to sail.

As Simon headed back toward Raphael, Clifford heard him shout excitedly, "Raphael, I am sailing to the West Indies!"

Satisfied that Simon would handle the groundwork, Clifford trekked back up the path. As he reached the landing, he stopped and observed the activities going on in preparation for the wedding. Gardeners spruced up plants. Painters with ladders were everywhere. Merchants delivered supplies and blocks of ice.

"Farce of a wedding," Clifford grumbled as he crossed the yard. He was the best man, but he was finding it hard to keep a good attitude. Jonah was marrying the woman who had publicly slapped him, a peasant! Of all the fine women in France, Jonah had chosen a peasant. In fact, his house was presently crawling with peasants.

No woman had ever slapped him without repercussion, and this one would pay as well. Starting now he would hide his true feelings. He would lay on the charm for her, make her comfortable thinking all was forgiven and forgotten. Then when she least expected it, he would pounce. It may take him weeks, no, months now because of the voyage, but he would have Catherine. He would take what he wanted from her, what was his due since the day he had seen her at the Marseille marketplace. He would ravage that sweet body, and she would not dare say a word to Jonah, not after he threatened to kill her precious parents and sister. Jonah was not always around. In fact, he was scheduled to take a voyage soon to Argentina.

His groin grew hot at the thought of joining Catherine in bed night after night. *After I have taught her well how to please me, she will no longer have an appetite for him. It will serve him right for marrying her and bringing her into my house.* He laughed wickedly. *He brought her right into the lion's den.*

CHAPTER 3

A flurry of activity was underway the night before the wedding. The house was festively decorated with pretty, white, paper-accordion wedding bells. The musicians had already arrived, and the band was setting up. Mouthwatering wedding cakes in attractive pastel colors were displayed on a mahogany table covered by a white, crocheted doily. Tons of food was being prepared in the kitchen.

Tonight the guests already on hand would enjoy *choucroute*, a favorite family recipe of cabbage simmered with pieces of sweet spicy sausage, accompanied by roasted potatoes and warm crusty baguettes with melted fromage. Escargots simmering in garlic and butter sauce would be served as the appetizer. For the dessert, a delicious mousse au chocolat had been prepared.

Clifford was in a wonderful mood, charming everyone with his handsome smile and funny antics. He was especially paying attention to Catherine.

Relieved to see Clifford so jovial, Jonah placed a friendly hand on his shoulder. "Thanks for making an effort to reach out to Catherine. It means everything to me for the two of you to get along. I knew you were too big a man to allow one little slap to bother you for long. She is sweet, kind, and funny. You will love her once you get to know her."

Clifford playfully slapped Jonah's shoulder. "Don't mention it. I have no doubt that I will love her too." Hiding his smirk, he walked away to get another drink.

Ivan and Jonah were the last to leave the parlor that evening. For a time the two men sat in quiet companionship. They both seem to be waiting for the other to speak.

Then hesitantly, as if he was searching for the right words, Ivan began. "Tomorrow you become a married man. I wish your mother were here. She would have been so proud." He paused and took a deep breath. With his eyes downcast, he continued. "Son, there's nothing like a woman who truly loves you. There is a certain peace a man feels when, in the depth of sleep, he turns and finds her warm body next to his. It gives him contentment to know that when he pulls her close, she is his heart, his soul mate, and she will always want the best for him. That is what I miss most since I lost your mother." His eyes were bright with tears when he turned to look at Jonah. "I believe you have found such a woman. Treat her well, son. Forget about the others. They no longer exist for you."

Jonah cleared his throat. "I have already forgotten."

"Good."

Ivan stood and hugged his son. Then he walked over to the crystal decanter and poured himself a glass of sherry. He sat back down and raised the glass to his lips, but before he took a sip, he said, "Now go to bed. You have a big day tomorrow. Leave an old man alone with his memories."

It was a perfect day for a wedding. A gentle breeze was blowing, and the weather was ideal. Catherine had hardly slept. She was dressed and ready to go. She wore a beautiful, white, satin dress, the bodice perfectly hugging the curve of her waist. Her hair was adorned with flowers woven through the lovely, brown strands.

When the soft knock on the door announced that the carriage was waiting, she eagerly lifted the heavy, satin dress and proceeded down the steps and through the open front door.

Dressed in similar shades of yellow, Suzanne and Marie followed closely behind her. Charles was already waiting by the carriage door, his short frame bedecked in a crisp, black suit. Suzanne's tears flowed freely as she helped her firstborn daughter into the carriage. Even Marie was unusually subdued.

Saint Marie's Cathedral was filled with people when the carriage pulled up to its doors. Jonah and Clifford stood together at the front of the church. Raphael was seated in the front row with Ivan, Rose, and Edward. Jonah had insisted that the old man, who was like a second father to him, be seated in a place of honor with his family. The old ruffian was dressed in his Sunday best. His white hair and beard had been neatly trimmed. He held a white handkerchief in his hands and occasionally blew his nose and wiped his eyes, gruffly complaining that all the fancy perfumes were bothering his eyes and nostril. Rose sat beside him, and she too was crying and delicately blowing her nose.

As Catherine slowly walked down the aisle of the crowded church, she kept her eyes only on Jonah. She had expected him to appear nervous but instead, he seemed poised and calm, and he was watching her just as intensely. Despite their guests, Catherine felt like they were the only two people in the church; that no one or nothing else existed.

He is mine, she thought. *For the rest of my life, he is mine.* This was indeed the happiest day of her life.

The party was in full swing by the time Clifford made his way to Catherine's side. He held out his hand to her and bowed. "May I please have this dance, Catherine?"

Catherine hesitated before answering. "Of course, Clifford."

He took her hand and led her to the dance floor. "My cousin is the luckiest man on earth to have found such a beautiful woman to be his wife," he whispered.

"Thank you, Clifford."

Catherine thought long before she spoke next. She wanted so much to make things right with him, if only for Jonah's sake. "I have been meaning to ask your forgiveness for slapping you that day in Marseille. I should not have done it. Please forgive me."

"It's all forgotten, Catherine. We need never speak of it again. Now let's enjoy our dance, shall we?"

Catherine felt a chill. She didn't believe for one minute that he had forgotten.

It was shortly after her dance with Clifford that Jonah came to take his bride away. They had danced with many of their guests, and now they went in search of their parents. Suzanne and Marie cried. Charles gruffly embraced his daughter. He cordially shook his new son-in-law's hand. Ivan hugged them and sent them on their way. They were heading out of the room when they found Rose. She threw her arms around them and wished them well. Edward was nowhere to be seen.

Jonah had yearned for this night for so long, and he was as nervous as a schoolboy. He could sense Catherine's anxiety as they walked to their chambers.

When they reached the door, he scooped Catherine up and carried her across the threshold. His fingers shook as he started to undo the satin buttons of her gown. He kissed each part of her body as he removed each article of clothing. When she was totally naked, he lifted her and placed her in the middle of the bed. Pausing to look at her, he caught his breath. Her pretty, golden eyes were looking at him so trustingly.

Jonah was a sea captain. It was the only trade he knew. As he looked at Catherine, he saw a glorious expanse of uncharted waters that was his alone to explore, and he would take a lifetime to explore her. He never wanted to do anything that would hurt her or would take away the trust he saw so nakedly revealed in her eyes.

He undressed and got into bed. He kissed her face, her neck, the two full twin globes of her breast, and he continued down the length of her body until she cried out his name, digging her fingers into his scalp. When he finally entered the wet, warm, silkiness of her womanhood, he felt an ecstasy of pure joy that he had never experienced before. He understood clearly now what his father had tried to tell him the night before—that nothing compared to the jubilation of a man who was confident the woman he loved was in love with him wholly and without reserve.

By the time Jonah and Catherine woke the next morning, their guests were gone. Catherine felt forlorn at the absence of her family.

She had woken to the weight of Jonah's arm secured tightly around her waist. At first she was confused when she felt the unfamiliar sensation of something anchoring her to the bed. Then she'd felt the warmth of his body pressed against hers. She'd tried to extricate herself, but her movements had only made him tighten his grip.

She really needed to pee, but the thought of waking him just to tell him was embarrassing. She shook him lightly. Next she poked his ribs with her index finger. Then she shook him a little harder. He was out cold. It had taken her quite a few minutes, but eventually she had managed to free herself, crawl out of the bed, and tiptoe to the bathroom. Then she crawled back into bed. She had laid there on her side for some time watching him and remembering last night when his eyes finally fluttered open.

He looked at her, smiled, and said, "Good morning, Mrs. Dusant." Pulling her close, he planted a kiss on her nose, and it had all started again, slow and sweet. Before leaving this morning, he placed an empty valise on the bed and told her to pack enough clothes for a week because they were taking a honeymoon voyage on the *Louise Catherine*.

She had just finished packing when she heard his footsteps. She turned to look at him, smiling as she watched him cross the room. He was energetic, happy, and full of life.

"Are you ready to go? Raphael and the *Louise Catherine* are waiting for us."

"You still haven't told me where we're going."

"You will know when we get there. Now let's get going." He teasingly slapped her buttocks when she walked past him.

Raphael was at the helm of the *Louise Catherine* with a limited crew on board. Jonah and Catherine were not leaving the waters of France, and Jonah had no desire to captain the vessel; his attention was needed elsewhere. He had planned this honeymoon trip for months and was anxious to get started. He and his bride were headed to Paris.

They toured the Louvre with its beautiful works of art. They saw the famous Mona Lisa painting. They walked through the Jardin des Plantes, the garden of medicine that had been created by Louis XIII's doctor, Guy de La Brosse, to cultivate medicinal plants. They visited the

Cathedral of Notre Dame and attended an opera in the heart of Paris. They meandered in and out of the many fine boutiques.

Despite her reluctance, Jonah insisted Catherine buy new dresses, and the proprietors wrapped each dress in delicate gauzy tissue once she was satisfied with the fit. He encouraged her to buy expensive French perfumes and little souvenirs for her family. He wanted her to feel like a princess because he knew she had spent her whole life in Marseille, only reading about these places in her school books.

They toured the city by day and made love in the captain's quarters by night. Jonah knew he would never be able to sleep in his quarters again without remembering these precious nights of loving Catherine. Her memory would be with him in the cold, dark, lonely nights at sea.

#

Catherine soon figured out the dynamics of the house. Rose had a firm grip on its daily operations, and she ran it like a military captain. She was firm but operated in such a manner that everyone gladly did her bidding. She was as quick to compliment as she was to criticize. Catherine knew the staff genuinely liked Rose.

Edward spent most of his days alone in the library. He clearly was a shrewd businessman who was used to getting his way. He was astute and secretive. Ivan was the more social cousin, and he handled the customer relations part of the business, but Ivan was a troubled soul who dearly missed his wife.

Catherine found herself with little to do to fill her days. She had daydreamed about cooking for Jonah, washing and mending his clothes like her mother took pleasure doing for her father, but it seemed that they had barely gotten out of bed when a servant would come and snatch the sheets to be laundered.

In the late afternoons, after Edward had left for the day, she'd slip into the library to explore the shelves. It was there that Ivan found her one afternoon. She had just returned a book of poems and was searching the shelves for something new.

Thinking she was alone, she let out a huge sigh. She jumped when she heard Ivan say, "That is a mighty big sigh, young lady. Is everything all right?"

"Yes," she answered quickly. "I am just a little bored."

Ivan smiled. "You sound just like Louise. She always had to be doing something. She could never sit quietly for long. She used to say it was a waste of good time. That's why I allowed her to get involved with the Jews down by the bay. It made her feel worthwhile. She was doing a good deed, and nothing lit up her face more than knowing she was helping someone."

He gazed away and then continued passionately. "I have never understood it. Edward is convinced the Jews willfully hurt her, but why would they? She was feeding and clothing them. She told me they looked forward to her visits. The day after Edward and I found her, I spoke with them. They were shocked and dismayed by her death. The women were inconsolable. Even the men had tears in their eyes. When they mysteriously disappeared shortly after her death, I began to think maybe Edward was right, that they had hurt her and now fled because they were afraid of repercussion. But something in here," he said, touching his chest, "tells me differently. They would not have hurt my Louise. Something else happened on that path."

Catherine was silent. She did not know what to say to him to ease the pain he so visibly carried.

Ivan smiled apologetically. He walked over to the table in the corner of the room, picked up the crystal decanter, and poured himself a drink. After taking a hefty swallow, he turned to her and said, "Please forgive an old man his grumblings. There's a nice patch of yard in the back garden. Louise used to grow beautiful flowers. You might want to try your hand at it."

"That's a wonderful idea," Catherine quickly replied, anxious to change the subject.

#

For days Lucinda had not been feeling well. She feared she had caught one of the annoying sicknesses that sometimes went around.

She was not worried about the dreaded fever because it had been years since there had been an outbreak. Still, she asked around and no one knew of any recent cases. She just had this unsettling feeling in the pit of her stomach. The smell of food made it worse, and it seemed that all she wanted to do was sleep. Despite her parents' accusation that she was being disrespectful, she had stayed away from the big house during the wedding festivities, and she had not gone to the ceremony.

Lucinda hated going over to the big house now that Catherine was there, but she had to go. She was assigned to help her mother in the kitchen. She should have been there from early this morning, but she had been so sick when she had woken. Now it was mid afternoon, almost the time when she would normally be leaving for the day. "Mama must be fuming," she mumbled as she crossed the yard and opened the back door. Her mother was nowhere in sight, but there at the stove stirring a pot of onion soup was Catherine.

Catherine smiled warmly, wiped her hands on her apron, and came forward extending her hand to Lucinda. "Hello. I'm Catherine. So very nice to meet you."

Lucinda looked scornfully at her outstretched hand. "I know who you are, and you don't belong here. Jonah is my man, not yours."

She dourly watched as Catherine turned pale and stuttered, "Ar … are you saying Jonah and you are …"

"I am telling you Jonah is mine, and you are a man thief." Then turning, Lucinda walked back out of the kitchen, leaving Catherine reeling against the stove.

Lucinda ran back down the pathway to the cottage, wondering what had compelled her to do what she had just done. She knew there would be hell to pay. Jonah would be stomping mad, and her parents would never tolerate such disrespect. Her head was spinning so badly by the time she reached the cottage that she sat on the wooden steps.

Clifford startled her when he sauntered over from the gallery to sit beside her. Rubbing the back of her neck, he whispered, "I've been waiting for you. I am in need of a little loving. When I didn't see you I figured I would just sit back and wait. I know your papa is out to sea, and your mama is in the kitchen at my house." He leaned over to kiss her. "So we have all the time in the world."

"Cut it out, Clifford. I don't feel well."

Clifford's eyes turned cold. "Since when do you tell me no?" He pulled her against him and started to undo the buttons of her blouse. At the same time, Lucinda felt the bile rise up in her throat. She could not control the vomit that spilled from her mouth all over his bulging crotch.

Nellie, the head cook, walked back into the kitchen from the adjacent vegetable garden where she'd been picking sweet peppers for the evening salad. "Hmm, that soup smells delicious. Your mama really taught you to cook. You can smell it all the way—" Nellie stopped short when she saw the ashen look on Catherine's face. "Child, what's the matter? You look like you've seen a ghost. Are you feeling okay?"

Nellie was short staffed today. Both her daughter and her main helper had not reported in this morning. Catherine had come to the kitchen to make a cup of tea and had noticed that she was in dire need of help. She had immediately dunned an apron and started to work. Nellie had been reluctant to accept help from the girl, knowing Rose would not approve of her working in the kitchen, but Catherine was a natural. She knew her way around a kitchen, and Nellie had really needed the extra hand. Now Catherine was stark white and trembling.

"I'm sorry. I need to get some fresh air," Catherine mumbled as she ran past Nellie.

Catherine didn't stop running until she reached the cliffs overlooking the bay. Her mind refused to digest the thoughts flowing through it. She couldn't even remember if she had turned off the stove in her mad dash out of the kitchen. That girl had said Jonah was her lover. If that were true, how could he have brought her here knowing his lover was here too? How could she continue to live here now? The pain she felt was so new to her, but she had to know the truth. She had to confront Jonah, and she knew he was down by the boatyard.

It was a good twenty-minute walk, and she was not wearing the right shoes. Her feet hurt, but she ignored the pain as she made her way down through the steep, rocky cliffs.

Jonah was lifting a bucket load of shrimp from the boat when he saw her, and a smile spread across his face. She had finally accepted his invitation. Lately she had been complaining about being bored. This morning he had invited her to come down to the bay. She had wiggled her pretty freckled nose and said the whole bay smelled like fish.

I should give her a big, sweaty bear hug.

Putting down the pail he was carrying, he started up the incline to meet her, grinning at the response he knew he would received when he scooped her up in his filthy condition.

His grin faded as he got a closer look at her face. *She's been crying!*

He increased his pace. "Catherine, what's wrong?" He reached out to touch her, and she brushed his hand away.

"That girl, the one with the long black hair, she said you are her lover, that I took you from her. Why didn't you tell me, Jonah? Why did you bring me here when you knew she was here too? I want to go home to Marseille."

The muscles in Jonah's jaws tensed. *Damn you, Lucinda!*

He took Catherine by the arm and led her under the shade of a large boulder, away from the watchful eyes of the men at the boatyard. Then he tilted her face to look into her eyes. "Catherine, I am not Lucinda's lover. I had a brief encounter with her years ago. It meant nothing to me."

Jonah swore as he watched a fresh batch of tears fall from Catherine's eyes.

"I never kept it a secret from you. You knew I had been with other women before I met you. But as God is my witness, since the day I fell in love with you, there has been no one else, and there never will be." He kissed her sweaty forehead. "Only you until the day I die."

"She called me a man thief," Catherine said with her head downcast. She hiccupped and swiped her hand across her nose. "I want to go home to Marseille, Jonah. I don't want to be here with you anymore."

Jonah's voice turned cold. "Take all the time you need to get over this, but know one thing. You are not leaving Toulon. You are my wife. You will stay here with me where you belong. You do not have to be with me until you choose to be. I will not force myself on you, but I will not entertain any further conversation with you about your leaving me. Do I make myself clear?"

"You cannot keep me here against my will if I choose to leave."

"I can and I will keep you here. Is that understood?"

She did not answer.

"Good. Now let's go home."

He waited for her to go ahead of him, and without touching her; he followed her back up the path to the house in silence.

"Catherine, are you getting dressed for dinner?" Jonah asked later that evening.

"No, I am not going down to dinner tonight."

"All right then, I will have a tray sent up to you."

Catherine didn't look up when Jonah closed the door and left, but the tears started fresh tracks down her cheeks. The matter with the black-haired girl had hurt her deeply. His blatant coldness, however, was far worse. He hadn't spoken to her since they'd argued earlier. She had come directly back to their chambers, but not him. In fact, she hadn't seen him again until he had come to bathe and dress for dinner. Even then, he hadn't said a word until he was fully dressed and ready to leave. This was a side of Jonah she had never seen before, and it frightened her. Still, she would not be held captive. She had a good mind to pack her bags and head for Marseille tomorrow.

Ivan looked up when Jonah walked into the dining room, immediately he asked, "Where's Catherine?"

"She's not feeling well. I instructed Nellie to have a tray sent up to her," Jonah replied, taking his seat. He had no appetite. He could barely swallow the food Nellie placed in front of him.

It didn't take Clifford long to notice. "It seems to me there's more to this than Catherine being sick. What happened, lover boy? You two have a fight?"

"Shut up, Clifford," Jonah snapped.

"Why? You don't want anyone to know the peasant isn't perfect?"

Jonah calmly put his fork down. He got up, walked around the table, and grabbed Clifford by the collar. Raising him up off the chair, he wrung the collar tightly around his neck. The muscles in his own neck bulged as he said through clenched teeth, "If I ever hear you refer to my wife as a peasant again, I am going to smash your face into oblivion."

"That's enough, Jonah!" Ivan ordered. "Release Clifford now!"

CHAPTER 4

Jonah let go of Clifford with such force that Clifford and the chair flew backward. The sudden jolt caused his bowl of onion soup to tilt off the table and land squarely on top of him. As Clifford bellowed, Jonah stormed out of the room.

Clifford struggled to get up. He was not only covered with onion soup, but the hot liquid had scalded his skin. He gingerly felt the back of his head where a painful lump was forming. His mother was holding his shoulders, trying to help him up, and his father and Ivan were leaning over him.

He angrily shrugged off his mother's hands. "Save your concerns for Jonah when I get my hands on him." Standing unsteadily, he walked out of the dining room.

"You really must have a talk with that boy about his explosive temper." Edward turned on Ivan.

"Clifford needs to know when to stop," Ivan replied. "He is constantly provoking Jonah."

"Does that warrant him attacking my son? These boys were raised in this house together. It is natural that there will be bantering between them. Jonah needs to toughen his skin."

"They're no longer boys, Edward. They are men. Your son is constantly making degrading remarks about my son's wife. It has to stop. You would have reacted the same way as Jonah if I had treated Rose the way Clifford treats Catherine. You seem to have forgotten,

Rose was a peasant too." Ivan gloweringly looked at Edward and walked out the door.

Rose sat at the table with tears streaming down her cheeks. Edward turned to her and said, "Will you please stop that silly crying!"

He sat back down, repositioned his napkin into his shirt collar, and reached for his fork. Before he put the fork full of fluffy white mashed potato into his mouth, he looked at Rose again and said, "Eat your food. There's no sense in letting it go to waste."

Glaring angrily at him, Rose threw down her napkin and left the room. Edward ate his food alone in silence.

Jonah walked around the estate for hours trying to calm his troubled mind. He realized he was angry because he feared losing Catherine. It had felt like she had sent a dagger straight through his heart when she said she didn't want to be here with him anymore. He knew she was hurting, and he knew he had reacted badly. He wanted to run back to the house, pull her into his arms, and beg her to forgive him.

He would deal with Lucinda soon enough, but Clifford was another disconcerting matter. He knew Clifford was jealous. He had been jealous most of their lives. He knew too that he pocketed money on the side, and for the sake of peace, Jonah had chosen to overlook it. Clifford was his blood, but he didn't trust him. He was concerned about Catherine's safety around him. He wasn't deaf to Clifford's snide remarks about his wife or blind to the way he looked at her. Jonah had a feeling the day was coming when all hell would broke loose between them.

Catherine was wide awake when Jonah entered their chambers. She pretended to be asleep, but she had laid there for hours wondering where he was at this late hour. Her mind had been her own worst enemy as she'd pictured him in that woman's bed. She stayed still while he removed his clothing, pulled down the cover, and got in beside her. She could feel his tension as he lay restlessly on his back.

Then suddenly he reached for her. "Catherine, please forgive me. I nearly lost my mind tonight worrying that you would leave me. I acted like a total fool today."

Catherine felt tremendous relief. No further words were necessary as he adeptly demonstrated his feelings on her body. Finally they slept, entwined in each other's arms.

It was late in the evening when Clifford went to the kitchen in search of an ice pack for his throbbing head. It had been a horrific day. First Lucinda had vomited all over his expensive pantaloons. The smell had been so horrid that he had chosen to dump them rather than have them laundered. Then Jonah had assaulted him, causing the onion soup to spill all over the brand new pair he had worn tonight. The lump on the back of his head was the size of an egg, and it hurt like hell.

Lucinda jumped with fright when he appeared in the doorway.

"What are you still doing here at this hour?"

She stopped washing the dishes and wiped the suds from her hands. "Since I wasn't feeling well, I didn't come in on time to work today. My mother was angry at me. To appease her I told her to go home and I would finish cleaning up."

"But it's after midnight. How come it's taking you so long?"

Motioning him to the kitchen chairs, she asked, "Can we sit for a while? There is something I need to tell you."

"Listen, Lucinda, it's been a long day, and I am not in a good mood."

"Please, Clifford."

"What's so important that it can't wait until tomorrow?"

"Don't be mad at Jonah. It's not his fault. It's mine."

"What? You want me to sit here in the middle of the night because you want to discuss Jonah? He's going to get his, Lucinda. No amount of your begging will stop me." He moved toward the door.

"I am here tonight because I am terrified of him," Lucinda said quickly.

Clifford stopped and looked at her disbelievingly. "You're afraid of Jonah. Phew, come on, Lucinda, you should know I would not believe that."

"Please Clifford, just sit down and listen to me."

Sighing, Clifford sat heavily in the chair. "This had better be good."

Lucinda took the chair beside him. "I am responsible for his bad mood. I caused it by confronting the peasant earlier today."

She went on to tell him what had transpired, finishing by saying, "That's why I am afraid to go home. I know he is coming after me. I thought if I just stayed here late enough until I am sure he is asleep, I will be safe, at least for tonight. This is the last place he would expect me to be since he knows I hate working in the kitchen."

As she had been speaking, a slow grin had been spreading over Clifford's face. Now he stood and pulled her up into his arms. "Lucinda, you are indeed my lucky charm. It takes a brave woman to do what you did, and I am delighted. There's no need to go home tonight. Come upstairs with me. I promise to keep you safe and warm."

Together they climbed the stairs to his chambers where he thoroughly collected on the full benefits of his invitation. As he was drifting off to sleep, he realized he had never gotten the ice for his head. The news Lucinda had given him had caused him to forget about the pain. His day had been wrought with troubles, but his night had ended ecstatically well.

#

Father Anthony was in the middle of his sermon in the crowded St. Marie Cathedral on Sunday morning, his nearly bald head gleaming with droplets of sweat. Today he was preaching on the virtues of patience, stating that God works in mysterious ways. His round face was filled with expression as he animatedly spoke to the congregation. The church was stiflingly hot. Dark, damp spots of perspiration were visible on everyone's clothing.

Nellie watched as her daughter got up from her seat for the second time, hurriedly squeezing pass the parishioners in her haste to get outside. Jacques, Nellie's husband, usually attended Mass with her, but today he had gone on a leisurely fishing trip with his brother, who was visiting from Brittany. It was rare that he saw his brother, and Nellie was glad to see him enjoy the day. She could see the Dusants sitting in their usual pew in the front of the church, at least the ones who regularly attended. Ivan, Jonah, Catherine, and Rose were always there. Edward came on alternate Sundays. Clifford hardly ever darkened the doors of the church.

Nellie's mind was drifting away from the sermon. Believing it was disrespectful not to listen attentively to the priest, she tried hard to keep her mind trained on Father Anthony. She wiped the sweat that trickled down her temples and tried again to refocus on the sermon, but her daughter dominated her thoughts.

Lucinda had always been secretive and sullen. Nellie knew she had fallen in love with Jonah years ago, but she also knew Jonah did not reciprocate those feelings. It must bother Lucinda that he had married Catherine and brought her home. She'd noticed that Lucinda had taken to spending more time with Clifford.

No, something else is wrong with her other than jealousy. She is always sleepy, and the vomiting … Jesus, Mary and Joseph—she is with child!

Nellie could not stay seated for the remainder of the service. She fidgeted until she had to get up and search for her daughter. She begged the parishioners' pardon as she squeezed out of the pew.

But who? Who is the father?

Her mind was in turmoil as she opened the door and stepped outside into the sunlight. *Oh no … not that squanderer. Not Clifford.*

Nellie found Lucinda on her knees, bent over a patch of grass, violently retching. She knelt next to her, moving the black hair away from her face. When Lucinda was spent, exhausted from the retching, Nellie pulled her daughter onto her lap, soothingly murmuring to her. The final hymn was being sung inside, the churchgoers' voices loud and filled with luster as they sang.

Nellie whispered to Lucinda, "This is not the place. We will talk about it when we get home."

Nellie went straight to her neat little kitchen and put on the kettle for tea. She cut slices of cheese and ham, warmed the croissants, and set two places at the table. She was glad Jacques was out to sea with his brother. Father Anthony was correct. God truly worked in mysterious ways. The situation would be much more difficult to handle if he were home.

Nellie waited until they had finish eating. Then she asked gently, "When was the last time you had your menses?"

"In March."

Nellie mentally counted. She was four months along. She took a deep breath. "Lucinda, who is the child's father?"

Tears spilled out of Lucinda's eyes. "Clifford."

Nellie's own eyes filled with tears. "Lucinda, why did you allow this to happen and with a man like Clifford? He is heartless and unfeeling. He is not what I would want for you, far from it. I will speak with your father tonight when you are asleep. We will have to go and talk to Edward. Clifford will have to marry you. There's no other way. You don't want to be a scorned woman in the province. Your father and I will come up with a plan to approach Edward."

Lucinda left her chair and knelt in front of her mother. She placed her head on her mother's lap and pleaded, "Please, Mama. Let me talk to Clifford first. I know him. He will be more receptive to marrying me if he thinks it's his idea. He will never agree if Edward forces him into it, and chances are Edward will not agree with you. Please let me talk to Clifford first before you tell Papa. Please, Mama."

Nellie smoothed her daughter's silky black hair. "Okay, I will give you until the end of the week, but then I must tell your father."

The heat of the noonday sun beat hard against the drawn curtains in Clifford's bedroom, making the room hot and uncomfortable. He moaned and tossed on the clammy sheets, his naked body flushed with the sheen of perspiration. Wiping the pasty film of drool that had gathered at the corners of his mouth with the back of his hand, he uttered a series of cusswords directed at the sun. His tongue snaked out to lick at his parched, cracked lips, and he smacked disdainfully at the taste of sulfur in his mouth. He smelled the foulness of his own breath. He dreaded getting up. He had a humongous headache brought on from his drinking binge.

Boredom had set in, and he had gone downtown to the local saloons in search of music, whisky, and women. Lucinda had not come to him. He didn't know what was wrong with her lately, but she was sick all the time. He hoped she got better soon because she was the sweetest piece of action he had going on. The women he had seen last night were not half as good as she was at pleasing him.

He rolled off the sweaty sheets and sniffed himself. Phew! He smelled awful! He reached for his pocket watch and squinted at its dials. It was a half past twelve. His father must be having conniptions. He was supposed to have taken a shipment of oysters down town to the merchants this morning. If anyone had knocked on his door or come into the room, he hadn't heard them. He had been out cold until the heat of the sun had disturbed him.

As he stood by the bed trying to gain his equilibrium, he heard the soft click of the bedroom door. Staggering, he turned to see who had come in.

"The stench in here is terrible," Lucinda said as she advanced inside. She walked directly over to the window, drew back the curtains, and opened the jalousies wide. The bright light momentarily blinded him, and he cursed as the pain in his head intensified.

"Your father is downstairs worrying about you. When you didn't come down this morning, he came up himself to check on you. He said you were out cold because you went out drinking last night. Jonah just took the shipment to town."

"Good," Clifford said, holding his head as he backed up and sat again on the bed. "Let the golden boy do it."

Lucinda came and sat beside him. "We have to talk, Clifford."

"Not now, Lucinda. My head is throbbing."

She ran a finger enticingly down his arm. "I can fix that."

Turning swiftly, he threw her backward on the bed, pulling off her blouse and brassiere in one sweep. "You know I never refuse an offer like that from you."

The rancid smell of stale liquor and sweat assailed Lucinda as he roughly removed the rest of her clothing and climbed on top of her. She gritted her teeth and bore the sweaty, filthy assault. She had to become a Dusant, and if this was the only way to accomplish it, it was well worth it. She was going to live in this house right beside Jonah and Catherine if it was the last thing she did.

As they lay together afterward, Lucinda soothingly rubbed Clifford's head. She watched as his eyes closed.

"Clifford?"

"Hmmm."

"I am having your child."

Clifford abruptly opened his eyes. Pushing Lucinda away, he sat up. His head was still throbbing, and he wondered if he had heard her correctly. "What did you say?"

"I am going to have your baby," she repeated.

"Are you sure it's not Jonah's bastard?"

Even as Clifford said the words, he knew they weren't true. Jonah had shown no interest in Lucinda despite all her efforts to entice him. He knew too that he had been keeping her too occupied. There was no way that the child could belong to any other man.

"I mean, are you sure you are with child?"

"I could not be surer."

He thought about how much she had been sick lately. "So what do you want me to do about it?"

"I don't know." Coyly Lucinda shrugged.

Clifford felt his stomach churning. He had not eaten since the evening before. "I am not a fool, Lucinda. I know you do not love me. You want Jonah, and you cannot have him, so I am the next best thing. You end up pregnant with my child, and now you're hoping I will marry you so you're not scorned." He got up off the bed. "I need to bathe and get something to eat. I don't want to talk about this anymore."

He left her there lying in his acrid stench.

Nellie was slicing a roasted duck when Clifford entered the kitchen. She greeted him as she would normally, all the while thinking about the seed he had planted in her daughter's womb.

"Nellie, would you mind giving me a few slices of that sumptuous duck? I would like you to make me a nice sandwich with it."

"Of course, Clifford, I will bring it to the dining room for you along with a nice hot cup of café. Go take a seat."

"Thank you, Nellie. You are a darling."

Clifford left the kitchen, and Nellie proceeded to vigorously slice the meat.

You had better do right by my daughter. If you refuse to marry her and she becomes a scorned woman, I may be a Christian woman, but I swear to God that I will take pleasure slowly poisoning you.

Clifford ate the sandwich and drank his coffee alone in the dining room. The house was quiet at this time in the afternoon. Beams of sunlight streamed across the room from the western windows. It forced him to move from his usual seat at the table to avoid the glare. He now sat in the same spot where Jonah had been seated the night Jonah had attacked him.

He frowned as he remembered. *You will pay, Jonah.*

His mind drifted to the news Lucinda had given him. He was going to be a father. *Ah, Lu, you are always full of surprises.*

He grinned when he thought of what she had done to Catherine. Lucinda had certainly sent Jonah into a tizzy, and nothing made him happier than seeing Jonah squirm. Marrying Lucinda and moving her in to "play house" with Catherine would certainly spark some lively entertainment.

He had been sitting at the table lost in thought for so long that he had not even seen Nellie when she'd removed his empty dishes. He realized he had made his decision. He would marry Lucinda. The smile on his face was pure evil as he thought of the effect it would have on Jonah and Catherine. He and Lucinda were two of a kind, cut from the same cloth of mischief. What better way to make Jonah's life miserable than to put the two women who loved him under the same roof?

He would talk to his father tonight after dinner. He knew Edward would not agree with his choice for a wife, but since when did he give a damn what his father thought? He got up from the table and stretched. He couldn't be more pleased with himself.

The afternoon sun beat down on Catherine as she worked in the patch of garden where her mother-in-law had once toiled. The huge chapeau she wore provided perfect coverage for her head and face, but it did little to prevent the sweat from pooling down her back. She hadn't intended to take her father-in-law's advice and tend the garden, though it was proving to be good therapy. She had been cultivating the soil for weeks. It kept her occupied and away from the house most afternoons.

Her gloved fingers dug into the moist soil as she planted a red rose bush. *Funny how we admire the splendid beauty of a rose while never noticing the thorns that could so viciously prick our fingers,* she mused.

The hard, cold side of Jonah she had witnessed still bothered her. He was his usual self again. Still, as much as she tried, she couldn't forget it. Maybe it was because he had forbidden her to leave. Her mother had told her she was too headstrong, that she would have to learn to be more acquiescing when she married Jonah, but she would never consent to being bullied.

Catherine had learned everything she could about Lucinda. She'd subtly questioned her father-in-law. She had gone in search of Raphael, who had become a good friend and confidante. She'd befriended Celeste, the young upstairs chambermaid.

From Ivan she learned Lucinda's father was one of the fishing boat captains, and her mother was none other than Nellie, the head cook. That had surprised her because she saw no physical resemblance between Lucinda and the friendly, blonde woman. Raphael had warned her to be careful around Lucinda while reassuring her of Jonah's love. Catherine smiled as she remembered her discussion with him. He had called Lucinda a few colorful words that a lady would never repeat.

But it was Celeste, the chambermaid, who had told Catherine the most surprising news of all. Lucinda was Clifford's lover! The pretty, freckled-faced girl had said, "Lucinda creeps into the house like a rat at all hours of the night. She sneaks into Monsieur Clifford's chambers, and she leaves early in the morning before everyone rises. She is a servant like me, but she acts like she is la femme de la maison. She treats all the servants like we are beneath her."

She liked Celeste. She reminded her of her sister, Marie, and oh how she missed Marie's playful antics. Since moving to Toulon, she had only received one letter, which had notified her that Pierre and Marie were engaged to be married the first week of December. It had made her all the more homesick for Marseille.

She pulled off her gloves and smiled with satisfaction when she surveyed the row of red rosebushes she had just planted. Reaching for the water can, she gave them a healthy dose of water. Ivan told her that Louise had loved roses. Tomorrow she would plant a row of pink rosebushes in her honor.

#

Clifford casually addressed his father after dinner that evening. "Father, I have a matter of great importance to discuss privately with you."

"Okay, I will take my coffee in the library. Let's go," Edward replied, reaching for his coffee cup.

"Is everything okay with you, Clifford?" Rose asked worriedly.

"Yes, Mother, everything could not be better. There is nothing for you to worry about. Father will discuss it with you when he is ready to do so."

When the library doors closed, Edward put his coffee cup aside and reached for the crystal decanter of sherry. "I have a feeling I am going to need this," he said as he raised the amber liquid to his lips. "What's on your mind?"

"Have a seat, Father. You will need to sit down."

Warily looking at his son, he took the seat opposite him.

"Tonight I am going to ask Lucinda to marry me," Clifford said unceremoniously.

Edward looked confused. He raised his hand and gestured, "Lucinda who? I don't know any of our friends who have a daughter by that name."

"I am speaking of Lucinda Perou, Father."

"Lucinda, the kitchen servant? Jacques and Nellie's daughter? Good Lord, man, have you totally lost your frigging mind?" Edward stood and started to pace. "I know you like to test me, Clifford, but I am warning you, you're pushing me too far. You cannot ask me to give you my blessings to marry a servant with whom you are already fornicating."

He resumed his seat. Exasperated, he tried another approach. "Look, continue to have fun with her. You don't have to marry her. There are many fine women of good lineage in France. You will eventually find the right one for you."

"I am not asking you for your blessings. I am telling you I am marrying her."

"Why, Clifford? Is she with child?"

"Yes, if you must know, she's carrying your grandchild, your blood. Now does that make a difference to you, Father?"

Edward stood again and poured himself another drink. "How far along is she? Maybe we can take her to one of those women in town who can handle this quietly for us."

"Damn it, Father!" Clifford bellowed, instantly on his feet. "How dare you even suggest that? This is my child. Your grandchild!"

Ivan opened the door. "Is everything okay in here?"

"Yes, everything is fine, Ivan."

Edward waited for his cousin to close the door, and then he turned back to his son. "How can you be so sure the child is yours?"

"Because I keep her fully occupied; when I am done with her, she has no strength for another man."

Acquiescently, Edward raised his hand. "Okay, you've made your point. I will speak to Father Anthony. Banns of marriage will have to be called."

"No, there is no time for that. I am leaving for St. Barthelemy in two weeks. We will be married before I leave for the voyage."

"But that's not possible. We need to—"

"Make it possible! We give enough money to the church for an exception to be made. Explain to Father Anthony that I leave in two weeks for months at sea, and I need to take a wife so that I do not commit sin by screwing all the natives. Tell him whatever you want, but get the date set soon. I don't want a big to-do. I just want"—he smirked at his father—"to use a word more suitable to your proper ears, I want to copulate legally as many times as possible before I sail." He walked to the door and opened it. "Oh, and by the way, tell Nellie to set an extra place at the dinner table tomorrow evening for her daughter. I am inviting my fiancée to dinner." Then he slammed the door shut behind him.

Clifford left the house and walked the short distance to the Perou cottage. A light drizzle was falling, but he could tell from looking at the night skies that it was going to pour soon. He picked up his pace. He had waited to give Nellie sufficient time to arrive home from her dinnertime duties. So that she didn't have to cook again after cooking all day, Ivan always allowed her to take home ample portions of each evening's meal for her family. He knew they would be having dinner now, but he couldn't wait all night.

As he neared the cottage, he thought of Ivan's unnecessary kindness to the family. *Ivan has always been a sap. No wonder Jonah is such an idiot.*

He climbed the wooden steps and knocked on the door. Lucinda opened it. The surprised look on her face delighted him.

She quickly stepped out on to the gallery, closing the door. "What are you doing here?

Clifford's eyes twinkled with mischief. "Come here and give me a kiss."

"I cannot play games with you now. I am having dinner with my parents."

"What makes you think I am here to see you?"

Her eyes locked with his, searching.

"Take my hand, Lu. We're going inside together to talk to your parents."

Lucinda gasped. Smiling, she reached for his hand and led him inside.

Jacques was just getting up to see who was on the gallery when the door opened, and Lucinda came in holding Clifford's hand. Immediately, he stood up straight.

"Good evening, Jacques, Nellie," Clifford said, taking off his hat. "I am here respectfully this evening to ask you for your daughter's hand in marriage."

Jacques looked at his wife and daughter, a puzzled expression on his face. Finally he cleared his throat. "My daughter is only a servant in your house. She is not of your status. She has no prominence. Why would you want to marry her?"

"Because we love each other, Papa," Lucinda responded quickly. "Love knows no status. I want to marry Clifford. Papa, please give us your blessing."

"If you love him, Lucinda, you have our blessings," Nellie interjected. "Your father has just been taken by surprise."

Jacques cleared his throat again. He found it difficult to speak. Clifford was his employer, and he did not want to disrespect him, but he did not like him. He had no regard for anyone, much less his employees. Still, his daughter had said she loved him.

"We will have to talk to Father Anthony. Banns of marriage will have to be announced, and—"

"That won't be necessary; I am leaving in two weeks for a voyage. We will be married next week."

"On no. Not so soon." Jacques was truly dismayed now.

"They want to be married before he leaves, Jacques. Surely you can understand the needs of young people. He will be gone a long time, and he wants her secured in the bosom of his family," Nellie quickly added.

"But she is secure here with us. They can wait until he returns. I do not understand this rush." Jacques looked at his wife, who nodded gently and persuasively at him. He then reluctantly turned back to Clifford and said after a heavy sigh, "But if my wife and my daughter desire this, I give you my blessing."

Lucinda cried out happily and flung herself into Clifford's arms.

"Thank you, Jacques. You don't have to worry about the arrangements. My family will take care of everything," Clifford said, reaching for Jacques's hand. Then he hastily bid them good evening, and Lucinda walked him out to the gallery.

It was much later that night as Jacques lay in bed with troubling thoughts about the sudden marriage when he realized Clifford Dusant had never said he loved his daughter.

#

Jonah was filthy and tired, and all he wanted to do was hold his wife. She had been on his mind all day while he worked at the boatyard. He had invited her to come down and keep him company, but she had refused. She had changed since the day they had quarreled, and he missed her playfulness and laughter. *Maybe a trip to Marseille will perk her up,* he thought.

He smiled as he climbed the second floor steps to his chambers. A trip to Marseille would indeed make her happy. He would tell her as soon as he got inside their chambers. Increasing his pace, he bounded into the corridor and bumped squarely into Lucinda.

Lucinda tried to pass Jonah, but he roughly grabbed her arms and pushed her up against the wall, pinning her there.

"Damn you, Lucinda! I told you to stay away from my wife and you didn't listen."

Her brown eyes were like chocolate pools as she brazenly held his stare. And then, leaning forward, she sniffed him. "Hmmm. I love a man who smells of sweat."

"I am going to have you banned from this house!"

"You're going to do no such thing, Jonah." Clifford's voice behind him was unruffled. "And I will thank you to take your filthy hands off my fiancée."

Jonah released Lucinda and turned around. "What the hell are you talking about, Clifford?"

Lucinda ran to Clifford, and he held her protectively.

"Lucinda and I are engaged. We will be married next week, so you cannot ban her from this house. In fact, the reason she is here right now is because she is moving her belongings into my chambers. From now on, she will be living right down the hall from you and Catherine."

Jonah looked at Lucinda. She smiled, mischief written all over her face as she held on to Clifford, her head resting on his chest.

"It's so damn pathetic, Clifford. You harass me, calling my wife a peasant. Then you up and marry a common kitchen servant, one who gladly opens her legs for anything that wears trousers. You're going to have to watch her carefully. She's likely to give you dozens of little bastards who aren't even yours."

Jonah turned around just in time to see Catherine close the parlor door.

CHAPTER 5

"Shit!" Clifford swore. All his careful planning had been for naught. He had so badly wanted to drop the news in their laps tonight at dinner. Then he grinned. He had to admit it could not have played out better had he carefully orchestrated the whole thing. The looks on Jonah's and Catherine's faces were priceless! Catherine had seen and heard everything. The golden boy was going to have to explain to his wife why he and Lucinda were locked together against the wall. He laughed heartily. But then he looked at Lucinda, and his grin faded. The bitch was still making sexual overtures at Jonah. Even now, after all of the trouble he had put himself through to make her an honest woman, she still wanted *him*!

"This obsession of yours for Jonah will stop, even if I had to beat it out of you," he snapped, grabbing her arm and pulling her down the hallway.

Jonah did not know how much Catherine had seen or heard, but he expected her to be upset. She was sitting on the sofa, and he sat beside her. They sat quietly for a time, she waiting for him to speak, and he attempting to regain his composure.

Finally he turned to her and said, "Catherine, I am truly sorry. I saw her there in the hallway, and my blood boiled. I had been waiting until I felt my temper was under control to confront her, but then just now when I saw her, I became angry again. What she said to you was inexcusable. She deliberately told you malicious lies to cause trouble between us."

He leaned back on the sofa and ran his hand through his hair. "Then Clifford showed up and made his explosive announcement. Unbelievable!"

"So what do we do now?"

"What do you mean?"

"It's obvious they plan to make us miserable."

"We will not allow them to believe their decisions have any effect on us. This house is big enough that the only time we have to really interact with them is at dinnertime."

"It will not be as easy as you make it sound, Jonah. That woman hates me." Catherine shrugged. "Oh well, at least she won't be working in the kitchen anymore so I can stop worrying about her poisoning me."

"I didn't know you worried about her poisoning you. If you had told me that before, she would have been removed from the kitchen long ago."

Jonah reached to take her in his arms, and she went willingly. He felt a rush of relief. He stroked her hair lovingly and kissed the top of her head. She smelled so good.

"Catherine."

"Hmmm?"

"You're not mad at me?"

"Why should I be mad at you? You were only defending me."

Her words sounded like music to his ears. "Please don't ever be afraid to tell me anything. I need you to talk to me. I can't stand it when you get quiet—and another thing." He took her hand, kissed it, and placed it on his chest. "Do you feel that? That's the heart that beats only for you. It was yours from the moment you raised the iron skillet at me on that first afternoon at your parents' home in Marseille."

She laughed, bringing a happy smile to his face. It had been so long since he had heard her laughter.

"Jonah?"

"Yes?"

"You really need to take a bath now. You are stinking up my sofa."

This time it was he who laughed merrily. "I am going to take a bath, and then when I am done, I am coming back to devour you, so you'd better be ready."

She looked at him seductively. "I will be waiting for you."

Lucinda took great pains to make sure she looked the part of high society. She swept her hair up in an elegant style, with loose strands framing her freshly powdered face. She selected the most elegant dress in her limited wardrobe. Her perfume smelled like lilies. She knew it was a bit overpowering, but it was all she had at her disposal.

When she entered the front door of the big house, she could smell the delicious, spicy aroma of roast beef. She recognized it as one of her mother's favorite recipes. She walked to the kitchen and slipped unobserved into the room, standing slightly past the entrance. She watched the hectic, final preparations underway for dinner. She looked at her mother standing over a big, boiling pot, her face red and perspiring.

"I will never be like you, Mama," she whispered. "I will never work so hard to serve people. People will serve me."

Catherine and Jonah were in a good mood when they entered the dining room. The extra place setting at the table was no surprise. They had expected Clifford to invite Lucinda.

When they were seated, Edward said, "I need to make a quick family announcement. Clifford has decided to take a wife. He has asked Lucinda for her hand in marriage, and she will be joining us for dinner. I know this is sudden, and believe me, I am surprised myself. Nonetheless, Clifford has made his decision. Let's do our best to make the young lady feel welcome."

No sooner had Edward spoken than Clifford and Lucinda appeared in the doorway. Clifford made a big show of escorting his fiancée to the dinner table. He pulled out her chair and seated her. Then he pleasantly addressed his family.

"A fantastic good evening to everyone. I am sure Father has already relayed the happy news that Lu and I are getting married next week." He looked down at Lucinda and smoothed the top of hair. "I know you're all thinking that this is too sudden, but think about it. Lu and I have been friends since childhood. We're very much alike in a lot of ways, and we enjoy each other's company. What better wife can a man want than a woman who knows his faults and accepts him anyway?" Turning to look at Jonah, he said, "I hope you don't mind, but I asked Simon to be my best man, and he has accepted."

"That's perfectly fine with me."

"I thought you would say that. Lu and I only want to have a quiet family dinner to celebrate after the nuptials. As you all know, I leave for the voyage shortly thereafter." He purposely looked at Jonah and Catherine. "Lu will reside in my chambers when I am gone. She will be a member of this family, and I expect all of you to treat her accordingly. Now, shall we eat?"

Clifford sat with a flourish, opened his napkin, and reached for his wine glass.

As Nellie served the heaping plates of roast beef and mash potatoes, she secretly studied her daughter. She had chosen roast beef tonight in honor of Lucinda since she knew it was her favorite meal, and it did not escape her notice that Lucinda was snubbing her. She listened to Clifford's grand speech all the while observing her daughter's facial expressions. Lucinda may not have realized when she actually became pregnant, but Nellie knew Lucinda had definitely set out to make it happen.

Clifford, you are more correct than you know. You and my daughter are indeed cut from the same evil cloth. You had better be careful though. She is much more cunning than you.

Thunder rolled and lightning flashed as Clifford and Lucinda exchanged their vows the following Saturday. Lucinda wore a simple, white dress that her mother had quickly sewn. Those in attendance consisted only of the immediate Dusant family, Lucinda's parents, and a few of Clifford's crewmembers from the *Marie Rose*.

As requested by the groom, there was no music for dancing after the ceremony, just a simple dinner where everyone wished them well. Then they bid good night and retired to Clifford's chambers.

When they were alone, Clifford unceremoniously removed his clothing. Lying naked on the bed, he watched Lucinda undress, noting that she was purposely taking her time. When she finally sat on the edge of the bed, he reached for her.

"Come here," he said gruffly.

"You were in a good mood all evening. Why are you angry now?" she replied, resisting his grip on the back of her arms.

He forcefully pulled her onto her back. Securing her hands above her head, he climbed on top of her. Then using his knees to force her legs open, he plunged himself inside her, and she closed her eyes.

"My good mood was for their benefit, not yours. Now open your eyes and look at me."

She kept her eyes closed.

Releasing his grip on her hands, he took hold of her face with his thumb and index fingers, squeezing the sides of her cheeks. "I said open your frigging eyes!"

Lucinda opened her eyes, and Clifford could see tears glistening in the corners.

"I want you to see that it's me, not Jonah, and if I ever see you flirting with him again, I will beat you senseless. Do I make myself clear?"

She nodded.

"Good."

He released his grip on her face, the imprints of his fingers leaving deep impressions on both sides of her cheeks. His hands moved to squeeze her breasts as he thrust into her again and again, finally collapsing heavily on top of her in a pool of sweat.

Three days later, the *Marie Rose* backed out of the boatyard to begin her voyage. Lucinda watched the vessel leave from the same window she had watched the *Louise Catherine* dock. She was relieved to be rid of Clifford. In fact, she couldn't care less if he never returned. She had achieved her objective. She touched her belly where the small bulge was growing. The child was the glue she needed to remain in good standing with the family. She had no further use for Clifford. He had been a means to an end. Now if she could just find a way to get rid of Catherine, she would then have a chance at the man she really wanted.

#

For its crew, each voyage starts out with boundless energy and excitement. There is something in the sea air that bewitches them, instigating the feeling of euphoria. Then midway through, the mood changes and restlessness sets in as the mundane days stretch on infinitely. Their disposition improves only at the first sight of land silhouetted in the distanced clouds. Then the gleeful whoops and hoorays rise like music.

And this will be a long one, Clifford thought. By the time he returned home, Lucinda would be ripe with child. He thought of her perfect body and tried to envision her big and fat with his child inside her. He could not deny it. He was looking forward to the child. He hoped it was a boy. He would finally be first at something. *Let's see you top that one, Jonah!*

He scowled. He was having trouble understanding himself. He wanted Lucinda to be a nuisance to Jonah and Catherine. Yet when he had seen her making sexual overtures at Jonah in the hallway, he had been overcome with jealousy.

He would have plenty of time out here at sea to come to terms with what he felt for Lucinda. Now he must remember to stash away some of those gold coins he was transporting. The simple-minded fools would never think to recount the coins against the bill of sale, and it always worked to his advantage.

"Trusting imbeciles." He laughed as he walked the length of his vessel, making sure that everything was fastened and properly secured for the night.

"Clifford, I see Saba," Simon called out.

Clifford joined him at the helm and looked at the steep mountainous island jutting straight up out of the sea directly in their line of vision. He perused the mariner's map lying on the counter.

"According to the map, St. Barthelemy should be just to the south of here."

Both men turned to look southward.

"I see it!" Simon yelled. "It's cloaked in clouds, but I can see its silhouette."

The jubilatory hoorays from the crew were contagious. It had been a long voyage, and although they knew there would be no oasis waiting for them on this little island, they were happy to put their feet on solid ground.

As he rowed the rowboat into the harbor, Clifford cursed at the throngs of seagulls squawking above him. The island's unique, natural beauty was lost on him. All he saw was the drought-parched hills.

Potential, phew! Unless you relished living like a caveman, there's no potential here. Ivan is so daft that he wouldn't recognize real potential if it walked right up to him and slapped him. What potential could he possibly see in this tiny island with its mountainous, dry terrain?

Onshore, he reached into his pocket and pulled out the name of the French government official to whom he was to deliver the cargo and pick up the outgoing one. He wanted to complete his business and leave this dismal place. He would give his crew a real treat and make a special stop when they sailed away. They would find the rum and revelry they wanted in the Spanish Isles. They couldn't linger too long though. It was the height of the gale season, and so far they had been lucky not to have encountered any of the bad storms.

#

Lucinda was furious the day she learned Catherine was pregnant. She and Jonah announced it demurely one evening at dinner. It was obvious they had already told Ivan because he had a doting look on his face. Nellie was serving dessert when they broke the news, and it irked her even more when her mother put down her serving tray to hug Catherine with such pleasure. The only one not involved in the commotion was Edward, who sat quietly observing everything.

Lucinda wanted to overturn the table onto Catherine's lap as she sat there bragging about how she was four months along and never sick.

Days later she was still plotting ways to inconspicuously push Catherine down the stairs. It angered her to share the spotlight with anyone, much less a woman she despised.

Jonah left for Argentina shortly after Clifford returned from St. Barthelemy. Catherine was besieged with loneliness. It didn't help that Clifford and Lucinda constantly made snide remarks when passing her in the house. She didn't trust them, so she kept her distance as much as possible. She took solace in the times she spent conversing with her father-in-law. He was a compassionate man whom she had come to love and admire.

Nellie and Rose were comforting as well. Nellie taught her how to knit so that she could make little booties and caps for the baby. Rose was like a mother hen, constantly checking to make sure she had eaten and taken her vitamins. Still, she wanted the comfort of her own mother. She yearned to go home to Marseille.

Most nights Catherine found it difficult to sleep, but it was raining heavily, and the sound of the rain melodiously hitting the galvanize roof lulled her into a deep sleep. At first she thought it was Jonah when she felt the hand slide up under her underwear and began to massage her private parts. From deep in the recesses of sleep, she slowly came to her senses.

As she opened her eyes, a hand clamped over mouth. "You remember when you slapped me?" Clifford whispered harshly. "I am here to collect payment. You're not going to say anything to anyone, because if you do, I will kill your parents and sister, but not before I screw Marie too. If you want to protect them, you will willingly open your legs."

CHAPTER 6

Catherine could smell the foulness of his alcohol-laden breath as he positioned his weight on top of her, keeping a hand clamped firmly over her mouth. She was terrified for her baby as his heavier frame pressed down hard on her belly. Whisky-reeking drool escaped from his mouth and dripped on her face. She was pinned to the bed, but he was drunk. She could overpower him given the right chance to act. Summoning her willpower, she forced herself to think clearly.

"Tonight you're going to be screwed by a real man. I am going to teach you tricks the golden boy could never teach you," he slurred as he bit her neck and roughly squeezed her breasts.

When he struggled to push her legs open with one hand, she seized the opportunity. She raised her right leg quickly with as much strength as she could muster, her knee catching him hard in the groin. He removed his hand from her mouth and bent over her in pain, holding his crotch.

Quickly grabbing the metal lantern next to the bed, she brought it down heavily on the side of his head, knocking him off the bed and to the floor. Then, trembling, she peered over the side of the bed. He was out cold. She jumped off the bed and ran to open the bedroom door and then the main door from the parlor to the hallway. Praying he was still unconscious, she ran back into the bedroom.

He was still lying on the floor where she had left him. An ugly, purplish-red bruise was developing on the right side of his forehead. He was shirtless, and his pantaloons were bundled around his feet, exposing his limp penis.

"Ugh," she said with a grimace.

She dragged him by his feet from the bedroom, through the parlor, and out into the main hallway. Then she quickly closed the door, pushing a heavy oak dresser behind it. Collapsing on the floor against the dresser, she cried, "Please don't let me have killed him."

Catherine sat on the floor against the oak dresser for the remainder of the night. She could not stop trembling. She felt cold, but her legs were too weak for her to stand. Her mind was not working correctly. It was surreal. Clifford had tried to rape her!

The fact that he had done such an unthinkable, cruel thing and the thought that she may have killed him were competing in her mind for preference. She envisioned him lying lifeless outside her door and Celeste finding him there when she started her morning chores. "Dear God, the gendarmes will come and take me away," she cried.

Her thoughts shifted. *What if he comes to and tries to break down the door?*

"Oh, God help me," Catherine prayed. He had threatened to kill her parents and Marie. What was she going to do?

Steep in turmoil, she lost track of time, and the sudden knock on the door startled her.

"Madame Catherine, I cannot get the door open."

Catherine quickly dried her tears with her palms. "Give me a few minutes, Celeste, and I will open it for you." Slowly she stood. Her feet felt wobbly as she walked to the bathroom to tidy herself.

Feeling a bit more composed, she pushed the oak dresser away and opened the door. She breathed a sigh of relief. There was no dead body! Celeste would be back at any moment. She walked to the bed and started to get on it, but then she paused, remembering what had nearly happened there. Grabbing a clean quilt from the linen closet, she headed for the sofa.

She was lying on the sofa when Celeste came into the room. If the young chambermaid noticed Catherine's red eyes and pale face, she did not comment on them. Instead she asked, "Is there anything I can do for you, Madame?"

"Please tell Monsieur Ivan that I am not feeling well, and I will not be joining the family for breakfast."

"I will go straight to him. You rest now. I will bring a breakfast tray for you. Is there anything special you want?"

"Only some hot tea and buttered toast."

"I will be back soon," Celeste said, leaving the room.

About midday Ivan became concern for Catherine. He had never known her to stay in her chambers all day. He ventured up the stairs and knocked on her door.

"Who is it?" Catherine's voice sounded tremulous.

"Catherine, it's me, Ivan. Please open the door."

When Catherine opened the door, Ivan immediately noticed her swollen eyes and tear stained face. She was still wearing her nightgown, and she appeared wobbly as she walked back to the sofa. Worriedly, he sat down beside her.

"Catherine, what is the matter?"

"I just miss Jonah and my family terribly," Catherine replied. "I want to go home to Marseille for a while. My sister is getting married in a few weeks. I would like to be there to help my mother with the wedding."

"Is that all that is troubling you?"

"Yes."

Ivan wasn't convinced that she was being truthful. None-the-less, he responded, "That's easy to fix. When would you like to go? I will escort you there myself."

"Tomorrow?"

"I will miss you greatly, my dear, but if it brings back your beautiful smile, it is worth my misery. You know," he said pensively, "Clifford is up to his old prowling ways again. He was in a brawl last night. There is a big, oozing gash on his forehead. That boy never learns. Well." He slapped his knees and stood up. "I will get a vessel ready to take you to

Marseille. Now cheer up." He gave her a fatherly kiss on her forehead. "See you at dinner."

Clifford was furious. The little bitch had kneed his groin and chopped him on the head. His head and testicles hurt. He had found himself on the floor in the hallway outside her door. He couldn't remember how he had gotten there. After she knocked him out, she must have dragged him through the rooms.

He gingerly wiped the blood and pus from around the wound with a handkerchief. When his mother had seen it this morning, she had wanted to call the doctor. She was sure he needed stitches. His father had given him a lecture on growing up and being responsible now that he was a married man. His so-called wife had said nothing. She showed no interest in knowing what had happened to him.

He had been drinking all evening. The alcohol had given him the courage to carry out his plan of extracting vengeance on Catherine. He had crept to her chambers in the middle of the night, excitement making the blood flow hotly to his loins as he thought of the delicacy he would finally sample. He had not planned on her so ferociously fighting back. She had successfully executed a counterattack. Clifford smiled wickedly. She was a fighter, and he thrived on a good fight.

Catherine took her time getting ready for dinner. She'd had plenty of time to think things through and calm herself. She would say nothing to Jonah or Ivan. She knew that if she did, Jonah would kill Clifford, and he would be sent to the gallows. She wouldn't risk losing her husband. Nor would she give Clifford the pleasure of thinking he had succeeded at intimidating her.

Let him sit there and squirm thinking I will say something to Ivan. He wants a fight? I will give him one, but it will be on my terms.'

She was poised and radiant when she walked into the dining room. She sat across the table from him and forced herself to speak amiably. She gazed brazenly at the ugly. oozing wound on his forehead and exclaimed, "Clifford! How did you get that awful looking cut?"

Clifford glared at her and mumbled, "I got into a fight last night."

She shook her head chidingly. "You know, Clifford, you really should be more careful who you pick a brawl with. The next time they might kill you!" She smiled knowing he was seething.

Marie squealed with delight when she opened the door and saw Catherine. It took a few seconds for her to realize her sister's father-in-law was also standing on the gallery.

"Oh, please forgive my manners, Mr. Dusant. I was so excited to see my sister. Please come in."

Charles and Suzanne smiled happily when they saw Catherine. After she greeted Ivan, Suzanne touched her daughter's growing belly. "Oh, Catherine, you're glowing."

"Yeah, like a giant pumpkin," Marie taunted.

"I do not look like a pumpkin!"

Suzanne turned to Ivan. "We're so thankful to you for bringing Catherine to us. Can I offer you some tea and something to eat? I have a chicken roasting, but it's going to be another hour or so before it is ready. We would be honored if you could stay and join us for lunch."

"A cup of tea will do just fine. I would be happy to join you, but I have a business meeting this afternoon. I am delighted to have brought Catherine home. I can see you miss her as much as she missed you."

Ivan stayed with the family for another half hour, and then Charles walked with him down to the vessel. The two men conversed pleasantly, Ivan doing most of the talking, deftly drawing Charles out in conversation.

#

"Stop bouncing like a damned jackrabbit and get the hell out of here." A grin belied the roughness in Raphael's voice. They had just pulled into the boatyard in Toulon from the voyage to Argentina.

"Huh?"

"You're almost shitting yourself in your hurry to get to Catherine. Now go, I will secure the vessel."

"You're sure?"

"Are you waiting for me to push your ass overboard? Get going!"

Jonah beamed Raphael a wide grin and bolted off the vessel. He didn't stop to catch his breath until he was in front of the house. He looked up at the second-floor galleries and windows, his eyes anxiously searching for Catherine.

That's strange, he thought. He was sure she knew he was coming home today. He fully expected to see the front door burst open. He lingered, waiting. After a few minutes, he proceeded across the yard. He opened the front door and groaned when he saw Lucinda sitting on the sofa.

She stood and walked toward him with her arms open, her protruding belly comically obvious. "Welcome home, darling. I know you must be hard up since you no longer visit your lady friends in the ports. I can take care of that for you." She ran her fingers down his chest, letting her hand fall lower.

"Cut it out, Lu," he said, brushing her hand away. "Go play with your husband. I am not interested."

"She's not here. The minute you left, she packed her bags and ran back to her mama in Marseille. She said she was leaving and not coming back." Lucinda pouted provocatively. "But I am here to take care of you."

Ivan saw the *Louise Catherine* dock. He knew his son would waste no time coming up to the house to see his wife. He had fully intended to meet him at the door and deliver the news that he had taken Catherine to Marseille. But as he descended the main staircase, it became apparent that he was not the only one who had been watching the *Louise Catherine's* progress. His anger grew as he watched Lucinda. The vixen had beaten him to the front door and was busy working her wiles on Jonah.

"That's enough, Lucinda! You should be ashamed of yourself. You're eight months' pregnant, and you are still hell-bent on seducing my son. Now, if you don't want me to tell your husband about your wanton disregard for your wedding vows, you will stop this nonsense. There is nothing but putrid lies coming from your mouth."

He paused to take a breath. "Jonah, your wife did not leave you. I took her to Marseille myself so she could help her family with her sister's wedding. Catherine fretted on the entire voyage over her concerns for you. She wanted me to make sure I explained to you why she left."

Swiftly turning, Jonah walked back out the door.

Raphael was still securing the *Louise Catherine* when he looked up and saw Jonah hustling back down the path. Without saying a word, Jonah climbed aboard the vessel and started to loosen the anchor.

Raphael immediately followed him.

"Now what the hell is wrong?"

"My wife is in Marseille. I am going to get her."

"Is everything okay?"

"Yes. She went back to help with the plans for her sister's wedding."

"And you can't wait until tomorrow morning to fetch her?"

"You don't have to come. I can handle it."

"You're right." Raphael scratched his beard. "I don't have to come with you, but I don't want you running the vessel into a reef because you're too blinded by love to see where the hell you're going. Now move out of my way. Let me handle this while you prepare to sail."

Strong, powerful arms encircled Catherine from the back. Warm lips caressed the arc of her neck, pausing only to inhale her scent and nip at the soft flesh. She smelled the intoxicating manly smell that was unique only to Jonah. Her knees went weak, and she felt the familiar heat between her legs. She dropped the ladle she was holding, and it clanged noisily onto the floor near her feet. The chicken stew cooking on the stove was forgotten. She turned in his arms and cleaved herself to his hard, firm body, her ample belly an encumbrance in her ardent need to mesh their bodies. She had missed him for so long. The smoldering scent from the stew permeated the room as they clung to each other.

Hazily they heard Suzanne's voice calling, "Catherine, something's burning." And indeed something was.

The sun was setting when Jonah and Catherine left Marseille that evening, promising to come back two days before the wedding. As the *Louise Catherine* glided over the waves, Jonah held his wife under the night sky filled with trillions of twinkling stars. Raphael was at the helm.

"God bless you, Raphael," Jonah whispered, his lips on the top of Catherine's silky head. He tenderly ran his hands over her belly. His child had grown so much in her womb since he had been gone. He was looking so forward to loving her tonight. He wondered if it would cause any harm to the child. He would have to remember to be very gentle, but God help him, he needed to love her tonight.

#

Lucinda was in her usual bad mood. She was so big with child that she waddled when she walked. Everyone kept their distance, including her mother. She barked orders at the servants, and nothing anyone did to try to make her more comfortable was appreciated.

She had woken with a craving for a *gâteau au chocolat*. At breakfast she had asked her mother to bake the cake, and it was almost noon. Grumbling, she maneuvered herself off the sofa and toddled toward the kitchen. Since the day she had married Clifford, she had never again set foot inside the room.

She stood at the door and hollered, "Mama, what can possibly be so hard for you that you cannot get a simple cake ready? I have been waiting too long now."

Nellie looked up from the pot she was stirring and grumbled, "Why has God given me such a cross to bear?" Then irritably she hollered, "The cake is cooling, Lucinda."

"I heard you. You're the cross that I have to bear, you're so slow. That cake should have already cooled. I want it now or—"

A gush of warm water suddenly exploded down her legs. She looked down at the shiny linoleum floor where the water was pooling around her feet.

A sharp pain hit her lower back, and the color drained from her face. "Mama, help me!"

Nellie turned off the stove and rushed to her daughter. "The baby is coming. Let me help you up to your chambers."

As her labor progressed, Lucinda's screams could be heard all over the house. Clifford was working down by the boatyard with Jonah, and Rose had asked one of the kitchen staff to fetch him. Edward and Ivan retreated to the library while the two older women tried their best to calm Lucinda.

After what seemed like an eternity, the sweet cries of a baby were heard, as well as the gleeful shout, "It's a boy!"

Noel came with cold, rainy weather and harsh mistrals. The Christmas logs were lit in the main parlor. The flickering flames cast a soft glow on the crèche that adorned the corner table proudly displaying Mary, Joseph, and the baby, Jesus.

The family gathered in the dining room and enjoyed *le réveillon*, the long feast, with roasted duck as the main course. After dinner they moved into the parlor, and Nellie served them generous slices of the Bûche de Noël. Despite the dismal weather, they were enjoying an evening of camaraderie. Clifford and Lucinda had not joined them in the parlor, opting to retire to their chambers with the baby, whom they had named Jacques after Lucinda's father.

As the family talked and enjoyed their dessert, Jonah drifted over to the crèche and gently picked up the little figurines. He liked this time of year because it reminded him most of his mother. She took such pleasure in decorating the house, and the manger was her favorite. Wistfully he smiled as the memories surfaced. He would leave his shoes by the fireplace, and his mother would fill them with treats and little toys, her face lighting up as she told him that Père Noël had come bearing gifts. Long after he had come to realize that it was his mother, not Père Noël leaving the little treasures, he still continued to leave his shoes by the fireplace in anticipation of his treats. She had never failed him.

#

"Oh, God, please help me."

Catherine whispered the simple supplication so calmly. Yet it was far from how she was feeling. The blood on her underwear could only mean one thing. Her baby was coming.

She sat, bewildered, on the commode watching the early morning sun cast shards of light on the hardwood floor before her. Nellie had said her belly had dropped in preparation for the birth, and that was the reason for her frequent peeing, but she wasn't expecting the child until the end of March, and it was barely the middle of the month. She wasn't feeling any pain aside from the normal prickly pains in her back.

Mama, oh how I wish you were here. Sighing, she pulled up her panties and waddled to find Rose or Nellie.

The women were both in the kitchen, and they immediately noticed her pallor.

"Are you okay?" Nellie stepped forward with Rose close behind her.

"I don't know." She explained what was happening.

Rose smiled and patted her hand. "It's going to be a while yet, but you're right, the child is coming.

It seemed to Catherine that the pains would never end. She had been in labor for almost eight hours, and the baby was finally crowning. Several hours before, Nellie had given her a slim vial of liquid to drink. It had dimmed her senses and given her some relief, but now the contractions were coming harder and faster. Nellie was wiping the sweat from Catherine's forehead when Catherine heard Jonah's voice. She cried out his name. She heard Rose tell him to leave, and she cried out louder, "No. Jonah, don't leave me!"

She saw when Jonah brushed Rose aside, and she sighed with relief when she heard him say, "My wife wants me here, and as long as she wants me, I am not leaving."

Jonah held Catherine's hands and whispered words of encouragement as she rode out each contraction. Finally she felt one last tremendous urge to push, and her body convulsed southward between her legs. She felt the relief as it finally expulsed the child, and then she heard faint cries that grew stronger as the newborn demonstrated the strength of its new found lungs. She watched Rose clean, bundle and hand the child to Jonah. His arms shook as he held the infant, and then tearfully he said, "Catherine, we have a son."

Jonah placed their son in her arms, and Catherine looked adoringly at her child. She counted every little toe and finger and kissed his little button nose. "Welcome, Marcel," she whispered.

"Marcel is a handsome, strong boy," Ivan said as he held his first grandchild. They were all seated on the main gallery enjoying the cool spring day.

Charles sat beside Ivan, and Susanne sat comfortably next to her daughter. She and Charles had just announced they would extend their stay for another week.

Raphael sat across from the two grandfathers, giving them orders on how to take care of Marcel. "He may be your blood," he told them flippantly, "but he is as much mine as he is yours. I am going to have him piloting the *Louise Catherine* in no time. He might turn out to be a better captain than his stubborn father." He poked Jonah playfully.

Jonah picked up the banter. "If you think you're going to have my son drinking whiskey and carousing like you, you'd better think again." He mischievously tipped Raphael's chapeau off his head. "Then again, you did bawl like a baby when you first saw Marcel. He is going to have you wrapped around his little finger, and you're going to spoil him rotten if I don't keep my eyes on you."

"That's right, I will spoil him 'cause he's my boy. Thank goodness he looks like his mother and not ugly like you," he bantered back.

#

The days flew by quickly, and everyone settled into their customary routines. The house was filled with the finicky cries and happy gurgling of two little boys who were oblivious to the discord that existed among their parents. Rose and Nellie doted on the children, knitting little sweaters, caps, and booties and cuddling them at every opportunity.

On the surface, the family appeared happy, but like the inward churnings of an angry volcano whose dome is destined to blow, the undercurrents continued to stir. Even the relationship between Ivan and Edward was strained. The only sons of two brothers, they had grown up together. Collectively, their fathers had owned the estate and had operated a successful fishing business. Ivan and Edward were barely in their twenties when they convinced their fathers to buy a trading vessel. To cut costs, they recruited family members and friends to crew the vessel, and they took turns captaining the trading expeditions. With Edward's cunning and Ivan's astuteness, they were soon making bigger profits than their fathers. It wasn't long before they were able to buy other vessels.

Ivan was aware of Edward's sometimes unscrupulous business ethics, but he turned a blind eye. He trusted Edward enough to be convinced that his vices were harmless. They both recognized their differences in character and personality were the very essence that made them so successful. Yet lately Edward hardly spoke to Ivan, and when he did, he was irritable and distracted.

Edward's behavior became progressively harder to discern. Rose was at her wit's end because she never knew what mood to expect. She worried that he was sick, and she begged him to allow her to send for a doctor. Something was deeply troubling her husband and its advent appeared to be connected to the birth of their grandson. It was baffling because he was deeply in love with little Jacques. The only times he seemed truly happy was when he was holding and playing with the child.

The animosity Lucinda felt for Catherine had not subsided, and Clifford encouraged it. He was hell bent on getting even with Catherine. Twice now she had gained the upper hand. His next plan for revenge would have to be precise.

The working relationship between Clifford and Jonah was also suffering. Whereas in the past they had managed to work civilly together for the good of the business, they now constantly bickered. One windy afternoon they came to blows down at the boatyard. Jonah had given an order to the crew to wash the vessels from the sea spray because the wind was particularly high and had blasted the vessels with salt. Clifford had immediately countered back, telling them to disregard Jonah's orders.

Jonah was outraged. "What the frigging hell do you think you're doing? I gave those men a direct order to wash the vessels. You have no right to pull them off the job."

"I can do whatever I want. I own this business too."

"You are willfully undermining me in front of the men."

"Yeah, I am. So what are you going to do about it, golden boy? Not a damn thing! It's about time you realize the world does not revolve around you and your peasant …"

Jonah had not given him the opportunity to finish his sentence. He punched him hard, knocking him to the sandy ground. Clifford got up and took a swing back at Jonah. He missed, and Jonah grabbed hold of the arm that had swung at him. The situation between the two men had become so heated that Raphael and Simon were forced to intercede, pulling them apart from each other's throats. The argument had continued that evening in the library in front of their fathers, who had sided each with his own son.

In the sultry heat of summer, the friction grew more fiercely until the dome finally exploded one stiflingly hot mid-August afternoon.

Catherine had been trying all day to keep Marcel cool. His arms, legs, and torso were red with a heat rash. She had taken off his clothes, leaving him only in his diaper, and they were on their private gallery trying to catch any little breeze possible. She too had stripped down to only a white chemise and cotton bloomers that reached down to just above her knees.

Her eyes scanned the purplish blue horizon, searching for Jonah and the vessel he was sailing. One of the captains of the fishing vessels had been out sick for more than a week, and Jonah was his replacement. She was worried because a storm was brewing. The waves were getting angry. She could see lightning and hear the rumble of thunder.

Wiping the sweat from her brow, Catherine glanced up at the sky. The air was thick and charged with tension. Definitely a bad storm was looming. She was hoping Jonah had turned around and was on his way home.

It started to rain, so she picked up Marcel and proceeded into the parlor, closing the jalousies because the wind was pushing the rain into the room. She placed Marcel in his crib, and as she straightened up, she felt the hair on the back of her neck rise. She turned around slowly.

Clifford stood stark naked at the entrance to the bedroom, his clothes in a rumpled pile on the floor. He had barricaded the main door leading to the hallway by pulling the oak dresser against it, just as she had previously done to keep him out of the room.

"So," he said menacingly, smacking his lips and rubbing his hands together. "What are you going to do now? There's no place for you to run."

Before she could react, he reached out and grabbed her arms, twisting them cruelly behind her back. The muscles and sinews in her arms and hands burned with the sudden pain as he dragged her into the bedroom and pushed her face-down on the bed. Roughly, he began to tear at her bloomers.

"You can scream all you want. It will only excite me further because no one can hear you above the sound of the rain."

He was lying on top of her back, his heavy weight pinning her to the bed. He was drunk again. She smelled the alcohol mixed with his sweat.

"'You should be careful who you pick a brawl with, Clifford,'" he taunted, mimicking her. "You're going to pay for it all now, bitch."

Catherine was terrified. The position in which he held her made it impossible for her to help herself. The tears fell from the corners of her eyes as she heard her son's screams.

"Shut up, you little bastard, before I come over there and permanently shut you up," Clifford yelled at Marcel while keeping Catherine pinned to the bed.

"Please, Clifford," Catherine mumbled, her mouth pressed against the sheet. "This is between you and me, not Marcel. Please don't hurt my baby."

"It's only you I want to hurt, and I plan to take my time hurting you."

Catherine figured if she kept him talking, she could delay the inevitable.

"You know that Jonah is going to kill you."

She realized she had said the wrong thing when she felt the hard slap against the back of her head. Then she heard the final rip of her bloomers and she felt his swollen penis against her bare skin. Feeling utterly helpless, she started to recite the rosary.

CHAPTER 7

A loud blast against the door and the sound of splintering wood
instantly halted Clifford's actions. She heard the dragging sound
of the dresser being pushed away and then powerful, angry arms pulled
Clifford off her. She saw Clifford fly across the room and land with a
heavy thud against the northern wall next to the jalousies.

She had never seen Jonah in such a murderous rage. As he repeatedly
smashed his fist into Clifford's face, Catherine heard bones breaking.
Blood spattered on the floor and against the wall. Shaken as she was, she
knew if she didn't find a way to stop Jonah, he was going to kill Clifford.

She ran and opened the jalousies. Bending over the railing she
screamed, "Help me. Anybody! Please come quickly."

Their chambers were located directly over the kitchen. She prayed
someone had heard her. Marcel was screaming, but she had no time to
tend to the child. She hurried over to Jonah and tried to pry him off
Clifford. He shrugged her away, throwing her off balance. She staggered
and came back at him. She begged and pleaded with him to stop, but
he was too far gone to hear her.

Catherine felt tremendous relief when she heard hurried footsteps,
and then Edward and Ivan appeared in the doorway. They were followed
closely by Rose and Nellie. It took all the strength the two older men
possessed to stop Jonah from pounding blows into Clifford. The older
men fell backward, taking Jonah with them as they fell. Still, he
struggled with them, trying to break free to get back to Clifford.

His father held him tightly, begging him to come to his senses.

Finally Ivan's persistence paid off, and Jonah stopped struggling. His knuckles were raw and bleeding, and he was panting heavily.

Clifford lay naked on the floor in a bloody, broken mess.

Rose started to scream when she saw her son's condition. He was conscious, but bleeding profusely.

Nellie turned to Lucinda, who was standing in the doorway. "Go get as many towels and sheets as you can find. We need to stop the bleeding."

Lucinda wordlessly followed her mother's orders, coming back quickly, her hands filled with linens.

Dazed and shaking, Catherine finally picked up her screaming son and silently began to rock him.

"What the hell happened here?" Edward thundered.

Nellie bent over Clifford. Covering him with a sheet, she began to treat his wounds. His nose was swelling rapidly. It was obviously broken, probably in more than one place. Both his eyes were swollen. The skin around them was puffy and turning an ugly purplish blue. He had multiple open wounds on both cheeks. His entire face was bloodied.

"I am going to clean you up as much as I can, but we're going to have to send for a doctor," Nellie told him.

"And the gendarmes!" Edward shouted. "That boy is not going to get away with it this time," he said, wrathfully pointing his finger at Jonah where he sat against the wall on the floor, his head resting in his hands, his knees bent.

"That's right, Edward. Go ahead and send for the gendarmes, because Clifford is the one going to jail," Ivan thundered back. "This is not the first time he has attacked Catherine."

Catherine stopped rocking and stared at her father-in-law.

"I know about it, Catherine. You were very brave and handled yourself well, not wanting Jonah to know in order to prevent something exactly like this from occurring. I am a quiet man, but I am not stupid. I observe a lot, and I know that it is you who gave Clifford the gash on his forehead that he sported for many weeks last year. That is also the reason you begged me to take you home to Marseille the very next day after it occurred."

Ivan turned to Jonah as he started to get up again. "Sit back down, Jonah! Your wife handled herself well, and she did it to protect you." He paused and looked at Clifford. "But this miserable excuse for a human being refuses to leave her alone. So please, Edward, go ahead and send for the gendarmes. I have had it with your son."

Edward turned to Clifford. "Is this true? Did you attempt to rape Catherine? Have you done so in the past?"

Clifford shrugged off Nellie's hand as she tried to stop a cut near his left eye from bleeding. "She was asking for it from the first day she slapped me in Marseille. I saw her first, and I wanted her, but Jonah had to pursue her just because he knew I wanted her."

"I asked you a question. Did you attempt to rape her?"

"Yes! I did! She had it coming for slapping me," Clifford shouted angrily.

Edward jammed his fist hard against the oak dresser, startling everyone. "Damned, Clifford! Where in hell did I go wrong with you? I gave you the best of everything. In fact, I worked hard so you could have life easy, and still you persist in being a good-for-nothing idiot. I have a good mind to—"

"Don't look at me like that!" Clifford interrupted his father through hacking sobs. "I am no different from you. I am just like you! You go after what you want, and you never let anyone or anything get in your way. That's how we got the boatyard. You got rid of those Jews, and you didn't let anyone stop you, not even Louise."

"What did you say about Louise?" Ivan asked.

"Leave him alone, Ivan. Obviously he's hallucinating from all the blows he received at your son's hands. Nellie has to finish tending to him. Let's all allow her space to work," Edward said quickly, trying to usher everyone out of the room.

Ivan dismissed Edward with the wave of his hand. Looking down at Clifford where he still sat on the floor, he asked, "What did you say about my wife?"

Clifford placed both hands on his head. Snot and blood intermingled and dripped from his nose. With his head bowed, they had to strain to hear what he was saying.

"I used to follow Father when he went down to the Jews' camp. I would creep down at a safe distance behind him. The first time I did it, I just wanted to be with my papa, so I followed him, hoping he would agree to take a swim with me once he saw me."

"That's enough, Clifford! I order you to say no more!" Edward shouted.

"Let the boy speak!" Ivan shouted back. "Please continue, Clifford."

Clifford exhaled as if a big load was being lifted from his shoulders, and then he continued. "When I got to the camp, I heard a woman crying. I crept up to the little hut and peered in the window. I saw Father holding a baby, and initially I thought how nice it was, but then I heard the tone of his voice as he spoke to a man standing a few steps away. I saw that his hand was covering the baby's mouth and nose, and the baby's face was turning blue. I saw the mother crying hysterically. I heard Father tell them that the next time he came and they were still there, he would kill more of the children."

There were loud gasps in the room, and Clifford momentarily stopped speaking. Then he continued, "I don't know if that baby died. I left before Father saw me. But I know other babies died because I followed him every time he went there.

"Father didn't know Louise was going to be down at the camp the day she died. She usually went on Sunday afternoons. This was a Tuesday. I was there before she arrived on her horse. I saw her and wanted to stop her from seeing what he was doing. She would never have understood, as I did, that Father was doing this for our good. But I didn't want anyone to know I was there, so I kept quiet.

"When she saw what was happening, Louise hurried right up to the bay and into the water where Father stood. He was holding a little boy of about two and was lowering him beneath the water when she called out his name. The mother was making such a ruckus, and I never understood why the fathers were so afraid. Father was just one man. They could have easily overpowered him.

"Louise did what the parents were afraid to do. She demanded he give the boy back to his mother, and Father did what she asked."

Clifford paused to wipe his nose, never once looking at his father. "But I could see he was upset that she had found him out.

"When the boy was securely in his mother's arms, without saying another word to Father, Louise turned and left. I believe he knew she was going straight to Ivan with what she had just seen. He followed her, and I followed him. I was only ten years old, but already I knew every shortcut through the cliffs. It wasn't hard to keep pace with him. It's how I was always able to follow him and remain unseen.

"I don't think he meant to hurt her, but it was obvious that she became frightened when she saw him pursuing her. He called out to her, asking her to stop. Instead she sped up, forcing the horse to go faster. I saw when the horse stumbled, and she fell off. I knew she was hurt badly from the way she had fallen. I expected Father to pick her up and bring her home, but he didn't. He came upon her, stopped, looked at her, said he was sorry, but that this was for the good of the company, and kept going."

The painful sounds that emerged from Ivan's throat were that of a severely wounded animal as he lunged at his cousin. Now it was Jonah's turn to hold his father back. He flew to his feet and caught hold of Ivan from the back of his waist.

"You son of a bitch! You left my wife to die on the side of the road like an animal, and all these years you led me to believe you knew nothing of what had happened to her. You accompanied me looking for her when you knew exactly where she was lying dead. You tried your best to make me believe the Jews had hurt her while all the time it was you."

Ivan's voice broke and he started to cry. "You preyed upon innocent, peaceful people who were so helpless and afraid of you that they wouldn't even defend themselves. You killed babies and you killed my wife all in the name of power and money. What kind of evil monster are you? From this day forward, you are no longer my family." Then he collapsed, crying inconsolably in the arms of his son.

Edward had become totally undone. He looked at Ivan, but the words he wanted to say couldn't come out of his mouth. His mind was in utter confusion. Nothing was making sense. The air was stifling, and he was having trouble breathing. He looked at his son and mumbled, "I am so sorry." Then he hurried out to the gallery. Rose and Lucinda followed him.

Jonah was busy tending to his father, and Catherine was sitting next to him on the floor, Marcel on her lap. Clifford was still sitting on the floor on the opposite side of the room, and Nellie had resumed tending to his wounds. When they heard Rose and Lucinda screaming, they rushed out to the gallery just in time to see Rose fall backward into Lucinda's arms. Lucinda was shaking so badly she could hardly hold on to the older woman's dead weight.

Jonah took Rose from Lucinda's arms and eased her onto the wet floor. Clifford looked over the gallery, and when he saw his father's broken body lying on the ground below, he fell to his knees against the railing. His screams were pitiful. Nellie was trying her best to pull him away from the railing. All the cuts she had tended were bleeding again in the heat of his anxiety. At the realization that his cousin was dead, Ivan too collapsed, hitting his head hard on the wet floor.

Jonah was lifting his father off the floor, and Lucinda was still trying to get Rose to regain consciousness when Catherine placed Marcel in his crib and ran downstairs to get help. She dispatched servants to fetch Raphael, Simon, Jacques, and the doctor. Then she ran back upstairs accompanied by Celeste. The perspiration dripped from her body. Holding on to the banister, she stopped at the top of the stairs to wipe the sweat from her face. It was then that she heard little Jacques crying. Realizing the child was awake and alone in Clifford and Lucinda's chambers, she instructed Celeste to collect him. Then she hurried back to her chambers.

Jonah had picked up Marcel. Ivan was still lying on the bed where Jonah had laid him. He was conscious, but pale. Lucinda was doing her best to comfort her mother-in-law, who was also conscious and wailing loudly. She sat on the floor with Rose's head on her lap.

Fully clothed now, Clifford sat in the same spot on the floor as before. Only now he was lamenting over and over, "I killed my father. I killed my father. It's my fault that he's dead. Oh Papa, I am so sorry."

Raphael and Simon arrived, followed closely by Jacques, who went immediately to Lucinda. He lowered himself to the floor beside her, and she laid her head on his shoulder. Raphael and Simon stood together at the entrance, their worn hats in their hands, their faces full of sorrow for this family that they held in such high esteem. Celeste was in the hallway, holding little Jacques, singing softly to him.

Jonah walked over to Catherine and handed Marcel to her. He cleared his throat. "I am going downstairs to attend to Edward."

"You will not lay your filthy hands on my father," Clifford yelled. "You caused this, you and that peasant! If you hadn't brought her into this house, this never would have happened."

All the fight had gone out Jonah, and it was clearly reflected in his voice. "Catherine has never said an unkind word to you, Clifford, but you keep using her as your whipping boy to get back at me. Today it's become clear that you are a troubled soul who witnessed things no ten-year-old boy should have seen. Yet it does not excuse your hatred and jealousy of me. Know one thing, though: you can continue to hate me all you want, but I will never allow you to hurt my family. Now I am going to take care of your father because you are in no condition to do so yourself."

Jonah turned and walked resolutely out the door, and Raphael followed him. They met the doctor on the stairs and directed him to Jonah's chambers.

Jonah and Raphael cleaned Edward up and laid him in the library where he had spent so many of his days. He would have to be buried by tomorrow, but today there were other pressing matters requiring immediate attention.

"Life is so strange at times," Jonah told Raphael as they positioned Edward on the sofa, being careful to make sure the massive wound on the left side of his head was not visible. "Just this morning he was seated at breakfast with us. He was in such good spirits that we all commented on it. Lately, he had been moody a lot."

"What happened up there?"

Jonah shook his head in bewilderment. "I left right after breakfast this morning to take Clovis's boat out. We were out a ways when the storm broke. It started to look so ominous that I decided to turn around and come home. As I entered the corridor to my chambers, I heard Marcel screaming. It was odd because Catherine always picks him up the minute he starts to cry. I hurried to open the door, and it wouldn't budge. Then I heard Clifford's voice. I broke down the door just in time to stop him from raping my wife."

The muscles began to pulse in Jonah's cheeks, and he clenched and unclenched his fist. "I wanted to kill him, and I would have if Catherine didn't scream for help. Father and Edward came and pulled me off him."

"You beat him up badly, but he needed a good ass whooping. I swear that boy's got his nose so far up his ass that all he smells in his own shit. I would have killed him too if I had caught him hurting Catherine or Marcel. I would have skinned his ass and hung it out to dry. But how did Edward end up falling over the gallery's railing?"

"I don't know yet. The only two people who know are Rose and Lucinda because they went out on the gallery with him, but the two of them have been in such a state that they haven't said a coherent word."

"The pieces aren't coming together here," Raphael responded, scratching his beard. "Why was he on your gallery?

"If you really want to know, you'd better sit down, Raphael. This is going to take a few minutes 'cause I am still coming to terms with it myself."

Jonah recapped what Clifford had disclosed about Edward, finishing with the truth about how Louise had died.

When he stopped talking, Raphael stood up and exclaimed, "Son of bitch!" He said nothing more as he paced the room. When he finally sat back down there were tears brimming his eyes.

"You know, they say it is bad luck to speak poorly about the dead, especially one who is right here in the room, but I have a good mind to wake his ass up and kill him all over again. Your mother was the nicest woman I ever knew. There was not a mean bone in her body." Raphael wiped his eyes. "You mean to tell me that bastard left her there to die like that? Ivan nearly lost his mind, and Edward watched him suffer." He shook his head unbelievingly. "And killing children! Oh! I am vexed as hell!"

Jonah had to admit that he felt the same way. Edward had not only robbed Ivan of his wife, he'd robbed Jonah of his mother, and he'd irreparably damaged his own son.

When they had completed all the pertinent tasks, which included wiping up the blood-spattered area where Edward had fallen and sending for the gendarmes, Jonah and Raphael rejoined the family.

The doctor was just closing his medical bag. Jonah escorted him downstairs to the library so he could give his official written report of Edward's death for the gendarmes. Then he returned upstairs to the family. They had to discuss what had happened before the gendarmes arrived.

Rose had regained most of her composure and was in the midst of describing what had taken place on the gallery. "Lu and I followed him out to the gallery because he was looking so dreadful. He kept saying he was sorry over and over again. He was mumbling other things too, but we couldn't understand him." She dabbed at her eyes with a white handkerchief and sniffed. "I mean we were all in shock by the things Clifford said. I still can't believe my Edward would have done such terrible things. Lately though, I knew something had been bothering him, and it started around the time little Jacques was born. Now I know that it was the sight of his own grandson that caused him to be haunted by those little children." She started to cry again, sniffing loudly.

Jonah walked over and knelt in front of her. "Rose, tell us what happened to him outside on the gallery."

"He slipped in the rainwater that had gathered on the floor. He was pacing back and forth, walking faster and faster, mumbling to himself. I tried to get him to stop, both Lu and I tried. When he slipped, he tried to regain his balance, but he kept sliding. His belly hit the railing, and he grabbed on to it. I thought he was fine, but then he did the strangest thing. He bent over the railing, and then … and then …Oh God, Oh

God! He toppled right over. Ohooooooo!" Rose held on tightly to Jonah as she moaned.

"Everything Mere Rose said is true. It happened just as she said," Lucinda volunteered.

Sighing heavily, Jonah stood. "The gendarmes will be here soon. As far as they are concerned, Edward slipped in the water and toppled over the gallery. That's *all* that happened here today, understood?" He paused, looking pointedly at each of them, his tone uncompromising. "Good; now Lucinda, if you don't want your husband sleeping in a jail cell tonight, please escort him to his chambers."

"Who the hell made you boss?"

"Shut up, Clifford," Lucinda retorted, looking scornfully at him. "You've caused enough mayhem because you couldn't control your dick. Now don't let your mouth and your bloodied, pitiful condition cast suspicion on your father. Let's go."

"Jonah, what about the doctor? Has he been taken care of?" Ivan's voice was weak, but it still sounded of authority.

"Yes, Father, he's been generously rewarded for his silence."

Nellie prepared stewed lamb for dinner, but no one had an appetite. No one wanted to eat dinner in the dining room where Edward's chair was so conspicuously empty. Rose enclosed herself in the library with her husband's body. When Catherine checked on her mid evening, her face was red and swollen from crying. She sat quietly with her for a while but left quickly when Clifford joined his mother. There was enough heartache within the family. Catherine wanted to avoid any further conflicts.

Word of Edward's death spread quickly within the province, and the house was filled with people paying their respects and offering their services. Ivan knew it was his duty to greet them, but he had no desire to perform that role. The pain was too raw, the hurt too deep. He was injured for life at the hands of his own blood.

Edward had lived, worked, and eaten with him. He had laughed with him, shared the joys of his son's marriage and the birth of his grandchild when all the while his hands were stained with Louise's blood. He lay in bed, and the tears fell freely as he thought of the cousin he had loved like a brother.

I will attend his funeral because I owe him that much, but I will not go downstairs tonight and keep vigil for him. If I did, I will end up pulling him from that coffin.

They buried Edward the next day. Even with such short notice, St. Marie's Cathedral was crowded. Rose could hardly keep up. Nellie's arms, as well as the smelling salts Nellie had brought along, were Rose's constant support.

When Clifford entered the church, faint gasps could be heard at the disfigurement of his face. The gossip being spread among the parishioners in hushed whispers was that he had finally met his match in one of his many brawls at the downtown saloons. It was the natural thing for them to assume.

Ivan was stately and welcoming. His calm demeanor belied the turmoil he was experiencing. He still looked frail, but everyone attributed it to the unexpected and sudden lost of his cousin.

Father Anthony was expounding on Edward's virtues when Jonah glanced over at Clifford. He felt his anger rise anew as he thought about Clifford's hands on Catherine's skin, touching the delicate flesh that until now had been untouched by any other man but him. The images running through his mind were too much for him to bear. Lucinda sat between him and Clifford, and he was trying desperately to quell the urge to reached across her and level Clifford with a fist. He felt Raphael's hand on his shoulder from the pew behind him, and it served its purpose of calming him for the time being.

For weeks after Edward's death, Ivan sequestered himself in the library. At times he hated Edward with such a passion that he wanted to strike out and smash something. Other times he felt an acute sadness at the loss of his cousin. Then there were times he blamed himself. Those were the most agonizing, and they haunted him. From the advent of their business ventures, he knew Edward was ruthless in his quest for success. Was he indirectly to blame for Louise's death? Why hadn't he ever confronted Edward about his misdealing? Had he done so, would Louise still be alive?

One dreary afternoon Rose knocked on the library door. She had lost weight, and the ready smile she had always possessed no longer lit up her face. There were more grays in her blonde hair, and her eyes carried a deep sadness. She gave him a halting smile as she walked slowly into the room.

When she reached the desk, she stopped. Uncomfortably wringing her hands, she said, "Ivan, can I have a few minutes of your time?"

"Sit down, Rose," Ivan replied without looking up at her, "and for God's sake, stop fidgeting. Since when have you been afraid to speak your mind to me?"

Rose's smile was melancholy. The frown between his brow and the tone of his voice brought an instant picture of her husband to mind. She stepped back and sat in one of the chairs opposite the desk.

Ivan put down the black ledger book he had been studying, took off his glasses, and gave her his full attention.

"I know," she began and faltered. She cleared her throat, took a deep breath and began again. "I know that you must be very angry with my husband and my son. They both hurt you deeply." She wiped her eyes and looked down at her hands. "To tell the truth, I am still having a hard time coming to terms with the terrible things Edward did. I know he had his bad ways, but nothing prepared me for this. I never would have believed him capable of those cruel acts.

Louise was my friend. She was closer to me than a sister. I loved her, and I grieved for her. When she died, I made a promise to look after her son as if he was my own, and I have always done that. I think that's one of the reasons Clifford is so jealous of Jonah. Knowing now that Edward was the cause of her death devastates me. There aren't adequate words to tell you how sorry I am and how badly I feel." She moved to the end of her chair. "But I need to know. Are you going to allow me to continue to live in this house? I would understand if you asked me to leave."

Ivan got up and came around the desk to sit beside her. He took her hands in his. "Rose, this is your home. I would never ask you to leave. I am not putting anyone out of this house."

"Thank you, Ivan. I can't promise you that it will do any good, but I am going to sit that boy of mine down and try to talk some sense into him." She stood, gave Ivan an awkward hug, and quickly headed for the door.

Ivan sadly smiled as he watched her leave. *Your son can stay because my son is leaving.*

CHAPTER 8

The following week, Ivan requested a meeting with Jonah in the library. What he had to say would be hard because he was about to alter the course of Jonah's life. Until now, Jonah had lived a privileged life. All that would change drastically, but Ivan was a man of vision. His son would endure hardship for a season. However, if the new land was toiled and tended properly, one day, with care and vigilance, Jonah would again live a life of plenty. He had confidence in his son. Now he only had to convince Jonah of the ingenious perseverance that was innately ingrained in his bloodline.

He had been carefully studying the unrest in Germany, and he knew with certainty that it was only a matter of time before Germany attacked France. He wanted his son well away from France when that occurred. He had meticulously planned his exodus. He had even planned his entourage.

When Jonah walked into the library, Ivan was taking a rolled-up document from the wall safe. He placed it on the desk and waited for Jonah to sit down. Then he took his seat behind the oak desk.

"Son, what I have here is a bill of sale for ten parcels of land in St. Barthelemy. Do you remember when I told you that I sailed there with a cargo on the *Ann Louise* when the island was still owned by the Swedes?" He waited for Jonah's acknowledgement.

"Well, I bought the parcels of land then as my own personal asset. It is located in the crest of a mountain with an unlimited view of the sea, just like here at home. The natives call it La Pointe. There is nothing there but dense brush at present, but the potential to build a house similar to this one is appealing, and the view of the surrounding seas is perfect to monitor your vessels."

"Wait a minute," Jonah said cautiously. "What are you getting at, Father?"

"I deeded the land to you, Jonah. It is solely yours. I want you to go to St. Barthelemy and build your home. I put together a listing of people who will accompany you and Catherine. You will take the *Louise Catherine.* The *Ann Louise* has been on dry dock for some time, but she is still a sturdy vessel. You will take her with you as well. Clifford can keep the *Marie Rose.*"

Jonah stood up angrily. "France is my home. I am not running away to some Godforsaken island in the middle of nowhere! You have taken too much liberty, Father! How dare you plan my life and make such drastic decisions for me? And what about Catherine? Have you given any thought to how this would affect her? You know how much she loves her parents. She would never agree to leave France. No." Jonah shook his head firmly as he started to pace the room. "This is madness! I am not leaving Toulon!"

"Jonah, think seriously about this. Clifford is not going to relent. He will attack you or Catherine again, and you will surely kill him. I will not watch my only son hang in the gallows."

"Then have Clifford leave this house, not me."

"You think that will solve anything other than making him more wrathful toward you and Catherine?"

Ivan stood up, walked over to the window, and gazed at the sea. When he turned around, he said, "I am also dissolving the export/import business. I am only keeping the fishing vessels and the house."

"Well, Father, you're full of surprises today. How can you make decisions that can so impact all our lives without first discussing it with us? Don't Clifford and I have a say in any of this?"

"I am the one in control of this business, and I will do what I think is best for it and this family! No one second-guesses me." Ivan took a deep breath and then continued more calmly, "I have been studying the events occurring in Germany. France and the United Kingdom just made an alliance to keep Germany in check, and in retaliation, Germany has threatened the United Kingdom's naval dominance. The situation is becoming tense. It's only a matter of time before Germany directly attacks France. When that happens, our economy will be destroyed, and our young men will be forced to join the French military. Our vessels may be seized for military purposes, and we would end up losing them anyway. It is best I close that part of the business before any of this occurs. You and your family should be far away from France's shores with two of the biggest vessels by then."

"And what about you, Father? Are you coming with me? Because you do not expect me to leave you behind, alone with Clifford!"

"Your mother is here. I could never leave her."

"My mother is dead. She would never expect you to sacrifice yourself. You have been doing that for way too long now. If I agree to this madness, I expect you to be on that vessel with me."

"Your mother was my life. You might consider it a sacrifice, but I will never leave her here alone. When I die, I will be buried right next to her." Ivan walked closer to Jonah and gently touched his shoulder to still him. His eyes were intense behind the round rims of his glasses. "You are a man of great character and strength, son. You come from a long line of valiant men, men who forged ahead and made their own fortunes. They broke new grounds and led the way for their bloodlines. Not all of us are like Edward and Clifford."

Ivan tapped his son's shoulder in a gesture of espousal. "You can do this. You have the stalwartness. I see it clearly in you. Now, I have charged you with much today. Take some time and think it through thoroughly. I won't suggest that you mention it to Catherine until it is clear in your own head. I will continue to put things in order for you. In fact, I have already broached the subject with some of our trustworthy relatives and friends. They are amiable to making the change and accompanying you. We're already into September. The ideal time to sail will be in approximately six weeks."

Jonah moved toward the desk and picked up the rolled-up documents his father had placed there. Then he staunchly said, "I will consider all that you have said, although I am not in agreement with any of it."

Catherine was playing happily with Marcel when Jonah entered their chambers. She looked up when he walked to the sofa and sat down heavily. Seeing the look on his face, she immediately placed Marcel into his crib and came to sit beside him. She knew he'd had a meeting with his father.

"What's wrong, Jonah?"

"You're not going to believe this," Jonah muttered. "Even I am having a hard time believing that Father would suggest such madness," he mumbled more to himself than to Catherine. Then he looked directly at her. "Father wants us to leave Toulon. He said he purchased ten parcels of land in St. Barthelemy many years ago, and he deeded it to me. He has taken the liberty of planning our future, even up to who will accompany us and which vessels we will take. He stated that it is of dire importance we agree to his madness on the following grounds; that Clifford will attack you again, forcing me to kill him; consequently, I will hang in the gallows; and Germany is on the verge of attacking France. If we're attacked, our vessels may be seized, so he wants us to pack up and set sail in six weeks."

The color drained from Catherine's face. Just yesterday she had received a letter from Marie in which she had expressed grave concerns for Pierre. The rumor of the pending war with Germany was widespread in Marseille. The Jews there were riled up and ready to fight, Pierre included. Marie was distressed and frightened for her new husband for more than one reason. She was pregnant.

"That might not be a bad idea." Catherine muttered.

"What?"

Jonah touched her forehead with the back of his hand. "Are you feeling okay? Do you understand all I just said?"

"Yes, Jonah. I understand clearly. I know I will be leaving Mama and Papa, but it does not mean I will never come back. We will have the vessels, correct?"

Jonah nodded.

"That means we will be able to sail back and forth. I only have one request. Marie and Pierre must come with us."

"Do you realize all that you will be giving up? This is a very small island. We will have to live in guest houses and perhaps tents until we finish building our homes. Father has this grand idea that the island has so much potential. I can't say I agree. I really don't relish the idea of living in uncivilized conditions, and I told him as much." He touched her nose. "And I also told him you would kick up a fit at the mere mention of it. I can't believe I was so wrong about you. Are you sure you don't have a fever?"

"I haven't always lived in luxury, Jonah. I remember the hardship my parents endured when they were building our home in Marseille. I was very little, but I remember that my mother pulled her weight. She didn't complain. She just got up each day and did what was necessary for that day. I also remember their elation and pride when it was finished. We can do this, Jonah. I know it won't be easy. We're facing the unknown, and it's always hard to do that." She sighed. "And I will be so very happy to be rid of Clifford and Lucinda. Your father is not the only one who worries about you killing Clifford. It torments me daily."

"You're sure about this?"

"Yes, but like I said, Pierre and Marie must come too. That's another thing your father is correct about. Germany will attack France, and all he told you will come to pass. It has been brewing ever since France declared war on Prussia. I don't want my sister to be a young widow."

Jonah's response was hesitant. "All right then. We're going to St. Barthelemy."

Ivan gathered the family in the library so he could make the announcement one week after his first conversation with Jonah. Nellie and Rose cried. Clifford could not hide his elation. He offered no objections when Ivan said he was dissolving the export/import part of the business.

"As long as you don't touch the *Marie Rose,* I don't care. I will start my own export/import business. I never wanted him as a partner anyway," he said, pointing his finger at Jonah.

"Yes, Clifford, the *Marie Rose* is yours. I will give you the papers to that effect."

"Well then, good riddance. Go live like the caveman you are.

But—wait a minute here." He turned his attention back to Ivan. "What about the estate and fishing business?"

"What about it, Clifford?"

"My father built this business and I—"

"Your father and I built the business," Ivan interrupted. "Now that he is dead, I am the sole owner, and I will make decisions at my discretion. I am well aware of your interest as well as Jonah's. That is why you are being allowed to continue to live in this house and work for this business despite your transgressions."

"My father is the one who had the guts to do what was necessary. You were always too much of a coward. You cannot eject me from this house or this business." Clifford chuckled menacingly. "You'd better be careful, old man. Just one slight push down the stairs and you won't be making any more decisions. The golden boy won't be around to protect you now that you have sentenced him to exile."

Jonah and Rose were instantly on their feet.

"Sit down, both of you!" Ivan commanded.

He walked over to Clifford and grabbed hold of his shirt collar, pulling him to his feet until they were both eye level. "I would consider that remark a threat, but I know you don't have the balls to lay a finger on me. You're too much of a whiny little wimp who never got the ass whooping you deserved when you were a young whelp. In the presence of your mother, I am warning you. I can and will evict you if you persist with your shenanigans. Now sit down so we can continue this discussion."

Catherine smiled. Jonah looked at his father incredulously. Lucinda appeared stupefied. Rose stood up and exclaimed her agreement, promising to help whoop Clifford's ass. But the look on Clifford's face was priceless. Sulking, he quietly sat back down.

Catherine needed to go home to Marseille. She wanted to see Marie and Pierre and convince them to come on the voyage, but more importantly, she wanted to see her parents. She had to be the one to break the news to them. She knew they would not take it well.

That evening after Marcel was sleeping, she broached the subject with Jonah. They were seated on the gallery enjoying the starry night. The full moon lit the ocean with slivers of shimmering lights.

"It is such a lovely night."

"Yes, it is."

"Catherine, have we totally lost our minds? Do we really want to give all this up? For what? An uncivilized little rock in the middle of nowhere? It's not too late, you know. I can still tell Father we're not leaving."

"Jonah, you know we have to go. Everything is already in motion. We can't change our minds." She looked down at her hands. "I need to go to Marseille. I have to tell my parents, and I have to convince Marie and Pierre to come with us."

"That's not a problem. We can go whenever you want."

"Not we, Jonah, just me and Marcel. This is something I need to do alone. I want to spend some time with my parents. They are going to take this really hard." She swallowed to remove the lump forming in her throat. "I want to give them time to play with Marcel and to adjust to the idea that we will be far away."

"How much time do you want?"

"Two weeks. Please, Jonah."

"You don't want me to come with you?"

"No."

"Well, I don't like it, but I understand. Can I at least sail you over to Marseille?"

Catherine arrived on her parents' doorsteps two days later, Marcel on her right hip and a valise in her hand. When she pushed open the front door, it struck her that the house was too quiet. She had expected to be greeted by Marie's happy laughter. It took her a moment to remember that Marie no longer lived there.

She put the valise down on the parlor's linoleum floor. "Mama," she called out, but there was no answer. Still holding Marcel on her hip, she peeked into the kitchen. It was spotless. No pots were cooking on the stove. No delicious smells drifted through the air. *Strange. Mama always has something cooking.* "Mama, Papa," she called out again.

Getting no answer, she walked through the house to the back door and pushed it open. She smiled when she saw them. Her mother was hanging laundry on the clothesline, and her father was bent over a patch of weeds in the yard, his fingers diligently pulling at them while he listened to her mother, who was so busy talking that neither of them heard or saw Catherine.

Silently she watched them, and then she walked down the steps.

"Hello, Mama, Papa."

Susanne halted midway in hanging one of Charles's pantaloons. Charles glanced up and quickly came to his feet, briskly rubbing his hands to dust off the dirt.

"Ohhh! Catherine!" Suzanne abandoned the pantaloon and ran to hug her daughter. Reaching for Marcel, she hugged and kissed him. Then she studied Catherine. "It is always good to see you, but this is so unexpected. Where's Jonah?"

"He's not here. It's just me and Marcel."

"What has that man done to you?" Charles roared. "I swear I will tear him apart if he has so much as laid one finger on you."

"Jonah hasn't done anything wrong to me, Papa," Catherine responded soothingly. "I am simply here because I wanted to see you."

"And because you have something to tell us." Suzanne interjected. "I know you, Catherine. There's something happening, and that's why you're here. Now what is it?"

Catherine wasn't ready. She needed more time. "Can I get settled into my room first? I need to change Marcel." She paused. "And I'm a bit hungry. Could you fix me something to eat? We can talk later." Taking Marcel from her mother, she hurried back into the house and up the stairs before they had a chance to ask any more questions.

Something was seriously wrong. Charles could feel it despite Suzanne's best effort to allay his fears. Even as she busied herself fixing supper, he could see she too was worried. Catherine had not come back downstairs. She was tarrying, which was a sure sign.

When the simple supper of fish and rice was ready, he went to the foot of the stairs and called for her to come down. She came downstairs alone, explaining that Marcel was asleep. Charles and Suzanne ate quietly with Catherine trying really hard to keep up a cheery conversation.

When he could stand it no more, Charles put down his fork. "Why are you here, Catherine? What has happened that you are so afraid to tell us?"

"There's no easy way to say this," she mumbled. Sighing heavily, she said, "Jonah and I and an entourage of friends and family are moving to an island in the West Indies called St. Barthelemy. We will be leaving in—"

"What the devil are you saying?" Charles shouted, throwing down his napkin and getting to his feet. "What kind of lunacy is this? You will do no such thing!"

"Sit down, Charles," Suzanne said, reaching for his hand. "Let her finish speaking."

Charles refused to sit. He walked back and forth, running his hands through his hair and cursing profusely as Catherine disclosed the entire saga starting with Clifford and ending with Ivan's theory that France would soon be engulfed in war with Germany.

"I want to go to Toulon and finish beating the hell out of Clifford. Good for nothing, high-falutin' … Jonah should have killed him! It would have been one less piece of rich trash to worry about." Charles continued to rant as he paced. "But this idea of your leaving is preposterous. Has that old fool, Ivan, lost his mind too? They're all crazy! The whole frigging lot of them! Bad blood, that's what is it!" He stopped and looked at Catherine. "I never wanted you to marry into that family. You know that! Now look at what has happened."

"Charles, stop your ranting. You're going to make yourself sick," Suzanne said. "Sit down. Let's talk this over rationally."

"There's nothing to talk over. My daughter is not going and that's final."

"Papa!" Catherine finally interjected. "You know I must go with my husband. Please calm down and listen to me."

The soft pleading in Catherine's voice made him pause, and he sat back down. Suzanne immediately stood up and began to massage his shoulders. They were all quiet for a few minutes.

Then Suzanne said soothingly, "Now Charles, Catherine isn't

finished. There's more on her mind. We need to hear her out." She looked at her daughter and nodded.

"Papa, I didn't agree to this move just for Jonah's sake. I did it for Marie as well. Just before I found out about Ivan's plans for us to leave, I received a letter from her. She was completely distraught over Pierre's anxiousness to fight the Germans. She expressed her grave concerns about losing him." She took a deep breath. "Papa, I intend to convince Pierre and Marie to join us on the voyage. I believe it would be the best thing to put a stop to Pierre's talk about going to war."

"Ohhhh, this nightmare has no ending." Charles stood up again. "You not only want to take away my grandson, you also intend to take away my daughter and my unborn grandchild." He placed his hands up defensively. "No more. I have had enough pain for one day. I am going to bed." He dejectedly walked toward the stairs.

Once Charles was out of sight, Catherine threw herself across her mother's lap and wept. "Oh, Mama, I never wanted to cause Papa and you pain, but I have no choice. I must go, and I truly believe taking Marie and Pierre with us is for the best. Now Papa hates me. Oh, Mama, I am going to miss you so much. I can't even imagine life without you nearby."

"It's not so bad," Susanne replied. "You will come back to see us. I agree that you should take Marie with you. I would feel better knowing you're together to look out for each other, and Pierre will be so useful to Jonah." Susanne sniffed. Smoothing back the dark hair from Catherine's face, she continued in the same soothing tone. "Your father could never hate you. He's just upset right now. Leave him to me. I will make him understand. Now, dry your tears and tell me more about this island. I have heard that there are a lot of French citizens already settled there, some of them from right here in Marseille. See, it won't be so bad. You will be surrounded by reminders of home."

The following morning when Catherine and Marcel went downstairs, Susanne was the only one in the kitchen. Charles had already left to tend to his fishing boat. She ate breakfast with her mother, chatting amiably, both of them avoiding any mention of the previous day. Then she left Marcel in her mother's care and went in search of Marie.

When Catherine arrived at the wooden gate that separated Marie and Pierre's house from the street, she reached over the gate to unlock the hook. She was unprepared for the big brown dog that accosted her. He bounded forward, and she immediately backed away from the gate.

She was pondering her options when she heard Marie yell, "Barlo, stop that dreadful noise and come here this instance!"

The dog whined and headed back toward his master as she rounded the corner and into view.

"You make way too much noise, you know that, you big lug. Now what's got you all riled up?" Marie looked up in the direction of the gate and blinked. "Catherine? Oh, Cathy, is it really you?"

Forgetting about the dog, Marie ran to open the gate and flung herself into her sister's arms. She pulled back, wiped her tears, and looked at Catherine, reaching for her hand to pull her inside the yard. "Let's go inside."

Catherine hesitated, looking at the dog.

"Oh, don't mind Barlo. He's harmless."

Once they were seated in the parlor, Catherine told her sister everything. She finished with the events of the previous evening, their father's dismay about her imminent departure, and her desire to have Marie and Pierre accompany them. When she was done, she at last felt emptied. It was all out on the table, and now it was up to Marie.

"You really have been going through a lot. I had no idea. Your letters gave no indication."

"I didn't want to worry any of you, and besides, I felt I had everything under control, until the day Clifford almost succeeded in raping me."

"It would be doubly awful for Papa and Mama. At least Pierre's parents have seven other children, none of whom are interested in fighting the Germans, not like Pierre, anyway. But Papa and Mama only have us. Still, I want to go. I will discuss it with Pierre this evening when he comes home. I will have to convince him that it is the best thing for us and the baby."

Marie touched her belly where a small bulge was showing and her eyes glistened with tears. "Oh, Cathy, you have no idea how worried I have been. All he talks about is fighting the Germans. He is filled with anger, and it is consuming him. He has joined forces with a group of men. They have secret meetings where they plan strategies for war. He is not my Pierre when he comes home from those meetings. He is tense and sullen. Cathy, you have to help me convince him by making it sound like Jonah desperately needs his help. We must not mention anything about Germany."

When Catherine left her sister's house, she was convinced that she had made the right decision in encouraging Pierre and Marie to join the voyage. There was no doubt in her mind now. If Pierre stayed in Marseille, he would die.

The next day, Pierre came to see Catherine. She was in the kitchen helping her mother fix lunch when he walked into the room with his cap in his hand, his suspenders gleaming against his starched white shirt. They sat at the kitchen table, and Catherine and Suzanne convinced him it was the right move; Catherine expressed their dire need for his carpentry skills, and Suzanne gave him her blessings. By the time he left after lunch, his decision had been made. He and Marie would accompany Jonah and Catherine to St. Barthelemy.

The days flew in a peaceful blurry. They were bittersweet because Catherine knew that this time when she left Marseille, her return would be clouded with uncertainty. She spent her days visiting with old friends and talking with her mother and sister. It seemed there was so much she and Suzanne needed to say to each other. Yet most days they were contented just to be together. Marcel's innocent playful antics were the balm that soothed their souls.

But Charles was another matter. He brooded and hardly spoke with Catherine or Marie. When he was home, he spent his time playing with his grandson or working in the yard. Catherine desperately wanted to bridge the gap that had developed between them. She didn't want to leave Marseille until she had found a way to reach him.

One afternoon she looked out the window and saw him working on the same patch of grass he had been tending the day she had arrived. She left Marcel in the house with her mother and went outside. Kneeling beside him, she started pulling at the weeds too.

"These weeds grow so quickly. I just pulled them up last week and already they are growing again. If I don't pull them, they'll continue to grow and choke your mother's flowers."

"You do a great job, Papa. The flowers are blooming thanks to your diligence."

They continued to work silently, their heads close to each other. Then she said gently, "Papa, do you remember when I was a little girl, and I would cry so much? You hated to see me cry. You would tell me that my eyes were melting, and you would make a big show of putting them back into my head. Do you remember that, Papa?"

He nodded, but he said nothing. His fingers continued to pull at the weeds.

"Well, Papa, my eyes are melting now, and I need you to make them stop. I can't stand thinking that you are disappointed in me. I love you, and I never want to cause you pain." She stopped pulling at the weeds and raised herself to her knees.

His fingers stopped moving. He turned around until he was seated on the dirt, and he motioned for her to sit as well.

"There is nothing you can ever do to make me disappointed in you. I love you too much for that. You and Marie are more precious to me than gold, and I have always protected you. It hurts me to know you will be so far away from me that I cannot protect you, and it makes me feel helpless." He smiled and touched her tear-stained face with both hands, leaving trails of dirt on her cheeks. "Now let's put those eyes back into your head so you can see again."

#

"No, Father, Raphael stays with you. Since you insist on staying, it will give me comfort knowing he's here. You said you don't want me to hang in the gallows, but rest assured I will kill Clifford if he harms you."

"Son, Raphael is too vital for your safety, both on land and on sea. He serves as the perfect proxy for me. No, he goes with you."

"And I say he stays. I will not leave you here alone with Clif—"

"Jonah, I agree with your father. We need Raphael. He's the most experienced of all of us. Clifford preys on women and people who can't help themselves. He's too much of a coward to try to hurt your father."

"Thank you, Catherine." Ivan looked determinedly at his son. "I don't need a bodyguard. Raphael goes and that's final."

They were in the library discussing the people who would be accompanying Jonah and Catherine. There were few people Ivan trusted without reservation, and he had handpicked them. Raphael was at the top of the list.

Josiah Dusant came in a close second. A cousin twice removed, he was an experienced mariner. He had sailed as first mate on many of the import/export voyages, but he preferred captaining the fishing vessels because he and his wife, Agnes, had three little girls all younger than the age of six, and he wanted to be close by when they needed him. His younger brother, Paul, was already in St. Barthelemy. It was the primary reason he had so readily agreed to the voyage. Josiah had heard that Paul was faring well on the island.

Alphonse Laroe was the head gardener on the Dusant estate, and he was well-known for his green thumb. His wife, Yvette, was his junior by ten years. They had no children, but as a prerequisite for agreeing to the voyage, Alphonse had insisted his two single sisters accompany them.

Alphonse, being the eldest, was very protective of Loretta and Philar Laroe, who were both quite eccentric. Their intuitive senses existed on a much higher level than normal. They could see and sense things the average person could not, and their dreams foretold upcoming events. They were midwives by trade, and they were well-versed in herbal medicinal poultices.

Vidal Ledee was the youngest fishing vessel captain in the company's crew. Ivan had met him twelve years ago in Normandy. He had been taking a stroll on the wharf while he waited for a signature authorizing the release of a cargo of gunpowder when he heard angry voices coming from a vessel anchored in the bay. He'd watched as two burly men tossed a young boy of about fourteen overboard. The boy had hit the water with a loud splash, immediately resurfaced, and began swimming briskly to shore. Ivan had noticed his malnourished state when the boy collapsed on the wharf.

Being careful not to frighten the lad, he walked over and crouched beside him. Gently, he asked, "Son, why did those men toss you overboard?"

The boy locked defiant eyes with his. "I am a stowaway. My father was a fisherman. He and his boat were lost at sea in a storm last year. I need to find a way to eat, and I have tried to sign on with so many vessels. But when they see how scrawny I am, they think I have the fever, and they quickly kick me off. I am not sick. I am just hungry, and I am a damn good sailor."

"Where is the rest of your family?"

"I have no family. My mother is dead. If they would only give me one chance, I don't want nothing for free. I want to work for my food."

Vidal's will to provide for himself had touched a chord in Ivan. "I will give you a chance. I have my own fleet. But I will expect you to live up to your word of being a damn good sailor."

"You will not be disappointed in me, sir," he had responded passionately, and true to his word, Ivan had never once been disappointed in Vidal. He was now a strapping, serious young man with broad, sturdy shoulders, and he was indeed an excellent sailor. Vidal would have taken the moon down from the skies for Ivan, so he had readily agreed to be first mate on the *Ann Louise* with Raphael as captain.

The two vessels would be laden with every imaginable provision needed to commence their new lives. Ivan had thought of everything, from lumber and nails right up to fabric, needle, and thread. The travelers, including the crew and their families, would be divided between the two vessels. Jonah would captain the *Louise Catherine* with Josiah as his first mate.

Charles and Susanne accompanied Marie and Pierre to Toulon the night before they sailed, but Charles remained displeased. From the first day he had come knocking in search of Catherine, he had known Jonah was going to be trouble for his family. Now he was taking both his daughters thousands of miles away behind God's face. It was ludicrous! They were leaving all the convenience and comforts of home to embark on a suicide mission. He could never condone this senseless departure to live in a God forsaken island where pirates and privateers still roamed.

That evening Charles sat alone on the gallery because he couldn't find it within himself to socialize. He looked up at the night sky with its trillion of twinkling stars and asked deploringly, "Why, God? What did I do so wrong to deserve these two men as sons-in-law? Why couldn't you have given me two good, devout, Catholic boys who would have kept my daughters safe and close to home? Instead you gave me a rich man and a Jew."

A crowd had gathered by the bayside to wish the travelers a bon voyage on the windy October morning. Suzanne had tried her best to persuade Charles into coming with her, but he had refused to budge, telling her, "You can go and watch them commit suicide, but I will not take part in it." Now amid so many people, she stood alone on the sandy shore as she watched her heart sail away with the *Louise Catherine*. The pain tore at her soul.

Ivan stood next to Rose and held her as she cried. He reminded himself that this decision was for the best. Yet his heart was not listening to his mind as tears glistened in the corners of his eyes. Nellie was on his other side with Jacques, who was holding his grandson.

Lucinda and Clifford stood a few feet behind them, and every so often Lucinda wiped her eyes. Clifford saw it and whispered in her ear, "You can cry for him all you want because you will never have him. He and the peasant have been sent into exile along with all their cohorts. It's too bad the old goat refuses to go with them, but it's just a matter of time before he croaks. Then all this will be mine. The golden boy won't be coming back. If the pirates don't kill him, the island will." He laughed wickedly, and Lucinda elbowed him.

As the *Louise Catherine* began her journey, Catherine stood beside Marie, their heads close together, tears making wet tracks down their cheeks as they gripped the vessel's railings. Their arms ached from waving to their mother, yet they continued to wave until they could see her no more.

Pierre stood next to Marie. He held Marcel in one arm and tried to comfort his wife with the other. Agnes stood next to them, holding one child in her arms while her other two children held on to her skirt. Her husband, Josiah, was busy helping Jonah with the vessel's departure.

The *Ann Louise* sailed at their side, its occupants, like that of the *Louise Catherine,* excited and saddened as they left behind the familiar and embraced the unknown.

The two vessels sailed away, side by side, from France's shore, their white sails billowing in the swift breeze. The travelers stood somberly on the decks, unwilling to miss the last glimpses of their homeland as it faded slowly into the horizon. Even as the sun beat on them with its implacable fury, and the wind prickled their faces with salty seawater, they remained vigilant. The children were unusually silent, as if they somehow understood that a momentous event was occurring. The silence was broken only by the sounds of the waves slapping against the hull of the vessels, the cries of the seagulls, and the shouts of the crew as they yelled instructions to each other. They were all of one accord, and the empathy between them was so strong that they understood each others' thoughts and feelings without the utterance of a single word. They were filled with the same trepidation about the future, but they had made their choice freely.

As the final shadows of France disappeared like the closing of a large curtain, it was as if a spell had been broken. Almost in slow motion, the travelers bowed their heads and made the sign of the cross. Then they began to move around on the vessels' decks, their chatter increasing in crescendo. There was plenty to do to make themselves comfortable in the close confines of the vessels. Each family had been assigned sleeping quarters, and albeit small and cramped, they were determined to make the best of it. Aside from making their personal living spaces comfortable, everyone was assigned with a task to make their communal lives run smoothly. After securing their lodgings, they set about familiarizing themselves with the vessels and the chores each person was expected to perform.

The journey had begun in earnest.

CHAPTER 9

From the helm of the *Ann Louise,* Raphael contemplatively observed the flurry of activity. This voyage was like none he had ever undertaken. There were women and children onboard and there were sure to be numerous bouts of sea sickness among the inexperienced travelers. They would be sailing through perilous waters down in the Caribbean. Pirates and privateers were rampant. As the vessel's captain, he felt an enormous responsibility for their safety.

Raphael could see the *Louise Catherine* in the not-too-far distance. He had promised Jonah that he would do his best to keep pace with the bigger and faster clipper ship, but already it was proving to be a challenge. The *Ann Louise* was an old girl, and she was giving it her best. He did not want to chance pushing the vessel too hard.

As he watched the *Louise Catherine,* he thought about Jonah. Raphael did not relish spending his last days on a dry rock in the middle of the ocean. Still he would have agreed to just about anything to keep the boy safe. That yellow-bellied snake, Clifford, would have continued to torment Jonah and Catherine, and Jonah would have killed him. It was that simple. Raphael could never watch his beloved Jonah hang in the gallows.

Yes, Ivan made the right decision, he thought. *He had the foresight to see the changes that will be coming to France. I only hope his vision of promise for this new land is on the mark too.*

Jonah was in a meditative mood as he steered the *Louise Catherine* through the waves. France had long-ago disappeared into the shadows.

Other than the shrouded silhouette of the *Ann Louise* behind them, they were alone on the vast expanse of sea.

For the most part, his passengers were busy acquainting themselves with the vessel. The earlier melancholy mood had been replaced with the eager task of getting settled. As he guided the vessel through the impending dusk, he looked for Catherine and Marcel among the people moving around on the deck. He spotted them with Marie and Pierre. Marcel was happily sitting on top of Pierre's shoulders. He was glad Pierre and Marie were onboard. Catherine had her sister, and he had a skilled carpenter. He worried about Marie's pregnancy too. Catherine would never forgive herself if something happened to Marie and the baby. For that reason, he was thankful Loretta and Philar were part of the group. The two women were the best known midwives in Toulon despite their quirkiness.

He watched as Agnes ran after one of her daughters, brown hair flying in the wind. Jonah smiled when she scooped the little girl into her arms and tickled her. The child's delighted giggles reverberated through the air. Josiah had confided to him that Agnes maybe pregnant again. That would make it two pregnant women in his entourage.

"Lord, help me," he groaned.

As the *Louise Catherine* maneuvered the waves en route to their new home, Jonah prayed fervently that his father had made the right call.

"Today was one of the worst days."

"I know," Catherine said soothingly.

She was holding Marie's hair away from her face while she leaned over the *Louise Catherine's* railing, wretchedly puking.

"This morning sickness is lasting from morning through night, and the constant motion of this blasted vessel is making it worse. I want Mama. This is all your fault. I should never have agreed to this miserable voyage. I want to go home."

"Marie, everything will be all right. At least you will never again have to worry about Pierre going to war."

"No, I am worrying about other things now," Marie snapped. "You saw the Spanish galleon yesterday. What if they attack us?"

"But they haven't. It was just another vessel passing us on the sea. There's nothing to worry about."

"They might still come back. What will we do then?"

"They won't come back, I promise. Things will get better."

"How can you say that, Catherine?" Marie cried, shrugging away Catherine's hands. "We have been on the sea for months now. It will be Christmas soon. The weather has been bad more days than good, and we still have months to go before we arrive. Ohhh, I feel like I am losing my mind." She began to cry in earnest.

Catherine felt helpless to assuage her sister's misery. She felt a certain degree of guilt for convincing her to come on the voyage.

She glanced down at the deck where Marcel played with wooden blocks his grandpa Charles had given him the day they sailed. She reached out to rub Marie's back, but again her offer of comfort was rejected. She stood awkwardly next to Marie, uncertain of what to say or do when she heard Pierre's familiar whistle.

"Are you feeding the fish again?" he asked Marie playfully as he took her into his arms, nodding to Catherine that he would take over from here.

Catherine felt like crying herself. She scooped up Marcel and made a quick exist. She went in search of Jonah, finding him in the galley talking to the cook. When he saw her, he immediately excused himself. Taking Marcel from her arms, he led her through a side door where they could talk privately.

"What is it?"

"It's everything, Jonah! It's this damned voyage. It's the heat, the cold, the wind, the sea sickness, the boredom." She paused, taking a deep breath. "And it's my sister. Jonah, she hates me. She's miserably sick, and she said it's all my fault. She said she wants to go home. I can't blame her. I want to go home too." Catherine laid her head on Jonah's shoulder and wept.

Holding Marcel in his right arm, he wrapped his other arm around her. When she was fully spent, he asked softly, "Do you feel better now?"

She nodded.

"Catherine, it is normal for you to feel overwhelmed. There are days when I am besieged with worry. You can cry on my shoulders anytime, but we must remain strong for all of them. Being pregnant adds an extra burden on Marie. Just continue to be there for her, even when she snaps at you." He tilted her chin so he could look at her. "I have to get back to work. Are you going to be okay?"

Again she nodded.

He handed Marcel back and kissed her. Mischievously he whispered, "All day today I have had exciting visions dancing in my head when I think of you. Tire Marcel out. I want him to sleep early tonight." Then playfully slapping her buttocks, he opened the galley's door.

In her small quarters, Agnes kept herself occupied by knitting a sweater for Josiah. Zelda, her one-year-old, was asleep on the triple layers of quilt on the floor. At her feet, five-year-old Jenny and three-year-old Flora were squabbling over a ball. She watched as Flora grabbed a handful of Jenny's brown hair and yanked hard, pulling the older girl backward. Somehow Jenny managed to twist herself around enough to grab hold of one of Flora's braids, and the two girls were now locked into a vicious, pulling circle.

"Stop it!" Agnes yelled as she put down her knitting and pulled the two girls apart.

She seated them in opposite corners of the room. Then she sat back down on the bed and resumed her knitting, but she couldn't concentrate. The room was too silent. She glanced at her daughters. Their little faces were pouting sadly as they sat quietly in their respective corners. She sighed heavily.

These listless days were wearing on everyone's nerves, and there were still so many more days to go. She and Josiah had been excited at the prospect of building a house that was entirely theirs. The letters from Paul had all sounded favorable. Still, there were so many frightening aspects to consider that, at times, she thought they had made a terrible mistake. She touched her belly where her fourth child might be forming. She hoped this one would be a boy, a strong son to help Josiah.

Taking pity on her two sad little girls, she carefully put aside her knitting and took out their favorite story book, motioning for them to join her on the narrow, hard bed.

As the night dew fell on the decks of the *Ann Louise,* the sweet melodic sounds of a guitar filled the air. The repetitious thump of a drum and the harmonious tune of a flute joined in to make merry music. The travelers sat around in the moonlight enjoying the respite of a beautiful, clear night. The ocean was calm, and a sweet sea breeze drifted through the air. Most of the preceding days had been dreary and tedious. Many of them had suffered the awful spasms of sea sickness.

Loretta sat next to her younger sister, Philar, enjoying the comforting sounds of the makeshift band. They were strikingly beautiful women with long, thick hair and petite, slim figures. Although Loretta was a brunette, and Philar was blonde, the sisters greatly resembled each other. Both women were in their mid twenties and had been born two years apart. They had no other relatives aside from Alphonse and Yvette.

It wasn't that they didn't want families of their own. As little girls, they had talked long into the night about future husbands and children, but the peculiar trait that existed in the women of their maternal bloodline had molded their fates. Not wanting her daughters to become pariahs like herself, their mother had encouraged them to hide their strange abilities, but it became increasingly difficult. Oftentimes they found themselves forewarning friends of events to come that inevitably led to the breakup of many friendships, including those of a romantic nature.

"Do you regret your decision to embark on the voyage?" Philar asked.

Loretta chuckled. "You ask as if we had a choice. Alphonse would have knocked us out, tied us up, and brought us along anyway." She leaned back on her elbows and looked at the night sky.

Philar waited, knowing Loretta had more to say.

Then with her attention still drawn to the sky, Loretta continued, "Do you remember Mama telling us when we were little that the clouds were representations of people who had died? Each one either had a pair of wings to indicate that they were heaven bound or a bundle on their backs, which meant they were on their way to purgatory. Look, there is a woman with a lovely pair of wings. It is such a beautiful night."

Sighing wistfully, Loretta turned and looked at Philar. "What you are really asking me is what I see in our future. It doesn't take any special ability to know that we're facing hard days of work in an unknown land with unknown perils. At least we will have an opportunity for a fresh start where fewer people know about us.

"Speaking of which"—Loretta nodded in the direction of Vidal, who was seated on top of a barrel on the far side from them, quietly observing everyone—"I believe you have an admirer. He's such a confident man, but I noticed whenever he's around you, he gets jittery. He is always studying you when he thinks you're not looking."

"Don't I wish," Philar responded wistfully. "He's interested now because he doesn't really know me. It's just a matter of time before I spook him away. He is awfully good looking though, isn't he? Hmm, look at those strong, powerful arms."

"Philar, you're drooling."

Christmas and New Year's found the travelers still at sea. The trade winds blew a steady stiff breeze, making the ocean turbulent. Still they celebrated the holy days in reverence as best they could, gathering together on Christmas and New Year's to pray, say the rosary, and sing the traditional noel hymns. The cooks on both vessels did their best to prepare festive meals, but their efforts were mostly wasted. Many of the travelers were too seasick to eat.

"I don't think I will ever be able to walk on solid ground again," Catherine said.

Catherine and Jonah were toasting the New Year in the privacy of their quarters. It was way past midnight.

"Don't worry. You'll stop wobbling after about a month on land."

"How soon will that be, Jonah? I am so tired of the sea."

"Another month-and-a-half or so, depending on the direction of the wind. We should arrive by late February. That should give us enough time to start building before the rainy season begins. It's going to be a lot of work, but we'll get it done. We're going to have to continue living on the vessels until we can find decent places to sleep."

"But you will allow us to go ashore."

'Yes, but first I need to make sure everyone will be safe."

It was the middle of January, and the ocean remained choppy. The constant rocking and the heavy spray kept most of the passengers inside. Except for a few hearty souls who braved the elements in search of fresh air, the decks on both vessels were deserted.

Raphael and Vidal had noticed a vessel trailing them. They had already alerted Jonah by activating the light signals they had prearranged for emergencies. Both vessels were prepared to react if necessary. By its large three masts and long elongated hull, they knew it was a Spanish galleon.

From the *Louise Catherine,* Jonah watched the galleon come closer until it paralleled the *Ann Louise.* Fear gripped him and his body went cold. He yelled to Josiah as he took the stairs by threes, "They're in trouble! Spin the rudder. We have to get back to them!"

Catherine and Mare were sitting in the dining area of the galley knitting, and Pierre and some of the men were playing cards a few tables away when Jonah sounded the alarm. The men rose to assist with the crises, and Marie leaped to her feet. Gripping Pierre's shoulder, she begged, "Please don't go. Don't leave me!"

"Marie, everything will be fine. Now stay here where you're safe with Catherine," Pierre said soothingly, loosening her grip on his shoulder.

As he headed through the door, she turned on Catherine. "See? I told you they would come back. Now we're doomed. They're going to kill our men and commandeer the vessel."

Catherine's mouth went dry with fear. She picked up Marcel and reached for her sister's hand. "Come; let's go quickly to your quarters. I will stay with you there. Let's not lose courage."

CHAPTER 10

Raphael, Vidal, and the men were armed with shotguns and rifles although they knew they were no match for the gun decks of the galleon. As its long beak slowed next to the *Ann Louise,* a tall, lean Spaniard appeared on the gangplank. Behind him on the many split-leveled decks, his crew was watchful.

"Take one step closer and I will blow your head off," Raphael said crossly. His insides were trembling but his hands were steady on the rifle. "What business do you have with us?"

The *Louise Catherine* pulled along the opposite side so that the large galleon was sandwiched between the two smaller vessels. Jonah and the men had their guns poised and ready.

"I mean you no harm. My name is Jaime Colon. I am the captain of the *Santa Elena.* My son is very sick with the fever. He has been delirious for days. I am hoping that you have medicine to help us. He will not endure until we reach land."

Raphael felt the nervous sweat running down his spine. He was mortally anxious for the safety of his passengers. With his rifle trained on the captain, he replied, "How do we know you're telling the truth?"

"I swear on my son's life. I would not lie about something like this."

"Then bring the boy on deck. Let us see him."

"I will not bring him out here," Jaime replied coldly, "You have a choice. It's either you decide to help me, or I will plunder your vessels and help myself." Motioning to his crew, he said, "They will attack both your vessels at a mere nod from me. Your puny guns are no match for my arsenal. Now which will it be?"

"He's telling you the truth," Philar whispered, coming up behind Raphael.

"Damn it, woman! Didn't I tell you to remain in your quarters?"

"Yes, but think about it," she said reasonably. "Is it not best to befriend him than to provoke his anger and create bigger problems for us?"

Raphael's attention was divided between the Spaniard and Philar. Keeping his rifle aimed at Jaime, he asked Philar, "How do you know he is being truthful?"

"I just know," she replied simply. "If you allow me to go onboard, I can help the boy. I know what you are thinking, and I don't agree. It is not a good idea to bring the child onboard the *Ann Louise*. That will expose us to his illness. Let me go onboard the *Santa Elena*."

"Confounded woman, how the hell can you tell what I am thinking?" He stole a quick glance at her. "Do you have any idea what kind of danger you're putting yourself into by boarding their vessel? I cannot protect you once you cross over there."

"I assure you, Raphael, they will not harm me." Locking her eyes with his, she asked, "Do you have a better solution?"

Raphael muttered a series of obscenities. "All right, just be careful."

Having his permission, Philar turned her attention to the Spanish captain and said calmly, "I can help you. Just let me get my medicine bag."

Alphonse immediately protested, "No! I forbid you. It's too dangerous."

She walked over to where he stood. Touching his face, she looked into his eyes and whispered, "We don't have a choice. We're in grave danger here, but I will not be harmed." Then she walked resolutely back inside the vessel.

She was back quickly with Loretta in tow.

"Now wait a damn minute. I will not allow both of you to go. One of you is enough of a risk. I will send a man to escort you, but not Loretta!" Raphael said adamantly.

Philar touched her sister's arm. "Stay here."

"I need a man to go with her," Raphael interjected. "I cannot allow her to board the galleon alone."

Vidal quickly stepped forward. "I will go with her."

"No, she's my sister. I will go! I don't trust those bastards," Alphonse shouted.

"Exactly why you shouldn't go," Raphael said. "Your damn hotheadedness might get us all killed." He nodded at Vidal. "You go."

"Anyone coming with me stands a risk of catching the virus," Philar murmured.

"It's a risk I will take," Vidal replied. "Now let's get this over with."

With the guns from both the *Ann Louise* and the *Louise Catherine* directed at the Spanish galleon, Philar and Vidal stepped toward the long vessel. Captain Jaime reached for her hand to assist her onboard. Vidal followed closely behind.

Without speaking, the captain escorted them through the vessel, past the galley, and up several decks. Philar felt the eyes of the crew ravenously following her. The corridors smelled of rancid food and male sweat. Just as they passed the galley, a huge, gray rat scurried by, its long tail brushing Philar's feet, and she didn't even flinch.

When they arrived at the door to his cabin, Jaime turned and looked at her sternly, his dark brown eyes searching hers. "How do I know you're not a scam?"

"You don't," she answered simply. "You will have to trust me, Captain."

"I do not trust anyone.

"How sad then your life must be."

He looked at her, perplexed, but he didn't reply. Instead he put his shoulder to the door and pushed it open. A young boy of about eight lay on the bed. His dark wavy hair was matted with sweat.

"What's his name?" Philar asked as she walked over to the bed and knelt beside him.

"Nicholas."

"Why is he here with you? Where is his mother?"

She opened her bag and began pulling out salves and vials.

"My wife, Elena, is dead. The boy always travels with me. The galleon is his home," Jaime answered brusquely.

Ignoring his abruptness, Philar spoke softly to the boy. "Nicholas, my name is Philar, and I am here to help you feel better." She smoothed his hair away from his face, and he groaned, grabbing at the tangled sheets.

Next to the bed was a simple oak dresser. A light-green enamel basin sat on top of it. She reached for it. Inside, the basin was chipped and dirty.

She handed it to Jaime. "Will you please wash this out thoroughly and fill it halfway with clean water?"

"I will not leave you in here alone with my son."

Looking directly up at him, she raised her eyebrows. "Captain, now you must decide. Do you or do you not want my help?"

Resolutely, he took the basin and left the room. Vidal stood observantly in the corner. Philar took her time ministering to the boy. She placed a handkerchief soaked in ointment on his forehead. Gently turning him on his side, she rubbed salve on his back, which was hot with fever. She pinned a little sack of camphor and herbs to his white chemise close enough to his nostrils so he could absorb the smell.

She glanced up as Jaime returned with the basin. Taking it from him, she placed it on the floor beside her. She took out a clean white handkerchief from her bag, dipped it in the cool water, and gently wiped Nicholas's parched lips. His mouth automatically opened, and his tongued reached out greedily to lap at the water. She carefully dripped droplets into his mouth.

Satisfied that his throat was reasonably moist to receive medicine, she raised his head and placed a thin vial of liquid to his lips. When she was finished, she asked his father for a clean quilt to cover him. She tucked the corners of the quilt securely under him. Finally rising to her feet, she handed Jaime a bottle of herbs mixture, giving him instruction to administer it to the boy at different intervals and warning that it would cause him to sweat profusely, thereby breaking the fever.

"Is there anyone else onboard who is sick?"

"There are a few who are showing signs."

Handing him a small sack, she said, "Have your cook grind raw garlic and onion, mix it with this and water, and have them drink it. It will taste terrible, but it will prevent the virus from spreading. Nicholas should be up and around in a couple of days. Just make sure that he doesn't overdo. His body will still be weak."

Taking one last look at the boy, she motioned to Vidal, and they headed toward the door. Jaime opened it, and they walked the distance back in silence. As they approached the gangplank, Jaime reached for her hand. "Senorita Philar, please accept this as a token of my thanks."

She looked at the gold coins he had placed in her hand and shook her head, "This is not necessary, Captain. Please take it back."

"Oh no, I insist," he said gruffly, folding her fingers around the coins. "I have never met a woman like you. Your bravery and kindness are unheard of, especially toward a man of my reputation. I will not forget you. Where is your final destination?"

"Do not answer that, Philar!" Vidal said quickly. "Stick with the business at hand, Captain. Our destination does not concern you. Now, this exchange is over." Placing his hand on Philar's back, he propelled her forward.

Ignoring Vidal and keeping his attention on Philar, Jaime blocked their path. With a mischievous twinkle in his brown eyes, he took her right hand in his, raised it to his lips, and kissed it. "Adios, Senorita Philar. Muchas Gracias. Until we meet again, and we most certainly will meet again." Then he stepped aside.

When Philar and Vidal were safely onboard the *Ann Louise,* and the *Santa Elena* had recommenced her voyage, her gigantic masts full sail again, everyone let out a collective sigh of relief. For the first time since their voyage had begun, Jonah boarded the *Ann Louise.* He wanted to personally thank Philar. She had bravely defused a potentially deadly confrontation. He also wanted to laud Raphael and his crew. He had waited anxiously aboard the *Louise Catherine,* feeling helpless while the episode had unfolded.

Vidal knew with certainty that he was in love. For months he had admired Philar. But aside from his occasional visits to the houses of ill repute, he had limited experience with women. Although he prided himself for being composed and confidant, he turned into a blundering, stuttering fool in her presence, so he had tried to convince himself that she was too ditsy for his liking. Of course he had also heard of her so-called gift. He didn't believe in such gibberish. Today though, he had seen another side of her. She had been the epitome of bravery, and her skillful and compassionate ministering to the child had impressed him. The Spanish captain had said he had never met a woman like her, and Vidal had to agree because neither had he.

He frowned as he thought of the Spaniard. He hadn't like the way Jaime had looked at Philar. When he had raised her fingers to his lips and kissed them, he had felt like pushing the obnoxious captain overboard his own vessel.

"Vidal."

He jumped when he heard her voice behind him. "Wh … what did you say?" he asked, tumbling over his words.

Philar laughed and reached for his hand. "I said come with me. I will not bite you, nor will I work my magic spells on you, I promise. I am taking you to my quarters where you will drink the bitter-tasting garlic-and-onion cocktail. I will not risk you catching the fever although you were very brave to accompany me today."

"You already have," he said softly, allowing her to lead him down the narrow corridor.

"What?" She stopped and looked up at him.

"You already worked your magic on me, and now I am hopelessly mesmerized," he said huskily, wetting his lips with his tongue. He brazenly pulled her into his arms and kissed her, taking time to explore the texture and taste of her mouth. Her hands encircled him, and his fingers entwined in the silky curls of her hair.

"If you two want to share spit, don't you think you should be doing it privately instead of putting on a show for anybody passing through here?" Raphael's booming voice brought Vidal out of his trance. "Vidal, my boy, I see you have been bewitched," he said with an amused chuckle as he continued down the corridor.

With his eyes affixed on hers, he pulled away. Philar again took his hand, and they proceeded to the quarters she shared with Loretta, who thankfully was not in the room.

She headed straight for the onion and garlic mixture. She poured a glassful and handed it to him. "Here, I want you to drink this. It will prevent you from catching any virus you may have come into contact with on the *Santa Elena.*"

He took the glass from her and sniffed it. "It smells awful."

"It tastes awful too. Now drink it."

He raised the glass to his lips and drank the bitter-tasting liquid in one gulp.

"Ugh. I hope this doesn't affect my bowels. Can I kiss you again now?"

She chuckled. "Not with that smell on your breath."

"Why? You bewitched me, and now that I drank your magic potion, I can't kiss you?"

"You can kiss me again later when my magic potion has gone through your system, and you smell better," she responded playfully.

He pulled her into his arms. "You know, I don't believe in such fallacies. You've bewitched me with your beauty and your sweet ways, but you're just an ordinary woman. All this talk about you is just rubbish."

"It's not rubbish." The tone in Philar's voice instantly changed.

"Of course, it is. You are beautiful, witty, and charming, and that, my dear, is the extent of your special gifts."

Philar pulled away from him. Vidal felt her aloofness even before she spoke. "You're thinking that it's all in my head. You're even finding it humorous. Well, it's not. It's very real. It's a part of who I am, and I will not fall in love with a man who cannot support my true essence."

"Philar, I"

"No." She raised her hand to stop him from speaking. "Say no more. Leave my quarters now."

"Philar, please!"

"I said leave!"

"Okay, I am leaving. But I am in love with you, and I intend to pursue you until you fall in love with me too." Just before Vidal closed the door, he winked and added, "I will be back for more sweet kisses when my breath recovers from your magic portion."

CHAPTER 11

The sun had begun its western descent in a blaze of yellows, oranges, and reds the afternoon St. Barthelemy came into view. The passengers on both vessels crowded the decks, craning their necks to get their first glimpses of the island's high hills and peaks. They had spent the day watching the chain of Windward and Leeward islands as they had appeared in view, and they were awed by their innate placement in an almost perfect half circle.

As they made their final approached, both vessels lowered their masts. The crew knew they needed to carefully maneuver around the many islets and reefs surrounding the eight-mile-long island in order to arrive safely in the mouth of its natural harbor. Mesmerized, the passengers watched as the vessels slowly entered the harbor and dropped anchors.

With one arm holding Marcel and the other clasped around Marie's expanding waist, Catherine gazed at the high hills and their sparse spattering of green grass and brown earth. There seemed to be rocks everywhere. She remembered Ivan saying the parcels were at the top of a high hill. She wondered which one of the hills it was and how they would get up there.

The pristine beauty of the water intrigued her. Leaning over the railing, Catherine watched fish and other colorful sea life just beneath the surface. She raised her face to the warm afternoon's sun and smelled the freshness of the air as the trade winds kissed her cheeks. She laughed with Marie as they watched the cumbersome pelicans with their long beaks and waddling gaits glide over the water in search of the many visible schools of fish. She listened to the frantic squawking of the seagulls, so plentiful here. She looked at the fishermen onshore securing their boats, their broad straw hats shielding their faces from the sun, and she felt an unfathomable contentment.

Rowboats from both vessels were lowered for the captains and their first mates. As Jonah rowed, he studied the U-shaped harbor of the capital city, Gustavia. A frigate was anchored in the bay, and fishermen secured their boats for the evening.

Jonah glanced up at the precipitous hills, noticing at once the three massive forts in strategic locations overlooking the harbor. A smattering of houses dotted the hills, and a more clustered group of buildings sat farther inland from the harbor.

When they arrived onshore, they set about securing the rowboats. Everyone on the island they had seen so far had opted to bow their heads rather than make eye contact, so the newcomers continued working securing the rowboats, not paying much mind to the galloping horse behind them.

"Josiah!"

Josiah abruptly turned around and called back, "Paul!"

The two men laughed and hugged, letting go only long enough to look at each other and hug again.

Finally Josiah said, "Jonah, this is my brother, Paul."

Jonah extended his hand. "I am so glad to make your acquaintance. We're going to need someone to point us in the right direction." He looked around and shrugged. "The few people we've seen aren't too friendly."

"They're a secretive bunch. They don't warm up to outsiders too quickly. Once they see you're here to stay, they'll come around. I received the same silent treatment when I first arrived. Don't let it bother you. I am glad to be of help. Tell me whatever you need, and I will try my best to get it for you."

"Well, to start with, we need to find safe, clean lodging."

"Not for Josiah and Agnes; they and the children will come home with me. I live in St. Jean, which is not far from here. I have a small house, but now that Josiah is here, we will add more rooms to it and eventually build another one. How many rooms do you need?"

"As many as possible. The crew can sleep on the vessels if need be, but the passengers need to come ashore."

"Ahh! I know the perfect place, Madame Clara's! We will go at once and see how many rooms she has available."

After tying the horse's rope to a wooden railing, Paul motioned for them to follow. He continued speaking as he led the way. "She is right here in Gustavia, just around the corner. She can be a bit cantankerous. Don't let her scare you with her sharp tongue. Her rooms are spotlessly clean, and she is a very good cook. The meals come with the rooms."

"How did you know we had arrived?" Josiah asked.

"You will find that on St. Barth, news travel quickly. Everyone was talking about the two vessels on the sea approaching the island. All I had to do was to see for myself. You can see the sea from every part of the island."

"So," Raphael said, "since they knew we were coming, where's everybody? Except for those few men down by the wharf, the place looks deserted."

"Oh, you can be sure they're watching you," Paul answered. "From behind every jalousie, they're scrutinizing you."

Paul led the four men through the narrow cobblestone streets of Gustavia. The houses they passed were modestly built, the yards enclosed by neatly formed stone walls. They soon rounded a corner and started up an incline. The smell of varnish tickled their nostrils. On their left, a joiner sat in a fenced in-yard beneath the shade of a large avocado tree, his head bent as he worked on an upside-down rocking chair. On the opposite side, an old lady stood on a wooden gallery watching them. Her head was covered by a white caleche, and she cradled a large, black and white cat in her arms. They bid her a good afternoon, but she didn't acknowledge their greetings.

The top of the incline gave way to another narrow, cobblestone street. Midway down the street, they arrived at a sprawling, bright-yellow house with white lattice trimmings. It contrasted with the smaller, more modest houses in the area. There was a general store next door, and a saloon occupied the space directly across the street. On both sides of the walkway leading to the gallery were pretty red and yellow hibiscuses. On the gallery, mahogany rocking chairs with woven straw seats swayed invitingly in the breeze. The main door was open, and the spacious parlor could be seen through the screen door. Paul clanged the brass bell.

"Hold on. I'm coming," a female voice answered.

They watched as a short, petite woman of about sixty approached, wiping her hands on a white apron. Her silver-streaked, blonde hair was pulled back in a loose chignon. Except for a smudge of flour on her left cheek, her appearance was impeccable.

Opening the screen door, she said, "Good day, Paul." She looked at the other men, but she did not greet them. "How can I help you?"

"Madame Clara, this is my brother, Josiah, and these are my friends, Jonah, Raphael, and Vidal. They just arrived from France today. Their families are still onboard the vessels. Josiah and his family are coming home with me, but the others are in need of rooms. Since it is well-known that you run the best boardinghouse in St. Barth, I brought them to you first."

"Humph." She frowned. "Like unwanted rodents, you just keep coming. Running away from France, are you? Well, St. Barth doesn't need any more outsiders."

CHAPTER 12

Raphael could not believe what Clara had just said. He couldn't stomach it. He had to say something. "And you run a boardinghouse with that nasty attitude? Woman, nobody never taught you no manners?"

Paul quickly interceded before Clara could reply. "Madame Clara, my friends are tired. They're good people. They can pay well. Please, do you have vacant rooms?"

Looking hard at Raphael, she replied, "Yes, I only have two boarders presently. There are six rooms available at four francs a day."

"That's ludicrous!"

"Shut up, Raphael," Jonah muttered.. Turning to Clara, he said, "We will take all six rooms. I can pay you in advance until the end of March. We will need the rooms for tomorrow by noon."

By noon the next day Jonah arrived on Clara's gallery with the passengers who would occupy the six rooms. After leaving Clara's yesterday, Paul had taken them to two other boardinghouses, one along Rue de la République, and another in Gustavia, closer to the waterfront. Some of the crew members would have to share rooms, but Jonah had managed to procure accommodations for everyone onboard both vessels. Madame Clara's establishment was by far the best. Pierre and Marie, Alphonse and Yvette, Loretta and Philar, Vidal , Raphael, and Jonah and Catherine would occupy the rooms. Raphael had protested, saying Clara's bad attitude would cause him to sin his soul, but Jonah had convinced him that he had to be near Marcel and Catherine to protect them.

Catherine was pleasantly surprised at the simple elegance and cleanliness of the boardinghouse. The parlor boasted several comfortable chairs and a bookshelf with assorted books. A card table was set up in the far corner of the room. A door to the right opened into a smaller room with a long dining table. Fresh flowers adorned its center in a simple glass vase. The savory scent of roasting chicken drifted in from another open door.

Clara greeted them civilly. With the help of a tall, black man in his seventies that she introduced as Oliver, their luggage was collected. They were escorted down a narrow hallway that opened to eight doors. In a no-nonsense tone she told them, "Breakfast is served at seven a.m. each morning. Lunch is served at noon and will consist of only sandwiches. Supper is served at seven p.m. each evening. If you miss out on those times, you will remain hungry because the kitchen will be closed. Wash day is Wednesday. Leave your clothes in the bags provided in your rooms outside your doors on Tuesday evenings, and we will collect them." She didn't ask if there were any questions. She proceeded to open each door and hand the occupant a key.

Catherine and Jonah were the last to accept their key to the last door at the end of the corridor. The room was small, but it smelled and looked clean. An average-size bed covered with a patchwork quilt occupied the center. A rocking chair and a wooden dresser with four drawers completed the furniture. A wash basin, a yellow soap, two towels, two washcloths, and a pitcher of water were situated on top of the dresser. A pleasant breeze blew through the only window in the room.

Catherine placed Marcel on top of the bed and sat next to him. "Well, we're finally here. What do we do now?"

He sat beside her. "Today we will take it easy. We all need the break. Paul promised to help us get to La Pointe tomorrow. The men and I will go up there and assess how to go about clearing the land." He touched her nose. "You will remain here with the women and explore Gustavia."

Jonah had to admit that Paul was right; Clara was an excellent cook. They enjoyed delicious roasted chicken and rice that evening. For dessert she had prepared pineapple tarts, which consisted of pineapples stewed in a sugary blend of spices and baked in a tasty golden crust. Clara didn't talk much, but she paid attention to every detail.

The other two boarders were both men. One was a Swede who was visiting the island on official business with the French government, and the other was a Dane from the Danish Virgins who was negotiating a contract to import sugarcane rum from St. Thomas. Both men were amiable, and the dinner conversation was lively.

Happy to finally be sleeping on solid ground again, Catherine fell into a restful sleep between the crisp, clean-smelling sheets. Marcel's cries woke her around four thirty a.m. He was hungry, and with dismay she realized she did not have any food to give him. Knowing she could not let him cry until breakfast was served at seven thirty, she quickly dressed. Being careful not to wake Jonah, she picked up Marcel and tiptoed down the long hallway to the kitchen. Judging from Clara's manner, she knew the older woman would be upset if she found her in the kitchen, but she had to find some fruit or cereal to feed Marcel.

The kitchen was dark, and Catherine did not see the woman coming in the back door until she was already opening the cupboard door.

"Who's there?"

Catherine jumped, hitting her head on the cupboard. A portly, black woman with a gigantic bosom carrying a kerosene lamp advanced into the room. She raised the lamp close to Catherine's face, and Marcel started to wail in earnest. The woman placed the lamp on the table and reached for the child. Backed against the cupboard, Catherine held on tightly to Marcel.

"It is okay, Missus. No need to be frightened. I won't hurt him or you." Her voice held a melodic lilt. "My name is Bella. I work for Ms. Clara. I come in here every morning to get things in place for breakfast. Now sit here with your youngster and tell me what you need," she said, pulling out a chair for Catherine.

Holding on to Marcel, Catherine backed herself into the chair. "He's hungry. I was just looking for cereal to feed him."

Bella smiled at her, the white turban on her head luminous in the semi darkness. "You one of them who come in yesterday on the boat," she said knowingly. "Just sit here while I make the boy some cornmeal pap. You want some tea?"

Not waiting for Catherine's answer, she placed two pots of water on the stove. Still unnerved, Catherine watched her as she moved about the kitchen. She had a distinct limp, which made her movements awkward. She guessed Bella to be in her seventies.

When the cereal was ready, Bella placed a bowlful in front of Catherine. "Be careful now. It's very hot. Blow on it before you feed it to the boy. This will fatten him up good."

The yellow porridge smelled and tasted delicious. Marcel hungrily ate the spoonfuls Catherine fed him. Bella placed a steaming cup of bush tea on the table, being careful to put it out of the child's reach. She continued talking to Catherine while she busied herself with her morning chores.

"Me and meh husband, Oliver, we work for Ms. Clara for years. She be good to us. Slavery ended here in St. Barth in 1847, long before it ended on the other islands. We was young then. We could a gone, but to go where, when we was done happy here. Most all the colored people left St. Barth, but not we. We stayed with Ms. Clara. Our bellies was full right here, and anyway, we does add some color to the place." Bella chuckled loudly at her own joke.

She shook her head sadly before continuing. "And then poor Ms. Clara. She had already lost her husband and two sons from the fever. We couldn't just up and leave her too. That was a bad year. More than three hundred people died from that fever. Fact is we had a lot of bad years. In 1837 we had a real bad gale that killed about fifty people and destroyed the Catholic church in Gustavia. Then in 1850 the whole town burn down. It was like God had turn He face from us." Bella stood motionless. From the faraway look in her eyes, Catherine knew her memories were transporting her back to another time.

Then wiping her hands on her apron, she sat across from Catherine. "Don't let Ms. Clara frighten you. She not a bad person. Inside she soft like cotton. She just went through a lot of bad times, which makes her think she tough. Humph, she really don't like French people though. She

French herself, but she always say they don't have no loyalty. According to her, we was better off with the Swedes than the French."

Slapping her knees, Bella rose slowly to her feet again. "Well, the child full now. I think you better get going. Ms. Clara don't like nobody in her kitchen but me and she. If you come again early tomorrow morning, I go fix you up with some more cereal for the boy. I got to go wake up Windy before Ms. Clara come."

"Who's Windy?" Catherine asked.

"Meh husband, of course."

"I thought you said his name was Oliver."

Bella let out a hearty laugh. "His name is Oliver, but I does call him Windy. You see, when we was first married, he use to pass so much wind. Up to now he still gassy. Anyhow, I started calling him Windy from then, and the nickname stuck. You go find out that around here everybody got a nickname."

Jonah and the men left right after breakfast. They had arranged to meet Paul at Gustavia's harbor. They would follow Paul on foot to St. Jean, where he had horses and donkeys waiting. It was a good half hour's walk, part of it uphill. By the time they arrived at the bayside in St. Jean, they were drenched with sweat.

Agnes, Josiah, and the children were walking along the white, sandy beach collecting seashells when they arrived. While the men chatted with Josiah and Agnes and admired the tranquil beauty of their surroundings, Paul slipped away to his house which was just a short distance from the beach. He returned in a few minutes, his hands laden. He handed each man a container of water and a brown sack containing a baguette and a generous slice of cheese wrapped in brown paper. "You're going to need this," he said. "Today is going to be long and hard."

Josiah kissed his wife and children, and the group left on their journey. They went back in the direction from which they had come, up the hill and back down through Rue de la République and Gustavia. They then started the tedious, slow climb up through the twisting hills that would take them to La Pointe.

There were long stretches of time with nothing but dense shrubbery. Cactuses with prickly needles threatened the animals' hoofs. Vines and catch-n-keep bushes reached out to snag them. Each man had brought along a machete or a sickle and periodically used it to disentangle themselves. The bushes and trees were so thick in some areas that it blocked out the sun, making temporary canopies above them. Iguanas lay lazily in the trees, watching the intrusion of their habitat, their long tails swinging languidly over the branches, their serrated ridged, leathery, lizard-like bodies blending in with the undergrowth. Black birds and yellow-breasted sparrows flew high above their heads. Mosquitoes and yellow jackets buzzed and ruthlessly attacked as the unfamiliar Caribbean heat bore down on them. Farther up the winding trail, they eventually came upon clearings with small houses surrounded by stone walls, but they were few and far between.

As they neared La Pointe, they came upon another such clearing. The yard was enclosed by mismatched wooden poles held together with wire. Two small houses were situated in close proximity in the middle of the yard, and a third structure was about ten feet away. Goats and chickens grazed in grassy patches. As they got closer, they saw four big dogs lazing in the shade of the houses' adjoining galleries.

Their approach alerted the dogs, whose boisterous barking immediately won their owners' attention. An older woman wearing a pale-blue blouse and a long, brown skirt appeared from the back of the houses at the same time a man about the same age dressed in overalls and a big, straw hat rounded the opposite corner.

"Okay, you can stop your ruckus now. I see them," the man said to the dogs. "Good day!" He greeted them, tipping his hat. "What brings you all the way up here?"

Jonah dismounted and approached the couple. "Good day. My name is Jonah Dusant. I own land not too far from here. It is called La Pointe. We recently arrived from France. My intention is to build a home for my family. We're here to survey the land and determine the best course of action."

"So," the man said studying him, "we're going to be neighbors. My name is Henri Turbe, and this is my wife, Emeline. The sun is hot.

Would you like to come in and sit in the shade for a while? You have another half hour's ride before you arrive at La Pointe."

The men looked at each other. They had not yet eaten, and the idea of a cool, shady place to stop and eat sounded appealing. They dismounted, tying their horses and donkeys securely to the fence poles. Henri opened the gate, and they took seats on the gallery.

Having done their job of alerting their owners to the strangers and satisfied that they posed them no harm; the dogs again lounged lazily on the gallery's floor.

"So, by some fluke, have we suddenly left St. Barthelemy? How come you folks are so friendly?" Raphael asked. "The people in Gustavia aren't too inviting."

Rocking in the chair next to him, Emeline chuckled. "Those townspeople are afraid of their own shadows, frightened that everybody means them harm. Up here, we hardly ever see anybody, so it's always interesting when people come along."

"Aren't you afraid though, to be isolated like this?" Pierre asked.

"Oh, we're not isolated. We go into town when we need to." She shrugged. "We've lived here a long time, ever since we came from Normandy in 1850. We have everything we need right here. For us, it's a lot better than living in town."

"Do you have any children?" Alphonse asked.

"We have a son and a daughter. They both live in St. Thomas in the Danish Virgins now. They said there was no future here for them." She bowed her head sadly and looked down at her fingers. "They come back every so often to visit us."

They chatted a while longer, and then Jonah said, "Thank you kindly for your hospitality. We'd best be on our way."

Henri stood, and the dogs automatically followed him. "You won't have much time for your assessment today if you intend to make it back to town before nightfall. You should bring enough supplies to last a few days the next time you come up. Emeline and I will be glad to help. She will be happy for the chance to have people to fuss over other than me, and I can help you with clearing the bushes and gathering the stones."

Jonah thanked him again, and the group left to continue their journey.

"Peculiar people," Vidal whispered as they rode away.

"Lonely people and gullible," Alphonse responded.

"Oh, come now. After all those sourpusses in town, they're refreshing. Nothing like that confounded Clara," Raphael countered.

"You see all those dogs?" Paul called out from the back of the group. "Any wrong move from any one of us, and those bloodhounds would have had us for supper."

Josiah nodded in agreement. "They've lived up here for so long that they've learned how to take care of themselves."

An hour later they crested the top of the hill, and Jonah set foot on the parcels that were his inheritance from his father. There was nothing but dense brush, and their spirits fell when they realized the enormity of the task at hand. They spread out, each man going a different direction to gain the full scope of their mission, making good use of the machetes and sickles to clear away the thick bushes and vines in their paths.

Jonah was in the thick of a cluster of thorny vines when he heard Raphael call out excitedly. He carefully extracted himself and headed back in the direction of Raphael's voice. He navigated his way through the trampled, broken vines and branches until he saw him and the other men standing near the edge of a stony overhang that sloped raggedly downhill.

Turning and seeing him, Alphonse proclaimed, "In all of France, I have never seen a view quite so astounding as this one. Come see for yourself, Jonah."

Jonah walked up to the men and gaped at the view. The ocean could be seen from every angle, with a clear, uninterrupted view of all the adjacent islands. The steep, high hills of St. Martin and St. Christopher, the flat lands of Anguilla, and the jutting, precipitous mountain of Saba were clearly discernible. The silhouette of other islands could be seen on the horizon. In closer parameter was a panoramic view of St. Barth.

In awe, his thoughts turned to Ivan. *How did you know, Father? This is so perfectly hidden away beneath the thorns and undergrowth. Did you too climb this wearisome hill and cut away at this jungle, or was it that cleverly honed insight of yours that led you to these particular parcels simply by gazing up at them from the streets of Gustavia? Whichever it was Father, bravo.*

#

"You want me to put my mouth where? Over that hole and tilt my head backward?" Catherine asked the man as Marie, Yvette, Loretta, and Philar laughed. "You can all laugh at me, but I don't see any of you volunteering."

She was holding a coconut. The tough, green outer husk of half of it was neatly cut away to reveal the hard, brown inner shell and a smooth, round hole. The shirtless vendor was giving her instructions on how to drink the sweet-tasting water directly out of the coconut.

"Okay, let's get this over with." She raised the coconut to her lips, tilted her head backward, and allowed the water to flow into her mouth. It was cool and thirst quenching. As the milky water dripped down the sides of her chin, she tilted her head again to get a second drink. Then she stretched out her hands to give the coconut to one of the women. "It's delicious," she said, wiping the corners of her mouth and chin. "Which one of you cowards will give it a try?"

"I will," Loretta said.

The two women shared the remainder of the water. Then the man cut the coconut in half with his machete, and they all shared the tasty, white flesh of the fruit.

They were enjoying a leisurely morning, strolling through the streets of Gustavia. Unlike the day they had arrived, today people were bustling around doing ordinary tasks. Vendors sold colorful fruits and vegetables. Fishermen occupied most of the wharf. The pungent smell of fish permeated the air as the pelicans and seagulls circled expectantly. Two large schooners were anchored in the bay delivering goods from the other islands. They received many curious glances, but in general, they were greeted politely.

Walking farther down the wharf, they came upon a woman sitting under the shade of a gigantic flamboyant tree, its branches ablaze with bright-orange blossoms. On a makeshift table in front of her was an array of hand woven, straw hats, purses, and baskets.

Catherine picked up a delicately woven green and white purse. As she ran her fingers over it, she felt a deep sadness.

"Do you like this hat?" Marie asked her, sporting one of the huge, straw hats on her head.

Catherine quickly brushed away her tears and smiled at her sister.

Soothingly Marie said, "Oh Cathy, Mama would love that purse, and I know how you feel. I miss her too."

From the wharf, they continued down the winding, cobblestone streets. Many of the old buildings that were once warehouses under Swedish rule had been converted into shops. They passed a butcher, a shoemaker, and a seamstress. They stopped to laugh at the antics of two barefoot boys chasing after a fat, brown hen. The boys slowed down long enough to smile shyly at the women and then continued their lively chatter as they sped up in pursuit of the clucking fowl.

Their wanderings led them to the most exquisite, little beach on the outskirts of Gustavia. They took off their shoes to feel the sand between their toes. The waves rolled in, its white caps lapping at their bare ankles. The beach was laden with shells of all sorts and sizes. Little Marcel took off running. Giggling, he plopped his bottom onto the sand. Leaning over, he reached out and grabbed a handful of the pretty, shiny shells, the sand drifting through his chubby fingers. The women came and sat on the sand, encircling the toddler.

"It's so beautiful here." Philar turned her face to the warm rays of the sun.

"Yes, it is very nice, but it will be a long time before it will feel like home," Loretta responded.

"What do you mean?" Yvette's fingers sifted through the grainy sand.

"Well, we can't continue living in the boardinghouse, and it will take time to build houses and get settled. I have a feeling the men have their work cut out for them."

"Are you saying they're in danger?" Marie eyes were filled with concern.

Loretta reached across and gently rubbed Marie's arm. "Oh no, nothing like that. I simply mean that there's plenty for them to take in today, it being the first day and all. They're not in any danger."

"Oh, thank God. They need to make quick strides in building those houses. That woman at the boardinghouse is just dreadful."

"Well," Catherine said, standing up and brushing off the sand from her long, beige skirt, "it will be noon soon, and we need to start heading back before she closes her kitchen. Remember what she said."

"If you miss out, you will remain hungry because the kitchen will be closed." They all laughed when Marie mimicked Clara.

Catherine picked up Marcel, whose hair and face were now covered with sand. She brushed him off as best she could, and they headed back in the direction of the boardinghouse.

They made it back in time to enjoy the chicken sandwiches Clara had prepared for lunch. There was no sign of her. The sandwiches were neatly wrapped and placed on a large, oval platter in the center of the dining table. A round bowl filled with sliced mangos sat next to it. A pitcher of lime juice, a pitcher of water, and two pots of hot, bush tea completed the spread. The women were the only people in the dining room, so they relaxed and enjoyed their camaraderie. They each retired to their rooms afterward for an afternoon respite.

Later in the afternoon, Catherine decided to explore the large backyard that was visible from the window in her room. Marcel was fretful, and she wanted to give him some play time in the fresh air.

The house was quiet as she walked down the corridor and opened the back door off the dining room. Stepping onto a dirt landing built up with stones, she descended the three wooden steps onto a flat surface where grass grew in patches amid the brown, stony dirt. She stood there for a moment to gain her bearings. Directly in front of her was a chicken coop, and she could hear the hens clucking. To her left in the vicinity of the kitchen was a platform with a large, round, gray, enamel basin. A wooden washboard was propped up in the center of it. An empty clothesline was situated to the far left. The whole area smelled musty.

Realizing that this was no place for Marcel to play, she turned around to leave.

It was then that she heard the soft bleating of the goats. She turned in the direction of the sound. There in the far right corner of the yard was a wooden pen filled with goats of all sizes. Enthralled by the animals, she walked toward the pen. She crouched next to the railing, placing Marcel securely on one knee. Instantly, the goats approached, sticking their cold noses through the cracks of the boards. She reached out her hand to touch them.

"What is it with you people that you always go where you don't belong?"

Catherine quickly pulled back her hand and turned at the sound of Clara's voice. Clara stood directly behind her, her arms encircling a straw basket full of eggs.

"I ... I was just showing Marcel the goats. He was restless, and I—"

"If I were you, I would not befriend those animals. They're going to end up on your dinner plate real soon. Out here is not the place for you and your boy. Now go back into the house where you belong," Clara said harshly.

Catherine was furious. "What is it with *you* that you are always so miserable?" Picking up Marcel, she stormed back into the house before she really lost her temper and said something more offensive to the older woman.

Clara had just reentered the dining room with a serving tray of sliced papayas when she saw the men taking their seats at the dinner table.

"You are not sitting at my table in that condition!"

"But Madam Clara, you said that we had to be on time for supper," Jonah said. "We just arrived back from a long, tiresome day, and we didn't want to risk missing our meal."

The men looked at each other, a sly smile on their faces. The women exchanged crafty looks. The other two boarders looked uncomfortable.

Clara placed her right hand on her chest. "Well, I am appalled. Is this how you behave in France?"

"Listen, lady, we're just following your orders. You said to be on time, and we're on time. You didn't say anything about being spruced up," Raphael bellowed.

Jonah quickly stepped forward. "Madam Clara, please accept our apologies. Just give us ten minutes. We will wash up, and we will be right back."

"You need more like an hour the way all of you look and smell," she countered back, wrinkling her nose.

Philar started to laugh, and the rest of the women could no longer contain their laughter. It was contagious. The two men seated at the table started laughing too.

Clara tried to keep a straight face, but the corners of her mouth gave her away. She shooed them out of the dining room. "Go take a good bath so you don't stink up my house. I will not hold up the dinner hour. However, I will fix a plate for each of you and leave it on the table."

Catherine whispered to Marie, "She's human after all."

The clean-smelling sheets were mesmeric. It was a marked improvement from the hard bunk Catherine had endured on the vessel for so many months, and it didn't take her long to fall into a deep sleep—until a blood-curling scream penetrated her slumber, causing her to bolt upright. She looked at her watch. It was 4:33 a.m. Was she dreaming? No. There it was again! She reached out and touched Jonah and Marcel, who were both sound asleep beside her.

A third cry broke the dawn's peacefulness. It sounded so close. She crept quietly to the window that overlooked the backyard. In the purplish blue of the early morning light, she saw the silhouettes of two people. She squinted and rubbed her eyes, peering more closely out the window. It was Clara and Oliver, and they were dragging something or someone between them. Catherine's heart began to beat faster and her mouth went dry.

CHAPTER 13

A s Clara and Oliver came clearer into view, Catherine saw that they were dragging one of the goats. A rope was tied around the animal's neck, and it was desperately resisting their efforts to pull it forward. She watched as they managed to pull the petrified goat under a big tree, securing the rope tightly around a thick, lower branch. She saw the gleam of the rising sun reflected on the shiny blade that Oliver pulled from a sheath at his side as Clara grasped the animal's head firmly and pulled it backward. She watched the blood spurt from the animal's neck, spattering liberally all over its slaughterers even as it continued to bawl piteously.

"Noooo!" The scream ripped from her own throat.

Jonah leaped from the bed. "Cathcrine! What's the matter?"

Catherine couldn't speak. She could only point toward the window. Jonah looked out and saw Oliver and Clara completing the deed, the limp, bloody animal in their arms.

"Oh, Catherine," he groaned, pulling her closely against him.

She buried her face in his chest and wept for the helpless goat. "Jonah, it was awful. How could they do that? I am so glad Marie's room overlooks the opposite side."

"Catherine." He gently pulled her away to look into her eyes. "Honey, this is how they eat. We have to adjust if we're going to survive here because where we are going to live is so far up that mountain that we're going to have to do the exact same thing."

"Jonah, I can't eat that goat, not after what I saw just now. I will choke if I try."

"You will have to learn how to get past this."

"No." She adamantly shook her head. "I won't!"

The following morning, Catherine woke with a nagging headache. She had not been able to fall back into a comfortable sleep. Her mind had kept replaying the bloodied slaughtering of the goat and its pitiful cries. Jonah suggested that they take a walk down by the wharf, telling her that the fresh air would help.

"So you're going to stay up there?"

"It's the only way we're going to get the land cleared and the houses built. We will never accomplish much going back and forth. It's too time consuming."

The tranquil beauty of the morning was lost on Catherine. She and Jonah were seated on the edge of the dock, their feet dangling over the side. Marcel was dozing on her lap. Jonah's announcement had served to intensify the pain in her head.

"We won't leave until tomorrow morning. We're going out to the vessels today to get the necessary items we need to build a camp. Paul procured two horse-drawn carriages to help transport the supplies. Thank God for him. He continues to be a big help to us."

Taking hold of her hand, Jonah said excitedly, "The view is unparalleled. Catherine, I am going to build a very big gallery where you and I will sit in the evenings and watch the sunsets for the rest of our lives. I can't wait to show you our land." He chuckled. "And wait until you meet Henri and Emeline. They're our closest neighbors, and they're charming."

Catherine raised her eyebrows. "Charming? Really? I have not met one person on this island I would consider charming."

"Yeah, I know, but Henri and Emeline are different. They offered to help us in any way they can. Oh Catherine, I am so excited about our new home."

Catherine smiled weakly. *How the tables have turned. I encouraged you into this. Now I am the one who is having second thoughts.*

Dinner conversation was lively that evening. It was the last night's stay for the Swedish and Danish gentlemen, and in their honor, Clara announced that she had made a guava cake for dessert, which she would serve with glasses of sherry.

"You mean you actually have liquor in this house?" Raphael teased. "What did you do? Take a walk across the street and steal a few bottles?" He looked at her coyly. "Clara, you're full of surprises."

Clara glared at Raphael. "I have never set foot in that place. I wish I had the power to shut it down." She went back into the kitchen and returned moments later with steaming platters of mutton stewed with potatoes and carrots. The spicy fragrance of the meat filled the air. Catherine felt her stomach turn as it was dished out and passed around.

"Mmm, this stew is delicious," Marie said, putting another forkful into her mouth. "The meat is so tender and perfectly seasoned."

Catherine halfheartedly smiled at Marie. All she could think about was that poor, helpless goat.

"Cathy, what's the matter? You're not eating?"

"I am not hungry."

"Well then, can I have yours? Remember, I am eating for two."

Catherine gladly passed the plate of mutton to her sister.

A short time later, she felt a gentle hand on her shoulder. "Mrs. Dusant, can I get you something else? Maybe a ham and cheese croissant? I have fresh croissants I am going to serve for breakfast tomorrow."

Catherine was pleasantly surprised by the caring gesture. "Yes, thank you, Clara. I'd like that if it's not too much trouble."

Clara nodded curtly and returned to the kitchen. She was back in a few minutes with the warm croissant.

As they were finishing dessert, Vidal reached across the table for Philar's hand. "It's such a beautiful evening. Can I entice you into taking a walk with me?"

"It's kind of chilly," Philar said hesitantly.

"It's lovely outside," Loretta interjected. "I'm going to the room to get a book. I plan to sit on the gallery and read for a while. I'll bring your shawl on my way back." She stood and headed to the room the sisters shared. She was back in no time with the book and a crocheted white shawl, which she slyly handed to Philar.

"Well then," Philar said a little too brightly. "Let's go take that walk."

They strolled leisurely in the direction of the wharf making light conversation. When they reached the privacy of the bayside, Vidal pulled Philar into his arms. She went willingly, yielding to his kisses and caresses. She knew what was on his mind, and she was trying to delay him speaking.

Inevitably he pulled away and nervously cleared his throat. "Philar, you're the most intriguing woman I have ever met, and I am hopelessly in love with you. I can't sleep at night. I think about you all the time." He got down awkwardly on one knee. "Philar, will you marry me? I don't have a ring yet, but I promise to get you a nice one soon."

"Stand up, Vidal."

Obligingly he stood, his eyes imploring hers.

"Let's give ourselves time to have a proper courtship. I have feelings for you too. However, I need to know you better, and you need to know me, who I really am, not who you perceive me to be. I agree to be your intended, but I am not ready to be your wife."

"So you agree to be my fiancée?"

"Yes, I do."

He picked her up and swung her around gleefully. "Then I can wait."

"What do you mean you told him not yet? Do you know how old you are and what a prize catch a man like Vidal is?

"I am younger than you, and yes, Loretta, I know his worth." Philar sat heavily on the bed. "I even believe I love him."

"So then what's your problem? Since you were quick to remind me of my own age, I will gladly take him away from you if you don't want him," Loretta replied, sitting down beside Philar.

"Oh Loretta." Philar threw herself backward on the bed. "Vidal doesn't believe in me, in my gift. He told me as much. How can I marry a man who dismisses such a big part of who I am?"

"Papa didn't believe Mama either, and they got married."

"And Mama lived her whole life trying to hide her true self to please Papa. I don't want to live like that. I am not ashamed, and I don't want to marry a man who will force me into being ashamed. I'd rather remain single."

Loretta mirrored Philar's action, throwing herself backward on the bed beside her. "I agree with you, except for the part of remaining single. I am still praying for someone to come along who will accept me for who I am." Turning her head to face Philar, she asked, "So what are you going to do?

"I am going to take my time, and whether I marry him or not will depend on him."

#

Clara couldn't fall asleep. She'd twisted and turned, fluffed the pillow, and changed into a cooler nightgown, but nothing worked. The clock said it was 12:37 a.m. Her days were so full and hectic that she should be able to fall asleep easily. Yet it was just the opposite. She'd work herself into such a frenzy all day attending to the myriad of tasks involved in running the boardinghouse that her body refused to settle down and succumb to a restful night's sleep.

She knew she could get away with doing a lot less and still make good money, but compromising her values was not part of her nature.

Deciding that a warm cup of chamomile tea might help, she put on her robe and started to make her way to the kitchen. When she entered the parlor, she noticed that the large hook on the main entrance door was unlatched. She had latched it herself before going to bed about two hours ago. She frowned. Did one of her boarders go out at this hour? They knew she locked the doors at ten p.m.

Well, if they are stupid enough to disobey my house rules, then they can just spend the night outside.

She walked over to the door and raised her hand to pull the heavy latch across. She paused. Even the music from the saloon across the street was silent. Who had gone out and where had they gone? She opened the door and stepped outside onto the gallery. The cool late night air felt brisk against her skin, and she pulled her robe more securely around her. Everything was quiet. The street was deserted.

"Hello, Clara."

She jumped. The voice came from the far end of the gallery. Turning in that direction, she could make out the shadow of a man sitting in one of the rocking chairs.

"Don't be frightened. It's only me."

Recognizing the voice, Clara sighed in relief. Then vexation took its place. She marched over to him. "Mr. Greaux, do you have no regard for rules? This door is closed for the night at ten o'clock. You know that! Now are you coming inside, or do I lock you out?"

"Oh woman, stop tongue lashing me and take a seat. You're going to make me go across the street and drink if you don't behave. The night is young and lovely. Relax. Come enjoy the sweetness of the dew and the splendor of the night's sky with me for a while. I promise to behave if you will."

"Mr. Greaux, I am not going to ask you again. Are you coming or—"

Raphael stood up, catching her off guard. He was so close she could smell the soap from his bath. It was disconcerting, and she felt lightheaded.

"Clara, when was the last time you sat on your own gallery for the pure sake of enjoyment?"

She didn't answer.

"I thought so. Please, come have a seat for a few minutes. That's all I'm asking," he said soothingly, nodding toward the rocking chairs.

She didn't know why, but she lowered herself into one of the chairs. Raphael reclaimed his and resumed rocking. The crickets chirped their merry tune.

Raphael broke the silence. "That was a nice thing you did for Catherine tonight. My room is right next door to hers. I heard the commotion with the goat this morning. Catherine is a light sleeper. I know she heard it too."

"I thought some of you might have heard," Clara replied. "But it was more than that with Mrs. Dusant. I found her and the boy in the backyard yesterday playing with the goats. I was a bit cross with her, and she let me know it."

Raphael chuckled. "Catherine always speaks her mind."

They were quiet again, and then he said, "You're not as hard and crusty as you want people to believe, are you?"

"I am woman running a business alone. Sometimes I have unsavory boarders who I have to keep in line. I cannot afford to let my guard down."

"What happened to your husband?"

A lump formed in Clara's throat. Even after all these years, it was still hard to speak about her husband and her sons. It was as if the pain waited silently inside of her, like a thief, ready to strike at her again each time she mentioned them.

"He and our two sons died from the fever in 1840. He was a Swede. I met him shortly after I arrived from Normandy. We built this house because we wanted to fill it with children," she said sadly. "My boys were only eight and ten when they caught the fever. My husband caught it soon after. I did everything I could to make them well. After they died, I wanted so badly to catch the fever too. But I never got sick. I kept right on living." Her voice broke. . "Eventually I realize I had to find a way to support myself. I had this big, empty house, and there was a need for rooms to rent. So," she shrugged, "I became a proprietress."

"I can relate to your sorrow. The woman I loved died from tuberculosis. I never had the opportunity to have a son." In a lackluster voice, Raphael continued, "I was very young. I never got over the pain. I closed my heart so it would never break again. Up until now I have lived my life on the sea."

"Somehow I got the impression Jonah was your son. You treat him like a son."

"I love that boy. I've known him since the day he was born. He's the reason I am here."

Will you stay on St. Barth?"

"I will stay as long as Jonah and Catherine stay, and for all intent, they're here to stay."

After a while Clara stood. "Well, Mr. Greaux, I was going to the kitchen to make myself a cup of chamomile tea. If you agree nicely to come indoors now, I will invite you to join me in the kitchen for some tea and a warm croissant."

"Lead the way, woman. I am right behind you. And for goodness sake, stop calling me Mr. Greaux. Raphael will do just fine."

He latched the door for her and together they walked to the kitchen. Clara didn't fall asleep until 3:16 a.m., but she slept peacefully. Her dreams were filled with an old seafaring ruffian.

#

"You finally come. I been looking out for you. I thought you would have come back sooner," Bella told Catherine when she entered the kitchen. The fragrant aroma of bush tea filled the room. Bella was sitting at the kitchen table peeling potatoes.

Catherine took a seat next to Bella, and Marcel immediately reached for one of the white, skinless potatoes lying in a pile. "Since my husband left for La Pointe, I have been having trouble sleeping. I toss and turn for hours. When I finally fall asleep, it's going on dawn."

Rising, Bella pushed the potato pile out of the child's reach. She walked over to the counter and picked up a white, enamel teacup. Lifting the kettle, she poured tea into the cup and placed it in front of Catherine. "Watch the boy so he don't get burn. Them fingers of his fast," she warned. Returning to the cupboard, she pulled out the container that held the cornmeal. Turning to Catherine, she said, "I am going outside to get water from the demijohn to make the cornmeal pop."

She was back in a few minutes with a small bucket of water. She poured some of the water in a saucepan and set it to boil. Wiping her hands on the apron around her ample waist, she resumed her seat.

"So you been having trouble sleeping?"

Catherine nodded, taking a sip of the tea. "Those crickets make such a ruckus."

"Be glad they singing a merry tune. You don't want to hear them singing slow and mournful. That means somebody go die."

Placing the cup back on the table, Catherine said, "You don't really believe that, do you?"

"Oh yes, Missus," Bella answered, nodding affirmatively. "A few months ago, them cricket was sounding so pitiful. A couple days later they find old Mr. Peter from the down street dead in he bed. You don't want to hear no dog howling neither, especially a she dog. They does see jumbies."

"Jumbies? What are those?" Catherine asked.

"Spirits of people who dead or go die soon."

Catherine nodded agreeably. She knew Bella was serious, so she tried not to make light of the older woman's beliefs. Changing the subject, she said, "My husband has been at La Pointe now for about a month."

"So you going to live up behind God's face at La Pointe?" Bella slowly rose to her feet to stir the cereal. "Humph. You just be careful up in them bush. All kind of strange things does fly around up there in the darkness of night."

She spooned the cereal into a small bowl and placed it on the table. Seeing the bowl, Marcel eagerly reached for it.

"The boy hungry. You best start feeding him now. You go have to learn how to cook it for him. I go tell you how."

Bella reclaimed her seat and started giving Catherine instructions on how to prepare the cereal. As she spoke, a bell started to chime. She paused in mid sentence, "'Tis six o'clock. The bell tower ringing. Ms. Clara go be coming soon. We got to hurry up. I hope you come see me before you climb the hill to La Pointe."

"Oh, I am not leaving the boardinghouse just yet. I will be back to see you. Even when I do leave, I will come back every time I return to Gustavia."

Catherine stood and hugged the older woman. Marcel reached out his chubby arms for a hug too, making Bella chuckle with delight as she enfolded the child against her huge bosom.

#

"My arms ache from carrying these damned stones," Paul groaned, lifting more stones into the wheelbarrow. It was almost full, and he would soon be pushing it up the incline over the jagged ground to where Jonah and Alphonse were mixing mortar. Pierre and Vidal were carrying the heavy bucketfuls of mortar over to the building site. Raphael and Henri were carefully arranging the stones between the mortar for the foundation of the first house.

Josiah was in St. Jean with Agnes and his daughters. He and Paul were taking turns going back and forth to check on them. Paul had shown him a shortcut through the steep, ragged hill that took him directly to St. Jean without going the roundabout route of Gustavia.

They had made tremendous strides in the month they had been at La Pointe. Cutting away at the thick, heavy bushes had been arduous work. They had undergone grueling days, working from sunrise to way past sunset. They had been stung by yellow jackets and honey bees and bitten by centipedes and scorpions. Their hands were rough and chapped, and their muscles ached from the strenuous chopping and lifting and all the bending. Still they persevered.

At night they slept on the hard ground beneath a roof of the most brilliant and copious stars they had ever seen. They were lulled into sleep by the melodic tunes of the crickets. They cooked their breakfasts at dawn on a wood fire, and they ate their suppers with Henri and Emeline. They sat on their gallery amid the dogs and two black cats they had not seen on their initial visit and enjoyed the simple meals and restful companionship after a long, tiresome day. Henri had been putting in a half-day's work every day with them, and an affable bond had been formed with the older couple. At the end of the evening, Jonah and his group returned to their campsite for a fleeting night of sleep. At dawn they rose and began again.

Jonah had offered to deed Raphael, Pierre, Alphonse, Vidal, and Josiah a quarter acre of land so each man could build a home for his family nearby. Pierre, Alphonse, and Vidal had accepted Jonah's offer, and each man had marked out his plot of land and the outline of his future house with twine.

Raphael and Josiah had declined. Raphael flatly stated that owning property went against his grain. He didn't want the responsibility it entailed, and he was more than happy to camp in a shack close to Jonah and Catherine.

Josiah opted to live in St. Jean. Agnes and the girls had fallen in love with the capacious, flat land. They were enjoying frolicking on the pristine beach with its soft, white sand and coconut and sea grape trees. Their time spent playing in the gentle surf and collecting shells had subtly tanned their once lily-white skin.

"When are we heading back down to Gustavia, Jonah?" Pierre asked one afternoon as they were taking a break under the shade of a gigantic tamarind tree. "Marie is probably having conniptions. I am going to catch the dickens when we get back."

Jonah chuckled. "I am sure you will. Actually, I've been thinking about bringing the women up here." He waited for the remarks he knew would come.

"You want to bring them here, under these conditions? You're not really serious, are you?" Alphonse asked.

"Yes, I am very serious. Before we left, I paid Clara for another month's' rent. It will be up soon. I am going to ask Henri and Emeline to allow them to sleep at their place. However, during the day there's plenty of work to keep them busy and help move things along more quickly."

Pierre whistled. "Man, you're really brave or really crazy. You know what chaos it's going to be with the women underfoot?"

"They're going to be an outright pain in the ass," Raphael chimed in.

Jonah laughed. "Actually, I think it's going to be quite entertaining."

At the end of the following week, the men returned to the boardinghouse in Gustavia. They were fatigued and sweaty, and they were looking forward to a bath and a good meal. Clara and Bella were in the parlor when they came hustling in the door.

"Phew! You smell horrible," Clara said, holding her nose. "Don't you dare enter my dining room! Go wash yourselves. You smell like a bunch of goats."

Bella laughed and continued dusting.

They obediently trotted past her, their hats in their hands. The smell of fried chicken coming from the dining room was making their mouths water, but they knew better than to disobey Clara.

"It's amazing how they make all those beautiful things from a plant," Yvette said as the women walked up the pathway to Clara's door. They were returning from an excursion to Corossol.

They had gone on horseback to the quaint fishing village known for its straw crafts. Nestled at the base of a steep hill close to the seashore, it was a community mostly made up of fishermen. The houses were simple, small structures, and they were built in close proximity to each other. Despite their simplicity, they were well cared for. The yards were neatly kept and separated with the same orderly, stone barriers as those in Gustavia.

In their leisurely wanderings, the women had stopped frequently to admire the calèche-wearing women plaiting the long straw blades of the latania plant, the strands deftly flowing between their fingers and the finished products lying on the ground around their bare feet.

Their presence had hardly been acknowledged. Only one kind soul had greeted them warmly. An older lady sitting in the shade of a wooden gallery had beckoned them over. The woman's heavily freckled hands had continued to swiftly plait the long, beige-colored strands as they came closer. Behind her against the wall of the small house, a black cat was stretched out on her side dozing while six black and white kittens suckled at her milk-laden breasts. Marcel squealed with delight when he spotted them, trying to break free from his mother's firm grip.

Putting down the half-finished plait, the woman smiled, her blue eyes shining in her wrinkled face. She proudly showed them her wares, taking the time to explain how the strands were stripped and laid out to dry in the sun for weeks to give them the pale coloring and make them flexible for plaiting. Her efforts had paid off. The women had each purchased several hats and handbags. She had almost succeeded in persuading them to take home a few kittens.

Now as they walked up the path to Clara's house, Loretta stopped suddenly. "The men are back."

Catherine looked around in happy anticipation. Frowning, she said, "There are no signs of them. How do you know?"

Loretta smiled at her. "They're here," she said with certainty.

At her words, Marie ran ahead of them. She flung open the door just in time to see Pierre heading into the dining room.

"Pierre!" she cried joyfully, flinging herself into his arms.

The women filed into the room, gleefully greeting their significant others. Loretta smiled forlornly. She was the only one with no arms to embrace her.

#

The screams pierced the evening's tranquility to such an extent that the dogs started to howl and the hairs on the cats' backs rose as they scampered for cover. It jolted Emeline and Henri out of a deep sleep. Grabbing the lantern, Emeline was the first to leap out of bed, her long, silver hair cascading down her back in disarray. Henri followed closely, holding fast to the strings of his pantaloon. They stopped short in front of the closed door to the room where the dreadful screams continued. Stepping in front of Emeline, Henri gave the door a forceful push. The scene that greeted them was comical.

The five women and little Marcel were standing on the bed in various stages of undress. The mattress frame had given way from the weight and the continuous movement of the women. Some of them had fallen into the crevice made by the mattress when it had collapsed, and they were desperately trying to regain their footing while they continued to scream.

Emeline made the sign of the cross.

Still trying to tie the strings of his pantaloon, Henri yelled, "What the hell is happening in here?"

Hiccupping from their constant screams, the women could only point to the floor and to the wall.

Catherine was the first to regain her voice. "That hideous thing on the floor fell from the roof onto Yvette's head. It entangled itself in her hair and then latched on to her shoulder. We finally managed to get it off her, but there's another one on the wall over there."

"It was cold and clammy, and it felt like it was sucking at my shoulder," Yvette interjected, rubbing her shoulder briskly. "It was awful."

Henri tried to hide his amusement. He bent over and picked up the dazed, offending mabouya, sending the women into a screaming fit again.

"It's only a lizard. It can't harm you. They eat the flies and insects on the wall."

"Well, it the biggest and ugliest lizard I have ever seen," Marie exclaimed. "I won't sleep in here with those things on the wall."

"Then I suggest you go outside while I try to catch the other one. This one was dazed from his rendezvous with you, so he couldn't run," he said, looking at the wiggling lizard he held firmly by his thumb and index fingers. Nodding toward the wall, he continued. "That little bugga up there is going to run. I'll give you ladies a chance to fix your clothes while I put this fellow outside. I will be right back. In the meantime, keep an eye on the other one. They move fast."

As he passed Emeline, he whispered, "Wait until they see the iguanas."

It was only their second night at La Pointe. They had arrived yesterday, replete with valises. After dropping off their belongings at Henri and Emeline's house, Jonah had whisked them up the hill to see the cleared site where their homes were underway.

But it was a rude awaking. Here there was no hot water warmed ahead of time for their baths. They bathed in cold water that they retrieved themselves with buckets from an assortment of drums and a concrete catchment in the yard. Food was not as plentiful. They ate whatever paltry servings Emeline could stir up, whether from killing a goat or chicken or from harvesting the local vegetables growing on the land. Except for the natural lighting from the moon and the trillion twinkling stars, the nights were dark and desolate. All five women were sharing a small room with only one narrow bed. Because Marie was pregnant, she slept on the bed. Marcel slept beside her. The other four women slept on the hard, quilt-covered floor.

They had only put in one day's work on the land, mostly gathering stones and arranging them in piles for the men, and already their hands were red and chapped. Not yet accustomed to the hot, strong rays of the Caribbean sun, they had perspired profusely in their full-length skirts and long-sleeve blouses. Their faces were sunburned a deep blistering red by the end of the day.

As the months wore on, the women grew stronger. Their muscles became more toned and their skin more tanned. They grew wiser, abandoning the full skirts for knee-length pantaloons and the long-sleeve blouses for sleeveless chemises. They grew braver. Although they would never make friends with the slithering, clammy mabouya, turning over a stone and finding insects no longer fazed them. Witnessing the slaughtering of an animal for food no longer disconcerted them. In fact, they learned how to perform the act themselves. They learned about the local fruits and vegetables from Emeline. They learned how to make salve from the cooling aloe plant to alleviate the sting of bees and insects and to soothe their sunburned skin. They learned how to plant and when to harvest. They worked alongside the men daily, hastily helping to make their new homes secure and livable before the gale season arrived.

CHAPTER 14

"**W**hy don't you just go over and talk to him? You know you want to." Philar teased Loretta. They were working side by side, piling stones in order of size and smoothness. "We've been up here almost three months, and you still haven't worked up the nerve to talk to Paul. If you don't make a move soon, I will take matters into my own hands."

"You will not." Loretta gave her sister a shove. "Beside, he's not interested in me. I heard Josiah say he's betrothed to a girl from Lorient. They have already come out publicly."

Philar stopped working to look directly at Loretta. "So what? He's not married yet. That means he's fair game."

"I am not that kind of—"

They both turned suddenly at the sound of a sudden crash followed by cuss words and moans. Immediately they ran in the direction of the sounds.

When Philar and Loretta entered the framed outline of a partially finished door, they saw the subject of their conversation sitting on the floor rubbing his left shoulder, the fallen ladder lying at his side.

Jonah and Pierre were leaning over him, trying to get him to stand.

"No! Don't make him stand," Loretta said with alarm. She squatted in front of him, her coyness momentarily forgotten. "Let me feel him first to make sure nothing is broken."

She looked at Paul, her green eyes expressive. "Other than your shoulder, is there any other part of you that is hurting? "

Paul gazed at her, taking a while to answer. "The back of my head feels numb."

On her knees, she came closer, encircling him with her arms to feel the back of his head, her fingers probing gingerly. "You're going to have a nice big lump back there, but there's no gash. Let me take a look at your shoulder."

Paul obediently turned slowly to give her better access. Loretta examined the area thoroughly. Frowning, she said, "You've got a good size bruise. You're coming with me to Emeline's house. My medicine bag is there. We need to get a poultice on that bruise and a potion for you to drink for your bruises inside."

She stood, extending her hands to him. "Take your time and stand up slowly. Jonah, can you give us a hand here? Help me get him on the horse."

Philar watched the entire scene unfold, a smile playing on her lips. She didn't intercede or offer assistance.

Paul left for St. Jean early the next morning, his shoulder in a homemade sling. He took more time than usual, cautiously maneuvering his horse through the steep, rocky path. His shoulder and the back of his head still throbbed, but it was his thoughts that were the most bothersome. Granted, the woman was beautiful. She exuded an extraordinary grace, so much so that it made her appear wiser than her years. She had adeptly attended to him. Her ministrations were compassionate, but she had done nothing to indicate that it was anything beyond that. So why was he having these disturbing thoughts? Why could he not stop thinking about her?

I am engaged, damn it! What the hell is wrong with me? Did the blow to the back of my head cause me to lose my mind?

He had to leave La Pointe! He had not slept at all. He kept remembering her touch and imagining those delicate hands caressing the secret parts of his body. He remembered the feel of her breast as she had pressed against him to examine the back of his head. He imaged her full lips, wanting so badly to kiss them until he felt fully sated. He recalled her smell, the husky softness of her voice, how his loins had grown hot with desire. He was going insane! At the crack of dawn, he had been packed and ready to go. He needed to get back to Beatrice and lose himself in her arms. He had to purge Loretta from his soul!

Paul knew that Jonah had been concerned when he had woken Jonah to tell him he was leaving. He had assuaged Jonah's worries as best he could, telling him he needed to get back to St. Jean so Josiah could come back to La Pointe. He could tell Jonah had not been convinced, but how could he tell him the truth? How could he tell him that he was suffering, but not from the fall? He was a betrothed man. It was inconceivable that he was suffering such angst over Loretta.

#

The pain woke Marie. She'd been feeling contractions all day, but nothing like this. She struggled to sit up. Marcel was asleep beside her. She rubbed her eyes, slowly adjusting to the darkness.

"Catherine! Catherine, please get up! Philar! Loretta! I need you."

The women stirred at once. Catherine was the first to sit up. "What is it, Marie?"

"The baby is coming!"

They sprang into action. Yvette picked Marcel up from the bed, placing him on the quilt. Catherine sat on the spot vacated by Marcel. She rubbed her sister's back as Loretta and Philar examined her.

"The child is already crowning!" Loretta turned to Philar, "Quickly, go and rouse Henri and Emeline. We need warm water and clean bedding, and Henri needs to go up the hill and get Pierre."

Before her sister had completed the sentence, Philar was out the door. Within minutes, she was back with clean sheets. "Emeline is heating the water, and Henri is mounting his horse," she reported.

"This little one is in a hurry. Marie, listen to me. You need to start pushing when I tell you," Loretta said calmly.

"I want Pierre," Marie cried as her body writhed with another contraction.

"He's on his way," Philar answered reassuringly.

Catherine continued to encourage her sister, holding her shoulders up when Loretta ordered, "Push!" It didn't take long for the little boy to be born. He came into the world screaming as Philar cleaned and bundled him. She gave him to Marie, who whispered softly, "Hello, Hypolite."

It was a little past midnight, and Jonah and Raphael had just put out the fire. The other men were already asleep. They had lingered to discuss the day's progress and their plans for the next day. In so many ways Raphael was a father figure for Jonah, and the counsel he provided him was priceless.

"So I am thinking about making a trip back to Toulon at the beginning of the New Year. By then, everyone will be comfortable in their new houses," Jonah said. "We're going to need to replenish our supplies." He paused, a frown appearing between his brows. "And I am very concerned about Father. I worry that Clifford will harm him."

"That whiney, little jackass doesn't have the balls to touch Ivan. I understand though, that you want to check on your father. I know you miss him, and he misses you."

"I am going to need you to stay here and keep an eye on things."

"I'd rather go with you. I miss my mistress—the sea—but I will stay behind and see to things for you."

Jonah stretched and yawned. "Seems to me you've forgotten about your mistress since you found a flesh and blood one. Think I don't know where you go on your excursions to Gustavia?"

"Yeah, that Clara, she's something else. She's really ..."

"Shh!" Jonah touched Raphael's shoulder. "Listen. Do you hear the sound of a horse?"

They reached for their rifles as the galloping grew closer.

"Should we wake the others?" Jonah whispered.

"Not yet."

The galloping stopped. They peered apprehensively at the blackness in front of them.

"Look over there." Jonah motioned to Raphael. The light of a torch flashed through the trees. They watched as it got closer, their rifles ready. Then they heard Henri's voice calling their names. Relief momentarily washed over them only to be followed by a new alarm. Something was wrong for Henri to come at this hour.

"Henri, what is it? Are the women okay?" Jonah asked anxiously.

Henri paused to catch his breath. "Marie is in labor. The child is coming fast. They sent me to get Pierre."

Jonah quickly woke Pierre, and the two accompanied Henri back to the house where the cries of an infant were clearly audible. At the sound of his child, Pierre started running. There was no sleep to be had that night. Jonah and Henri joined the women on the gallery. They stayed there until dawn, giving Pierre and Marie privacy to bond with their son.

#

"I do not want to go back up to La Pointe! I think we have put in enough time helping them, and besides, we have to start building your house. It's crowded in here with your pregnant wife and three little daughters." Paul was adamant as he faced his brother.

Josiah had just returned to St. Jean from a month's stay at La Pointe, and he was trying to persuade Paul to go up one more time to help Jonah and the others.

"Paul, I gave Ivan my word that I would help Jonah. A man is only as good as his word. They are almost finished. One more trip; that's all I am asking."

"Josiah, I have a job at the salt pond. I have my boat. I have a fiancée. I have a life. I do not want to go back up there!"

"All right then." Josiah sighed. "I have no choice. I will rest tonight and go back up to La Pointe myself in the morning."

Josiah started to walk away dejectedly when Paul called out to him. "Your wife and daughters miss you. They need you to stay here. I will go this last time, but after this, no more."

Josiah turned around, walked backed to Paul, and hugged him. "Thank you, Paul. God will bless you for your kindness."

What I need God to do is to erase from my soul a certain green-eyed beauty that you're forcing me to see again, Josiah.

The powerful feelings he had experienced a month ago had waned. Still she crossed his mind too frequently, and he would have preferred not to have to see her again.

"Please, Vidal, do not go down to Gustavia today. I dreamt last night that your horse lost its footing, and you tumbled over the cliff," Philar implored.

"Philar, I asked you before to stop this nonsense. You work yourself into a frenzy believing you have special powers to see things that aren't there. I am going to Gustavia. Nothing will happen to me."

Vidal turned to walk away, and she grabbed his arm, "Vidal, I am begging you not to go today."

He shrugged off her hand and she started to cry.

Loretta immediately put down the bucket of water she was carrying and ran to her sister. Putting her arms around her, she said, "Let him go, Philar. You tried to warn him."

Paul had just finished filling the wheelbarrow with another load of stones when he saw and heard the exchange between Philar and Vidal. He wasn't the type to interfere in matters that did not concern him, but he hated to see a woman cry.

Securing the wheelbarrow, he walked the short distance to them. "Maybe you should listen to her, Vidal," he said, stepping into his path, blocking him. "Dreams can have meaning. What harm will it do to change your plans until tomorrow?"

"Vidal groaned. "Not you too, Paul. I have an appointment in Gustavia today, and I am going. Please don't encourage her. I have had just about enough of these shenanigans." He walked over to his horse and mounted it. Taking the reins, he trotted off down the hill.

Wrenching herself from Loretta's arms, Philar ran in the direction of the lookout at the edge of the cliff.

"Shouldn't you go after her?" Paul asked Loretta.

"No, she needs some time to calm herself." Exasperatedly, she exhaled. "I hate to see her like that. The two of them have been arguing way too much lately. He is pressing her to get married, but it's exactly that closed-minded attitude that keeps her from agreeing."

"What do you mean?"

"I am sure you've heard that Philar and I are ... different. We see and dream things before they happen."

"So?" Paul shrugged. "What's so wrong with that?"

"Vidal has a problem with it. He thinks it's all in our heads."

"Really?" Paul replied. "I believe some people are born with special abilities. My mother was always warning Josiah and me about her dreams. We used to laugh at her. We made light of it, but we took heed. More than half the time she turned out to be right. Vidal is a good man. He'll come around. Give him time."

"He'd better not take too long." Loretta sighed.

Paul looked at the ground. After an awkward silence, he said, "I never did thank you for tending to me. You did a good job. I really appreciated it."

"I looked for you the next day. Jonah told me you left suddenly. I was worried. How is your shoulder?" Loretta's hand automatically reached out and touched his left shoulder.

Her touch reverberated through his body. He felt weak. "It ... it's fine," he stuttered. "Uh, I need to get back to work. They're waiting for the stones."

Avoiding her eyes, he stepped around her and headed back to the wheelbarrow.

Loretta watched him quickly walk away. She silently cursed the fates. Here was a man who was perfectly suited for her, yet he belonged to someone else. She was not the type of woman who would intentionally hurt anyone. Paul had been back at La Pointe for almost three weeks now. She had tried to keep her distance from him. She knew he was doing his best to avoid her too, but the pull was so strong.

As the morning wore on, Loretta found herself making excuses to walk past Paul. He had taken off his shirt, and his tanned, muscular torso glistened with droplets of sweat. She envisioned him naked, his body cleaved to hers, sweat consuming them in passion, and finally, she could stand it no more. *Oh God, please forgive me for what I am about to do.*

"The sun is very hot. I thought you might like a cool drink of water."

At the sound of Loretta's voice, Paul's hands stopped moving. He had been so busy sorting stones to fill the wheelbarrow that he hadn't noticed time passing. He knew he had been up and down the incline many times today, but he had done so perfunctorily. His mind was too consumed with thoughts of her.

He pulled out a damp handkerchief from his pantaloon pocket and mopped the sweat from his forehead. Then wordlessly he sat on the dusty ground and took the cup she offered. Nonchalantly she sat beside him as he drank the water.

"So," Paul said, breaking the silence. "How do you like St. Barth?"

"It's different from France in some ways, yet similar in others. I think it's because so many people from France live here. What truly enthralls me is the sea. I'd liked to be able to take a swim and enjoy the sandy beaches. Living all the way up here, I don't have much opportunity to do so."

"I can take you. There is a nice sandy beach just down the backside of the hill. It's called Le Gouverneur."

Paul couldn't believe what he had just said. Yet not wanting to lose his nerves, he pulled out his pocket watch. "It is slightly past noon. I am due for a break. We can go now if you like."

"I would love to go. Give me a half hour. I will fix us some sandwiches."

Loretta felt excitement rise within her. The air between them was so charged. It was a heady feeling, mixed with guilt and pleasure. She should have stopped this. Tell him no—but she didn't want to stop it. She wanted to seize this day. She wanted to embark on this forbidden tryst with Paul.

They set out on Paul's horse down the backside of La Pointe. Loretta had not yet seen this part of the island, and the view was just as magnificent as the other side. The vast expanse of shimmering sea dotted with neighboring islands took her breath away. Halfway down the hill, they turned off onto a steep, rocky path, the trail barely discernable. They traveled quite a distance with Loretta holding tightly to Paul's muscular back, the scent of him wreaking havoc on her senses.

The trail finally gave way to the most brilliantly white sand she had ever seen. The azure waves rolled invitingly to the shore in a secluded half-circle cove. They dismounted, and Loretta immediately took off her shoes, luxuriating in the feel of the warm sand between her toes. She looked around, breathing in the distinct smell of the sea. Other than the pelicans, they were alone. Stretching lazily, she began to strip off her clothes until she was gloriously naked. Without looking at Paul and knowing the effect she was having on him, she walked slowly into the white-capped surf.

Paul watched her every move, his mouth dry and his body ripe with anticipation. He had never wanted a woman as badly as he wanted this one. Yet he was contrite with guilt over what he was about to do. With his eyes fixed on her as she frolicked in the water, he removed his own clothing. She stopped moving and boldly admired him as he walked to the water's edge. Locking eyes with her, he entered the warm seawater. His excitement grew as he waded out to her where the waves reached just beneath her full, lily-white breasts. The water had made her nipples hard—or was it the expectancy of him that had caused the tantalizing effect? He pulled her into his arms and kissed her hungrily as her hands roamed freely over the places she had touched in his dreams. He groaned with pleasure as he kissed and licked her salty skin. The feel of her sweet, slender body pressing against his was intoxicating.

When he could stand it no more, he cupped her face in his hands and looked deeply into her eyes. Lord, how could he say what was on his mind? As it was, he was delirious. Yet he had to say it. "Loretta, I am out of my mind with wanting you, but my being with you will not change the fact that I am getting married to someone else. You must understand. I don't want to hurt you."

"Ssh." She put a trembling, wet finger to his lips. "I know." Paul saw the agony in her eyes as she said, "But I cannot live the rest of my life without having loved you just this once."

She pulled him tightly against her, wrapping her legs securely around him as the water gently rocked them. He lost all ability to reason as he buried himself deep within her. Together they rode the crest of their passion. Paul knew she had given him a priceless gift, something she could never give again to any man. He also knew without doubt that he had lost a piece of his soul on Gouverneur Beach.

After they had eaten the chicken sandwiches Loretta had prepared, they spent the duration of the afternoon lazing under the shade of the sea grape trees, the cooling trade winds blowing briskly against their naked skin. Conversation flowed easily. The intimacy they shared was as natural and as old as time. It was as if they had always known each other.

As the brilliant afternoon sun set in a spectacular blaze of color, they rode home silently, Loretta's head resting trustfully on Paul's back, her arms securely around his waist. Paul was mystified. He had spent months avoiding her, and in just one afternoon, all his good intentions had been totally, irrevocably shattered.

CHAPTER 15

"Vidal's hurt. I know it," Philar cried. "It's been four days since he went to Gustavia."

"If he's not back by tomorrow afternoon, we will go down to Gustavia to look for him." Loretta tried to console her.

They were all sitting on Henri and Emeline's gallery. Sunday evening's supper with the older couple had become a tradition. Only Loretta, Philar, and Yvette still slept at the house, but soon they would be moving too.

As dusk fell in purplish-orange hues, and the shadows of night gradually descended, lending its cooling shade to the unrelenting tropical heat, they shared each other's company. Catherine sat next to Marie, admiring little Hypolite. Jonah and Pierre sat on the floor rolling a ball with Marcel. Paul sat beside Henri on the steps, trying to listen attentively as Henri gave him advice on how to keep pigeon pea trees free from bugs.

Every so often Paul looked at Loretta, but she didn't return his glances. The few times he had caught her eyes, he had seen her anguish. But damn it! He was in misery too. Every part of him ached just to hold her. She had closed herself off from him, and it made him angry. Yet he knew he had to find a way to respect her decision. He was not a free man.

They all heard the galloping horses. They watched as two gendarmes trotted up to the gate. Henri yelled at the dogs to quiet them as he and Jonah went to greet the gendarmes. The pall that fell over everyone was perceptible. In hushed silence, they watched as Henri opened the gate. They strained to hear any audible bits of conversation. They saw when Jonah and Henri hung their heads. They waited anxiously as the two men shook hands with the gendarme and walked back to the house.

"What happened to Vidal?" Philar asked, not waiting for them to speak.

Jonah put his hand on her shoulder. "I am so sorry, Philar. He is in a coma. Two men found him three-quarters of the way down the hill. They saw the horse wandering around, and they realized something must have happened to its owner, so they went looking. Apparently he fell over the cliff. They brought him down to Gustavia. People there remembered him staying at Clara's, and they took him to the boardinghouse. Clara called the doctor. He has several broken bones, including his collarbone."

Philar started to cry. "Why didn't he listen to me? I need to go to him."

She started to head toward the gate when Loretta grabbed hold of her. "You can't do that until tomorrow. I will go with you first thing."

"I will accompany you," Paul interjected. "It's time for me to return to St. Jean anyway."

Paul knew that he had willfully said the words in hopes of sparking a reaction from Loretta, and he felt gratified when he saw her frown. He barely heard when Jonah said, "I am coming too. Vidal is on St. Barth because of me. His welfare is my responsibility."

Vidal looked dreadful. Aside from the purplish, blue bruises that covered the right side of his face, he was deathly pale. His head was wrapped in white gauze. Spots of blood had seeped through the gauze, making a striking contrast on the white fabric. His left leg, right arm, and shoulder were also wrapped in bandages.

Jonah was troubled by Vidal's condition. Vidal had always been dependable and loyal. It was because of his unwavering dedication that Ivan had chosen him for the voyage. Leaving Philar and Loretta in the room with Vidal, he went to find Clara. He wanted to thank her for helping Vidal, but more importantly he wanted to pay for his expenses.

There were medical and rooming charges that needed to be covered. Philar would stay on at Clara's for as long as necessary, and Loretta had agreed to stay with her.

He found Clara in the kitchen with Bella.

"Clara, may I please speak with you privately."

Clara nodded and wiped her hands on a dishcloth. Telling Bella she would be back momentarily, she motioned for Jonah to follow her. Jonah couldn't help but notice how the formidable proprietress had mellowed. He smiled as he thought of Raphael. The old ruffian had softened up around the edges too.

With everything arranged, Jonah returned to La Pointe the next day. Sadly he had no good news to report to everyone waiting for word on Vidal. He had left him in the same condition in which he had found him.

As the week wore on, Vidal did not improve. The doctor, a thin, middle-aged man wearing round spectacles that were too big for his face, came every two days. He would sit at the edge of the bed and watch Vidal, barely examining him. Then he would shake his head dismally, mumbling that there was no hope. Philar had had enough of the dispiriting doctor by the end of the week. She ordered him not to return, telling him bluntly that he was on a death watch rather than a mission of healing. He stiffened his thin body in offense, pursed his almost nonexistence bottom lip, and mumbled, "As you wish, Mademoiselle."

The next morning Vidal developed a high fever that would not break despite Philar and Loretta's best efforts. He burned with fever all day and into the evening. At their wit's end, the women turned to prayer.

They were saying the rosary when Bella poked her head inside the room.

"Hello, Misuses. Can I come in?" Not waiting for their answer, she shuffled into the room, closing the door. She held a brown bag filled with fragrant, green leaves. "I hear you're good with herbs, but you're not having much luck this time." Glancing at the bed, she said, "Tis time you learn about the local bush."

She beckoned them closer and opened the bag wide. "I got something here that go broke that fever quickly. This here is soursop bush. Tis the best medicine for fever. Crush up the leaves and put them in he socks and tie some in a handkerchief around he head. In the middle of the night, replace the old leaves with fresh, crushed ones. By tomorrow morning that fever go broke."

Desperate to try anything to help Vidal, Philar took the bag and thanked Bella. Then she immediately started crushing the leaves.

Bella watched for a few minutes and then shuffled toward the door. Her hand was on the door knob when she turned around again.

"And oh! The soursop bush does make a good tea too. It helps you sleep soundly. The tree does bear a prickly, green fruit. It's tasty when it ripe, all white and creamy. You could tell when it ripe by gently squeezing it. It go be a little soft against your fingers. Make sure you spit out the black seeds though."

True to Bella's words and to the relief of both women, Vidal's fever was broken by morning. Philar and Loretta had taken turns through the night crushing and changing the leaves. They thought his coloring had improved as well.

It was the middle of their second week in Gustavia. Loretta had gone to her room for a well-earned afternoon nap. The sisters seldom slept in the room, opting to sleep on the floor of Vidal's room to keep watch over him. He was slowly showing signs of improvement. The ugly bruises had faded, and his natural coloring had returned.

Loretta was drifting off to sleep when Bella knocked on the door and announced that Mr. Dusant was calling on her in the parlor.

She entered the parlor expecting to see Jonah. When she saw that it was Paul, she quickly turned around and headed back toward her room.

Taking double strides, Paul reached her partway down the corridor and grabbed hold of her arm. "I came to enquire about Vidal."

"Then you should call on Philar. I have nothing to say to you," Loretta said, trying to pull her arm free.

He nodded in the direction of the main door. "Take a walk with me to the waterfront."

She raised her eyebrows. "Aren't you afraid your fiancée will find out you're strolling with me in public?"

He didn't answer. She started to pull her arm free again when a door opened, and a middle-aged couple stepped into the corridor. Not wanting to become a spectacle for anyone's entertainment, Loretta sighed and allowed him to lead her to the door.

When they were a good distance away from the boardinghouse, she turned on him. "What is wrong with you? Why are you pestering me?"

"I just wanted to see you. I miss you."

"Listen to me. You didn't force me into anything. I was a willing partaker. So stop feeling sorry for me and leave me alone. Go back to St. Jean where you belong."

She started to walk away. He grabbed her arm, forcing her to turn around and pulled her roughly against him. "I'm leaving," he growled, his face close to hers. "I am going to marry Beatrice, and God help me, I will forget you ever existed." Pushing her away, he stormed off down the cobblestone street.

Loretta watched Paul until he was out of sight, wanting desperately to run after him. In this close-knit, devoutly religious community, being betrothed was as good as being married. If he left Beatrice to be with her, it would destroy the life he had built for himself on the island. Loretta couldn't let that happen. Still, she was inexplicably angry, and it puzzled her. After all, she was the primary instigator of the illicit tryst they'd shared. She had known fully well that he was already betrothed, and in the height of their passion, he'd even made certain that she understood it would not change his plans to marry Beatrice. So why was she feeling so hurt and jealous?

With her head hung low to hide her tears, she walked back to her room at Clara's. She couldn't ever remember a time when her spirit felt this low, and she didn't know how to begin to remedy herself.

At the end of the second week, Vidal opened his eyes. Loretta had gone for a stroll after dinner. Philar was sitting on the bed beside him thinking about her sister. Although Loretta was doing her best to hide it, Philar knew that something was wrong, and she knew it had to do with Paul. She was thinking she needed to sit Loretta down so they could talk it over when she felt Vidal touch her arm. Surprised, she turned quickly to look at him.

"Hi," he said weakly. "Where am I?"

Philar was elated. She leaned over and kissed his forehead, tears of relief flowing down her cheeks. "You're at Clara's," she said, wiping her eyes. "You've been unconscious. You fell off your horse."

He lifted his left hand and started feeling his body, taking note of all of the bandages. A frown developed on his face, causing the smile on hers to fade. She knew what was coming next.

"This is your fault," he said hoarsely. "You and your damned predictions. You made me so nervous on my way down the hill that I lost my concentration." He cleared his throat. "This will stop now, do you hear me? You will never talk about this nonsense again. Not now or ever when we're married."

Philar felt like she had been slapped. Getting off the bed, she went to stand by the open window. The saloon next door was busy. The swinging doors were in constant motion. With her back to Vidal, she watched people go in and out of the building. The rowdy revelry of laughter from inside grew louder every time the door opened. Her mind drifting, mostly to avoid the hurtful words Vidal had just spoken, she thought of Clara. She could understand why the staunch woman disliked the saloon being so closed to her business. It went against everything she stood for and believed. She could empathize with Clara. The man lying there on that bed was betrothed to her. He represented her future. Yet he was the complete opposite of what she stood for and believed. How could she spend a lifetime living beside him when he was so opposed to the very quintessence of her being?

"Philar, are you hearing me? I said I need a drink of water."

Wordlessly, she picked up the pitcher of water on the nightstand and poured some into an enamel yellow cup. She sat on the edge of the bed and carefully lifted his head. Placing the cup to his dry lips, she advised him to sip slowly. When he was finished, she returned the pitcher and cup to the nightstand. Telling him she had a dreadful headache, she quickly left the room.

Philar was still hurting from Vidal's cutting comments even though days had passed. Every day he grew stronger. He could now sit in the chair and enjoy the view from the window in his room although he complained to no end about the inappropriate activity of the saloon across the street. She spent as much time as possible outdoors to avoid his bickering. On this particular morning, she slipped out the boardinghouse and headed for the wharf.

The seagulls were squawking boisterously as they competed with the pelicans for the small fries jumping in the water. Philar watched as an ambitious seagull snatched one of the little silvery fish out of the gigantic beak of an offended pelican. The pelican lumbered away to another spot on the iridescent ocean's surface, and the brazen seagull followed, ready to again snatch away its prized catch.

Today the wharf was teeming with activity. There were many crafts in the water. Vessels were unloading goods being imported from the neighboring islands. Fishermen were busy with their early morning catch. The many lively variations of French dialects resounded through the air as people bustled about purchasing fish and vibrantly colored tropical fruits. She laughed as she observed the antics of a shirtless young man holding up a red lobster. He was bartering with a stout, older woman, but she was animatedly arguing that the price was still too high.

Philar raised her face to the sun and breathed deeply. The smell of bread baking mingled with the heady aroma of the sea filled her nostrils. She loved early mornings like this in St. Barth. It made her feel alive and effervescent.

She picked up a spiny, green soursop from the table of a vender and squeezed it gently for softness as Bella had instructed. The fruit was definitely ripe. Absentmindedly, she continued to think about Vidal. Despite all the lovely scenery outside his window, the only thing he could focus on was the saloon. She was so tired of seeing this side of the man she thought she loved. She had agonized about it, and her decision had not been easy. She would nurse him back to health, but she could not marry him.

She was paying the vendor for the soursop when she heard a familiar, deep, masculine voice at her shoulder.

"Buenos dias, Senorita Philar. I knew we would meet again. Oh, but why such a sad frown on such a beautiful face?"

She turned and looked into the soulful brown eyes of Captain Jaime Colon.

CHAPTER 16

Jaime's sudden nearness startled Philar. Quickly gathering her wits, she finished paying the vender and managed to mumble, "How … how are you, Captain? What brings you to St. Barth?"

His brown eyes teasingly studied her. "Would you believe me if I told you the truth?"

Strolling away from the gaping vender, she answered coyly, "Can I believe the words of a rogue Spanish captain?"

"Yes, because I am speaking truthfully. I knew your destination was St. Barth despite the protestations of your cowardly companion. I have been here twice before looking for you. It was only a matter of time before I found you." He touched her cheek. "And here you are, even more beautiful than I remember."

She backed away from his touch. "How is Nicholas?"

"As strong and as healthy as a young horse. There he is," he said looking over her shoulder. "Nicholas! Come here. Come say hello to the beautiful woman who saved your life."

A tall, lean boy with a mass of shiny, black, curly hair ran up to them. Not taking his gaze off Philar, Jaime introduced them.

"It is so good to see you looking so robust, Nicolas." Philar reached out to shake his hand.

With a flourish, the boy took her hand and raised it to his lips. "Muchas gracias, Senorita. My father speaks of you often." Then he hustled away again.

Philar turned and watched him disappear into the throngs of people. "Aren't you afraid to let him go off on his own like that?"

"Not at all; the boy knows how to take care of himself."

He reached for her left hand. "Come have breakfast with me."

"I ... I don't think that's a good idea. What will people say?"

He looked around. Then he whispered conspiringly, "It's too late. You are already in trouble. They are all gawking. Come. Let's go."

Still holding her hand, he led her away from the waterfront. They walked to a narrow, twisting path where the undergrowth was thick with tall grass. They continued until they reached a clearing where the grass grew in smaller patches through the sandy ground. She could smell the sea nearby. Passing the clearing, they turned a corner where a big, black stallion was tied to a tamarind tree. She hesitated. She had been caught up in the excitement of the moment, but now reality was intruding.

"Hold on a moment," she said as he began to loosen the knot on the rope. "I agreed to have breakfast with you, not to sashay away to unknown parts with you on a horse."

Dropping the rope, he put his hands on her shoulders. "Philar, you are safe with me. Let me show you St. Barth in ways few people seldom see it. Now come, let's enjoy the day while it is young."

She was under a spell. It was the only logical explanation for why she allowed Jaime to help her mount the horse.

With Philar holding on securely to his waist, they rode past Rue de Public up the hill toward St. Jean. Then they took a left turn in the direction of Colombier, where the latania plants grew thickly in droves. From there they trotted on a narrow, descending path en route to Flamands. They stopped on the crest of a hill to overlook an expanse of blinding, white sand, the waves from the cobalt sea roughly lashing at its borders. Proceeding down the incline, they arrived at another narrow, flat, rocky trail that led them to Petite Anse. Goats grazed indolently in grassy patches on both sides of the trail, undisturbed by their presence.

Jaime stopped the horse and they dismounted. "I promised you breakfast, and you will find that I always keep my word."

He took her hand and led her through another track road

inconspicuously hidden by tall grass. They proceeded down steps made of big, flat rocks to a wooden house whose dreary, weather-beaten exterior had obviously seen better days. The structure stood precariously on the edge of a precipice, and it looked to Philar like it was in danger of sliding down the jagged, rocky cliff into the crashing waves of the sea at any moment. Still holding her hand, he pushed the door open. Inside, the room was dusty and cluttered. Philar heard a female voice singing in the adjacent room that was separated from this one by a beaded curtain.

"Renata," Jaime called out, and the singing stopped.

"Jaime, is that you?" A pretty brunette stuck her head through the beads, and Philar inexplicably felt a jolt of jealousy.

The woman emerged, revealing a generously curved body with thick, curly ringlets cascading to her waist. Not waiting for an introduction, she greeted Philar, her brown eyes warm and friendly. Then she turned and backhanded Jaime across his head.

"Oww! What the hell was that for?"

"You lousy scoundrel, you made me cook for you last night, and you never showed up. I don't have food to waste, you know," she replied hotly, her hands akimbo on her full hips.

Rubbing his head, Jaime replied, "I am here now. Let's eat."

Renata sighed loudly. Taking Philar by the arm, she mumbled, "Come. Let the jackass stay in here by himself."

With Jaime following, she led Philar through the beaded curtain to another cluttered room with an oversized, cloth hammock secured by thick ropes and anchored to the north and south walls with heavy hooks. They proceeded through a back door that opened onto the steep, rocky cliff. Off to the right side of the narrow strip of space that served as a backyard was a rudimentary lean-to, where a black pot was simmering on burning coals. A crudely made wooden table and three chairs were situated in the middle of the lean-to. In the corner next to the lean-to were three steel drums, each covered with a white cloth that reflected brightly in the sunlight. A rope was tied securely around each of the rims, firmly holding the cloth in place.

Philar stood unobtrusively to the side, watching the lively exchange between Jaime and Renata, perplexed both by the jealousy she was experiencing and by how easily Jaime had persuaded her to come with him.

She watched Jaime walk over to the coal pot, lift the lid, and stir its contents. The spicy, fragrant steam immediately escaped. She felt nauseated when she heard him say, "Hmm. Turtle stew."

Feeling like an intruder, she turned away and looked out at the sea. She was too vulnerable, prone to these feelings because of Vidal.

"Come eat, Philar. Despite her many faults, Renata is a good cook."

His voice so close startled her, and she lost her footing. He reached out with both hands to steady her.

"I ... I don't think I can eat turtle."

"Why not? Turtle meat is delectable, and it is good for you. It heightens your sexuality." With his hand on the small of her back, he nudged her toward the table.

Despite her misgivings, the turtle stew was delicious—or was it the flavorsome sugarcane rum that dulled her senses? It must have loosened her tongue too, because as Renata filled her glass again with the golden liquid, she heard herself ask, "So, are you Jaime's lover?"

Renata put down the rum bottle and laughed boisterously. "No way in hell. He's all yours. The baboon is like a big brother to me."

Suddenly serious, she continued. "I was raised on the sea. My mother abandoned me at birth. She was high society French. My father was a sailor, and a very good friend of Jaime's. No one in my mother's family wanted me, so my father took me with him." She lowered her eyes sadly. "He died when I was twelve. By then, I was already proficient at taking care of myself, but it made Jaime's ego feel good to believe he was my protector."

"She never needed my protection. She can curse and swear better than any man I know, and she is dangerous with a dagger."

Ignoring Jaime, Philar asked her, "How did you end up living here?"

Just as swiftly, Renata's mood changed again. She smiled, revealing deep dimples in both cheeks. "The salt of the sea is in my blood. I cannot stay away from it for long. When it calls to me, I must go. But I needed a place of my own. You know, some place to get away by myself. We're always roaming the Caribbean and Atlantic waters, but we seem to have a particular penchant for St. Barth." Gesturing to her surroundings, she continued, "I noticed this castle from out there on the sea. I kept an eye on it every time we sailed past here. When I was convinced it was unoccupied, I decided to fix it up and make it my own. It's perfect for me. My bateau is anchored right down there."

She pointed to her right, and Philar saw two boats bobbing in the waves of a small sandy bay situated in the crevice of two oblique hills, one of which jutted out way into the open ocean.

Jaime picked up the conversation. "The *Santa Elena* is anchored just behind that hill. One of those boats is mine. Look up there," he said, turning her in the opposite direction.

Philar gazed upon a tall, rocky hill that seemed to reach the sky. Amid the various-sized boulders, there was a huge grotto nestled into the hill, its jagged wide opening resembling a giant mouth.

"See that cave? That's my playground. The crew and I sleep up there sometimes."

Her head and legs felt funny from the effects of the sugarcane rum. Yet she raised the glass to her lips and drank the last drops. Renata's gumption enthralled her. She turned again to her and asked, "Aren't you afraid to live here all by yourself?"

"Phew! Not at all. No one would dare bother me."

Jaime laughed. "I pity the poor soul who tries. He's liable to find himself gutted wide open like a fish."

Nodding agreeably at Jaime, Renata continued. "The crew comes by when they're in port, and when the sea calls to me, I rejoin them on the *Santa Elena*." She shrugged. "I have the best of both worlds."

"Well," Jaime said, standing up. "Thank you, Renata. The food was delicious as always, but I promised to show Philar the splendors of St. Barth. We need to get going."

Philar thanked Renata, and they headed back through the house.

As Renata hugged Jaime good-bye, she whispered in his ear, "She's not your type. She's an innocent. Behave yourself!"

He didn't answer. He just looked mischievously at her and winked. From high above the cliff, Renata watched Jaime help Philar into the rowboat. She watched them paddle away until they rounded the curve of the hill. Judging from the unfamiliar glint in Jaime's eyes, she was certain she hadn't seen the last of the blonde-haired beauty. She only hoped the girl was spirited enough to handle a man like Jaime.

Philar knew she was behaving out of character. On a normal day, she would never have wandered off with Jaime, but this was not a normal day. She was on the threshold of something new, a bend in her life, and she was embracing it. She'd had another moment of hesitancy as she'd climbed into the rowboat, but it had been fleeting. All she'd had to do was think of Vidal and the stifling, unbearable alternative he represented. She was quiet as Jaime paddled the boat expertly in the rough seas. As they rounded the hill, the *Santa Elena* came into view, and instantly she remembered her first encounter with the vessel. She'd known then too that it would not have been her last. Sometimes she wasn't sure if this so called gift was a blessing or a curse, but she was coming to understand that she couldn't fight destiny,

True to his word, Jaime proceeded to show her St. Barth from a totally different perspective. He told her that most of the *Santa Elena*'s crew was onshore, and the few onboard would make themselves scarce when they saw him with a woman. As the sea breeze caressed her face, and the sun kissed it, she began to relax and enjoy the excursion. Jaime kept the sails at a cruising level so she could see everything at a leisurely pace.

Philar was riveted by the magnificent beauty of St. Barth from the sea as they circled the eight-mile-long island. Jaime took particular care in the north and east sides, maneuvering the vessel a safe distance from the coral reefs. The rolling high hills, with Morne du Vitet being the tallest, and the many valleys and white sand beaches were enthralling. The island was surrounded by so many islets. *Like little jewels guarding the bigger gem,* she thought.

They made quick stops in Bonhomme close to Flamands, L'Ane Rouge by Colombier, and Coco islet near the Grande Saline, but it was the islet of Fregates that Philar liked best. It was their final stop on the way back, and by then the sun had begun to descend in a kaleidoscope of brilliant colors. It was just two tiny strips of land connected by a long stretch of sand, but it offered something that the other islets hadn't, protective shade from the sun. Aside from the Fregate birds that populated the islet, there were coconut palm trees whose long shadows cast cooling shade in the sand.

Tired and sunburned, but feeling mellow, Philar sat in the shade of the palms, and Jaime bent his long legs and sat beside her. They had spent the entire day amiably together. Yet they had hardly spoken. Now as they sat close to each other enjoying the spectacular sunset, Philar felt the tension between them.

"Mi amor," he finally whispered. "We cannot stay here very long. If I am going to get you back to Gustavia at a decent hour, we must start heading back soon."

Philar trailed her fingers in the sand, making random patterns.

"I don't want to take you back, and I know you don't want to leave me either."

Wordlessly, she brushed the sand from her fingers and hugged her knees. There were numerous little tunnels in the sand made by tiny, silvery sand crabs. She watched as one timorously emerged from a tunnel near Jaime's feet only to scuttle back in at a slight movement of his foot. Another little crab close to his hand scurried away to the safety of its hole, its ten little legs moving speedily. Like the little crabs, part of her wanted to run away from him too. She felt the intensity of his stare. With little effort or perhaps not even being aware of it, he exuded a potent sexuality, and the element of danger about him only enhanced it. She curled in her bottom lip and bit hard into it. Her mind was churning with so many questions. Then, emotionally flustered, she blurted out, "How can you live like this, roaming the sea day after day, having no place to call home, no family, no one to love you?"

"Oh, but I do have a family and a home, and I had love too. The crew is my family, and my boy, Nicholas. *The Santa Elena* is my home, and Elena was the only woman I loved ... until now."

Philar looked deeply into his brown eyes and he returned the look, searching hers as well. "I am betrothed," she said simply.

"I know. I also know that if you marry that coward, you will be miserable for the rest of your life. You're too much woman for a man like him."

"And am I enough woman for you?" She studied his face. There were deep grooves forming parenthesis around his mouth. He was at least fifteen years her senior.

"From what I know and have seen of you, you'll do."

"I am not sure that I am equipped to handle your lifestyle."

"You're better equipped than any other woman," he countered, leaning backward onto the sand.

"I see and dream things before they happen."

"Excellent. I will always be prepared to handle things ahead of time."

"I am afraid to venture out."

Jaime gently pulled her backward until she lay on her back besides him. Raising himself on one elbow, he ran the back of his fingers over her right cheek tantalizingly close to her mouth. "I believe it was Christopher Columbus who said, 'You can never cross the ocean unless you have the courage to lose sight of the shore.'"

"So you're quoting Columbus?"

"Why? You think because I am a vagabond sailor, I am not a learned man?"

"I am afraid of you." Her voice was barely audible.

"Don't be. I will never harm you." He lowered his head, claiming her mouth in a kiss that made her weak. She felt the heat exploding between her legs. Vidal's caresses had never made her feel like this. After thoroughly devouring her mouth, he feathered her face and neck with light kisses. His fingers kneaded her nipples through her blouse, making them hard and needy. Trembling, she began to quickly undo the buttons to give him easier access when he stilled her fingers with his hand.

"No, Philar. We will make love, but not here and not now," he whispered huskily. He took her hand and brought it to his bulging crotch. "I am burning for you too, mi amor, but I want to make sure you really want me before I take you because then you will be mine for life. I can pleasure myself with any woman. That's not what I want from you." He stood up, pulling her up with him. "Now come, the sun has set. I need to get you home."

Philar felt confused and embarrassed. Brushing the sand from her clothes, she silently followed him back to the vessel.

Jaime was brooding and silent on the ride back. He remained aloof until they were in the stark darkness of the track road where the horse was tied above Renata's house. Then he pulled her tightly against his hard body and passionately kissed her again.

When he had finished arousing her, leaving her breathless for the second time, he whispered gruffly in her ear, "This is what is going to happen. I am going to give you twenty-four hours to decide if you want me. The day after tomorrow at precisely noon, I will be waiting for you on Gustavia's harbor. The *Santa Elena* sails for Martinique that evening. If you want to be my woman, you will come to me publicly. I cannot promise you a life of luxury. My life is a rough one. I live by the dagger, and sometimes I steal and lie to get what I want."

Smoothing back her hair, he bit her earlobe. Her knees buckled and she leaned into him. "But I can promise you passionate, undying love. I can offer you excitement and adventure. I can guarantee you that twenty years from now, your body will still go weak from wanting me." His tongue licked the inside of her ear, and she moaned, bending her head sideways to give him better access.

Abruptly he pulled away. "Let's get you back to Gustavia."

Loretta was beside herself with worry. Gustavia was buzzing with the news that Philar had been seen traversing around town with the Spanish captain, and that had been very early this morning! Now it was almost four p.m., and still there was no sign of her. She had been fielding Vidal's questions all day. She'd told him Philar had a stomach ailment and was resting in her room, but he was feeling much stronger now. He had insisted on joining the other boarders for lunch. Then he had proceeded down the hallway to the room she shared with Philar. It had taken all of her wiles to convince him not to open the door. She had finally succeeded by reminding him that Clara would regard his visiting Philar's room a mortal sin, and they would all be thrown out of the boardinghouse.

But where was she and what was she doing with that Spaniard? Had she totally lost her mind? Loretta didn't know whether to pray or curse as she paced the boardinghouse's gallery. She was becoming more and more agitated. It was a stupid thing to do. Didn't she know that her reputation was being ruined by keeping company with that vagrant? He was a perfidious man, dangerous and untrustworthy. What if Vidal found out? She had done everything in her power to keep it from him, but gossip was commonplace in Gustavia.

Exasperated, she sat down heavily in one of the rocking chairs. Philar had always been capricious and frivolous, but she had never done something this dimwitted before.

Oh God!! What if she doesn't come back?

Loretta was so blinded by tears that it took her a moment to recognize the man coming up the path. She groaned when she realized who it was. "Paul, please, not now. I can't cope with arguing with you today," she said as his foot touched the bottom step.

"I am not here to argue, Loretta. We need your help. Agnes has been in labor since yesterday. Josiah said that she always has long labors, so we weren't worried. But now she's bleeding, and despite all of her pain, the child isn't coming. We sent for the doctor. He's all the way in Marigot with another patient." He looked at her imploringly. "Loretta, will you please come with me?"

Loretta didn't hesitate. "Let me get my bag and tell Clara I won't be here for supper. I will be right back."

Relieved, Paul sat on the gallery's steps. She had been so angry the last time he had seen her that he had been afraid she would not be willing to come with him. He should have known better. Loretta was intrinsically kindhearted and a natural healer.

She had been crying. His heart leaped. Was she pining for him? He had been longing to see her, but he'd disciplined himself to stay away. Besides, he had needed a legitimate excuse. The last time he'd used the ruse of enquiring about Vidal, and he had left hotly without ever finding out about him. He shook his head, secretly smiling. She was indeed a sight for his sore, yearning eyes. Suddenly penitent, he wiped the smile from his face. He was of course deeply concerned for Agnes. "Ayyy!" He groaned, slapping his knee. In his elation to see Loretta, he had forgotten that Beatrice was back at the house in St. Jean.

#

Clara was coming down the corridor when she heard a loud crash in the dining room. She hurried to the open door, knowing Bella was the only person in the room. She had left her there just a few minutes ago polishing the dining table. Her heart immediately palpitated when she saw her rotund legs suspended above the straw seat of one of the chairs, her back lying flat on the linoleum floor.

"Bella! Oh, Jesus! Are you hurt badly?"

"No, Miss Clara. I just got the wind knocked out of me." Bella answered from her horizontal position. "Just give me a minute; let me catch meh self."

Clara felt weak with relief. She sat on the floor next to Bella. "How did you fall?"

"Well, I keep seeing these two, big, blue sea flies flying around in here. You know it mean somebody coming from overseas to visit you. I take it to mean that more French people was coming here from France, and I know you don't like it when that happens. So I was trying meh best to catch them for you."

"Oh, Bella, we run a boardinghouse. If sea flies come to herald the arrival of overseas visitors, then the whole house should be swarming with them all the time."

When Loretta entered the dining room to tell Clara not to hold supper for her, she found the two women on the floor with Bella still lying on her back, her legs suspended against the chair.

"Are you ladies okay?"

"Yes," Clara replied. "Bella had an escapade with a couple of sea flies. Can you help me get her up?"

"I go need to drink a glass of sugar water just in case I got any bruise blood," Bella said with certainty as both women helped her to her feet.

#

Paul and Loretta rode the distance to St. Jean in silence. As they were about to enter the house, he took hold of her arm to still her. "I need to tell you something."

She looked at his hand on her arm and then up into his eyes, waiting.

"Beatrice is in there. I haven't been spending much time with her. This morning when I returned from the Salt Pond, she was waiting for me. She coerced her brother into bringing her here to spend the day." He looked at her, his eyes begging her to understand. "He's going to come back to take her home before nightfall."

"Let go of my arm."

He did as she asked, and she turned and walked to the door.

Loretta could hear Agnes's moans before she even entered the house. When she pushed open the door, the three little girls were huddled together in the corner of the parlor. Their father sat at the opposite end of the room looking totally distraught. She went quickly to hug the girls, murmuring to them reassuringly. Then she patted Josiah comfortingly on the shoulders as she passed him on the way to the bedroom.

Agnes was writhing on the bed, drenched in sweat. Loretta could tell she was delirious. The white sheet under her lower torso was stained red with blood. A young, slender, blonde woman of about eighteen was seated at her side holding her hand.

The girl looked up with worried eyes when Loretta entered the room. "Oh thank God you're here. She's in so much pain, and I don't know what to do to help her."

Loretta acknowledged Beatrice with a faint smile, going straight to the bed. Smoothing back the damp, dark hair from Agnes's forehead, she spoke to her comfortingly, all the while assessing her condition. Beatrice stood up and made a motion toward the door.

"No, please don't leave. I am going to need your help," Loretta said quickly. "Continue to hold her hand. I need to look and see what's happening with the baby, and it's going to cause her more pain."

Beatrice silently nodded and resumed her position at the side of the bed.

The baby was breeched.

"Lord, please guide my hands," Loretta whispered a fervent prayer. She looked around the room for a clean towel, spotting some on a wooden shelf above Beatrice's head. Taking a thick, white one, she rolled it into a long, tight wad.

Going around the side of the bed, she took Agnes's other hand and said calmly, "Agnes, I am going to have to turn the baby. It's going to cause you some intense pain. I want you to bite down hard on this to help take the edge off it. You're going to be okay."

She walked back to the foot of the bed, greased her hands with an herbal potion, and proceeded to grease Agnes's enormous belly. As Loretta began the critical task of externally massaging and manipulating the child's head into the birthing position, Agnes's body convulsed and twisted with pain. Loretta could hear her teeth grinding as she bit down hard on the towel. Beatrice's eyes were round with fear, but to her credit, she stayed put, allowing Agnes to mercilessly squeeze her hand.

After some excruciating minutes, Loretta finally had the baby's head securely in position, but Agnes was so fatigue she could hardly put forth the effort to push the child out.

"You can do this, Agnes." Loretta kept encouraging her after each push. She saw the strain in Agnes's face as she mustered her strength and pushed until her fourth daughter emerged.

The little girl was bruised and battered from her harrowing trip down the birth canal, but she was alive and wailing. After Loretta cut and clamped the umbilical cord, she cleaned and wrapped the infant in a soft, white blanket. She looked over at Agnes, but she was barely conscious. She had no choice but to place the child into Beatrice's arms so she could return to tending to Agnes.

"Olivia."

"What did you say?" Loretta didn't want to like Beatrice. Until now she had been faceless, and it had been easy to dislike her. Now she saw a courageous, fresh-faced young woman, and she felt even more tormented. She had transgressed against Beatrice, and God help her, she couldn't be sure she wouldn't do it again.

"The baby, her name is Olivia. Agnes told me she was hoping for a boy this time, but if turned out to be another girl, she would name her Olivia."

Loretta sent Beatrice into the parlor with the baby while she completed her ministrations on Agnes. When she finished, she sank wearily into the chair. It had been a very difficult delivery. She had been gravely concerned about both mother and child, and she was relieved that it had turned out so well. She felt spent, drained of energy, and she rested her head on the back of the chair, closing her eyes. She could hear the happy laughter coming from the parlor as they admired the child. Beatrice was exclaiming on how deftly and calmly Loretta had handled the complicated birth, and the tears slipped quietly from Loretta's eyes when she heard her say, "When Paul and I have our baby, I want no one else to deliver me but Loretta."

"Excuse me, Loretta. May I please come in to see my wife?"

Opening her eyes she saw Josiah standing before her looking anxiously at the bed. He held the tiny infant gingerly in his big arms. His body automatically made gentle rocking motions.

"Of course, Josiah."

Handing the child to her, he nervously approached Agnes's bedside. He touched her face, and then he bent over and kissed her.

"Don't worry. She's going to be fine. She's just exhausted from the ordeal." Loretta's voice was soft and assuring. She could see that Josiah was having difficulty taking his gaze off his wife. When he finally looked at Loretta, there were tears in his eyes.

"Oh, Loretta, I was so afraid. How can I thank you enough for saving my wife and child?"

"There's no need, Josiah."

"Surely I must pay you. If the doctor had come, I would have had to pay him, and he would not have been as compassionate as you."

"We wouldn't be so settled in La Pointe without your hard work. You have done so much to help Jonah and the rest of us, both you and

Paul." With one hand wrapped securely around little Olivia, she rubbed the back of her neck with the other. "I must head back to Gustavia soon. I will come early in the morning to check on them. Agnes will sleep through most of the night, and the child will not cry to be nursed tonight as long as she is warm and snugly wrapped. I'll stay just a little longer to make sure that everything continues to be okay."

Josiah came around the bed to hug her. "God bless you, Loretta. St. Barth is lucky that you decided to come here."

Her thoughts again on Philar, Loretta was anxious to leave when Paul came into the room a short while later. Agnes was sleeping soundly. The infant was swaddled warmly, and she was safely ensconced in the wooden cradle her father had built for her. Her cheeks were pink and healthy, and her little rosebud mouth made gentle sucking sounds as she slept.

"How is Agnes?" He stood awkwardly just past the door.

"She's going to be fine. She just needs to rest now."

"Beatrice is gone. Her brother came to take her home."

Disregarding his comment, Loretta replied, "Can you please take me back now?"

"Yes, let me get the wagon ready. The dew is falling heavily. You will be warmer in the wagon."

She nodded, and he quickly left the room.

For a time all that could be heard in the darkness was the steady clicking of the horses' feet. Occasionally the pungent smell of kerosene drifted through the cool night air as another lantern was lit in one of the houses they passed. The reflections of the flickering flames could be seen through the open windows.

"Thank you, Loretta," Paul said, finally breaking the silence. "Agnes and the child would have died tonight if it wasn't for you."

She didn't answer, and they continued on in silence again.

"She's so young. She must be at least ten years younger than you." Loretta's voice was barely a whisper.

"She is," he replied simply. "The women here marry young, and they look for older men who are already settled. Most times it's their parents who make the decision as to who they will marry."

"So in their eyes, I am an old maid."

He didn't answer, not knowing what to say.

"She was brave tonight. Please convey to her my thanks."

"She wanted to go back into the bedroom to say good-bye to you. I discouraged her."

"Why did you do that?"

He shrugged. "I don't know."

Loretta sighed, pulling the knitted shawl more tightly around her shoulders. "I've decided to return to Toulon with Jonah when he makes the trip in January. There's nothing for me here."

Paul glanced at her sharply. "I am here. What about your brother and sister?"

She looked at him pointedly. "You don't count. There is nothing between us. We had a brief moment of intimacy, but that's all it was. It meant nothing."

Paul felt slighted. "It meant something to me."

"Then you're delusional," she said coldly. "My brother is settled and content in La Pointe. Although he will argue strongly against my leaving, he doesn't need me as an encumbrance, and my sister ..." She wiped tears from her eyes. "Philar has taken all leave of her senses."

In a sad, low tone, Loretta told Paul everything about Philar, Vidal, and the Spanish captain, ending with how worried she was that Philar wasn't coming back. When she was finished, he whistled in astonishment.

In the distance two cats yowled, their inherent mating song evoking a series of frantic barking from the neighboring dogs. The stillness that followed the animals' shrilled outburst was eerie. Then Paul suddenly halted the wagon.

He turned to look at Loretta, trying to find the right words to tell her what he was feeling. "You've made it clear that you don't want me, and that what we shared meant nothing to you. That's not true for me. What we shared is engrained in my heart, but I can accept that you don't feel the same about me." He cleared his throat. "But right now, I can see you're hurting, and I have been so longing to hold you. Please, Loretta. Let me hold you."

He opened his arms, and she allowed him to enfold her. He held her for a long time, smoothing back her hair and placing light kisses on her forehead. He realized these precious moments of holding her would have to last him a lifetime, and when he finally released her, he saw that his shirt was wet from her tears. Having no adequate words, he silently resumed the journey

It was nearing the ten o'clock hour when Paul and Loretta arrived at the boardinghouse. The streets were mostly deserted. Paul secured the wagon just a few feet away from the pathway to the boardinghouse. Three men lingered outside the saloon doors in drunken stupors, talking loudly amongst themselves. Helping Loretta down from the wagon, he insisted on seeing her to Clara's door.

As they walked up the path, they saw two people locked in a passionate embrace on the gallery. When Loretta realized it was Philar and the Spaniard, she was both relieved and angered. She watched as the Spaniard ardently kissed Philar one more time before disentangling himself from her. Passing them by, he muttered a curt good evening.

Stretching dreamily, Philar put her hand on the door to open it, acknowledging Loretta and Paul only with her eyes. Loretta hastily stepped in front of her to block her entrance.

"Do you have any idea what you put me through today or do you even care?"

"Don't start with me, Loretta. I am not in the mood," Philar frostily replied.

"You've always been selfish and impulsive, but what you've done today beats all. Do you know what people are saying about you, gallivanting with that good-for-nothing, dangerous vagabond? He's bad news, Philar! If Vidal finds out—"

"Okay, Loretta, you want to argue? Then let's have it out," Philar said, moving away from the door. "But first, you don't know anything about Jaime, so please refrain from badmouthing him."

"You're defending him! Don't tell me you let that man make love to you."

Philar backed against the wooden railing as Loretta closed the space between them. Loretta sniffed and then gasped. "You've been drinking!"

"Oh stop being so damned self-righteous! So what if I had a few drinks? You ought to try it sometime. Maybe you wouldn't be so priggish, and it's none of your business who I screw."

"Philar, I am warning you."

"Or what? What are you going to do, Loretta?" Philar gestured with her arms, taunting her sister. "I didn't look down my nose at you when you screwed Paul."

Paul stood uncomfortably on the side. Loretta stole a nervous glance at him, and it didn't escape Philar's notice.

"That's right, Paul! I know my sister screwed you," she yelled over Loretta's shoulder. "You want to know what else I know? She pines for you. She mopes during the days, and she cries herself to sleep at night. She is in love with you, but she's too much of a frigging martyr to tell you. So she chases you away to convince you otherwise." In a singsong voice, she taunted, "Poor little Loretta. The man she loves is a betrothed—not married, mind you! Only betrothed! But she doesn't have the gumption to fight for him."

"That's enough, Philar!" Loretta said, reaching out to grab her arm.

Philar swung away wildly, staggering. "I don't give a shit if Vidal finds out. He can take his high and mighty attitude and stick it up his opinionated ass!" Her voice was rising higher and higher. "You know what? I had fun today. I felt alive and adventurous, and no, I didn't even have to screw Jaime to feel that way." She poked a finger at Loretta's chest and said with emphasis, "But I want to screw him, and I think I will."

"I will not have this vulgar behavior on my gallery. It is ten o'clock, and my door is closing. Are you coming in or do I lock you out?"

They turned at the austere sound of Clara's voice.

"Please give us a minute, Clara. We are coming right now," Loretta responded apologetically.

Clara glared at the two women and then looked at Paul with distain.

"I am appalled to see you here at this hour, Mr. Dusant, much less partaking in such tasteless conversation. These are two single women. This is not good for your reputation. Beatrice's family would be very upset if they knew."

"Oh just shut your old, pompous ass and go back in the house," Philar blurted, surprising everyone.

Clara gave a loud, offended gasp and slammed the door. They heard the sound of the heavy latch as it resolutely locked them out of the boardinghouse.

Loretta was visibly dismayed. Wringing her hands, she turned to Philar. "Now look what you've done. We're locked outside with no place to spend the night."

Philar shrugged nonchalantly. "It's no problem. We'll just curl up in the rocking chairs. She has to let us into our room in the morning."

Paul was stupefied. What kept replaying in his head was that Loretta loved him. Coming out of his daze, he told the sisters, "Both of you are coming home to St. Jean with me. I was coming to get Loretta in the morning anyway so that she can check on Agnes. This way I won't have to make an extra trip."

Philar turned to Loretta. "Agnes had her baby?"

"Yes, another little girl this afternoon. The child was breeched, and it was very difficult."

"I am so sorry I wasn't here to help you."

"It's okay. I am just so relieved that you're here now."

Paul was again astonished. The sisters had just been arguing bitterly. Now they were hugging each other, their heads close together like it had never happened.

"Please, Philar, reconsider your decision," Loretta begged. "You're not yourself right now."

They were walking along the tranquil shores of St. Jean's beach. Although Paul had done his best to make them both comfortable, they had barely slept. Loretta's distress was tantamount to last night's. Philar had dealt her another blow with the news that she was joining Jaime on the *Santa Elena*. Now the sun was rising in amazing hues of oranges and yellows as they strolled barefoot along the beach, tears staining their faces.

"My decision is made, Loretta. I am leaving tomorrow at noon with Jaime. I won't change my mind."

"But you hardly know him," Loretta cried. "The life he lives borders on insanity. It's perilous. It's no place for a woman like you."

Philar stopped walking and looked directly at her sister. "A woman like you could not live that life, but I am different from you. I am not meant to live a fettered life, and that's what I would have if I stayed here and married Vidal. With Jaime I get to see more of the world. There's excitement and adventure." She put her arms around Loretta and said softly, "You knew this was going to happen. We both did. Be happy for me, not sad."

"But do you love him?"

Philar laughed through her tears. "I know that he's a passionate kisser, and he makes me weak with excitement. Does that count?"

The sisters spent the rest of the day with Josiah, Agnes, and the children. Agnes was still looking tired, but she was up and nursing Olivia when Loretta checked in on her. Philar helped Josiah with the other three girls, bathing, feeding, and playing with them. Her decision made, she was back to being her jovial self, and the little girls delighted in her playful antics. She had decided not to return to the boardinghouse, not wanting to tangle with Clara or Vidal. Loretta would go back that evening to collect her belongings and bring them to St. Jean tomorrow.

Vidal was missing Philar. Initially he had believed Loretta when she had told him Philar was sick with a stomach ailment, but now he knew the truth. Philar was terribly upset with him. As he hobbled into the little corner store in Gustavia, he vowed to make it up to her. She was the reason he had come to Gustavia that fateful day of the accident. It had wrecked all his plans, but now he was almost well again.

A man with a thick, dark mustache greeted him from behind a glass counter. "Hello, Vidal. I have been waiting for you. I was beginning to think you had changed your mind."

"Not at all, Luis. I had an accident that laid me up. Do you have it?"

"Yes, I do. "

The man went into the adjacent room and returned with a red velvet pouch. He made a grand show of opening it, slowly pulling out a dazzling diamond ring with small rubies surrounding the diamond. "It is magnificent," he whispered.

Vidal picked up the ring and studied it, a satisfied smile spread across his face. "Yes, it is indeed magnificent, but not as precious as my Philar. Do I owe you any additional charges?" he asked, reaching for his billfold.

Luis smiled and shook his head. "May you and your fiancée have a long, fruitful life together."

Vidal thanked him and walked back into the bright, tropical sunlight. Despite his lingering injuries, there was a spring in his steps as he walked toward the waterfront en route to the boardinghouse. It was close to noon, and he wanted to make it back in time for lunch. Hopefully Philar would be in the dining room today. He hadn't seen Loretta this morning either.

The narrow streets had a steady flow of people, and he kept bumping into them. His mind was preoccupied with Philar. She had a right to be upset with him. He had reacted badly when he woke and found himself bedridden. He had been such an idiot, and it could have cost him dearly, but he was determined to make it up to her. He would have to learn to live with this so-called gift of hers. He would never believe such twaddle. What was more important was that she believed it, so from henceforth, he would indulge her. Having been raised on the sea, he had never been exposed to a proper courtship. Jonah seemed to be a connoisseur though. When he returned to La Pointe, he would beseech Jonah to teach him the gentle ways to treat a woman. Yes indeed, from this day forth he would make Philar a very happy woman. He had a new lease on life, both physically and romantically.

As Vidal crossed the street, he caught a glimpse of Philar just up ahead. She was wearing his favorite yellow dress. A huge canvas bag was slung over her shoulder. She was walking with a determined stride as if she was late for an appointment.

Immediately, a smile lit up his face. He picked up his pace to catch up with her. He was going to hug her tightly and plant a passionate kiss on her sweet lips. Then he was going to tell her how sorry he was and how he planned to make it up to her, but she was walking so fast.

"Philar!" he called out. She didn't hear him.

"Philar!" he called again, hobbling faster now, forgetting about his soreness. He stopped to catch his breath, angry that he was still not yet in good form. He was almost close enough to touch her.

"Philar!" he yelled, but a conch shell horn blew loudly, announcing the arrival of a new boatload of fish, and she didn't hear him above the noise.

His head and right side were throbbing, and he felt winded. Her name was on his lips again when she raised her hand excitedly to greet someone on the harbor, and he followed her gaze. His heart plummeted as his eyes made contact with the subject of her interest. He watched in utter horror as Philar ran into the arms of the dastardly Spaniard from the *Santa Elena*.

CHAPTER 17

Jaime deliberately held Vidal's stare, smiling smugly as he passionately pulled Philar against him, running his hands boldly over her body. Then to the consternation of Vidal and the gaping public, he bent his head and claimed her mouth. When he was finished making his conquest publicly known, he possessively put his arm around her waist and led her to the waiting rowboat.

Vidal hung his head and made his way blindly back to the boardinghouse. He was conscious of the buzzing gossip. He heard the unsavory names being attached to Philar. He felt the piteous looks, but he had slipped so far within himself that he was numb, oblivious to everything but the intense loss he was feeling. She had left him, and there was no one to blame but himself.

Loretta and Vidal returned to La Pointe the next day. They rode up the hill solemnly, barely speaking the entire length of the journey. Loretta was suffering doubly. She had not only lost her beloved sister to Jaime and the sea, she had also lost the man she loved. Wedding plans were in full swing in St. Jean and Lorient; it was the talk of Gustavia. The nuptials of Beatrice and Paul were to take place within two weeks.

Catherine was hanging laundry on the clothesline when she saw them coming up the hill. Her initial excitement tapered when she noticed their postures. The absence of Philar was telling enough. Dropping a wet shirt back into the basket, she went to greet them.

Yvette had also seen them and called out for Alphonse as she joined Catherine.

"Where is Philar?" Yvette asked.

Loretta dismounted the horse and ran into her brother's arms.

"She ran away with the Spaniard from the *Santa Elena,*" Vidal answered, grimacing as he slowly tried to get off the horse.

"What? This is some kind of joke, right? You're not serious?" Alphonse exclaimed. He pulled Loretta away from his chest to look into her eyes. His gaze was wild and full of questions. "What the devil is he saying, Loretta? Tell me this is not true. You would never allow our little sister to do such a foolish thing."

"I tried to stop her, Alphonse. I pleaded. I begged, but it was like she had become someone else," Loretta sobbed.

Pushing Loretta aside, Alphonse advanced on Vidal. "What about you? What did you do to stop my sister from leaving? Or was it because of you that she left? You always gave her a hard time about her gift. Did you argue with her, ridicule her?" He grabbed Vidal's collar and twisted it. "I swear on my mother's grave that I will beat you senseless if you are the cause of Philar performing such an imprudent act."

"That's enough, Alphonse!" Jonah bellowed.

Alphonse released Vidal and turned away, sobbing loudly.

Silently Jonah beckoned for Vidal to follow him. Yvette took Loretta by the arm, and the small group disbursed.

In Jonah and Catherine's parlor, Vidal commiserated his sorrow over losing Philar. He expressed his desire to return to Toulon, stating that there was nothing left for him in St. Barth.

Two days later Loretta sought out Jonah. He was on the far side of the property chopping wood for the coal pit when he saw her strolling forlornly in his direction. She appeared so sad that in hopes of making her smile, he said playfully, "I hope you've come to tell me that there's gold buried up here. Better yet, just show me where to start digging."

Loretta smiled weakly. "I've come to ask you to take me back with you to Toulon."

Jonah shook his head regretfully. "I cannot agree to take you back without your brother's consent, and he will never agree to let you go. You are a single woman. Apart from Alphonse, you are alone in the world. There is no one in Toulon to look after your welfare."

"I do not need Alphonse's permission, and I most definitely do not need anyone to look after me. I am not a child." Loretta took a deep breath filled with vexation. "My brother is not my keeper. As it is now, he barely speaks to me. He blames me for Philar leaving. If you do not take me back with you, I will find another vessel. There are plenty of them in Gustavia's harbor."

Puzzled, Jonah watched her walk away. Catherine had mentioned that she believed there was something else bothering Loretta aside from the business with Philar. Judging from her behavior lately, he tended to agree. As he picked up the chunks of wood for the coal pit, he wondered what else it could be that had the usually tranquil woman in such a tizzy.

With his decision made to return to Toulon, Vidal more closely resembled his old self, but Loretta had profoundly changed. Her lackluster attitude was so evident that they all now suspected something drastic had affected her during her time in Gustavia. Two weeks later, the veritable reason for her despondency came to light.

They were gathered together at Pierre and Marie's house to celebrate Marie's birthday. Raphael had purchased a new banjo from a shopkeeper in Gustavia, and he was happily strumming the five strings, making everyone laugh with the funny lyrics he was making up about them. Marie had adopted a puppy from a litter of one of Henri and Emeline's dogs, and the black and white puppy was yelping loudly outside. The puppy was so used to making a ruckus that no one paid attention until they heard the knock on the door. Everyone was already in attendance, including Henri and Emeline, so the presence of someone at the door startled them into silence. They all looked at each other wondering who it could be. Then Pierre walked over and opened the door.

Josiah, Agnes, and their four children stood on the threshold. The expressions on their faces were troubled. Agnes held the baby in one arm. She held Jenny's hand with the next. Josiah was holding Flora and Zelda.

"We had to leave St. Jean in a hurry. They were stoning the house," Josiah said simply. "We need a place to stay, and the only place we knew to come was La Pointe. We were headed farther up to Jonah and Catherine when we heard the revelry. We figured we would find everyone here, so we stopped."

Catherine came forward to take the baby from Agnes. Marie was right behind her. She ushered the little girls into the house.

When the family was settled among them in the parlor, Jonah asked, "What's going on, Josiah? Why would anybody in their right mind stone your house?"

Agnes wiped the tears that escaped down her cheeks, and Josiah slipped his arm around her shoulder. They seemed reluctant to answer.

"It is because of me." The strong, masculine voice came from the direction of the door. They all watched as Paul advanced into the room, his eyes steady on Loretta. "I broke my vow to marry Beatrice."

There was a series of loud gasps and then total silence as Paul continued in a steady monotone. "I have known for some time now that my heart belongs to someone else. I tried to ignore it. In fact, I fought it like the devil. I viewed it as an imposition. I was already committed, and there would be hell to pay if I reneged." He sadly shook his head. "But I couldn't fight it any longer."

Walking over to Loretta, he pulled her to feet. Holding her hands, he said, "My heart belongs to you, Loretta. You are the other piece of my soul, and if I can't have you, then I fear I will lose my mind." He kissed her hands and then got down on one knee. "Loretta, in front of your brother and the rest of our friends and family, will you please put me out of my misery and marry me?"

The celebratory claps and applauds filled the parlor as Loretta nodded her approval, and Paul's arms encircled her. In the excitement of the moment, no one noticed Alphonse's clenched fists or the frown of worry on Jonah's face. Beatrice had been publicly scorned and abandoned by Paul. Now it was understood why the house was being stoned. Paul had become an outcast.

Jonah cleared his throat. "I am sorry to put a damper in your glee. We all recognized that something was dreadfully wrong with Loretta." He smiled. "Now we know. However, we have a serious problem here. By walking out on Beatrice, Paul has placed himself in a very precarious position. He stands to lose everything he has built for himself in St. Jean, and he is also in danger of blows. If they catch him alone, they will beat him up."

Marie rose and beckoned the little girls into the bedroom. The birthday party was forgotten.

"Josiah and his family are involved by association," Jonah continued. "Josiah being Paul's brother and living in the same house. I believe Josiah will be embraced again in St. Jean, but it will take a long time before Paul is accepted again." Jonah turned and looked at Paul. "Do they know you left Beatrice for Loretta?"

"Beatrice figured it out, and I didn't deny it."

"That means they know you came here," Jonah continued. "We're all going to have to be vigilant. I wouldn't put it past them to come up here after you."

"Just wait a damned minute," Alphonse growled. He came forward, a scowl on his face, and pointed a reproving finger at Paul. "He publicly dishonors a young woman, drags my sister's good name into his muck, and you want to harbor him here? For all you know, he deflowered that poor girl. If she was my daughter or sister, I'd want to skin his ass too." He moved to stand menacingly in front of Paul. "How dare you involve Loretta in this? Stay the hell away from my sister or I—"

Loretta stepped between the two men. "Stop it, Alphonse! I have been involved. I love Paul, and my heart aches for Beatrice, but what Paul did, he did for me." She emphatically touched her chest. "He loves me enough to sacrifice everything to be with me."

"He should have spoken with me first and properly ask for your hand, not barge in here in front of everyone and go directly to you. He disrespected me," Alphonse replied angrily.

"You are correct, Alphonse," Paul interjected, "I should have approached you first, and for that, I humbly ask your forgiveness. But I want you and everyone else to know the truth. I did not deflower

Beatrice." He looked lovingly at Loretta, and she returned his gaze. Then he looked back at Alphonse. "I love your sister. I give you my word that I will always protect and cherish her." He took a deep, nervous breath. "Alphonse, may I please have Loretta's hand in marriage?"

Still looking hurt and angry, Alphonse remained silent. The room was virtually still.

"Oh, come on now, Alphonse. Stop being such a hard ass. You're standing there so stiff it looks like you're holding back a hot shit," Raphael bellowed. "Hell, for all it's worth, you have my blessings, and if them assholes are brazen enough to come up here looking for trouble, let them come. We look after our own around here."

"You damn right, Raphael. They will have to get past all of us," Pierre agreed.

Reluctantly Alphonse opened his arms and enfolded his sister. Reaching past her, he offered his hand to Paul. "I promise you that I will personally feed you to the fish if you hurt Loretta."

Jonah felt the improved ambience in the room as the men slapped each other's backs in solidarity, and the women visibly exhaled. He turned to Josiah and Agnes. "You are more than welcome to stay with us. I know Agnes loves St. Jean's beach, but we have a very exquisite one just down the backside of the hill. It is called Gouverneur."

Loretta looked up at Paul, and they both smile surreptitiously.

The weeks passed, and no one came up to challenge Paul and Loretta. Jonah and Catherine escorted them down to Gustavia a month later to speak with the Catholic priest about marrying them, which he flatly refused to do. Instead, the old priest, a man in his seventies with thinning spikes of gray hair and a face filled with an intricate pattern of lines, lamented on Paul's long list of sins against the church. He expounded in-depth on the penances that Paul must perform as evidence of his sorrow if he ever hoped to be forgiven. When he had finished tongue-lashing Paul, he turned his derision on Loretta. Having heard enough, Catherine faked a fainting spell, leaning heavily on both men as they presumably escorted her from the stiflingly hot rectory.

Clara was sweeping the gallery when they returned to the

boardinghouse. "Go wash up. Lunch will be served momentarily," she said without looking at them. She glanced up as they began to walk past her, and abruptly, she stopped sweeping.

"What's wrong" she asked, looking at Catherine.

Catherine took a seat in one of the rocking chairs, and the others followed her example. "Jonah and I want to see Paul and Loretta respectfully married so that the gossip about them can stop, but the priest refuses to marry them."

Clara pursed her lips. "Surely you can understand why. What they have done is offensive to the entire community."

"There is nothing offensive about my love for Loretta!"

Jonah gave Paul a furtive look and motioned for him to be quiet.

"They are both good, decent people," Catherine said. "Jonah and I can vouch for that. Clara, is there anyone you know who might be able to help us?"

With her arms folded, Clara studied Catherine. She formed her mouth to speak and then stopped. Her inward wrestling was obvious. Then she unfolded her hands. "I am going against my better judgment, and if I ever hear that you mentioned my name in reference to this conversation, none of you will be welcomed here again. Do I make myself clear? "

They all nodded.

"I take it that you need a Catholic priest?"

They nodded again.

"I have a good friend who is a Catholic priest. We have a deep respect for each other. If I give my blessings, I know he will marry them." She looked at Loretta and Paul with distaste. "The only trouble is, he is stationed on an island just off Guadeloupe called Marie-Galante."

"That is not a problem," Jonah injected quickly. "We can sail there."

"Very well then, I will write him a letter that you will take with you. You can leave in the morning. Now go wash up. I need to help Bella in the dining room." She dismissively put the broom aside and walked into the house.

Paul and Loretta were married on a bright November day by Father Degout, a middle-aged priest with a friendly demeanor, a stark contrast to his good friend Clara. The ceremony was held in an old stone Catholic church on Marie-Galante, an island with nearly one hundred sugar mills. Apart from two nuns dressed in full, black habit, Jonah and Catherine were their only witnesses.

#

In late January, Jonah and a small crew, which included Vidal, set sail for Toulon. With Jonah's permission, Vidal had signed over his interest to the small parcel of land Jonah had deeded him to Paul and Loretta. By the time the *Louise Catherine* sailed, Paul, with the help of the other men, had already begun to construct a house.

From the moment Jonah arrived back on the family's estate in Toulon, he was the center of attention. Ivan, Rose, and Nellie looked overjoyed to see him, and Lucinda blatantly flirted with him, which only served to antagonize an already-irate Clifford.

At dinner on the first evening, they listened raptly as Jonah regaled them with stories of life on the island. They applauded happily when he told them Catherine was expecting their second child.

Clifford's anger grew as he watched his mother and his wife idolize Jonah. Nothing had gone according to plan. The golden boy had not languished on the island. Instead, he had returned a hero.

"Oh stop this absurdity!" Clifford hit the table so hard that the china rattled. "You're all carrying on as if Jonah is some kind of god. I am sick of it. He's playing in the sun all day getting bronzed while I am busting my ass here trying to keep us afloat. Nobody thanks me for that! But the golden boy returns, and the fatted calf is slaughtered." Pushing away from the table, he threw down his napkin. "You all make me want to puke. Are you coming, Lucinda?"

"No, I haven't finished eating," Lucinda answered insolently, "and besides, I am enjoying the conversation here."

Clifford's wrath intensified as Lucinda dismissed him with the wave of her hand and turned her attention back to Jonah.

"Well, you'd better wipe the drool coming down your chin and keep your bloomers on because if you think you're going to get a chance to screw him, you're badly mistaken." He spitefully gave the tablecloth a quick yank, spilling the contents of the wine glasses. Smirking, he walked out of the dining room.

Rose was quick to apologize. "I am so sorry for his behavior, Ivan." Rose

"It's okay, Rose, let him have his tantrum," Ivan said affably.

After dinner, Jonah joined his father in the library. He was pleased to see him looking so well, but as he watched Ivan pour sherry into two crystal glasses, he got his first inkling that something was wrong. Ivan's hand shook when he handed him a glass, and then he took a seat beside him. Taking a hefty swallow of the amber liquid, he said, "So, from all indications, you appear satisfied with your new life. I am pleased."

"Catherine wanted to come with me, but because of her pregnancy, she and Marcel had to stay behind. I am going to Marseille to visit Charles and Suzanne by midweek. I have letters and photographs to deliver from both Catherine and Marie."

Ivan ran his hand over his face and groaned. When he looked at his son, his eyes were sorrowful. "There's no easy way to say this, so I am just going to say it." He took a deep breath and let it out slowly. "Both Charles and Suzanne died within the last four months."

"What?" Jonah mirrored his father's reaction by running his hands over face. "H-how?" he stuttered. "Catherine received a letter from Suzanne not long ago. She gave no indication that anything was wrong. On the contrary, Catherine said she sounded upbeat and cheerful."

"You must remember that correspondences between France and the island take several months for delivery, sometimes up to half a year. But from what I gathered, Suzanne was sick for a while, and it is highly probable that she purposely set out to make everything sound cheery in her letters to her daughters."

Ivan got up to pour himself another glass of sherry. "Would you like another sherry, son?"

Jonah shook his head, and Ivan resumed his seat. Clearing his throat, he continued. "I found out quite by accident that she was sick. I was in Marseille on business, and I decided to swing by and visit them. I knew right away that something was wrong when I saw the yard. It was full of weeds. Charles is always weeding and tending the flowers. I knocked on the door, and he opened it. Poor man, he was totally discombobulated. I was not two steps inside the house when he flung himself into my arms and bawled. You know he was a proud man." Ivan leaned over to place the empty glass on the parlor table. "So this behavior was totally out of character. When he had composed himself somewhat, he led me into the bedroom. I was dismayed to see Suzanne lying on the bed deathly pale. The handkerchief she held was tinged with blood, and she was coughing horrifically."

Ivan ran his hand over his face again and sighed heavily. "Oh, Jonah, I felt so sorry. I told them I would locate the best doctors in the provinces to attend to her, and I did, but it was too late. I was also angry. Had they contacted me months ago, she could have been saved. Their stubborn pride prevented them from reaching out to me."

He shook his head sadly. "I spent a lot of hours sitting by her side in those last days. She claimed she didn't want me to know of her illness because she didn't want her daughters' new lives to be hindered. She said she knew I would have found a way to send word to them, and they would both want to return to France immediately. She didn't want that for them, but she wrote them both letters. I have the letters to give you."

Jonah's eyes were wet with tears. How could he go back and deliver this dreadful news to his wife and her sister? "What happened to Charles?"

"We're not certain. After Suzanne died, he just folded. I tried to get him to come here to Toulon, but he wasn't interested. He was found early one morning on his boat in the harbor. There were no bruises or cuts on him. From what I heard, he just appeared to be sleeping." Ivan nodded perceptively. "I know how it feels to lose the only woman you've ever loved. The man died of a broken heart."

The following days were hectic as Jonah and Ivan worked together to fill the supply list for the return trip to St. Barth. As they were organizing the delivery to the *Louise Catherine* at the end of the week,

Ivan looked at Jonah sadly and said, "I am going to miss you all over again. It has been such a pleasure having you home."

"I won't stay away for long, and the next time I come I will bring Catherine and your grandchildren."

So as not to offend his father, Jonah carefully formulated his next words. "Father? Aside from a few businesses in town that have closed, I don't see much change in Toulon. In terms of the war, I mean. You were so adamant that major changes were coming."

"Oh, it's already happening. Those businesses closed to avoid further losses. It's a domino effect. One business closes its doors and it affects another. France's economy is losing strength daily while Germany is gaining strength both economically and demographically. They are now considered the number-one manufacturer of steel in the world. The Franco-Prussian war has made the German Empire a powerful nation. When they succeeded in annexing Alsace and most of Lorraine, they obtained large amounts of iron and ore, which stimulated their military power. It's not a question of whether they will attack France; it's a matter of when."

"Will it be safe then for me to bring Catherine and the children on my next trip?"

A frown appeared between Ivan's thick eyebrows. "I am so looking forward to seeing them. When do you plan to come back?"

"About this time next year."

"I will find a way to get word to you to let you know if it's safe to bring them."

#

Jonah arrived back in St. Barth on a late, balmy afternoon in early May. It was twilight by the time he had finished securing the vessel, so he decided to spend the night at Clara's. Unlike his initial arrival to the island, people stopped and greeted him warmly by name on his walk to the boardinghouse. It came as a pleasant surprise. He was no longer considered a stranger in this tight-laced community.

"So how is the mother country?" Clara asked as she escorted him to his room.

"I was only in Toulon, so I cannot speak for the rest of France. Everything is about the same, although my father is certain war is imminent with Germany."

"Humph," she snorted. "That means more of you will end up on St. Barth's doorstep."

"Like rodents, you mean? I thought by now your opinion of us had improved. Raphael is one of us, you know. So are you for that matter," Jonah gently chided.

Clara wriggled her nose and looked up at him. "Some of us learn how to appreciate the unique beauty and the peaceful way of life of this little island while the rest of us, the rodents, pillage it, thereby getting fat and wealthy through ill-gotten means. My dealings with you and your wife have proven to me that you're not one of the rodents, but believe me when I tell you, not all French people are like you and me."

"That can be said about all nationalities, Clara."

"I am aware of that," she replied. "Still, I can only speak from experience." She opened the door to his room, quickly gave it a glance, and then handed him the key. "Welcome home," she said with a genuine smile. "It is nice to have you back on St. Barth."

As Jonah rode up the hill the following morning, he fervently prayed for guidance to help him deliver the news to his wife and her sister of their parents' deaths. It occupied his thoughts the entire length of the journey. Catherine was pregnant. The news would devastate her and possibly harm the child. He thought of not telling her at all until after the birth, but he knew she would never forgive him. After agonizingly mulling it over it, he came to the conclusion that he would stop and speak with Pierre before going home. He would let him tell Marie. He knew he would have enough tribulation telling Catherine.

Being the foremost house on the incline of the hill, Paul and Loretta were the first people he saw when he came into the clearing. Paul was raking the yard while Loretta worked on the flowerbed. He could hear the repetitious thumps of a hammer coming from inside. As they looked up and saw him, he quickly put his index finger to his lips to shush them.

"Who's inside the house?" he asked, dismounting.

"Pierre's putting in some cabinets for us," Paul replied.

"Is Marie with him?

"No. What's wrong, Jonah?"

"I have troubling news. Let's go inside. I need to talk to Pierre."

They followed him into the house, where he related the sad news about Charles and Suzanne. He asked Pierre to go home and speak with Marie. The sisters would need each other, and it would help if they both found out simultaneously. Clearly perturbed, Pierre dropped everything and headed home, and Jonah followed him up the hill.

Catherine was on the gallery putting out bowls of sugar for the birds, humming happily as she situated each bowl on the wooden railing. Marcel was playing with a ball on the floor.

For a long time, Jonah stood silently watching her. Her belly had grown substantially which meant the child would be here soon, and she looked so content. The news he was about to deliver would shatter that contentment.

"Oh, Catherine," he groaned. Gathering his strength, he softly called her name.

Turning gleefully at the sound of his voice, she flew into his arms. Marcel's chubby little arms happily encircled his feet. Jonah felt a sudden surge of anger. He had yearned for this moment. Now the distressing news would ruin his happy reunion.

As he held and kissed her, Jonah knew Catherine felt his sadness, and so he tried to pull her tighter, trying to delay the inevitable. Pulling away, she looked up into his face, her eyes searching his. "What is it, Jonah? What has happened?"

"Let's sit down, Catherine."

"No." She adamantly shook her head. "I don't want to sit. Just tell me!"

"Catherine I …" The tears sprung unwillingly from his eyes. He couldn't speak.

"Is it Ivan? Oh God! Has something happened to him?"

Jonah shook his head. "No, it's not Father."

"But then who? Who would have you this upset?" The puzzled looked on her face changed into utter shock as it hit her. "My parents?" she murmured incredulously. "Mama? Papa? Which one?"

"Both. They're both dead." Jonah's words were barely audible.

Catherine let out an agonizing wail. Being frightened by his mother's screams, Marcel began to cry too.

"No, you're lying!" She pounded his chest. "Why do you want to hurt me by telling such a vicious lie? Tell me you're lying, Jonah. Mama and Papa can't be dead. They just can't be. Nooooooo!"

Jonah tried his best to hold on to her as she writhed and cried in his arms, but eventually she slipped down his body, collapsing to the floor. She curled into a fetal position as best she could with her gigantic belly.

"Catherine, please get up. You're going to hurt yourself and the baby," Jonah begged, but she wasn't hearing him as she called out for her parents over and over in singsong intonations. He sat beside her on the floor, helplessly holding Marcel. This was far worse than he had imagined.

"It's okay." Gentle hands touched his shoulder. "Get up and take Marcel for a walk. I will take care of Catherine. Yvette and Agnes are with Marie." Loretta's voice was soothing.

"But I can't leave her like this," Jonah cried, his face writhing in agony.

"Go, I have her. Marcel shouldn't see his mother in this condition." Loretta tugged at him until he raised himself to his feet. Then she pushed him and Marcel through the door.

Loretta resumed Jonah's position on the floor. She shifted Catherine's heavy weight so that she could hold her more comfortably. Murmuring soothingly, she rocked her. Eventually Catherine stopped crying, hiccupping softly as she lay in Loretta's arms.

"We need to get up now, Catherine," Loretta whispered. "Let me take you inside. You can sit on the sofa while I get you a glass of water, okay?"

Catherine nodded and allowed Loretta to help her into the house.

Loretta was just coming back into the parlor with the glass of water when Marie burst through the front door with Yvette right behind her. She flung herself onto the sofa beside Catherine, and the two women began to bawl again in earnest.

"Agnes is with the children, including Marcel," Yvette told Loretta as they helplessly watched the sisters' grief. "This is just awful. I wish there was something we could do."

"There is," Loretta whispered, setting the glass of water on the parlor table. "We can leave them alone." She took Yvette's hand. "Come, let's go. They have each other now, and that's the best solace for them. Let's give them privacy. We will check on them in a little while."

The ensuing days were hard ones for Catherine and Marie. They wanted to know what had caused their parents' death, and they hounded Jonah for every detail. He patiently repeated several times what his father had told him, and he gave them the letters addressed to each of them in their mother's delicate handwriting. Marie had torn hers open immediately, but Catherine couldn't find the will to rip the seal. The depth of her emotions was too raw.

At times Catherine felt guilty for having left France and for encouraging Marie and Pierre to do so too. She felt responsible for her mother's sickness and ultimate death. She should have been there to take care of her and nurse her back to health. Then there was the anger, and it raged within her with a fierce fury. Why hadn't her mother sought help? It was her mother's foolish behavior that had caused her own death and ultimately caused her father to die as well. Her grief was so profound that she could barely function. She was lethargic. She had no appetite, and she was losing weight. She knew that it was not good for the baby, but she had ceased to care about anything. She hadn't bathed or combed her hair in days.

Marie seemed to have bounced back to her old happy self, and that too angered Catherine. How could Marie continue on so easily? Didn't she feel the acute loss of the two pillars that had supported and encouraged them their entire lives?

"Catherine, this has to stop. It is not good for you or for the baby," Jonah told her sternly one Sunday afternoon. She was huge and ungainly, and the baby was due any day now.

"Henri and Emeline are expecting us. Are you coming?"

"No," she replied listlessly from the sofa

Jonah picked up Marcel and sighed. "You know, you have to remember that you have a son, an unborn child and a husband. *We* didn't die with your parents." Then he walked angrily through the door.

Catherine didn't even turn her head to watch him leave. She couldn't understand his anger. She had suffered a double blow with the death of both parents. His father was alive and well in Toulon. How could he even begin to understand her anguish?

"Let him be angry," she mumbled, repositioning herself on the sofa.

As she pulled the blanket up to her head, her eyes caught the edge of the white envelope jutting out from under the Bible on the corner table. She quickly closed her eyes. The image of the envelope loomed behind her eyelids. She felt drawn to it, and she fought the feeling. She turned her back and tried to sleep, but the restlessness persisted. Sighing heavily, she threw off the blanket and reached for the envelope. Her eyes filled with tears again at the sight of her mother's handwriting. She lifted the envelope to her nose, breathing in deeply, hoping for a whiff of her mother's scent. There was none. Dejectedly, she ripped the seal.

CHAPTER 18

My dearest Catherine,

I will not write of sadness for there is no need. Dry your tears. Live your life to the fullest. Embrace your God-given talents and blessings. In so doing, you honor your father and me.

You and Marie are my flowers. Like natural flowers, you must lift your faces to the sun and absorb its rays so that you can bloom brightly, and you must withstand the rain and the dew, for it will only strengthen your roots, sending them deeper for substance, thereby feeding your soul.

Know that you were planted on this earth for a purpose. Soon enough your own seeds will grow and multiply. Trust in yourself and in God Almighty. When you need fortification, look inward into your soul and draw from the wellspring of faith that dwells there, and know that I am always with you, my precious flower. I am the root from which you grew, and I am indelibly a part of you.

Affectionately,
Your mother,
Suzanne

J onah subconsciously watched as the little spider laboriously spun her web between the boards of the gallery's wooden railing. The intricately detailed web spanned the length of three boards now, and still the spider toiled.

"Did you hear a word I just said, Jonah?" Raphael sat on the step besides him.

"Huh?"

"I was telling you that I am going down to Gustavia tomorrow, but you're so preoccupied with that spider web, you didn't hear me. Still worried about Catherine?"

Jonah stretched out his long legs on the lower steps. They had just enjoyed a supper of stewed mutton and rice with Henri and Emeline. Now they were all relaxing on the gallery.

"Yeah, I am more worried than ever. I have never seen her like this, and I don't know what to do to make her come out of this malady. The baby is due any day now. I feel like I've lost my Catherine."

"From the looks of her, she doesn't look lost to me."

Jonah glanced sharply at Raphael. "What? What are you talking about?"

"Look over there." Raphael nodded in the direction of the path.

Jonah turned so quickly that he heard his neck crack. She was slowly walking down the hill, her ungainly girt waddling.

"The baby must be coming!"

Jonah bounded up the hill to meet her. "Catherine, are you okay. Is the baby coming?"

His gazed went from her belly to her face. She was flushed with sweat from her walk in the afternoon sun, but her face was serene. She was smiling! She had on clean clothes, and her hair was combed.

"My feet hurt, and I am awfully hungry. I hope you didn't eat all the food. Where's Marcel?"

Jonah sighed heavily with relief. Then a happy grin spread over his face. "No, there's plenty more stewed mutton left. Marcel is on the gallery with everybody else. Come; let's get some food into you."

As he took her hand, he asked, "What happened to suddenly make you feel so much better?"

She looked up at him and smiled. "I read my mother's letter."

Catherine was frolicking with Marie in the Mediterranean Sea just down the hill from her home in Marseille. The brisk waves felt invigorating. Laughing playfully, Marie cupped her hands, filling them with water and splashed her. She shrieked. Giggling, she reciprocated, vigorously splashing back. A wave rocked against her and she lost her balance. Steadying herself, she watched the whitecaps foam as the wave moved past her. Her gaze drifted to the shore. Her mother and father were walking hand in hand on the white sand. They smiled and waved cheerfully to her.

"Mama, Papa!" she tried to cry out.

She watched them walk farther down the bay, their backs to her now.

"Mama, Papa, please wait!"

She could hear the words inside her, but they wouldn't come out of her mouth. She whipped around in the water, frantically looking for Marie. Where did she go? The waves seemed to have gotten rougher. She started to struggle against them in her frenetic efforts to get to the shoreline. Her parents were walking farther and farther away. She needed to stop them from leaving! She felt the energetic tug of a gigantic wave as it pulled her backward, overpowering her and wrapping her in its watery grip. She couldn't breathe. She was falling into a deep, dark abyss. She heard a loud pop and the sea engrossed her entire body.

"Jonah!"

The shrill sound of Catherine's voice woke Jonah instantly. "Wake up, Catherine. You're having a bad dream."

Catherine opened her eyes, blinking rapidly to try and focus. She was wet. Her entire back felt damp and sticky against the sheet. "Jonah, I … I believe I peed myself," she said, trying to sit up. She was halfway off of the bed when she felt a soaring pain in her lower back and belly. "Oww," she cried out.

"Catherine, you didn't pee yourself. The water is from the baby. It's coming."

Jonah leaped from the bed. Grabbing his pocket watch, he peered at it. "It's a little after three a.m. I am going to rouse Loretta. Will you be okay until I get back?"

"I don't have a choice, do I?" she snapped. "Go, but please hurry. The pains are coming hard and fast."

Jonah left the house with his pantaloon in his hands. He didn't bother to grab his shirt. He ran down the hill in the chill of the early morning dew, simultaneously trying to get his feet into the legs of the pantaloon. He pounded on Paul and Loretta's door so hard that the fowls in the chicken coop immediately started to cackle, and the roosters began to prematurely crow.

Francois came into the world just a few short hours later. His boisterous cries pierced the early morning stillness. As Loretta cleaned, wrapped, and handed him to his mother, she felt the distinct feeling that something was peculiar about the little boy, but she was unsure as to what it was. He seemed perfectly normal, with his funny little tuft of brown hair. His coloring was good, and he was a healthy weight. Still, Loretta couldn't shake the feeling that he was different.

#

"Spit it out."

"Huh?"

"Don't give me that look," Jonah said. "This is the third time you've hit your thumb with the hammer. Now what's bothering you?"

Raphael put down the hammer and sat on the rocky ground beside it. Pulling out a dirty handkerchief from his pocket, he mopped the sweat from his forehead. The look on his face was an interesting blend of contemplation and discomfiture.

"Well? I'm waiting."

"It's not so easy to talk to you about these things," Raphael replied hesitantly. He absentmindedly played with his beard, still reluctant to express his thoughts. Then he blurted, "I am going to marry Clara."

"That's wonderful!"

"Well, I wouldn't call it wonderful. I don't like the idea of being henpecked."

Jonah shrugged, looking puzzled. "I don't understand."

A painful look crossed Raphael's face. "I have this problem, down there," he pointed to his crotch. "My balls hurt."

"Why?" Jonah was trying hard to hide his laughter.

"Boy, don't tell me you never wanted a woman so bad that your balls didn't hurt like hell. Wipe that stupid grin off your face. It's not at all funny. It's painful."

"So that's your problem." The laughter ripped from Jonah. "You're lusting for Clara, and she won't give you any unless you put a ring on her finger."

"I know she is passionate in bed"—Raphael looked sheepishly at Jonah—"but I am going to have to marry her to find out for sure."

Jonah chuckled harder and gave Raphael a congratulatory slap on the back. "You old dog, you've been sniffing under Clara's tail, and now she's got you begging with your tongue hanging out. Goes to show you can't judge a book by its cover."

Clara and Raphael were married two months later. It was a simple ceremony held in the Catholic church in Gustavia. The only invited guests were Jonah, Catherine, Oliver, and Bella. Clara hadn't wanted a big to-do. She wore a beige dress, and her gray-streaked blonde hair was combed in its usual chignon. She was composed and unruffled.

Raphael, on the other hand, was fidgety. The old ruffian was spruced up to the max. His salt-and-pepper hair was slicked back, and his beard was neatly trimmed. Still he looked uncomfortably like an old caged rooster.

As Jonah watched them, he thought back to his conversation with Raphael and a smile wickedly played across his lips. The image of Raphael and this ascetic woman in the throes of passion was hilarious. He was happy Raphael had finally found love. He and Clara were complete opposites, but they complemented each other well.

#

Francois was approaching his first birthday before Catherine fully realized there was something wrong with his social development. He seemed unmindful of the sounds around him, and although he would smile when she played with him, he did not try to interact with her as his brother had done. Yet he was thriving in his physical developments, prompting Jonah to put up gates to keep him from harm's way.

As time wore on, she attributed the little boy's lack of social skills to a stubborn streak. It began to aggravate her. He ignored her warnings not to climb the gallery's railing. He didn't respond when she called him. He didn't dance when Raphael played his banjo, and he refused to repeat the words she tried to teach him. In fact, he didn't try to formulate words at all. Eventually her irritation turned to distress. Something was wrong with her little boy. He seemed to be living in a world of his own.

It all came to a head one day when she accidentally dropped an empty iron pot. It fell with an awful loud clang on the floor next to where the two little boys were playing. Marcel instantly screamed and came running to her, but Francois was unperturbed.

Holding Marcel, she picked up the pot and purposely dropped it again. Totally unaffected, Francois continued to play with his blocks. Bewildered, she sat on the floor beside him. She placed her hand next to one of his ears and snapped her fingers. He didn't respond. She snapped her fingers next to his other ear; still no response. She put her lips to his ears and yelled out his name. Still there was no reaction from the little boy.

"Oh God!" she cried. "He's deaf!!"

She pulled Francois onto her lap next to Marcel. Holding her two sons, she cried. She felt remorse for all the months she had gotten upset and irritated with Francois. She blamed herself for his deafness. She had grieved for her parents deeply, and it had affected her child. She bowed her head and absorbed the sweet-smelling scent of his hair, her tears falling on top of his head.

Marcel wiggled from her arms, intent on returning to his game, but as if knowing she needed to hold him, Francois stayed nestled against her.

#

"I am pregnant and I want you to deliver my baby."

The earnest announcement came so abruptly that Catherine was taken aback. She and Loretta were seated on Clara's gallery rocking lazily in the mahogany chairs. Marcel and Francois were playing at their feet. Feeling a yearning for a change of scenery and a chance to explore the shops, they had accompanied their husbands on a supply trip to Gustavia. The two women had become close confidants, and they enjoyed each other's company.

"Oh, that's wonderful news." Catherine reached over to hug her. "I am honored you think so highly of me that you would trust me to deliver your baby, but I don't know if I can do that, Loretta. You're better off with the doctor."

"Catherine." Loretta took hold of Catheirne's hands. Looking deeply into her eyes, she said, "I trust you more than any doctor, and besides, he's never around when he's needed. You can do it. I will talk you through it."

"But what if I end up hurting you or the baby? I would never forgive myself. Oh, I wish Philar were here."

Catherine blurted the words impulsively and immediately felt contrite when she saw the sad look on Loretta's face. "I am so sorry, Loretta."

"It's okay. I think about her all the time. I wonder where she is and how she's doing. I had hoped the *Santa Elena* would have returned to St. Barth by now, but ..." Loretta shrugged, her eyes downcast.

"Why the two a you sitting out here looking so gloomy?"

Engrossed in their conversation, they hadn't seen Bella and Oliver coming up the path, their hands laden with sacks. In his usual quiet manner, Oliver tipped his hat in greeting and proceeded through the gallery door, but Bella claimed the closest rocking chair. Placing the sacks on the floor, she fanned herself with her hands. Beads of perspiration dotted her face and dripped between the double folds of skin on her neck.

"Phew, that heat out there ain't making joke today. You see how it drizzling and the sun shining so bright? That means the devil beating he wife. It go be even hotter tomorrow." She stopped fanning herself to closely peruse the two women. "Did I hear something 'bout a baby?"

"Yes," Loretta replied, "I am going to have a baby."

"Good for you, but you ain't the only one." Bella turned to Catherine and then pointed at Francois, who had his chubby hands firmly planted on the floor. His little body was arched and his head was bent over looking between his legs.

"You see what your boy doing? He looking for he brother or sister. You go get another baby yourself soon."

Catherine was so accustomed to Bella and her foibles that she chuckled. "Oh, Bella, don't wish that on me. These two boys are enough of a challenge."

Bella nodded with surety. "Another baby coming soon. Well." She braced her hands on the arms of the rocking chair. "I got to go put away these provisions." Then she slowly raised herself from the chair and lumbered into the house, leaving the two women chuckling.

#

The brisk Christmas winds habitual to the Leeward Islands started in early December, lending a cooling respite from the tropical heat. It heralded the Christmas season for the islanders, who alleged that if you lifted your face to the wind and breathed deeply, you could smell the sweet fragrance of the season. For Catherine, it was a stark contrast to the cold, harsh mistrals of Toulon, and she had come to look forward to the cooling breeze that sometimes lingered way into March. True to Bella's words, with the Christmas breeze came the news that she was pregnant again.

In January, despite her pregnancy and against Jonah's better judgment, Catherine insisted on sailing to Toulon. Ivan had hired a caretaker for her parents' house in Marseille. Still, she wanted to assure herself that the house was being tended properly. She had asked Marie to come with her, but Marie declined, saying she had no desire to brave the long and tedious voyage.

Catherine found that the dynamics in the house in Toulon had not changed. Rose still ran the household, and Nellie still cooked and served the meals. Although there were more wrinkles in his handsome face, Ivan still looked stately.

Lucinda greeted Catherine with the same animosity, choosing to ignore her while she blatantly flirted with Jonah. However, there was an enhanced element of antagonism about Clifford, and it didn't take long for Catherine to feel its sting.

"So, you've come back for more," he menacingly whispered when he cornered her in the hallway on the first evening. Picking up a lock of her hair, he taunted, "This time you won't get away, my little island savage."

"One of the skills this island savage acquired is the precise ability to slice the neck clean off a goat. If you do not relish becoming a eunuch, you should stay far away from me," she replied coolly.

Their eyes had been locked in silent battle when Celeste's soft voice intruded. "Monsieur Clifford, Madame Catherine, is everything all right?"

Clifford instantly dropped Catherine's hair and turned on Celeste. "What do you want, you little church mouse?"

Celeste's eyes darted between Clifford and Catherine. Subconsciously stroking the linens she held tightly in her arms, she said, "Madame Catherine, Monsieur Ivan would like you to come to the dining room right away."

"I am on my way," Catherine replied. Giving Clifford an icy stare, she whispered, "I would take pleasure in castrating you." Then she sidestepped him and walked confidently down the corridor.

Jonah could see more clearly now the slow degeneration that had taken place in Toulon. More than half the businesses in town had closed, and there was talk everywhere about the impending war. Heavily armored gendarmes now guarded the huge naval arsenal yard in the harbor. They were also situated at strategic points on Mount

Faron. People were antsy, and they were holding tightly to their limited resources. As a direct result, his father's fishing business was losing revenue.

Knowing Clifford as well as he did, Jonah understood his increased restiveness. Not only could he could no longer afford his elaborate lifestyle, he could no longer enjoy his drinking binges because most of the saloons in town had closed. Just like on his prior trip, Jonah kept his distance from him because every time they were in close proximity, he felt the urge to pummel him.

Jonah and Catherine returned to St. Barth in time for Catherine to deliver Loretta's son, Manuel, and in turn, Loretta delivered Catherine's only daughter, Sarah. In due course, Catherine would have two more sons, Charles and Victor, and Loretta would have two daughters, Loren and Philarine. Marie would bear another son, Benjamin; Yvette would finally conceive a daughter, Julie Ann, but Agnes would never have the son she so desired.

Jonah consistently made annual pilgrimages to France, sometimes taking Catherine and the children with him. He started taking on cargo on the yearly voyages, and as the demand grew, he expanded his business to include cargo from other Caribbean islands.

So the residents at La Pointe endured and proliferated. They raised their families together, each looking after the other. They stayed true to France's traditions while embracing the customs indigenous to the Caribbean. They toiled, and the parched, rocky soil capitulated under steadfast hands and bore fruit. They tenaciously battled hurricanes and droughts, and they persevered.

But the winds of change affecting France would soon blow in the direction of the Caribbean, and the looming new century would bring problematic changes and people to the tranquil, little island of St. Barthelemy.

CHAPTER 19

Roger Dusant ducked under the eaves of the La Rouge Saloon in the upper town by the railway station to escape the heavy raindrops. He looked thirstily at the swinging doors of the only saloon still open. He sure could use a drink, but his pockets were empty. He glanced out at the weather. The rain wasn't letting up. He wondered if he could swindle some foolish soul into buying him a nice, frothy beer. The sneer on his face widened as he contemplated the thought.

Roger was far from what anyone would consider a saint. He had lied or cheated his way out of every job he had ever held. Even his cousins, Ivan and Edward, had fired him on the spot when they had caught him stealing red-handed. They had immediately ousted him from his comfortable cottage on the estate. He couldn't understand why they had been so upset. He was family after all, and he was entitled to a few perks on the job. Now he lived in an old dilapidated shack not far from Boulevard de Strasbourg.

Normally he was able to persuade the thugs in town to hire him to carry out their seedy deals. He was wily enough to pickpocket the gendarmes, but this mess with Germany and the Jews had even the thugs wary. He had a wife and children to feed. He swore, cussing the rain and his fate.

A movement across the street caught his attention, and he watched as Jonah Dusant closed an umbrella and sauntered under the protective covering of an open-air restaurant. Forgetting his plans for a drink, he studied Jonah as Jonah shook hands with the proprietor and together they took seats at a table. Clifford had been so pleased when the old man, Ivan, had sent Jonah away. He had been sure that Jonah would languish on that tiny Caribbean island in the middle of nowhere. Roger snorted loudly. The man was the picture of health.

The joke's on you, Clifford. That island can't be that bad if Jonah looks like that.

Then, like a lightning bolt, it hit him. The insidious thought grew within him until it reached its full proportion. He laughed loudly at his own genius.

"Business is just not good, boss. People are holding tightly to their money. We're trying our best to sell the catch," Simon said, nodding toward the cache of unsold fish, shrimp, and lobster.

"Either you try harder or you find yourself another job. I will be damned before I continue to feed a bunch of lazy imbeciles."

Fuming, Clifford turned and walked back up the steep path to the house. The proceeds from the fishing business had fallen drastically, and his export/import business was nonexistent.

"Damn those German bastards," he grumbled, "and damn the Jews too. They're everywhere! The whole of France is infested with them."

Reaching the landing, he paused to catch his breath. Even the elegant old house had lost its luster. It had been recently repainted, and the grounds were still neat and clean. Yet it was as though the cloak of economic despair that was hovering over France had already taken a glancing blow at the estate. The atmosphere of unrest was palpable. Germany was becoming more aggressive, so much so that France and Russia had formed an alliance. Jews were streaming out of Germany, and the vast numbers of misplaced Jews were becoming more incensed for retaliation. Mistrust was rampant. The French believed that not all the Jewish evacuees were genuine. They were displeased and leery of the large influx, so the Jews felt like pariahs in France.

The whole thing aggravated Clifford. He couldn't even venture out anymore without encountering public uprisings. He had gotten caught in the middle of a heated fracas just yesterday downtown. His lavish lifestyle was in serious jeopardy, and he was helpless to change his circumstances.

It didn't help that Jonah was thriving on St. Barthelemy. Clifford wanted to smash the golden boy's face each time he arrived for his yearly visits. Jonah was robust and muscular and lavishly content while Clifford wallowed away in misery and financial privation. The peasant had bore him more children, and she too was still slender and attractive. It was preposterously unjust.

Broodingly, he crossed the yard and opened the main door. Lucinda was lounging on the sofa. Their two-year-old daughter, Lenia, was playing on the floor. He had passed his son, Jacques, in the yard, and he had not stopped to tell the little brat hello. He had been intent on passing Lucinda too when he smelled an awful stench.

Glancing at the child, he groaned, "Lucinda, the least you can do is clean Lenia. She's plastered in shit!"

"I told Rose a half hour ago that Lenia's diaper needed changing." Lucinda stretched lazily.

Clifford walked over to the sofa, grabbed a handful of Lucinda's long, black hair, and pulled her to her feet.

"Ouch! You're hurting me."

"My mother is not your servant. Now take that child upstairs and bathe her."

He let go, pushing Lucinda forward onto the floor. Grudgingly she picked up Lenia. Keeping her at arm's length, she started up the stairs.

Roger knew if he hung out long enough at La Rouge Saloon, he was bound to bump into Clifford. He had been dawdling here every night, waiting. His wife, Solange, would throw a fit when she found the money missing. She thought he didn't know about her pathetic attempt to hoard money. Stupid woman, she should know that nothing escaped him. He rubbed his hand over his face. An unusual twinge of guilt was gnawing at him for invading her secret stash, but he couldn't just sit here in the saloon dry-mouthed. Besides, his plan would benefit her and their boys. Picking up the mug from the counter, he took a swallow of the frothy beer.

Because of the unsavory nature of his particular skills and its vigilant prerequisites, he never allowed himself to get drunk. He absentmindedly rubbed the six-inch scar on his left arm. He had learned that lesson the hard way.

Bored, he ignored the big-bosomed blonde giving him the eye a few stools down and glanced again at the door. This part of town was not Clifford's usual haunt, but the other saloons were closed, and Roger knew it was only a matter of time. Yawning, he ordered another beer and resigned himself to waiting.

The fight with Lucinda emulated all the others. The only dissimilarity was Clifford's reaction. Given their present financial state, it had angered him when he walked into their chambers and found Lucinda lovingly running her fingers over new lingerie and shoes. Calmly he had opened a drawer of the oak dresser and withdrew a pair of scissors. Then he'd picked up the closest pair of pink bloomers and started cutting away. Before Lucinda could react, he'd reached for a second one.

"Clifford! Have you lost your mind? Give that back to me!"

"I've warned you that I cannot afford your extravagances, but you persist in defying me."

Lucinda tried to stop him, but her efforts were no match for his superior strength. When he was finished shredding the lingerie, he'd picked up a black, shiny slipper and proceeded to apply the scissors to the leather.

Wailing loudly, Lucinda had taken hold of the end of the slipper and tugged wildly. In the ensuing scuttle, she'd fallen backward onto the floor, knocking down the kerosene lamp. The loud clamor had woken both children, and they started howling along with their mother. Their strident wails and the pungent smell of kerosene had immediately summoned the rest of the household. Of course Ivan and his mother had sympathized with Lucinda, openly chastising Clifford. He'd felt so stymied. Ivan was demanding that he cut costs, yet he had interfered in his efforts to preempt his wife's senseless spending. In vexation, he'd turned and walked out of the room.

"You must be frigging crazy if you think for one minute that I would trust your sorry ass. Now get out my face and let me enjoy my whiskey."

Roger had seen Clifford the moment he'd walked into the saloon, and he had wasted no time. He needed to talk to him while he was sober, before the effects of alcohol clouded his reasoning.

"We're in the same boat, Clifford. We're both suffering from this mess with Germany, and we're both shrewd and calculating. You see how good Jonah looks. That island is agreeing with him, plus he's far removed from all this nonsense of war. Why can't we have the same advantage? Your vessel is sitting in dry dock slowly rotting, of no use to you. Why not put a crew together and sail away to the good life?"

Roger watched Clifford, letting his words sink in, and then he delivered his clincher.

"Jonah has always made you look like a fool. You always come in second to him. Are you going to let him have the upper hand again? Why should he enjoy prosperity while you languish here in misery? Come on, Clifford, you're too smart for that. We would make a good team."

Clifford did not respond. Roger could see the muscles in his jaw tensing. He said nothing as Clifford ordered another whiskey and swallowed it in one gulp.

"I wouldn't take you anywhere. You're nothing but a common thief. You don't even have the scruples not to steal from your own family. You don't deserve to carry the Dusant name."

Roger coolly raised an eyebrow. "Really, Clifford? Are you forgetting the many times I helped you steal goods on the trading expeditions? Wasn't that stealing from your family too? When Edward caught me with those gold coins, you were as guilty as I, but you let your father expel me from the estate. You were too much of a coward to tell him about the coins hidden in your own pockets."

Clifford ordered another whiskey, again swallowing it in one gulp. "It's not my fault if you were so daft that you got caught."

Roger felt his anger growing at Clifford's nonchalance. Realizing anger would get him nowhere, he forced it back. "You owe me, Clifford," he said softly. "I took the blame for you. I could have told your father the truth. All he would have had to do was check your pockets. If that's not trust, what is? Think about it. We have the power to change our circumstances and sail to a better life. I will be awaiting your answer." He lightly touched Clifford's shoulder and walked away.

Clifford had only one more drink. The seed Roger had planted instantly took root, and he walked the streets of Toulon in a mix of bafflement and excitement. It was a genius idea. Why hadn't he thought of it himself? But he would never consider taking Roger. Simon was his man.

He couldn't sleep in his eagerness to speak with Simon. At the first crack of dawn he headed down to the bay. Sure enough, Simon was already up. He was sitting shirtless on the pier, his bare feet hanging over the edge, a fishing line dangling from his hands. An empty, yellow, enamel coffee cup and a half-eaten croissant lay on the pier beside him.

"No, boss, I am not going. I am not deserting the motherland. I am ready to defend her against Germany."

"Come on, Simon." Clifford uttered a profanity. He could hardly hear himself speak over the noise from the damned seagulls eying the croissant. "What the hell is this sudden allegiance to France? "What I am proposing here is a chance for a better life. Why muddle yourself in this war?"

Diverting his eyes from the sea, Simon looked at Clifford and said passionately, "I am a Frenchman. It is my duty to defend my country. Sorry, boss, I wish you safe travels, but you will have to find another first mate."

Still smarting from Simon's rejection, Clifford reluctantly went in search of Roger. He didn't want to align himself with his ill-reputed, second cousin. Seven years his senior, Roger more closely resembled Clifford than Jonah. Though Clifford was a bit heavier, they had the same ruddy complexion, unruly blond hair, and unsavory morals. Yet identifying with Roger's depravity was the very reason Clifford distrusted him. A thief couldn't trust a thief. Roger was the most unscrupulous man Clifford knew, but if he was going to embark on the voyage, he had no other choice. Aside from Simon, all the other imbeciles on the estate were dotingly loyal to Ivan.

As Clifford passed Boulevard de Strasbourg in downtown Toulon, his thoughts shifted to his family and the reactions they would have when they learn he was sailing to St. Barthelemy. Ivan would vehemently protest, and his mother would bawl. Lucinda would be the only one happy. The chance to be near Jonah again would supersede all of her misgivings. Clifford frowned. If needed, he would allow Lucinda to use her wiles to ensnare Jonah. He still intended to extract revenge on Jonah and the peasant, and to that end, Lucinda could be instrumental, but if she made any moves without his permission, he'd beat the shit of out her.

Clifford rounded a corner, and a series of dilapidated houses came into view. He picked his way down the grubby, dusty path until he stood in front of Roger's address. The dingy appearance of the rundown shack Roger called home made his skin crawl. A shirtless, skinny, little boy of about seven answered his knock. The child immediately looked at his hands and then looked up at him with wide, blue eyes. "Did you bring food?"

"No. Where is your father?"

Leaving the door open, the boy backed into the room, calling, "Papa, there's a man at the door."

Clifford could see another shirtless little boy sitting on the torn linoleum floor eating a piece of bread. Inside, the room was sparsely furnished, with only a beat-up old brown sofa and a chipped corner table holding an old kerosene lamp. Roger emerged from the only other room, his hair disheveled.

"You look like hell."

"Shush, Solange is sleeping. She worked the night shift cleaning the hotel down the street."

"And why isn't your sorry ass up fixing food for your sons? They're hungry." Clifford intentionally raised his voice.

"Ain't nothing to fix."

Clifford reached into his pocket and took out a few coins. "Go down to the bakery and buy them food. It is one thing a Dusant does not do is neglect his bloodline. It's shameful that you're neglecting yours. We're sailing in two weeks. Be ready. And know that I will have no qualms in throwing your ass overboard if you pull any shit on me."

#

"What is wrong with these people? It's like we have the plague," Clifford mumbled.

Their arrival on St. Barth was greeted with the same aloofness that Jonah's entourage had initially experienced. Clifford tried to stop several men to ask for directions. Some just ignored him, using their large straw hats as subterfuges, and others mumbled incoherently in their haste to get away.

"I didn't like this place the first time I saw it years ago."

"You're using the wrong approach," Roger replied.

"What the hell are you talking about?" Clifford snapped, wiping the sweat from his face.

"Think, Clifford." Roger looked squarely at him. "They're leery of us because we're strangers, but if we had a connection to someone they knew and trusted, they might be more agreeable. Tell them we're related to Jonah."

Clifford looked at Roger, understanding dawning in his eyes. He smiled slowly. "You might be worthy of being a Dusant after all."

"Clifford, why did you bring me here to die in this awful heat?" Lucinda whined.

"Why don't you do me the favor and die already," Clifford retorted, shoving her into the small shop they were passing.

The space inside was clustered with an assortment of wares. A large, round pan was set up in a corner, a big block of ice occupying its center. Bottles of assorted drinks were propped around the ice. Bumping shoulders, they headed straight for it, their mouths parched from the unaccustomed tropical heat.

As they were paying the proprietor, Clifford casually broached the subject. Adjusting his voice to an affable tone, he said, "We need help." He paused and sighed for effect. Hemming and hawing, he continued.

"We just arrived from France to visit with our cousin, Jonah Dusant. He's going to be so happy to see us, but …" He picked up his daughter and rested her head on his shoulder. Rubbing her back comfortingly, he gave a meaningful look at the other three children. "We don't know how to get in contact with him, and the children are so tired."

The proprietor, a stout gray-haired man, listened attentively to Clifford. Then he shook his head. "I can direct you to a boardinghouse, but I will not tell you where Jonah lives. If you are his relation, he will know you have arrived and will come looking for you."

Henri and Emeline avidly listened to the conversation between the strangers and the proprietor while they kept their attention on the charcoal, iron goose they had come to buy. As they filed past them through the constricted walkway, Emeline whispered to Henri, "They are Jonah's relation. You can see the resemblance. We have to help them."

Henri nodded in agreement, and they followed them out of the store.

"Hello, my name is Henri. This is my wife, Emeline. We are Jonah's neighbors. We can take you to him."

Clifford didn't try to hide his excitement, "Thank you most kindly." Then purposely he frowned. "There are eight of us, including the children. We cannot impose ourselves on Jonah and Catherine. Do you know of a place nearby?"

"Yes, we can impose on them," Lucinda spurted from behind him.

Roger nudged her hard from the back. "For once shut up and let the man speak."

"I suppose you are correct," Emeline was saying. "Catherine just birthed her fifth child last month. Not that she would mind," she interjected quickly. "Catherine is such a gracious woman." She looked at Henri excitedly. "Why don't they stay with us? We have plenty of room."

"Oh no," Clifford feigned, excitement building within him. "No, no, no," he shook his head. "Thank you for your very kind offer, but we cannot burden you."

"Nonsense," Henri replied. "Relations to Jonah are relations to us. Besides"—he leaned forward and winked—"you would be doing me a favor, giving her those little ones to fuss over."

"Well, since you put it like that," Clifford replied, ascertaining that there was enough hesitancy and appreciation in his voice. "We have no choice but to accept. Lead the way."

Emeline chuckled with delight and took the little girl from Clifford. "Henri, you go finish up our purchases while I take them to the wagon."

Raphael cursed himself profusely. Had he not lingered in bed this morning with Clara, he would have seen the *Marie Rose* making her way into the harbor. He was usually a very early riser, but the boardinghouse was rarely void of guests. He had seized the opportunity and persuaded Clara to stay in bed. She had been doing such tantalizing things to him, and afterward he had fallen back into a deep, contented sleep. She had risen, dressed, and was working in the house while he slept in oblivion.

When he had finally meandered into the kitchen in search of food to satisfy his grumbling belly, Bella was tattling away about the new vessel from France in the harbor, and how its occupants were touting their relations to Jonah. She'd gone on to say that Henri and Emeline had taken the strangers up to La Pointe.

Alarm instantly gripped him. He dropped the cup of bush tea on the counter with such a heavy thud that the amber liquid splattered liberally out of the cup, startling Bella into silence. Paying no mind to her agape mouth, he walked over to the window and opened the jalousies. Sure enough, it was *the Marie Rose.* Cussing every profanity he could think of and forgetting about food, he hurried back to his chambers. He ridiculed himself for his sensual respite. "Damn my age," he grumbled as he dressed hurriedly. He needed to get to Jonah.

Even before he reached Henri and Emeline's house, Raphael could hear the children's laughter. He groaned as he watched Emeline pick up a little boy of about five and hug him.

She waved excitedly when she saw him, beckoning him to stop. "Come, Raphael. Jonah's cousins are here. We found them in Gustavia. When I told them Catherine had just had a baby, they reluctantly agreed to stay with us. That was so considerate of them." She clucked on as Raphael tied his horse and followed her to the house. "Just like Jonah and Catherine, they're very nice people. Well, that's not entirely true about Lucinda. She complains a lot. Solange is a sweetheart though, the way she looks after those children."

"Solange?" Raphael's expression was puzzled.

Emeline glanced at him quizzically. "You know, Roger's wife. That Roger is a charmer. He's so polite and helpful. The other one"—she paused as if trying to remember his name—"Clifford? He is nice too, but he seems to have a superior air about him."

At the mention of Roger, Raphael's spirit sank further. Clifford could not have aligned himself with a more devious man. They were all in danger, but how could he possibly make Henri and Emeline realize the plight they had so trustingly brought upon everyone? Already Emeline was bonding with the children. He decided it would not be wise to say anything at present. He steeled himself to face the two men as Emeline ran excitedly ahead of him.

"Everybody come quickly, Raphael is here."

"Hello, Raphael, it is good to see you," Clifford said, coming forward to hug Raphael.

With an indomitable stare, Raphael allowed Clifford to embrace him. "Whatever shit you're planning, it won't work," he whispered. "I'll skin your ass before I let you get near Jonah and Catherine."

Clifford pulled away and slapped Raphael good naturedly on the shoulder. "I know how happy you are to see me. You remember Roger."

Roger stepped forward. "How is Jonah? That sweet little wife of his must be even more beautiful now that she's in full bloom." His eyes mocked Raphael, taunting him.

"Why don't you all go up for a quick visit now? Raphael can take you," Henri interjected.

"That sounds good," Lucinda chirped, perking up.

"No, we're all fatigued. It will be too much for the children," Clifford quickly replied. "We will go see them tomorrow when we're rested."

"Very well then," Raphael said ascetically. "Jonah and Catherine are expecting me." Nodding farewell primarily to Henri, he turned and headed out the gate.

"That's strange," Henri muttered as he watched Raphael mount his horse.

"What, dear?" Emeline asked distractedly.

"Raphael didn't say that he would convey the news of their arrival to Jonah."

"Oh, I wouldn't worry about Raphael," Clifford quickly interjected. "He's always been possessive when it comes to Jonah and Catherine. He likes having them all to himself."

Henri looked pointedly at Clifford. "I have never gotten that impression in the years I have known him."

An uneasy feeling was stirring within Henri. Frowning, he glanced at the radiant face of his wife as she played patty-cake with the little girl. He let the conversation drop, tucking it away to mull over later.

Catherine was cooking supper when Raphael hustled through the front door. Always happy to see him, she quickly wiped her hands on her apron to greet him with the customary hug. She stopped abruptly in the kitchen doorway. Raphael was shaking. She could not recall a time when she had seen him this furious.

"Raphael, what's wrong?"

Ignoring her question, he asked, "Where is Jonah?"

"He is up by the goat pen fixing the fence."

He turned and briskly walked out of the house, and totally alarmed, Catherine followed.

"Looks like a storm is brewing," Jonah told Pierre as they hammered nails into the new fence. He glanced at the sky as another ripple of thunder echoed in the sweltering afternoon heat.

"It's no wonder, it has been so hot," Pierre answered. "We'd better hurry up before we get drenched out here."

Jonah glanced again at the ominous skies, and his eyes caught on the man quickly making his way up the incline. "Raphael?" he muttered.

"Catherine is following him. Something is wrong," Pierre said, dropping the hammer on the ground.

The two men abandoned their task and hurried toward them.

"Raphael, what happened?" Jonah's voice was filled with worry.

"Clifford and Lucinda are at Henri and Emeline's place. Roger is with them."

"Roger? Who Father and Edward expelled from the estate? Clifford despises him. Why would he bring him here?"

Disgruntled, Raphael replied, "The heat must have gone to your head because you're totally missing the point here, Jonah. Clifford has joined forces with that belly-crawling snake, and now they're down there kissing each other's asses. Their families are with them. It's our bad luck that Henri and Emeline just happened to be in Gustavia, overheard them saying they're your relations, and happily invited them home." He angrily swiped at the sweat running down his face. "Lucinda's grinning like a damn hyena, pissing herself with glee to get to you while those two bastards are plotting their moves."

The rain began to fall in big, heavy drops, but they stood still, perplexed by the troublesome news.

"Let's get out of the rain," Jonah said as a bolt of lightning lit up the gray skies. Taking Catherine's arm, he led them back to the house.

"We must warn Henri and Emeline," Pierre said.

"I agree, but how?" Raphael responded. "Emeline is already stupefied over the children. She's clucking like a damn mother hen all around them."

"Henri is the more amenable one," Catherine offered. "We can get him by himself and reason with him, but it has to be soon. They're way too susceptible to cope with the likes of Clifford."

"I will speak with Henri," Jonah replied, "but we have a bigger problem. Raphael said they are planning on coming up here tomorrow, and I will be damned before I let them set foot on this land." He clenched his fists. "Clifford is in my territory now. He stills wants to tangle with me, well, he's about to engage himself in the battle of his life, no matter the demons he brought with him. He will never succeed against me. He might be my blood, but these are my people and my parcels. I will passionately protect and defend them."

#

"You don't really expect me to sleep on that hard cot." Lucinda glared at Emeline.

"It's not so bad," Solange interjected.

"What would you know?" Lucinda turned her venom on Solange. "From where you come from, this must feel like heaven, but it is pure hell for me. I am not sleeping on that thing."

"Lucinda." Clifford's voice was falsely soothing as he walked into the room. He pulled her into his arms. "You knew it was going to be uncomfortable for a while until we get settled," he said sweetly, wringing a hard pinch at her waist. She squirmed and he pinched harder. "Now behave yourself and help Solange put the children to bed."

He turned to Emeline, who was still standing in the doorway. "Please forgive my wife's rudeness. She gets grumpy when she's tired. Where's Henri?"

"He already retired for the night," Emeline answered meekly.

"Then you should too. Let me handle this." Clifford put his arm around her shoulder and propelled her out the door. "We're already indebted to your kindness. Pleasant dreams, Emeline."

When Cliffford was certain Emeline was gone, he roughly grabbed Lucinda's cheeks and said, "I am warning you, do not screw this up for us. I am going outside to speak privately with Roger. You had better be happily lying your ass on that cot when I get back."

The dogs growled when Clifford and Roger stepped onto the gallery. Clifford muttered a curse and roughly kicked one out of his path. Wining piteously, the dog cowered and retreated to a darkened corner. The others bared their teeth and took a stand, but they too retreated when Roger accosted them from the back, hitting them hard with a wooden stick. Spurred on, Clifford spitefully pushed the sleeping cat off her perch on the gallery's railing. She fell with a startled meow into the adjacent bougainvillea bush. Grinning maliciously, they walked into the yard and out of earshot.

"Did you hear them say they own ten parcels of land here?" Roger whistled. "Do you know what we can do with that many parcels? There's so much potential."

Clifford snorted. "Now you sound like the old goat, Ivan. All I see here is a bunch of rocks."

"I don't agree with you. We have to come up with a plan."

"For what?"

"To own these parcels. We came here to share in the good life Jonah is living, remember? Well, it seems to me we have already fallen into a goldmine."

"You think they're just going to give it to you?"

"Don't be an ass, Clifford. We're going to beguile them out of it. You heard the old lady say their son and daughter live in the Danish Virgins and hardly ever come back. We just need to convince them just how unfair they're being treated by their children. Kill them with kindness."

"And what about Jonah and the rest of them? They're not going to sit back and make it easy."

Roger laughed. "You so easily forget our forte, cousin. We just need to take our time and play our cards right. When we're finished with those old people, they will want nothing to do with any of them."

"The old man is already showing doubts about us."

"Then getting rid of him will be the first order of business."

Lucinda was up early and in good spirits the following morning, although she had hardly slept. Her back ached from the hard cot. She'd twisted and turned for most of the night in the god-awful heat listening to Clifford and Roger snore in the adjacent, smaller room. It had annoyed her that Solange basked in sleep, comfortable on the hard floor next to the children. Then toward dawn she'd seen the ugliest, lizard-like creatures crawling on the ceiling. She hadn't tried to close her eyes since, intent on keeping watch to make sure those things didn't come near her.

Putting her night of misery aside, she left the room early. She found Emeline in the kitchen and willingly took the bucket she handed her. She submissively followed Emeline outside to the well. Without argument, she cast the roped bucket into the well and pulled up the full, heavy pail. She didn't protest too much about bathing in the yard or about the first icy splash of water that touched her skin. None of this misery mattered because she would be seeing Jonah today. He would rescue her from this hell that had suddenly become her life. Surely he would take them all in, no matter the strife between him and Clifford. Jonah was a Dusant, and he was honor-bound to look after his blood. Yes, most assuredly her life on this god-forsaken island would improve after today.

"Where are you going all spruced up, and why aren't you helping Solange with the children?" Clifford asked when he found her sitting on the gallery a short while later.

"Solange already has them dressed. They're in the kitchen eating. You need to hurry up. It's already hot. We need to make it up the hill to Jonah before it gets hotter."

"You do know the golden boy is not going to be hospitable," Clifford said, taking the seat beside her. "He's not going to welcome you with open arms and take you in. In fact, we will be lucky if he doesn't send a posse to chase us away from here."

"Then you don't know Jonah. He would never turn away his own blood."

"Still carrying a torch for him, aren't you?"

"Jonah is a real man. He doesn't hold grudges, like you. Now are we going?"

Clifford stood up abruptly, sending the chair into a tilting spin. "Yes, damn you. We're going. If only to prove to you how wrong you are about him."

With a freshly baked gateau from Emeline, by mid morning they were on their way to La Pointe. Clifford and Roger knew their visit would not be welcomed. It was all part of their stratagem. The hostile greeting they were expecting would serve to sow the seeds of doubts they had already planted.

As they crested the hill and caught sight of the well-built houses and neatly manicured yards, the grin on Lucinda's face grew.

The sound of galloping horses followed by the sight of rifle-toting men wiped the widening grin from her face. Clifford slyly watched her as she coughed, blinking to clear her vision as the group of men came to an abrupt stop, surrounding them in a cloud of dust.

Jonah was at the center of the group, and the stern, hard look on his face was far from welcoming. He cocked the trigger and aimed his rifle at them, the others in his group following suit.

"Turn around and get off of my property. You're not welcome here,"

"Please, you're scaring the children," Solange cried, grouping them around her as they began to whimper.

"Then you should not have brought them here. I am not going to say this again. Get off my property."

Clifford and Roger stepped forward, their hands raised and visible. "You're not going to shoot unarmed men in the presence of their families, now are you?" Clifford asked tauntingly.

"Don't tempt me, Clifford," Jonah replied.

"We've come to share the good life you so obviously found here. Since we're of the same blood, we thought for sure you would welcome us." He glanced around at the group of men and then purposely let his eyes rest on Lucinda.

"You thought wrong."

Clifford smirked and looked at Roger. "We're not welcomed here, Roger. What should we do?"

Before Roger could respond, a shot was fired on the ground near their feet, causing a large plume of dust. The women and children screamed.

"That's the only warning you're going to get. The next shot is going to ricochet right up your asses. You heard the man—get off of his property or we will carry your carcasses off. You've got three seconds to start moving." Raphael's tone posed no option.

Clifford nodded to Roger, conveying silently that their mission had been completed. They rejoined the women in the wagon. Solange and the children were crying. Lucinda looked stupefied.

"This is not over, Jonah," Roger said menacingly. You're going to have to watch your back from now on. You will never know when we're going to strike."

Jonah and the others kept silent, their rifles still trained on them.

As the wagon pulled away, Lucinda broke her stupor and cried out, "Why, Jonah? When did you become so hard and unfeeling?"

Clifford's grin was filled with mirth as they rode away from La Pointe.

"Oh my God! What happened?" Emeline exclaimed when she saw the sad looks on their faces.

"Those bad men shot at us, and made Mommy and Lucinda cry," Oswald, Solange's five-year-old, piped up.

"What bad men?" Emeline asked, wiping the tears off his cheeks. "There aren't any bad men up here."

"Yes there is." Jacques, Lucinda's son, and Olie, Solange's eight-year-old, simultaneously nodded.

"What the dickens are they talking about?" Henri boomed. "Who shot at you?"

"It's okay really," Clifford feigned. "They were not expecting us, and we shouldn't have taken the liberty to just go on up there. We should have known from our experiences back in Toulon that they are sometimes quite irrational. Jonah has always had an explosive, dangerous temper. Why, he once beat me almost to death just for talking to Catherine. You remember that time, Roger? I had so many broken bones." He shook his head sadly, letting his voice trail off.

"Yeah, I remember," Roger agreed. "He and his band of cohorts up there were always in trouble with the gendarmes. That's why the old man arranged to have the whole group of them leave Toulon and come here. He was afraid Jonah would end up in the gallows."

"Oh Lord!" Emeline placed her hands to her mouth. "We have made friends with terrible people. What kind of men would shoot at women and children? We have slept in the same house with them, eaten our meals with them."

"Wait a minute," Henri interjected. "If they are as bad as you say, why did you choose to come here in search of them?"

"Because our living conditions had become unbearable in Toulon. In desperation, we came, hoping they had changed." Roger shrugged. "I see now we have made a terrible mistake."

"I don't believe you," Henri said flatly. "I have spent years with those people at La Pointe, and nothing you said sounds credible from my experiences."

"But Henri, they shot at them," Emeline said incredulously.

"Did you see them do it? How do you know they're telling the truth? Before I side with anyone, I am going up there to have a talk with Jonah myself."

Henri reached for his hat and headed out the door.

"You need to get them out of your house, Henri. They are dangerous."

"They are saying the same things about you, Jonah. How do I know who is telling me the truth?"

"Henri." Jonah looked directly into the older man's eyes. "You have known me for more than ten years. In that time, have you ever known me to be dishonest or deceitful?"

"No, I haven't," Henri conceded.

"And I am being straight with you now. You must expel them from your property."

"I don't know how I am going to do that. Emeline is entranced with those children, and she already believes the lies they are saying about you."

The two men sat for a long time as Jonah filled him in on the family's history.

"I am sorry, but as long as they are there, we will not be joining you for Sunday suppers."

Henri nodded sadly. "I will find a way to get rid of them."

"We can help you; just say the word."

"Yes, I know, but it's a delicate matter with Emeline's emotions. Just promise me you will be here when I need you."

Days drifted into months, and still Henri had not succeeded in ousting his unwanted houseguests. Solange remained likeable, but with each passing day the others revealed more of their malevolent ways. Even the animals shied away.

He had told them several times they needed to find someplace else to live. He had even gone so far as to threaten to call the gendarmes. Each time he had done so, he and Emeline had engaged in terrible arguments. Without question, he knew she was duped. Her self-imposed blinders had totally obscured her vision, and she adamantly fought against him in defense of her houseguests. He hated arguing with her, so without fully realizing it himself, he began to relent. He still missed his good friends at La Pointe, and occasionally he took a ride up the hill to visit with them, but it was not the same.

The months wore on and the rainy season begun. It was the wettest November that he could remember, and the old house sprung additional leaks from the continuous heavy rains. Buckets and pans were placed all over the floor to catch the constant drips.

"I am going to have to go up on the roof on the first dry day to fix some of those leaks," he mentioned one evening at supper.

"We will go with you to help," Clifford volunteered.

Over the course of days, the rain gradually subsided. Then one morning the sun rose brightly. Henri retrieved the ladder from the shed and whistling softly, he made his way onto the roof. He was not happy, but he had made his peace with the situation. Emeline was his life, and since the children had come, she was full of life. He hated when they quarreled, and they no longer did now that he had acquiesced.

He had been up on the roof for at least an hour when he looked up and saw Clifford and Roger getting off the ladder.

"We promised to help you. Why didn't you tell us you were coming up here?" Roger asked.

"Because I am capable of fixing my own roof without help," Henri replied, not bothering to look at them.

"Well, we're here. Show us what to do," Clifford said.

Henri stood up, his back aching from bending over.

"Okay. You see that section over there? There's a hole under the galvanize. Clear away the loose section of the galvanize so I can get leeway to the hole to fix it."

They nodded and headed in the opposite direction. Glad to be rid of them, he continued hammering the new boards in place. He was almost finished. Good thing too because the sun was getter hotter. Emeline was cooking his favorite pigeon peas soup, and he loved the little cornmeal dumplings she made. Every so often the enticing aroma drifted toward the roof, making his mouth water and his belly growl.

His thoughts were on a nice hot bowl of soup when Roger called out to him, "Can you come over here? We are having trouble lifting the galvanize."

Annoyed, Henri put the hammer down and made his way across the sun-glistened roof. "Why are you so close to the edge? The area I showed you is higher up," he said as he neared them.

"We know," Clifford said calmly, "but we can't push you off the roof from that spot. Today is the day you meet your maker, old man."

Henri never had a chance to defend himself. Roger came at him at full speed and violently shoved him off the roof onto the rocks below.

CHAPTER 20

Clifford looked over the edge at Henri's broken body and muttered, "Sorry, old man, but you were getting in the way of progress." Then he looked at Roger and smiled. "Shall we go down now and deliver the grim news?"

"Yeah, let's go tell the old crone that her Henri won't be eating any more soup." Roger's grin was pure evil.

They walked into the house and headed for the kitchen, their pretentious faces somber.

"Oh God, Oh God! My Henri." Emeline's piteous bawling could be heard for miles as Solange rocked her.

"I am so sorry, Emeline. I didn't know that part of the roof was still wet," Clifford said, wiping tears from his eyes. "He slipped and we tried our best to catch him, but we were just not fast enough."

"Don't worry, we will take good care of you, Emeline," Roger soothed. "We will never leave you alone."

Jonah's gut instinct told him Henri's death was not an accident, and he blamed himself. It was because of him that his good, trusting friends had taken in Clifford and Roger. On the day of the burial, he could stand it no more as he watched Clifford's pretentious performance, and his temper got the better of him.

He walked up to the coffin where Clifford stood and collared him, nearly pushing him backward onto the corpse.

"You have everybody fooled, but I am too familiar with those crocodile tears to fall for them. I swear if I find out you are responsible for Henri's death, I will kill you myself."

"Stop it, Jonah!" Emeline cried. "Have you no respect for my husband's body? Get out of my house, you and all your followers. Today I see for myself what they have been trying to tell me for so long. You are a dangerous, devious man, and you are no longer welcome here. Now go before I have Clifford and Roger throw you out."

Shaking with vexation and embarrassed by his actions, Jonah bowed his head and quietly left the burial. Solemnly, Catherine and the others followed him.

It was times like these when Loretta regretted being clairvoyant, times when the knowing made her feel helpless, times when she wished she had the additional ability to change things. She was exhausted, and it showed. She knew she worried Paul, and her sweet husband did his best to empathize, but he was incapable of easing her angst.

In her spirit she was disturbed by visions. In her dreams she was haunted. Henri's spirit was restless, and he roamed her sleeping hours seeking restitution. Even in bright daylight, his specter pursued her. She was privy to knowledge she dared not share with anyone, in particular Jonah, for with certainty he would act on his vow to kill Clifford. She yearned to reach out to Emeline, to break her dense stupor and warn her of the imminent dangers she faced of losing everything including her life, but the shroud they had placed around her was impenetrable. Trying to reach her would further endanger everyone else.

Clifford and Roger's arrival on St. Barth heralded an epoch of perilous times. The quandaries they would cause would have a daunting impact on them all. The fingers of trouble would reach out to touch future generations, and despite having the knowledge, Loretta was powerless to change it.

"We've prepared everything for you. You need only to sign it as you promised," Clifford said, handing the document and pen to Emeline.

Emeline put the soup ladle down on the table and took the document from Clifford. She missed Henri so much that on Saturdays she still cooked his favorite pigeon peas soup as she had done for years. She could smell him in the kitchen with her, and it comforted her. At night she held his pillow and cried, and she could swear she felt his hands in her hair. Had it not been for the children, she would have surely lost her mind.

"I don't know if I am ready to sign this."

"Come," Roger replied, taking her by the arm. "Let's sit down and go over this again." He propelled her to the kitchen table and forced her to sit. "For the last year we have been the only ones taking care of you. I think we were divinely sent to you, seeing how Henri died within the year of our arrival." He shook his head for emphasis. "What would you have ever done without us?"

"But If I sign all the parcels over to you, I will be leaving nothing for my children."

Roger snorted. "You mean the same two children who could not even take the time and come back for their father's funeral? They have no use for you, Emeline. They've already forgotten about you and St. Barth."

"They sent word saying that they did not have the money for a voyage, and they promised they would come soon," Emeline responded in her children's defense.

"So where are they?" Roger said, spreading his hands wide. "Listen to me. If they really wanted to come back, they would have found a way."

Clifford took over. "Oh, Emeline. The four little children you have living with you now, they're your future. They love and adore you. You're their *grandmere*. Do it for them. Sign the document ensuring their future here on St. Barth. They will stay with you. We all will. Oh no, don't cry, Emeline," he said soothingly, wiping her tears. "You know you're doing the right thing."

Emeline looked at both men, tears brimming over her wrinkly blue eyes. With trembling fingers, she took the pen, and with her son and daughter weighing heavily on her mind, she signed away all ten parcels to Clifford and Roger Dusant.

"Good work, Clifford, we did it!" Roger slapped Clifford's back in glee later that evening. "Told you we could. Hell, it was as easy as taking sweets from a child. You know, this is only the beginning. One of these days we're going to own this entire hill, including the untouchable La Pointe." Roger looked at Clifford, mimicking reverence. "We're going to build houses and shops and make tons of money, starting with these ten parcels. The question is, what are we going to do with the old woman now that she has become dispensable?"

"Oh, she's not useless yet," Clifford replied. "She cooks, cleans, and watches the children, both she and Solange. If we had to wait on my sorry excuse for a wife, we'd starve and be living in filth. No, let her live out her days of usefulness. But I like your idea of owning La Pointe." He rolled his right hand into a fist and slapped it into his left. "That would be the ultimate coup. It would crush the golden boy once and for all."

When Emeline died a few months later, Catherine was filled with guilt and grief. She regretted not having tried harder to reach out to Emeline, and she was saddened that she could not attend the funeral, but she would not defile Emeline's memory by provoking a scene.

Feeling Emeline's children had been purposely kept away so Clifford and Roger could take possession of the land, and unaware that Emeline had already signed it over, Catherine made it her mission to send them word of their mother's death. She and Jonah escorted them to their homestead two months later, where they were hostilely greeted and refused entry. Deeply shaken, they summoned the gendarme, who demanded that Clifford and Roger produce the legal document they alleged Emeline had signed relinquishing her legal rights. Lucinda tauntingly danced and waved the deed in Jonah's face before handing it over the gendarme, who after thoroughly examining it, woefully shook his head and announced that it was, in fact, an authentic document.

#

There's not a decent store in this pathetic place to buy a good pair of shoes," Lucinda whined.

"You don't need another pair of shoes, you already have too much." Clifford uttered a series of curse words in annoyance. His hands were laden with her purchases. He was tired and sweaty, and he wanted to get home before dark.

He should never have agreed to bring her to Gustavia, but she had been an ardent lover the night after she shook the deed in Jonah's face. He too had been pumped by their coup. It had resulted in a night of explosive passion, and in its throes, she had extracted the promise of a shopping spree. She hadn't let him forget it. She'd whispered the naughtiest pleasures of an encore in his ears, but only after the trip to Gustavia.

"We need to get started up the hill before darkness falls." Clifford determinedly headed in the direction of the wagon.

"My feet hurt," Lucinda wailed. She sat on a stone wall and rubbed her ankles.

"We don't have time, Lucinda!"

Reluctantly, she stood. "The clouds are making up. It's going to rain, and we'll get soaked."

"Serves you right for dawdling all morning; I told you to hurry up and—"

"Clifford, look! There's Clara's boardinghouse. Why can't we stay there for the night?"

Clifford looked at the yellow and white sign just up ahead. He didn't relish riding back up the hill either, and it had started to thunder. He knew Raphael was married to Clara, the owner. He had seen the woman before in Gustavia. She was prim and proper with not a hair out of place. How the hell she had hooked with a loser like Raphael was beyond his conception. He'd heard that her boardinghouse was the finest in St. Barth, but in light of her entanglement with Raphael, he'd stayed away. He glanced at the clouds as a clap of thunder rolled. With her decorousness, surely she wouldn't be brash.

"Clifford, it's lightning! Let's go to the boardinghouse."

"Let's go," Clifford conceded.

Not bothering to clang the bell, they hurried through the door as a loud bolt of thunder crackled.

Bella was polishing the parlor table. "Lawd, send help. This go be stinging nettle in here today," she mumbled in a singsong voice, straightening up to face them.

Clifford's tone was commanding. "Go call your master; we need a room."

"Meh what? Nobody ain't tell this white boy that slavery done over?" Bella folded her arms over her bosom and glared at him.

"Look, I don't have time to waste. Call your master."

"Bella is my family, Mr. Dusant. She is not a slave. I take offense at the way you are addressing her."

Clara had entered the room so quietly that they had not been aware of her presence. "Furthermore, you're not welcome in my home, so kindly turn around and go back out the door."

Lucinda gave an insulted shriek. Clifford kept his stance. "This is a business establishment. You are compelled to provide service despite your prejudices against us." He purposely looked around. "Where is the old goat anyway?"

Clara reached behind her, opened a drawer, and retrieved a pistol. She cocked it, pointing it directly at them. "Perhaps you didn't hear me when I asked you politely to leave. Now I am warning you to get your asses out of my house."

"But there's a storm!" Lucinda cried.

"Then you'd better hurry to one of the other boardinghouses." Clara advanced on them, and glaring at her, they backed out the door.

As Clifford and Lucinda hurried away to find shelter from the storm, Clifford muttered, "One of these days I am going to make them all pay for their transgressions."

#

Like the sand trickling slowly through the delicate mahogany-cased hourglass that perpetually sat on Jonah's oak chest, time moved on. More people settled and built homes amid Jonah and Clifford on the steep hills of La Pointe. As the population increased, a new generation of Dusants matured and came of age, and the lines that defined the feud became opaquely obscured among the younger generation. Jonah did not try to prevent them from socializing, although he made it clear that Clifford, Lucinda, and Roger remained unwelcome at La Pointe.

Marcel, being Jonah's eldest son, felt a sense of duty to be ever-vigilant at protecting his birthright. He tolerated Lenia, Oswald, and Olie, but he disliked Jacques who had grown to be the spitting replica of his father, Clifford.

Faithfully every year, Jonah continued his pilgrimage to Toulon. As his children grew, he insisted they accompany him so they could know and appreciate the motherland. The three oldest, Marcel, Francois, and Sarah, were avid sailors. To Catherine's dismay, Sarah was the one who was most passionate about the sea. Her only daughter was an outrageous tomboy who could handle the helm of a vessel and keep up with her brothers.

To Clifford's delight, Jacques was courting Julie Ann, Alphonse's daughter. His son's affiliation with the family was the key to infiltrating them. While he persuaded Jacques to ask for the girl's hand, he secretly plotted how he could use the nuptials to his advantage.

He and Roger had continued to add ill-gotten land to their mounting cache. Through their sleazy dealings, they had become affluent in real estate holdings. In the beginning, their neighbors had been susceptible to their false-hearted flattery, making it easy for them to take advantage. Now they were circumspect, and to a degree, intimidated by Clifford and Roger.

Thanks to Solange's supplications, Roger eventually eased up on his unscrupulous ways, content with his now-comfortable lifestyle, but the more Clifford and Lucinda acquired, the greedier they became.

Since the day Jonah had turned them away from La Pointe, Lucinda had become vengeful. She goaded Clifford on in his quest to purloin La Pointe from Jonah, and so, while they kept a wide berth from La Pointe, they watched and waited.

CHAPTER 21

"Well, look at you, all domesticated and contented." Loretta's hands froze on the cast-iron skillet she was scrubbing. Could it be? Slowly she turned and looked into the brown eyes of a gypsy. She gasped as she took in the white, frilly blouse and the long, colorful skirt. Her eyes perused the large, dangling earrings, the deeply tanned, freckled skin, and then the smiling face that so resembled her own.

"Oh my God! Philar, is it really you, or am I seeing a vision?"

Trembling, Loretta came forward to touch her sister's face, and then embracing her, she cried with joy. But then anger overtook her, and she pushed Philar away.

"I should put you over my knee and spank you for all the misery you put me through. You missed my wedding, the birth of my children. Philar, you've missed out on my life," she cried.

"No, I haven't," Philar answered softly. "I came back several times and observed you from afar. Don't look so surprised. You knew I was here. You felt it in here." She took Loretta's hand and placed it on her chest. "I stayed away because I knew seeing me and then watching me leave again would be too hurtful."

"That's nonsense and you know it," Loretta retorted. "You put Alphonse and me through unnecessary suffering. You cheated your nephew and nieces out of knowing you. Now look at you. You look like a gypsy." Loretta ran her hand through her hair and agitatedly sat at the kitchen table.

Philar took a seat beside Loretta, and reached for her hands. Her voice was soft and soothing when she said, "I know them." She chuckled. "It's funny how your Manuel is as serious as Alphonse, and Loren is just like you. Philarine is my image. For her sake I hope she turns out more like you. I also know Julie Ann. She looks just like Alphonse. Do any of them have the gift?"

Despite her anger, Loretta was so happy to see her sister that she began to relax. "I don't know about Julie Ann, but both my girls do."

"Don't do like Mama did; don't make them repress it because it only makes it harder to cope."

Ignoring her statement, Loretta asked, "How did you get in here unnoticed?"

Philar laughed; the sound reverberated in the quiet room. "I am a gypsy, remember? We are crafty and shrewd. Paul and Manuel are visiting Josiah in St. Jean, and your girls are up at Marie's house. See? I did my homework," she said lightly, the impish smile Loretta knew so well playing on her face.

"How is Jaime?"

Philar's smile brightened, "He's wonderful and sexy. What?" she exclaimed. "Don't tell me you're still prudish?"

Ignoring her gibe, Loretta touched her hand softly. "Philar, I am sensing that there's something else. What is it? Are you okay?"

Philar got up and meandered around the room, stopping at the family portrait on the wall. She let her hands brush across it. "That's a lovely portrait," she muttered. Sitting back down, she said, "Loretta, I do not regret my choices. I am happy with the life I have chosen, so put your mind at ease. There are no worries there. But there is another reason I am here, and it has to do with Jonah's daughter, Sarah."

Startled, Loretta asked, "You know where she is? Jonah and Catherine have been out of their minds with worry. She's been missing for months. I sense she is alive, but I keep seeing the sea."

"She's with Nicholas on the *Santa Elena*. They're in love. They want to be married."

"Oh, so it's Jaime's boy that has caused all this trouble. Jonah only knew that she met a boy while sailing and lost all her good sense. He forbade her to see him, and she ran away. You must bring her home, Philar. Her parents are sick with worry."

"That's why I'm here, but it's not as simple as that. She's pregnant."

"Oh, Lord," Loretta groaned. "Jonah is going to have conniptions, and poor Catherine."

"Still, she needs her mother. God knows I am not capable of mothering anybody. I am heading up there to speak with Jonah and Catherine. They need to understand that she loves Nicholas. Keeping her away from him will only serve to antagonize her."

What are you suggesting? That she marry Nicholas and wander the seas with him? Jonah will never agree to that."

"I know, and I am trying to do the right thing here. I dread it, but I need to start heading up there."

"Are you going to see Alphonse?"

"If I have time, I have to get back to the *Santa Elena*. I left them in Renata's charge." She winked and laughed mischievously, the light sound vibrating through the quiet room. "We have to keep an eye on them 'cause they're going at each other like rabbits."

"Philar!" Loretta chided.

"Oh Loretta, life is too short not to enjoy a bit of humor." Standing, Philar slipped her arms around Loretta's waist. "I promise not to stay away too long again, okay?"

Loretta locked her in an embrace. The sisters hugged for a long time and then having no adequate words to say good-bye, Philar slipped silently out the back door.

With vigorous movements of her upper arm, Catherine tried to swipe at the tears that were constantly threatening to overflow. She was leaning over the wash basin, scrubbing one of Jonah's pantaloons, her hands elbow-deep in suds. The mid-afternoon sun was dancing in the yard, parching the hibiscus trees that had proudly sported bright red and orange blooms earlier in the day. Now the pretty flowers had begun to wilt, succumbing to the sun's unrelenting heat.

Her aggravated effort only served to make her eyes sting as the sweat pooling on her forehead seeped into them. Murmuring with frustration, she wiped her hands and dabbed at them with the collar of her blouse. She could hear the happy antics of her two younger sons in the parlor as they bantered over a card game. Normally it brought her joy to listen to them. Today it only reminded her of the empty hollowness in her heart. Her daughter was missing.

In a sudden fit of ire, Catherine lifted the washboard from the basin and flung it across the yard, sending spatters of sudsy water scattering. Putting her head down on the rim of the basin, she cried, emptying this fresh vestige of tears.

It was the not knowing that tormented her, and the fact that she had begged Jonah not to be so hard on the girl. Sarah was young and impressionable, and willful as well. The more her father had forbidden her from seeing the boy, the more determined she had been to defy him.

Catherine was so lost in her misery that she didn't immediately feel the hand on her shoulder. The subtle chime of bangles, and the sweet, unfamiliar perfume didn't register right away.

Finally sensing she was not alone and startled by the strangeness, she turned and looked into soulful, brown eyes.

"Philar?"

Philar put a finger to her lips to quiet her. "Yes, it's me."

"How did you get in here past the boys?"

Philar smiled. "That seems to be the question of the day. Let's go find Jonah," she said, gently lifting Catherine from her knees. "Stop worrying; Sarah is fine. She's on the *Santa Elena,* and she wants to come home, but I must speak with Jonah first."

Catherine's heart started beating faster as her mind assimilated Philar's words. Sarah was alive and well, but it would be foolhardy to involve Jonah at this point.

"Wait!" She clutched Philar's arm. "Take me to Sarah. Leave Jonah out of this. She will listen to me, but if her father is there, she will be obstinate."

Catherine could see Philar's hesitancy. "Please, Philar!"

"Okay, let's go."

"Wait, I have to tell the boys I am stepping out."

She was back quickly, and together the two women left La Pointe.

Catherine followed Philar through a dense area where the catch and keep bushes were thick, their thorny branches reaching out to scrape her bare arms. She didn't feel the sting of the scratches, nor did she pay any mind to the sweat pooling down her face and back. Her mind was steadfast on getting to her daughter.

Amid the brush, they came to a heavily shaded flamboyant tree where a brown stallion was tied, lazily grazing on grass.

Philar helped Catherine mount the stallion and then climbed up in front of her. "Hold on tightly. We're headed down the steepest, rockiest part of the hill."

Catherine only nodded as she slipped her arms securely around Philar's slender waist.

They rode through desolate, stark paths across the island and then down the perilous cliffs of Flamands. Catherine soon realized she would not be returning home today. She wondered what Jonah would do when he found her missing, and she steeled herself against the pain she knew she would cause him.

Night had fallen when they finally got into a rowboat. For the first time, Catherine wondered about her hasty decision. No one knew her whereabouts. She had not seen Philar in years. Her characteristics were foreign from the woman she had once known, and she had clandestinely sneaked into the house. She could easily dispose of her in the turbulent waters surrounding them. Trying to calm her troubled mind, she reminded herself that Philar had no reason to want to harm her.

"There's something you need to know before you see Sarah."

Up until now they had been preoccupied with the journey and had barely spoken. Now as Philar rowed the boat toward the darkened silhouette of the *Santa Elena,* her attention was turned fully on Catherine.

"You said she was fine."

"And she is," Philar replied, "but she's pregnant."

Oh God!," Catherine cried out. "It's all that boy's fault. He filled her head with trickery, lured her into his vagabond ways."

"Now hold on here." Philar's voice was soothing but firm. "There are two people involved. It's not all Nicholas's fault, and he's not a bad boy. He's steadfast and stalwart, and he adores Sarah. He wants to marry her."

"And take her where?" Catherine retorted angrily. "Out here on this perilous sea, to live like a vagrant?" She was shaking with vexation. "How could this happen to my little girl?"

"She's not a little girl, Catherine. She's clever and wise beyond her years. She doesn't want to stay on the *Santa Elena*. She needs you, but she's afraid of your reaction, in particular her father's. She asked me to come and speak with you. She wants to come home, but she's determined that she will not give up Nicholas. If you want to keep your daughter, you and Jonah will have to accept that Nicholas and the child are part of her life now."

Catherine did not reply. She knew she would do whatever was necessary for the well-being of her daughter, even if it meant accepting Nicholas into their lives. It was Jonah who worried her. His mulish rejection would lead to a terrifying impasse if she could not find a way to break through to him.

"We're here, Catherine."

A large splash in the darkened water behind Catherine startled her, and she stood too quickly, causing the rowboat to bob. Feeling dizzy she held on to Philar's arm to steady herself.

"Finally, I was beginning to worry," a strong masculine voice boomed. "I am pleased to make your acquaintance, Madame Dusant," Jaime said, reaching for her hand to help her into the vessel.

Having been confined to her cabin years ago when they had first encountered him on the sea, Catherine had never met the Spaniard. The image she had conjured of him was not far from the imposing stature who now stood before her. Even in the darkness she could sense his arrogance.

"Hello, Captain," she replied curtly. "Can you please take me directly to my daughter?"

"She is waiting for you in the galley," Jaime replied just as tersely.

"Go ahead and take her to Sarah. I will secure the rowboat," Philar volunteered.

Nodding at Philar, Jaime turned to Catherine. "Please come this way."

Catherine followed Jaime down the wooden planks toward the starboard side, passing gun-toting, gruff-looking men who brazenly eyed her. She could hear music and rowdy laughter coming from the opposite side of the vessel. The light from the half-moon cast ominous shadows in the murky crevices of the deck, and she shuddered. She heard muttered profanity and smelled the pungent odor of overpowering cigars as they passed an open window, and for the second time she wondered at the wisdom of her impromptu decision to undertake this venture without Jonah. She wondered too about Philar. How could she have so easily adapted to this itinerant lifestyle? She seemed so at ease.

They finally stopped at a door midway of a long, damp corridor.

"Aye, Captain." A thin, scruffy man with a patch over his left eye greeted Jaime, his grin revealing rotted front teeth as he slinked away from the door to allow them entry. "They're in there," he said. Then conspiringly, he leaned closer to Jaime. "Renata is landing them hell."

"Eavesdropping again, Pedro?"

"No sir," he quickly replied, fidgeting as he backed away. "Just going 'bout my business."

"Then be bout your buisness. Next time I catch you, you will walk the plank."

"Oh no, Captain, not the plank!" Pedro yelled, scurrying away.

Jaime laughed at the man's clumsy dash down the corridor, and then he opened the door.

"Mama" Sarah cried, flinging herself into her mother's arms.

Catherine felt her knees go weak with relief. She was cognizant of the others in the room, but she didn't care as she held her daughter tightly, savoring her familiar smell.

Sarah finally pulled away, and still holding her mother's hand, she pulled her forward.

"Mama, this is Nicholas."

Loosing Catherine's hand, Sarah took hold of Nicholas's arm.

"Mama, I love him. We want to be married." She gently touched her belly. "We're going to have a baby."

Unwillingly the tears sprung from Catherine's eyes. She finally allowed herself to take a look at the young man who stood protectively next to her daughter. Aside from the dour look on his face, he was handsome, tall, and muscular with thick, curly black hair. He was also much older than Sarah, and Catherine fought hard to keep her emotions under control. She wanted to reach out and slap him for the turmoil he was causing her family.

A pretty, full-figured woman stood beside him, cagily watching. Stepping forward, she said, "Hello, Madame Dusant. I am Renata. This monkey here seems to have swallowed his tongue." The woman thrust Nicholas frontward. "Where are your manners, boy? Introduce yourself properly and wipe that look off your face before I smack you."

Giving Renata a dogged look, Nicolas offered his hand to Catherine. "Pleased to make your acquaintance, Madame." Then he stepped back and reclaimed his position next to Sarah.

Again, Sarah held onto his arm. "I want to come home, Mama. I don't want to have my baby here, but Nicholas must be welcomed to visit me, and I know Papa will not allow it."

Catherine felt a myriad of emotions. She found herself saying words that resounded in her head from another time in the voice of her own mother.

"Leave your father to me. I will make him understand."

"You just let your mother walk out the door, not caring?" Jonah's voice blared at his two younger sons. Marcel and Francois stood next to their father, their faces creased with worry.

"She said she was stepping out," Charles replied. "We thought she was going to see Tante Marie, Yvette, or Loretta."

Noting his father's growing anger, Marcel turned and faced the small group that had gathered. "According to my brothers, my mother left before noon. It's almost six o'clock. You're sure none of you have seen her?"

Everyone turned to look at each other, but no one could say they had seen Catherine.

"Let's get the horses and start checking the track roads. I don't trust those bastards down the hill," Pierre said, moving in the direction of the horses.

"We have to hurry. Darkness is falling," Alphonse agreed, following closely behind Pierre.

"Wait!" Loretta cried out. "She left with Philar."

"What?" The chorus of voices simultaneously reacted.

"Loretta, Philar has not been here in years," Paul said hesitantly.

"She was here today. She sneaked into the house this morning. I thought I was seeing a vision."

"Philar was here, and you said nothing to me? Don't you think I had a right to know, Loretta?" The offended look on Alphonse's face was obvious.

"Give her a chance to finish speaking, Alphonse," Paul interjected. "Catherine is missing. There are more pressing matters at hand."

"I asked her about seeing you, Alphonse. She said she would if there was time, but she had come on a more pressing mission." Loretta diverted her eyes from Alphonse and looked at Jonah, "Sarah is on the *Santa Elena*. It is Jaime's boy with whom she ran away. Philar came to speak with you and Catherine because Sarah wants to come home, but she is afraid of you."

Jonah sat down and ran his hands through his hair. "Why didn't you say something sooner, Loretta?"

Loretta raised her chin defiantly. "I wanted to give Catherine a good lead ahead of you. Had you gone with her, there would be no success in getting Sarah home. Your pride would have gotten in the way." She stopped and cleared the lump from her throat. "I know you're angry with me, but Catherine will be fine. She will do what's necessary to bring her daughter home."

The tension in the room was thick. With bated breath, everyone looked at Jonah. He rose slowly from the chair, his jaws were visibly tense. "How dare you presume to know what's best for my wife and my daughter? I am going to tear that boy apart limb from limb. We should have let him die of the fever, but thanks to Philar, he lived to cause me trouble."

Loretta held his gaze coolly. "Philar saved all our lives that day, and you know it."

"Do you know where the *Santa Elena* is docked?"

"No, but I know Catherine is unharmed."

"Why? Because your so-called visions told you?" Jonah snapped sarcastically.

"I will not permit you to speak to my wife in that tone, Jonah," Paul said warningly.

"Your wife let my wife go unattended to parts unknown with her wayward sister. For all I know, she and that Spaniard conspired to kidnap Catherine. If anything happens to her, I swear—"Jonah!" Marie stepped forward. "I know my sister, and I am positive Philar did not persuade her to go without you. That was Catherine's doing." She took a deep breath. "And I understand Loretta's delay in telling you. I would have done the same."

Jonah hit the wall so hard that the room vibrated. "Get out of my house. All of you."

For a moment they remained stock-still. Then Marcel took the lead and nudged his brothers toward the door. The others followed quietly.

Like sails that had lost their zest in the absence of breeze, Jonah sunk into the nearest chair. "Oh, Catherine," he groaned.

She was his life, the wind that kept his sails aloft. He lived and breathed Catherine. Twenty-five years of marriage and five children had not dimmed his passion. She was as beautiful and desirable as the day he had married her. He knew she thought he was too hard on the children, Sarah in particular. He ran his hands angrily over his face. He had four sons, and none of them could compare to the tribulations of Sarah. Despite her mother's best efforts to defend her, Sarah was willful and deliberate in her actions.

Jonah prayed Loretta was correct, that Catherine would indeed return safely with Sarah in tow. There was only one solution to keep her away from the Spaniard. It entailed taking drastic measures that would terribly upset Catherine, but she would have to understand that his actions were best for the girl.

Catherine spent a sleepless night on the hard bunk in the small confines of the cabin. The room was musty and reeked of stale sweat, but truth be told, she would not have slept if she was in the finest hotel in Paris. Not even the loud, repetitive groaning of the vessel infiltrated her thoughts. Her mind was a whirlwind of worries. She had to get Sarah off this grimy vessel and safely home. She also had to mollify Jonah's temper and somehow make him agreeable to Nicholas's visits, and therein lay her greatest dilemma. She wrestled all night, trying to come up with a plan, and finally toward dawn, she decided not to tell Jonah of Sarah's pregnancy. She knew inevitably he had to know, but she needed time to break it to him.

She glanced at her sleeping daughter lying next to her and lovingly smoothed back a strand of hair from her face. With her features relaxed in sleep, she looked vulnerable, much like the sweet child of infancy. She would have to convince the headstrong young woman not to spitefully spurt the news to her father. The oncoming days would be wrought with vexations, but they would be worth it if she could manage to keep Sarah safe and sound.

A sudden outburst of cusswords halted her thoughts, and she reached for her pocket watch. It was 4:53 a.m. She shook Sarah to awaken her. Philar had said they would start the journey early, and Catherine was ready to take her daughter home.

"Thank God!" Jonah exclaimed when Catherine and Sarah entered the house. He went to his daughter first, carefully inspecting her. "Are you okay?'

"Yes, Papa." Sara's voice was contrite.

"Good, now go to the bedroom. I will deal with you after I talk with your mother."

Jonah waited until he heard the door close, and then sighing deeply, he pulled Catherine into his arms. When he felt comforted enough by her body, he put his hands on her shoulders and pushed her backward so he could look at her face. "Don't you ever, ever put me through this again. I died a thousand times in the last twenty-four hours."

"Where are the boys?"

"They're somewhere on the estate, avoiding me. I haven't been easy to live with lately."

Catherine smiled faintly and took his hand. "Come, let's go outside to the gallery where we can talk privately."

They sat together overlooking the phenomenal view while she related to him everything that had happened. He listened quietly. Finally, she took a deep breath and said, "Sarah wants us to allow Nicholas to visit her. She said they're going to get married, and if we don't allow her to see him, she will run away again."

"Okay."

Catherine whipped her neck around. "What?"

Jonah shrugged. "I don't like it, but what choice is she giving me other than locking her up?"

#

"Hypolite! I wasn't expecting you home until Sunday. Is everything okay?" Marie asked her firstborn son when he bounded through the kitchen door. He had started working for Clara at the age of twelve, so he spent most of his time in Gustavia.

"The flag is up. A gale is coming."

"What are they saying in town? Is it a bad one?"

"Telegrams from the islands down south say it is. I helped Raphael board up the boardinghouse. Luckily they only have three guests. Clara told me to go home so you wouldn't worry."

Marie put down the dish she was wiping and walked outside. Hypolite followed her.

"The sun is shining so brightly. It's hard to believe there's a gale coming."

"The birds, they're gone," Hypolite mumbled in wonderment.

"What did you say?" His mother looked up at him, confused.

"Bella said that if the birds all left, it is a sure sign of a bad gale."

"Well, let's hope that Bella is wrong, okay? I'm glad Clara sent you home. There's plenty to be done before it gets here. Go to the shed and get the boards while I go tell your father and the others. After we're finished securing the house and the animals, we will go up to Jonah and Catherine's and ride it out. There's safety in numbers."

Loretta knew the tempest was coming before Marie knocked on her door. For days she had been dreaming of it. She hadn't said anything, partly because it was irksome to always be a bearer of bad tidings and partly because there was nothing that could be done to prevent an act of God.

When Marie left, she called Loren and Philarine out of the bedroom. "There's a gale coming, and I want you to start securing our belongings while I go get your father and brother. Once everything is secured, we will go up to Catherine and Jonah's, but we need to hurry. It will be here soon."

"It's going to be a bad one, Mama," Loren said. "I saw it in my dreams."

"I did too," Loretta replied, hugging both her daughters. "We will have a grueling night, but you know from your dreams that we will be okay."

By late afternoon, they were all settled in at Jonah and Catherine's house. They were not overly worried. In the years they had lived at La Pointe, they had experienced numerous gales. As darkness fell, they heard the distant echo of conch shells heralding from every direction the onset of the gale. Then the wind gradually increased until its dramatic crescendo engulfed them. It screeched unrelentingly against the walls of the house, demanding entry. The rain fell in noisy spurts, driven by the wind. As the weather worsened, they cowered in a narrow, inner hall. For hours they crouched together. Then the wind stopped. The stillness was eerie.

"It's gone," Philarine whispered.

They untangled themselves and stretched. Warily they ventured out to the gallery.

"Phew, we have never seen a gale like this one before," Paul said.

"What time is it?" Alphonse asked.

Jonah pulled out his stop watch. "It's half past one."

"Look at the trees, they're leafless," Yvette commented.

"We will have a mess to clean up with all those leaves and branches," Pierre inputted.

"It is so calm and clear now. We can see every star," Catherine remarked.

"It's not over. We're in the eye," Loretta said. "It's coming back more furiously than before. We need to go back inside now."

"She's right," Jonah replied. "We're experiencing the full effect. It's right over us."

"What? It can't be any worse than what we just went through," Marie cried.

The wind was back within minutes, whipping mercilessly at everything. They felt the pressure in their ears as they hunkered down, this time holding mattresses atop their heads for protection as the walls popped, and the galvanize groaned, lifted, and flew away. They heard the grunts of the heavy furniture being bullied by the wind. They felt the harsh pellets of rain and the sting of objects grazing their skin, and one by one they lost their grasp on the mattresses.

"Papa, help me," Julie Ann cried when the wind began to pry her loose from her mother's grip. Jonah, Pierre, and Paul held on to Alphonse as he pulled his daughter back to safety. Then they made a human chain, locking arms securely, crying and praying while sitting in a pool of gathering water.

When the wind finally subsided, they looked up into the early dawn sky that had replaced the roof. Slowly they stood up. Dazed, they made their way through the twisted jumble that had once been Jonah and Catherine's house. Mindlessly, they picked up objects as they staggered through the rubble.

Outside it looked as though France's war with Germany had put in an appearance in St. Barth. The landscape was stark, raped of the beauty that had existed only hours before. The trees were leafless, utterly undressed, and left as a castigating sign of the gale's wrath.

None of their homes had escaped unscathed. They had lost the better part of their material possessions. Yet they were thankful. Together they were strong. They would rebuild, and the process would begin immediately.

The advent of this latest hurricane and its devastation would spiral hard economic times for the island. Clara's boardinghouse had survived with minimum damage, but there had been widespread destruction to Gustavia and its port.

St. Jean too had been hit hard. Josiah and his family had spent a harrowing night, barely escaping with their lives. For the second time they sought shelter in La Pointe.

I received an urgent telegram from Father," Jonah told Catherine a few weeks after the hurricane. "He wants me to come to Toulon to settle some estate matters. I am leaving at the end of the week."

"But it's been less than a month since the gale." Catherine's dismay was obvious. "There is still so much to do. Can't it wait for a few more weeks, at least until the gale season is over?"

"No, it's best I leave now. We're already in October, and I would normally sail in January anyway. This way I will be back earlier in the New Year. I am taking Francois and Sarah with me." Jonah kissed the top of Catherine's head and smiled at her reassuringly. "Don't worry, everything is under control here, and I will be back soon, I promise. It won't be a long trip."

"Leave Sarah here with me. Take Marcel instead. I don't want the two of you knocking heads on the sea."

"But she wants to go. She's all excited about seeing her grandpere."

"You spoke to Sarah before telling me?"

Jonah rubbed Catherine's arms reassuringly. "Stop worrying, Sarah and I have been getting along much better. You see how smoothly it went when the Spaniard was here last week. I didn't say an unkind word."

"Nicholas."

"What?"

"The Spaniard, Jonah; his name is Nicholas. You never say his name. Why is that?"

"Oh, Catherine, I don't mean anything by it. I promise to do better, okay? Now, I have to go to Gustavia. I am meeting Raphael. We're preparing the *Louise Catherine* for sailing. He's not coming with me, so you can send for him if you need him."

Later as Jonah trotted down the hill, he thought about the Spaniard, and his anger grew.

I will remember his name all right, when I banish him from my daughter's life once and for all.

"Sarah, why did you agree to sail to Toulon with your father before discussing it with me?" Catherine asked her daughter as they sorted through the brown paper bags of sugar apples they had picked from the trees prior to the gale's arrival.

"Putting the sugar apples in the paper bags was a good idea, Mama," Sarah said, running her fingers over the knobby rinds of the round, green, tropical fruit. "There are enough ripe ones in here to share with everybody."

"Sarah, you're willfully avoiding answering me. You and your father are like oil and water. You are bound to knock heads, and he still doesn't know about the baby. It's not safe for you to be on the sea. Tell him you've changed your mind."

Sarah closed the bag on her lap and turned her attention fully on her mother, "I am feeling fine, Mama. Papa and I have been getting along better, and I really want to see Grandpere. I won't be able to sail next year, and Grandpere is getting up in age. The *Santa Elena* just left for Venezuela, so Nicholas will be gone for a while too."

Lovingly, Sarah touched her mother's arm, her amber colored eyes, replicas of her mother's, glowed with sincerity. "Don't worry. Francois will be with me. He knows about the baby, and he's been overprotective of me since I told him." She chuckled. "A real pain; that's what he's been, but I know he wouldn't let anything happen to me. I promise I will tell Papa myself on the return voyage, just before we arrive back so that you can buffer me from him. I truly want to go, Mama."

"All right then," Catherine sighed. "You were born with gills. I never could keep you from the sea. Just promise me you will control that temper you inherited from your father, and you won't let him rile you into arguing."

"Jonah, I know you are preparing to sail, but I need to speak with you before you leave." Alphonse's hands were shaking uncharacteristically as he stood at Jonah's front door.

Jonah was busy with the final preparations for the voyage, but noting Alphonse's tension, he led him to the gallery. "What is bothering you, Alphonse?"

Alphonse looked down at his hat, his fingers playing with the rim. "Jacques has asked me for Julie Ann's hand. Given the discord between you and his father, I haven't given him my blessings yet, and Julie Ann is miserably upset with me."

Jonah's eyebrows creased into a frown. "That boy is just as pompous as his father."

"I see that for myself, Jonah. I tried to discourage the relationship, but my daughter is in love with him. She is my only child, and I don't want to be estranged from her." His eyes begged Jonah to understand. "They won't be living here at La Pointe, so you wouldn't have to encounter Clifford and Lucinda too often. Of course you will have to see them at the wedding, and I would want you to be there. You're my best friend."

"It seems to me you have already made your decision, Alphonse. I am not pleased with Julie Ann's choice for a husband, but I cherish you and Yvette. Catherine and I will do all we can to help you with the nuptials, and we will be at your side at the wedding. This does not change our longstanding friendship."

Alphonse stood up, relief clearly displayed on his face. Reaching to shake Jonah's hand, he said, "Thank you, Jonah. Your understanding means plenty to me. I will go tell Yvette and Julie Ann to invite the boy back now."

"It is unnatural, that child's fascination with the sea," Clara remarked as she handed Loretta a glass of lime juice.

"Who are you referring to?"

"Catherine's girl, Sarah, she sailed out this morning with her father to Toulon."

"Sarah went with her father?'

"That's what I just said. Are you feeling okay, Loretta? Suddenly, you've turned pale."

"I just have a dizzy spell. If you don't mind, I will go and sit on the gallery in the fresh air for a while."

Loretta walked outside, away from Clara's discerning eyes, and eased herself into one of the rocking chairs. She, Paul, and their son, Manuel, had been in St. Jean for the past month helping Josiah repair the gale damage. Agnes and the girls were still at La Pointe. Loretta had opted to come with Paul, alternating her time between St. Jean and the comfortable boardinghouse. The news of Sarah embarking on the voyage with Jonah had sent chills through her, and she wished she had been at La Pointe to warn Catherine not to let Sarah go. Yet she would have been faced with a familiar quandary. How do you tell your best friend that her husband's persuasive words are filled with trickery?

Please God, just this one time, let my dreams be wrong.

CHAPTER 22

Agnes and Josiah's four daughters were attractive women. Their beauty was the talk of St. Jean, and Josiah had his hands full with the hopeful suitors who flocked at his front gate. He grumbled profusely, for he had yet to see one who was worthy of his daughters' hands. Well, with maybe one exception—Jonah and Catherine's boy, Francois.

Olivia was slender and tall with expressive hazel eyes. Her beauty attracted the best of suitors, but unlike her sisters, she showed no interest in any of the young men who came calling. She'd roll her eyes in distain and retreat to the bedroom should any of them seek her out. She was neither frivolous nor chatty, and he often likened her to Clara. With her analytical nature, she could easily run a successful business given the opportunity. She went after what she wanted, and it seemed her heart was set on Francois.

Faithfully by midday every Sunday, Francois arrived on his horse. Josiah could set his clock by him, and he smiled as he thought of the boy's ritual. He'd come galloping down the road at high speed, slowing the horse to a trot as he approached the gate. After securing the horse, he'd take out his handkerchief and wipe the sweat from his face and neck, covertly sniffing his underarms. Satisfied, he'd pull out the small sash of raison chocolates he bought each week from the General Store across the street from Clara's. It was Olivia's favorite. Then running his hands through his hair, he'd approach the gate.

Amid good-natured teasing from her sisters, Olivia would run out to meet him. They would sit on the gallery for hours laughing and conversing only with their hands. Josiah would look out the window and sigh. Francois was a good boy from a good family, but he was deaf. How could he properly provide for his daughter?

He'd already broached the subject with Olivia. She'd rebutted immediately in support of Francois.

"Don't let his deafness fool you, Papa. Francois is very intelligent. He's strong-minded and resourceful. He's a workhorse. I love him, Papa. We will look after each other."

"He's your cousin."

"Yes, but far enough removed."

Are you sure you love him, or do you just feel sorry for him because of his condition?

"What condition?" she'd replied smartly. "He's perfectly fine as he is."

"He has not asked me for your hand as yet."

"Oh, but he will, Papa," she'd said with a twinkle in her eyes.

Francois thought Olivia was flawless, and he adored her. They were kindred spirits who had been drawn to each other from childhood. She was the one who stood up for him when the other children made fun of him, mimicking his hand signals and calling him a dunce. She was the one who made sure he was in the know and included in all the games and festivities. It was with her prodding and no-nonsense stance that he had perfected his hand signals so that he could socialize and communicate. She was the one who told him that he was handsome and strong and perfect just the way God had made him, and she was his love. With her, he wasn't deaf. He was gifted and skilled, and he could accomplish anything. He sought and cherished her approval, and he could not wait for the day when he was in a position to ask her father for her hand.

#

"I am always glad to see you, but I can't help wondering why you are here so early," Ivan told Jonah on his first night back in Toulon.

"A son can't come to see his father anytime he wants?"

"Yes, but my son appears anxious, which is a clear sign something is wrong."

Jonah didn't answer. He got up and walked over to the counter to pour himself a second glass of sherry. When he was seated again, he said, "Downtown is almost deserted. On my way here from the dock, I overheard several conversations about a world war being imminent."

"Yes, it is. Britain just allied itself with France and Russia, a very sad thing for our already-emaciated economy."

"How are you really faring here, Father?"

Jonah couldn't help but see the frailty of the man who had seemed to be a giant when he was a boy. He noted the cane Ivan was now using. Each time he left now, he wondered if he would see his father again.

"We're doing fine. I prepared well for such a time as this, but you are deliberately avoiding the subject. What brings you here early?"

Jonah looked down at the amber liquid in his glass, and immediately he thought of Catherine's beautiful eyes. He felt guilty for having withheld his true purpose from her, and he knew he would have hell to pay when he returned.

"I am leaving Sarah here with you at the end of this week." He told his father all about the Spaniard and about Sarah's disappearance for months.

Ivan listened quietly and then asked, "Is Catherine in favor of this?"

"She doesn't know."

"I respect your reasons, but I don't think you are doing the right thing. If she truly loves the Spaniard, forcing her to stay here will not change her feelings, and it will only enhance her derision for you, not to mention the predicament it will create between you and Catherine."

"My mind is made up, Father. I am not going to tell her anything. I will just leave before dawn when she is still asleep. I will not permit her to destroy her life with that little vagabond. He says he wants to marry her. The audacity of him to think he can take my daughter to live like a common drifter on the sea! It will never happen as long as I am alive!" Jonah touched his chest passionately. More calmly, he said, "I will come back for her next year. By then she should have come to her senses."

"It's amazing how time can change a man," Ivan remarked. "When you were young, and I forbade you from marrying Catherine, you told me quite brazenly that I could not prevent you from marrying the woman you loved. Thank God you were right, and I was wrong. I am saying this only to offer you perspective. I recommend you change your mind and take Sarah home. It will be a joy for me having her here, but this covert move of yours will backfire on you."

"I will not take her back to that Spaniard!"

"Very well then, just be prepared to deal with the consequences."

The early morning hues of dawn had not reached their peak of beauty when Jonah roused Francois and signed to him to get dress. Jonah waited while he put on his clothes and collected his satchel, and then the two of them went down to the library where Ivan was waiting.

Noting that his sister was nowhere in sight, Francois signed to his father about her whereabouts. Jonah signed back that she was already onboard the *Louise Catherine* with the crew.

The two men bid Ivan good-bye with robust hugs and hurriedly walked down the steep, narrow path through the cliffs to the boatyard. As they neared the yard, Francois's eyes roamed the *Louise Catherine*'s decks for Sarah. He felt unsettled. How could she be onboard the vessel at such an early hour, and why were they leaving so hastily? He touched his father's arm to get his attention and again signed about Sarah.

"She's on the vessel," Jonah signed back.

No sooner had they boarded than the anchors were pulled. Feeling really apprehensive now, Francois searched the entire vessel for Sarah. Not finding her, he made his way to his father at the helm.

"She's not here!" he signed angrily.

"She is staying behind with Grandpere," Jonah signed back.

"You lied to me!"

"Had to be done to protect your sister from the Spaniard."

"Go back!"

"No."

"Go back!" Francois reached for the rudder.

"Stop it!" Jonah wrestled his hands away.

Francois struggled with his father, pushing him hard. Jonah fell, hitting his temple on the side of the counter. Francois spun the rudder swiftly, pointing the vessel back toward Toulon. Jonah regained his footing, blood spurting from the gash on his temple. Again they struggled for control of the rudder. The erratic motion of the vessel alerted the crew, and several men came to Jonah's assistance. They subdued Francois, wrestling him to the ground where he appeared to sit submissively while they tended to the bleeding cut on Jonah's face.

The loud splash drew their attention, and they turned to see Francois frantically swimming in the turbulent waters below.

"Jesus!" Jonah cried. "Go after him before he kills himself!"

Francois woke later to find himself tied to his bunk. His father was standing over him, a bulky gauze covering his right temple. Francois immediately started to struggle against the ropes.

Jonah put a calming hand on his Francois's chest. "Stop fighting me, son," he said sadly. "What I have done is for the best. You don't want Sarah to live a life of misery, do you? Well neither do I. I know you love your sister, but I love her too, and I want the best for her, for all of you. Now if I untie you, will you promise not to dive overboard?"

Francois vehemently shook his head.

"Well then, I guess you will remain tied up for most of the voyage. Let me know when you change your mind." He patted Francois's chest and walked out of the room.

Sarah woke and stretched lazily. She had a wide view of the sea from the high four-poster bed, and she loved that it was the first thing she saw in the morning. As her gazed spanned the glistening sea, something odd gnawed at her subconscious. She closed her eyes and started to doze again. Then she bolted upright. The *Louise Catherine* was missing!

"Grandpere, where is the *Louise Catherine*?" she asked hastily when she rushed into the library.

"Sit down, Sarah," Ivan answered sadly. "There's something I must tell you."

Sarah was profoundly despondent. Weeks had passed, and hourly she relived the dreadful moments of her father's treachery. She loved her grandfather dearly, and she tried not to show the true depth of her pain to protect his feelings. He was old and fragile, and he had always treated her kindly. She knew none of this was his doing, and she knew too that her mother and Francois had been duped as well.

She had to get back to St. Barth and to Nicholas, and daily she plotted her escape, pilfering supplies required for her survival at sea. She needed a vessel sturdy enough to withstand the voyage, and she had already scouted out the one she planned to steal from her grandfather's fleet. She would have to go it alone, but she was not worried. She was strong and healthy despite the pregnancy, and she was an ace at sailing. She needed to leave soon though, before she became too big with child.

Like every experienced mariner, Sarah knew it was bad luck to set sail on a Friday, but she wasn't worried about bad luck when she climbed aboard the vessel on a cold Friday morning. Grandpere had left for Marseille the evening before, and she seized the chance. She wanted to be long gone before he returned. She knew Rose would send word to him the minute she found her missing.

After the first few weeks of rough seas, the weather improved, and Sarah sailed with little trouble. The solitude did not bother her. There was something enchanting about the mystical beauty and terror of the sea, and she had always felt an indescribable kinship with it. She had plenty of time to think, and she thought often about her mother and how upset she would be with her father. She thought about Francois and how he must have felt when he realized their father was leaving without her. She searched her heart, and there she found forgiveness for her father. He had done what he believed was right to protect her, and somehow she would find a way to make amends with him. She thought about St. Barth, the exquisite, little island of her birth, and how much she missed it. But mostly she thought about her unborn child and his father. She couldn't explain it; she knew it was a boy. She yearned to see her child and to hold Nicholas in her arms.

The sea remained calm and the weather clear as she entered the lower Caribbean Sea, and she breathed a sigh of relief. She was almost home.

She didn't see the rogue wave until it was almost on top of her. There was little she could do but hold her growing belly and brace herself.

The silhouette of a vessel far out on the horizon caught Catherine's attention as she crossed the backyard. *Could it be the Louise Catherine already?*

Quickly she went into the house to get the telescope. She placed it to her right eye, squinting her left eye for a clearer view. "It is *the Louise Catherine!*" Going back into the house, she called out to her sons, "The *Louise Catherine* is coming in. I want to go down to Gustavia to meet it. Which one of you is coming with me?"

"I will," Charles responded.

"I think we should all go," Marcel said, pulling Victor off the sofa. "Papa is going to need help getting the supplies off the vessel. I will go and hitch the horses to the wagon."

Raphael, Clara, and Olivia were already on the wharf waiting for the vessel to drop anchor by the time Catherine and her sons arrived. Catherine could barely stand still. She was so anxious to see Sarah. She'd worried about her the whole time they'd been gone, and she wondered about Jonah's reaction when she had told him about the baby. Sarah had said she would tell him just before they arrived.

Catherine got her first inkling that something was wrong when she saw Francois's vexation as he disembarked. He and Sarah were always together, so she craned her neck to see if Sarah was behind him.

"Francois!" she called out to him as he attempted to pass her by in route to Olivia, forgetting for a moment that he was deaf.

Grabbing his arm, she signed, "Where's Sa—"

Catherine's hands stopped moving when she saw Francois's tears. Lifting her skirt, she barreled across the short distance to the *Louise Catherine*, pushing the crewmembers out of her way as she boarded the vessel.

Francois turned to Raphael and signed, "Go with her."

Quickly, Raphael followed Catherine. Clara, Marcel, Charles, and Victor were right behind him.

Jonah appeared on the gangplank at the same time they caught up to her.

"Jonah, where's Sarah?"

"Sarah is in Toulon. I left her with my father."

Catherine began to tremble. "Did you even tell her you were leaving her?"

"No. It was the best thing for her. I will be damned before I let her be with that Spaniard. I will go back for her next year."

"You will go back for her now! There was no telegram from your father, was there? All the while you made us believe you were okay with Nicholas visiting, you were plotting to take Sarah away. Turn this damned vessel around and go for my child or I will do it myself." Catherine's voice had risen so high that a small crowd gathered on the wharf.

"Catherine, I—" Jonah tried to reach for her.

"Don't you dare touch me, you lying, deceitful … .your daughter is pregnant!"

"What?"

"That's right, Jonah. She's pregnant, and now you've sentenced her to have her baby alone."

"You kept crucial information from me. I had a right to know that my daughter was with child." The tone in Jonah's voice now rivaled Catherine's.

"We were afraid you would act like the stubborn jackass you are and go kill the boy." Catherine angrily swiped at the tears that were blinding her. "Sarah was building her courage to tell you on the return voyage. She was so happy to be getting along better with you." Catherine's voice broke, and she turned and buried her racking sobs into Raphael's shoulder.

Clara sized up the situation and took action. She turned to the gaping, growing crowd on the wharf and barked, "Go home, you bunch of nosy busybodies. The opera's over. There's nothing more here for you to see."

Automatically the crowd began to move away, whispering amongst themselves.

Turning to Catherine and Jonah, she said, "There's already been enough of a public spectacle. Come on, let's go over to the boardinghouse where we can sit down and solve this rationally."

"The only solution I want is to have my daughter safely here with me," Catherine said when they were seated in the privacy of Clara's office.

Raphael looked at the two people he loved so dearly. It pained him to see them so badly at odds. "Jonah, I will put a crew together and take Catherine back to Toulon to collect Sarah. Marcel and Charles can come with me. You take Victor home, have Marie or Loretta pack a valise for Catherine, and send him with it in the morning. We will leave early."

"I will go with Catherine," Jonah replied.

"No, you won't because I might just push you overboard!" Catherine retorted.

A knock at the door halted the conversation.

"Come in," Raphael ordered.

Hypolite opened the door and handed Jonah a white envelope. "The telegraph office just delivered this for you. They said they received it a couple of days ago, but they knew you were abroad. They saw when you just came in here."

Jonah stood to take the envelope. He remained standing as he ripped the seal, his hands trembling. His eyes perused the paper, and then it slipped from his fingers as he hurried out the door. The room was quiet. All eyes were on the simple slip of white paper lying obtrusively on the floor. Then Marcel walked over and picked it up.

He read it and then looked sorrowfully at his mother. "It is from Grandpere."

"Read it," she barely whispered.

"Dear Son. It is with a heavy heart I relay to you my fears that our Sarah is lost at sea." Marcel's voice broke as he continued. "She took one of the vessels and ran away. I immediately sent Vidal and Simon to find her when I discovered her missing. They traversed the sea, finally giving up when other mariners advised them of rogue waves being reported in the Caribbean Sea. I am so sor—"

"Nooooooo!" The screamed that ripped from Catherine's throat was agonizing. There was no consoling her as she writhed and screeched, finally passing out cold in Clara's arms.

CHAPTER 23

"C atherine, you have to leave," Clara said as she entered the darkened guest room. She walked over to the jalousies and pulled them open. Sunlight streamed into the room, revealing the gauntness in Catherine's face. She raised herself to her elbows, shielding her eyes with one hand. Then she reached for her purse. "I c-can pay," she stuttered.

"I don't want your money, Catherine," Clara said, sitting on the edge of the bed. "It's been three weeks since you've been lying here. You know I am known for speaking my mind, and I am going to be frank with you now. You've been coddled by Bella, Loretta, Yvette, and your sister, and I let them in here because you needed that kind of handling, but too much coddling is going to make you a weakling, and you're too strong a woman for that."

"I don't want to go home. I can't face Jonah," Catherine whispered, reaching for a handkerchief.

"It has to be hard when the person you need the most to comfort you is the one causing you pain," Clara said compassionately. "But Catherine, listen to me because I might be the only one brazen enough to tell you this, and you need to hear it." She took a deep breath and plunged on. "You're not entirely blameless. You withheld the knowledge of Sarah's pregnancy from Jonah."

"I did it because he—"

"Shush, hear me out. I know why you did it, but maybe had he known he would have handled things differently."

"So you're blaming me for my daughter's death?" Catherine cried.

"No, Catherine, I am saying your husband is a good man who only wanted to protect his daughter, just like you. I am not saying he was right," she added quickly.

"Do you have any idea how it feels? I can't bury her. I can't go to a grave to visit her."

"No, I don't know how that feels," Clara replied sadly, "but I know how it feels to lose more than one child within a matter of days. I lost both my sons, Catherine. You have four sons who need their mother more than ever. Francois is hurting so badly. He won't even look at his father. He moved into a shed in Josiah's yard. I haven't seen the other three, but I know they must be hurting too. Your husband is thin and pale. He comes almost every day to check on you although he's afraid to upset you by coming into the room. Your family is broken, Catherine, and you're the only one who can fix it. You can't do that lying on this bed."

"How do I fix them when I am broken myself?"

"One step at a time. Tonight you bathe, comb your hair, put on a clean dress, and come to the dinner table. I want you out of my boardinghouse and back at La Pointe with your family by Friday."

"How did you get so wise?"

Clara smiled faintly as she headed for the door. "It's a curse of old age." Then sternly she added, "Be at dinner tonight."

Hypolite came to collect Catherine's valise early on Friday morning. He had been ordered by Clara to escort her to La Pointe, but Catherine asked him to detour the wagon over to St. Jean.

"Good morning, Catherine." Josiah's voice was filled with joy when he saw her standing at his gate. "It is so good to see you. How are you feeling?"

"Better," she said simply. "I came to see my son. I hear he's been sleeping in your backyard."

"Yes, he's on the back gallery with Olivia."

"Do you mind if I go around there? I will go in to see Agnes when I am done."

"Please go right ahead."

Catherine walked around the yard to Francois. He got up to hug her, and Olivia quietly went inside the house.

"I've come to ask you to go home with me," she signed.

A frown quickly appeared on Francois's face as he fervently shook his head. "No!"

She looked him straight in the eye as she signed forcefully, "If I can forgive your father, so can you."

"She died, Mama," he signed back angrily. "Sarah died, and I couldn't protect her like I promised her I would. He left her there! I fought with him to go back, and he wouldn't! He tied me to my bunk." Francois's green eyes, so much like his father's, were filled with anguish.

Catherine opened her arms, and he buried his face in her hair as the heavy sobs racked his body. She held him, his much bigger frame dwarfing her until the sobs subsided. Then gently pushing him back, she touched his face and signed, "We must forgive your father and ourselves too. We are still a family. It's time for us to go home. Your father and your brothers need us, and we need them."

#

"There's something you need to know before you go up to La Pointe," Raphael told Nicholas and Philar when he intercepted them in Gustavia three weeks later. "Sarah is not up there. She drowned in a rogue wave on the return voyage from Toulon."

"You're lying," Nicholas said, trying to bypass Raphael. "You want to keep me from her. Move out of my way, old man."

"I am telling you the truth. Why do you think she came with you?" Raphael asked, nodding at Philar. "Ask her."

Impatiently, Nicolas said to Philar. "Tell this old geezer to get out of my way."

Gauging the truth in Raphael's eyes, Philar looked at Nicholas and said softly, "It's true. I dreamt it; that's why I told you I would come with you."

"No! Sarah is the best sailor I know," Nicholas said adamantly. "This is a plot to keep me away from her and my child. I am going up there. No one is going to stop me."

"That would not be wise. They're just beginning to recover. Seeing you will set them back." Raphael said firmly.

"They can't shut me out. I have a right to—"

"Nicholas." Philar touched his arm. Looking into his eyes, she signaled that she had a plan. "Let's come back another time."

"Okay," Nicholas agreed. For Raphael's benefit, he shouted, "But I am coming back. I am going to find out what's really happening with Sarah."

"It won't work, so don't even try it," Philar said as they furtively rode up the rocky back way to La Pointe.

"What won't work?'

"The idea you're playing with in your head to ride ahead of me up to La Pointe. I am just as fast as you on a horse, and you'll nix any hope of getting my help then. Not to mention that I might just let Jonah skin you and feed you to the goats."

"Bruja," Nicholas whispered.

"I heard that. I'm not a witch."

"You know they're lying. Sarah didn't drown."

"I wish I could tell you that's the truth. I understand your need to know. That's why we're going to see my sister, but we're not going anywhere near Jonah, understood?"

Nicholas turned tormented brown eyes on Philar. "She did not drown, Philar. I am going to find her. If it takes my life, I am going to find Sarah!"

"You have to stop this," Loretta cried when Philar wrapped her arms around her from the back. "You're giving me heart palpitations."

"Admit it; you knew I was around."

"So to what do I owe the honor of seeing you this time?" Loretta asked as she reached for two teacups.

"Better make that three."

"Huh?"

"Nicholas is outside. I needed to talk to you first before I brought him inside. He's obsessed with finding Sarah. Raphael stopped us from going up to La Pointe, but Nicholas is still insistent that he is going up there, so I brought him here."

"Do you know what really happened?" Loretta asked.

"Raphael told us she drowned on the return voyage. I knew he wasn't speaking the entire truth. I have a feeling Jonah is responsible, and that's why I left Nicholas outside. I don't want him to know that part because there would be bloodshed between him and Jonah."

Loretta quickly told Philar the details, and then agreeing to keep their story straight, Philar went to get Nicholas.

When Loretta finished speaking, Nicholas said passionately, "Sarah is a strong swimmer. I have no doubt she survived the wave and swam to a nearby island. They should be out there looking for her!"

"Her grandfather dispatched several vessels to look for her. They only found debris."

"They would see debris. Many vessels would have been destroyed in the rogue waves. That doesn't prove Sarah is dead. She's alive; I know it, and I won't rest until I find her."

The two women looked at each other; neither had the heart to disagree with Nicholas because, as gifted as they were, neither could vouch that Sarah, had in-fact, died.

#

"Do we really have to go?" Catherine asked Jonah as he buttoned the back of her dress.

"How would it look, Catherine, if we didn't go?"

"Just the thought of being around Clifford curdles my blood."

"It's only for one day."

Jonah's hands lingered on Catherine's shoulders, and then he rested his chin sadly on the top of her head. "Alphonse's daughter is marrying a man he dislikes, yet he didn't do anything foolish like me. I can't imagine how you must feel today."

Catherine turned swiftly into his arms. "I am not entirely blameless,

Jonah. I should have told you about Sarah's pregnancy. Instead, I withheld it from you. I have to live with that regret too." She touched his cheeks. "You're still the love of my life. We hold Sarah in our hearts, but we're not looking back."

They had both indelibly changed. Catherine's eyes reflected a new acuity tinged with sadness, and the gray strands in her hair had multiplied. Jonah had lost weight, and there was a perpetual frown between his eye brows. They had managed to pull together to salvage their relationship and their family. Still, the facets of their lives at La Pointe were changing.

"Welcome to my humble home, cousin. May I offer you my condolences?" Clifford said, extending his hand to Jonah. "I was saddened to hear about the loss of your daughter."

"Thank you, Clifford," Jonah replied, accepting his hand. "May I offer you congratulations on your son's wedding?"

"They make a handsome couple, don't you think?"

"They do." Jonah nodded discomfortingly. He was struggling to make small talk with Clifford. It was the first time he had set foot in Henri and Emeline's old home site since the day he, Catherine, and Henri and Emeline's son and daughter were jeered away. Poignant memories of the hours spent there with his old friends and the antagonistic feelings he still harbored for Clifford were wreaking havoc on his emotions. The old house had been replaced by a huge, white structure replete with chandeliers and split-level galleries. No vestige of its former character remained. There was only a handful of wedding guests mingling around, and Lucinda was gleeful as she socialized with them.

In the awkward moments that followed, Jonah glanced around for Catherine. She was on the opposite side of the room helping Yvette and Solange share out cake. He turned his attention back to Clifford just in time to see Lucinda entwine a hand through her husband's arm.

"Well, if it isn't the golden boy himself. Forgot your rifle tonight, Jonah?"

"Shut up, Lucinda," Clifford warned.

"Why?" she blabbered loudly.

"You're drunk. Go sober up before you shame your son and me."

Ignoring Clifford, she kept her attention on Jonah. "Poor Jonah." She puckered her red lips provocatively. "He tried so hard to keep us away, and just look at what Julie Ann and Jacques did."

"I am not going to tell you again to shut—"

"Hello, Jonah," Roger said, coming up behind Clifford. "This is the first I am seeing you without your rifle. I just had a talk with your sweet little wife. She's still a looker, slim and curvy ..." he said suggestively, letting his voice trail off.

Jonah was about to respond angrily when he felt a firm hand settle on his shoulder. "Everything okay here, Jonah?" Paul asked as he and Pierre flanked him on both sides, their stance leaving no room for doubt.

"Yes, everything is fine. Thank you for your hospitality, Clifford, Lucinda." With eyes of green steel, he looked at Roger. "I will pass your compliment on to my wife. She is indeed a desirable woman. Men have been known to lose body parts from lusting over married women like her. Now, if you'll excuse me, I am going to get a slice of wedding cake."

Clifford watched Jonah walk away, Paul and Pierre at his side. Then he turned angrily on Roger and Lucinda. "You two idiots! You just ruined my plan to get on his good side. How are we going to ever get our hands on La Pointe if you persist on being Neanderthals?"

CHAPTER 24

The following year, 1914, Germany declared war on France. They had declared war on Russia two days prior. France did not back down. It rose to the conflict and prepared its troops, ready to reclaim Alsace and Lorraine, which they had lost to Germany in the Franco-Persian War.

The first group of German soldiers gathered on the borders of Belgium, demanding access across their territory to invade France. Despite Britain's support of France and Russia, it was not committed to joining the war. However, Belgium ports were near Britain, and Germany could pose a serious threat if they were successful in defeating Belgium. Thus, within hours of Germany declaring war on Belgium, Britain declared war on Germany, and World War I was started.

The trickledown effect on St. Barth was disastrous. The island relied on France for economic support. With France engulfed in war, the island's monetary life vein shriveled. It had never recovered from the last hurricane, and now to make matters worse, it was suffering from a serious drought. Without rain, the vegetation was dying. Even the plentiful latania plants were parched and yellowed. The islanders were suffering on many levels, and so, as a means of bettering their plights, once again they set their sights on the neighboring islands.

#

The sharp pounding on the door sounded ominous. Catherine warily walked across the room and pulled it open. She was so tired of bad news, and she knew the knock heralded more of the same.

Three months ago her son, Victor, had announced that he was joining the French Marines. She had begged, cajoled, and cried, but ultimately she couldn't stop him from packing his valise. He had argued that there was no future for him on the island in its present economic condition, and he wanted to explore the outside world while he defended the mother country. With the war raging in Europe, she worried constantly about his safety. In essence, Catherine felt like she had lost two children.

Then shortly after Victor's departure, a telegram had arrived from Vidal advising of Ivan's passing. Jonah had wanted to leave immediately for Toulon, but Vidal had strongly advised against it, stating that war conditions were perilous. He and Rose had handled matters precisely as Ivan had directed, and everything was secured until a time when Jonah could return safely to France.

Now Catherine braced herself as she looked into Hypolite's sad eyes.

"Clara sent me. It's almost time. She wants you and Jonah to come now."

"Go back to her at once. I need to wake Jonah. We will be right behind you."

Bella opened the door on the first knock, her arthritic body trembling as she greeted them. "Come this way. Ms.Clara waiting for you in the room." Shuffling forward painfully, she led them down the corridor, and with tears brimming her eyes, she opened the door.

The immaculately clean room harbored the acrid smell of death. Clara sat on a chair next to the bed, holding the freckled, mottled hand that she had so come to cherish. She looked up when they walked in; her eyes were clear and free of tears. "He has been asking for you, Jonah," she said calmly.

Jonah touched her shoulder softly. "Do you mind if I have a few moments alone with him?"

"N-no," she stammered, rising to her feet. "That's what he wants. I need to speak with you and Catherine privately when you're through. Bella will sit with him while we talk."

The women left the room, and Jonah claimed Clara's chair. He found himself choking on his own tears as he picked up the hand that Clara had been holding.

"Hey you, why don't you get your lazy ass off that bed? The *Louise Catherine* is waiting for us."

Raphael smiled weakly. His words were barely audible. "'Fraid you're going to have to go it on your own now. I won't be getting off this bed again."

Jonah couldn't control the sob that escaped his lips.

"Now don't go getting all snotty over me. I am old, and I have lived a good, long life." A wistful look crossed the pallid shadows of his face. "St. Barth has been good to me. It gave me my Clara. Look after her, Jonah. Pay no mind to her toughness. It's going to be hard for her without me." Nodding for Jonah to come closer, he lifted his hand to touch Jonah's cheek. "And thank you for giving me the chance to be a father. You have made me so proud. I love you."

"I love you too, Raphael, with all my heart."

Jonah bent over and kissed his forehead and then, overcome with emotions, he silently slipped out of the room.

While Bella sat with Raphael, Jonah and Catherine sat with Clara in her office. Given the circumstances, they were amazed at the older woman's composure.

"It's just a matter of time until I am gone too."

"Clara, I don't feel like having this conversation now.

"Jonah, I am eighty-five years old. I can't live forever. I wouldn't want to, not without Raphael." Her voice broke, and she quickly recomposed herself. "You're the only people I trust." Looking at Catherine, she said, "I am bequeathing the boardinghouse to your sister's son, Hypolite. He's an honest, studious young man, and I would have been lost without him these last years."

Opening the desk drawer, she withdrew a single white sheet of paper. "When I am gone, I want you to see that these instructions are carried out. Other than seeing to a smooth transition for Hypolite, I only have one other request, and that is for Bella to be taken care of comfortably. Since Oliver died, I am the only family she has, and she has always been here for me." Chuckling softly, she continued. "She's ten years older than me, but I have a feeling she will live to be a hundred. Can I trust you two to fulfill my last wishes?"

Silently they nodded.

She abruptly stood and smoothed down her skirt. "Very well then, I need to get back to Raphael now."

Clara's hand was on the door knob when she paused and turned back to them. "Thank you for bringing him to me. When I saw him on my gallery on that very first day all those years ago, I would never have believed I was meeting my soul mate."

#

It was the hardest decision Josiah had ever had to make, and he was agonizing over it. Even the move from Toulon to St. Barth had not affected him this emotionally. Yet as the head of his household, he was obliged to do what was best for his family. Times were hard. His main livelihood was his fishing boat, and faithfully he cast out his nets. The problem wasn't that he didn't make a good haul. There were ample fish in the sea, but there were ample fishermen too and just not enough customers. Money was scarce. He usually supplemented his income with his vegetable garden, but the drought had destroyed all his plants. Reluctantly he had agreed to allow his daughters to find jobs in Gustavia, to no avail. No one was hiring.

Word had spread quickly that Eduard Tomas, an affluent resident of St. Barth who had sailed to St. Thomas in the Danish Virgins years ago, had returned and was inviting people to sail back with him. He was holding gatherings in Gustavia, and in sheer desperation, Josiah had gone to listen to him speak.

Josiah was surprised to see the throngs of people standing on the wharf, including his brother, Paul. He stood on the perimeter of the crowd, mesmerized by Tomas's depiction of the fourteen-mile-long island and its majestic rolling hills and busy natural harbor. He said the island was thriving with many coal docks and warehouses, and since it was governed by Denmark, it was not directly affected by the war. He spoke about the two already established settlements of people from St. Barth on separate sides of the island. Those on the south had settled in a hilly niche near the west side of the harbor, and they were making a decent living fishing and straw working. His proposal was for the settlement in the north where the land was rich and rife for farming. He had said there were plentiful opportunities to fish in the pristine Atlantic waters on the north as well. He promised wages and lodgings to the aspirants. He would be in St. Barth for three months, giving enough time to get affairs and families in order for the voyage.

Josiah had not slept that night. He'd sat on his gallery watching the subtle dance of the moonlight in his yard. He was simultaneously filled with excitement and trepidation as he contemplated the possibilities.

"So, you went to hear Tomas. Then you sit out here without speaking to me?" Agnes asked softly as she sat beside him on the step. Josiah had been so lost in thought that he hadn't even heard the gallery door open. "Oh, Agnes," he said with a sigh, "it sounds so enticing. There were so many people there, including my brother and his daughters."

"Is Paul thinking about leaving too?"

"No, he only accompanied his daughters to the gathering. They're the ones who want to go. Despite how good it sounds, Paul says he will not leave St. Barth, and he is distraught over Loren and Philarine's interest in the voyage. Of course when they saw me, they started badgering him about going along with me, although I didn't tell them I would go."

Stretching his legs out on the bottom steps, Josiah sighed. "But I want to go. I don't know how I am going to tell our daughters, in particular Olivia. She won't want to leave Francois. Tomas says he won't be leaving for another three months, so there's time."

"You are sure about this, Josiah?"

"I am not sure at all. We've raised our daughters and built our lives here. It's not as easy as when we left Toulon."

"The important thing is for us all to stay together," Agnes said. "The girls will squawk, but they will adjust, including Olivia. Let's just find out everything we need to know before we make a decision."

#

For days Jonah had been suffering from a persistent pain in his chest. At first he was sure it was a gas pain, but it had continued intermittently. His shoulders and neck ached as well. He hid his symptoms from Catherine, not wanting to worry her. They had suffered way too much sorrow lately, starting with Sarah. A piece of his soul had died with her. He had broken the sacred vow of fatherhood. He had failed to protect his daughter. Worse yet, she had died at his hands. Catherine had forgiven him, but he could never absolve himself.

I am not going to let a nuisance pain get me down.

Jonah picked up the ax and headed for the coal pit. As he walked up the incline, he felt winded and had to stop to rest several times before he made it to the crest.

When he raised his arm to swing the ax, the pain sliced at his chest again, and he gasped for breath. He sat down, resting his back against the trunk of a tamarind tree. He felt weak. Cold sweat dampened his body.

He would rest for a few minutes and then start again. He had to get the wood chopped today. There was no one else to do it. Marcel and Charles were out fishing with Paul and Pierre, and Francois spent every spare moment in St. Jean with Olivia, particularly now that Josiah had officially announced his plans to move to St. Thomas. Jonah hadn't said anything to Catherine, but he knew it was only a matter of time before Francois decided to join them. It would serve to further break her heart.

Jonah knew he could have called Alphonse to give him a hand, but their relationship was strained ever since Julie Ann's marriage to Jacques. It was only natural that the boy would spend time at his in-laws' home. However, several times Jonah had stopped by to see Alphonse and Yvette, only to find Clifford and Lucinda comfortably seated in their parlor. Now that Julie Ann was pregnant, he could only expect to see them there more frequently. He couldn't blame Alphonse. Yet inanely he felt a certain degree of betrayal. He did not want to say anything about Clifford that would place Alphonse in a compromising position, so he had begun to keep a polite distance. His gut instinct told him Clifford was still plotting, ready to strike at the first vulnerable opportunity.

Oh how I miss Raphael, he thought as he finished chopping the wood. He placed them in a neat pile to be burned tomorrow morning, and then he started back down to the house.

Inside, the house smelled like lemons. Catherine had told him she was going over to visit with Marie.

She must have mopped the floors before she left.

Jonah bent over and took off his shoes so that he would not track dirt onto the clean floor. The house was so quiet and smelled so good that he sat on the sofa to enjoy the solace. The pain had eased, but he was feeling tired. He decided to lay back and close his eyes for awhile, at least until Catherine came home.

"So have you been trying to make better friends with Marcel?" Clifford asked Jacques as they put the final coat of paint on a new rental house Clifford had recently acquired.

He prided himself on his acquisitions. Thus far he owned six rental properties and two small businesses. This house would make number seven, and he had tenants already committed to moving in on the first of the month.

"No, Father, I haven't been able to make any more leeway with Marcel."

"How about with Charles and the dunce?"

"Neither."

"Have you even been trying?"

"Why should I want to be friends with people who clearly dislike me?"

Clifford put down his paint brush, walked over to his son, and grabbed his arm roughly. "All my life, Jonah has taken everything from me. Your mother wanted him more than she wanted me. He even took my birthright. That property up there is rightfully ours. The old goat, Ivan, swindled it for his son. I am hell bent on getting it back, and you're going to help me."

"Julie Ann's parents are their friends. I don't want confusion with them."

"Damn Julie Ann's parents! Why do you think I encouraged you to marry her?" In a more soothing voice he said, "So that we can get back what rightfully belongs to us. Everything you see here, everything I've done is for you. I don't want you to suffer the injustice that was done to me. Now be a good son and do your father's bidding. Make friends with them, okay?"

Jacques nodded obediently, and Clifford pulled him into his arms for a hug. He felt gratified when he saw the new tenacity in his son's eyes. The boy was too soft. He didn't have gumption, but he did have allegiance. The only way to manipulate him was to lie.

I believe I've finally convinced you, Clifford thought as he watched Jacques pick up the paint brush, dip it into the can of paint, and vigorously attack the wall. *Now do what's embedded in your bloodline and help me vanquish the golden boy. We will take everything from Jonah. It's only a matter of time now.*

"Jonah, you know I don't like it when you lay down all sweaty and dirty on the sofa." Catherine had just returned from her afternoon visit with Marie. "I was able to salvage these limes from Marie's tree. They're kind of dried, but I believe I can still get some juice from them. I know how you like your lime juice," she said lightly, passing him en route to the kitchen.

Placing the limes on the counter, Catherine reached for the bananas she planned to boil and mash for supper. Then she opened the kitchen drawer.

"Jonah, did you move the knife again? I want to slice the limes, but the knife is not in the drawer where I put it. Jonah, are you hearing me? Jonah?"

Catherine walked back into the parlor and over to the sofa where Jonah still lay. "I hate to wake you from such a good sleep, but you have to get up now," she said, gently shaking him. "The boys will be back soon and—Jonah!"

Noticing that he was too still, she shook him harder. She tried lifting his hands. They fell back lifelessly. She slapped his face. She placed her ear to his heart, and then she starting wailing.

Marcel and Charles found her sitting on the floor, her head lying on the side of Jonah's chest, her hand smoothing back his hair, murmuring incoherently to him.

It seemed all of St. Barth had turned out to pay their final respect to Jonah Dusant. The entire day of the wake, people traversed the winding roads to La Pointe, bringing food and kind words. He had come to St. Barth a stranger, but he had died a native son. They buried him on the land that he had loved and protected. He rested not far from the tamarind tree under which he had last sat. It was a peaceful, shady spot where the trade winds rustled through the trees and birds chirped happily. It was also where Jonah had spent numerous hours of work with Raphael and the others

It was the first time Clifford and Lucinda had set foot in Jonah and Catherine's house. To avoid discord, Catherine had given orders not to turn them away. Lucinda was wailing loudly, blowing her nose and holding tightly to her son, Jacques, who couldn't help but remember his father's words about his mother and Jonah when he saw her reaction. Clifford said all the right things and behaved appropriately while he secretly let his eyes feast on La Pointe

Catherine managed to sufficiently pull herself together. Without Jonah to captain her, she realized she had to chart her own course. She missed him terribly, and at night her pillow accepted her tears. Still, she knew she had to remain strong for her family. In her moments of weakness, she thought of Clara. She too she was gone now, but her strength and guileless wise counsel still resounded in Catherine's head.

Jonah must be having a conniption, Catherine thought when she saw Clifford walking toward her.

"Catherine, I am so sorry, I want—"

"No, you're not," she said coolly, cutting him off. "I've allowed you to stay because I don't want my husband's funeral tarnished by disturbance. However, don't think for one minute that his passing gives you leeway to come onto my property. You, Lucinda, and Roger are still not welcome here. Now if you will excuse me"—she stepped around him—"I have genuine people to receive."

Clifford had timed it perfectly. He knew Catherine would react precisely as she had. He had waited until she was in close proximity to Jacques before approaching her. His son had overheard the entire conversation, and judging from the offended look on Jacques's face, Clifford's plan had been successful.

He sauntered over to Jacques, making sure to look appropriately affronted. "Every time I try to reach out to them, they hurt me again."

"It's okay, Father. I saw how she just treated you. I promise you, one day I will turn the hand of justice in your favor," Jacques replied, rubbing his father's shoulder.

#

"I asked all of you to come here today because I have something important to tell you," Catherine said, trying to control the tremor in her voice.

She looked at the dear faces of the people crowded into her parlor. The memories of the times they had shared, the hardships they had endured, and the lives they had built together flooded her, and she fought hard against the lump in her throat to continue speaking.

"I have decided to go back to France. Marcel and Charles will accompany me. Although I would prefer otherwise, Francois has signed up to sail with Eduard Tomas to St. Thomas. Marie's son, Benjamin, is going with him."

The murmuring instantly began, and Catherine raised her hand to stop it. "Please, hear me out before I lose my nerve." She took a deep breath and cleared her throat. "When Jonah's father died, he left behind his estate in Toulon for Jonah to settle. Jonah's plans were to sail to Toulon this coming January. He didn't live long enough to do that." Glancing at Marie, she continued, "My sister has advised me that she has no desire to return to Marseille, so that leaves our parents' home for me to attend to as well."

Catherine looked down at her trembling hands. "My sons will come back to St. Barth often to check on our estate. This is their home. However, I don't plan on coming back. I can't live here without Jonah. The memories are too painful."

The silence in the room was thick. Yvette was the first to speak. "Oh, Catherine, won't you please reconsider? La Pointe will not be the same without you."

"Please stay," Pierre added. "I don't know how I am going to handle Marie without your help. You're the only one who knows how to settle her down." He wrapped his arms around Marie, who was overcome with tears.

"There's no need to leave, Catherine," Alphonse said. "Time will ease your sorrow."

"Stop it, all of you." Loretta said, going to stand beside Catherine. "You're not making this easy for her. We have to accept that things are changing around here. Both my daughters are leaving with Josiah and Agnes for St. Thomas, so I know how it feels. It tears at me to let them go, but I have to do it."

She looked lovingly at Catherine. "You are closer to me than a sister, and I will yearn for you, but I release you and let you go with blessings. Only you know what your heart needs to heal your soul. We will be parted physically, but we will never be parted in here." Loretta touched her chest for emphasis and then opened her arms.

Catherine couldn't hold back her tears any longer. She buried her face in the hollow of Loretta's neck and sobbed. There was not a dry eye in the room.

Catherine heard the soft knock on the door, but she didn't have the strength to rise from her seat at the kitchen table. It had been an emotionally draining day. It hadn't been easy to tell everyone she was leaving. St. Barth had been her home for longer than her years in Marseille.

"Madame Catherine, may I have a word with you please?"

Catherine looked up into Olivia's hazel eyes. "Please sit down, Olivia. I didn't know you were still here."

Catherine had always liked the girl. There was an aura of candor about Olivia that she found refreshing. She had a graceful walk that reminded Catherine of a swan, and she carried her beauty so unpretentiously that Catherine wondered if she knew just how beautiful she was.

Olivia took a seat across from Catherine and reached out her long, graceful fingers to take hold of her hands. "I know you are deeply worried about Francois. I want to reassure you that I love him with my heart and soul. We will look after each other, and I will write letters to you every week so you know how we're doing. I promise you that you are not losing your son." Olivia looked down at their entwined fingers and said demurely, "I'd like to believe you're gaining another daughter."

Catherine squeeze Olivia's fingers softly, "Thank you, Olivia. I appreciate your saying that, and I will anxiously look for those letters. Just remember Francois is as stubborn as his father."

Catherine didn't sleep the night before Eduard Tomas and his group sailed for St. Thomas. She was up at dawn with Francois as he packed away his last few belongings. For once she was glad he was deaf because it would have been difficult for her to speak with the huge lump blocking her throat. Behind his back she trailed her fingers lovingly over his pillow.

When he was packed and ready to go, she touched his arm. Taking his hand, she placed a small sack of gold coins in his palm. Then she signed, "I want you to take this and buy a few parcels of land. You cannot marry Olivia without a home to take her to, and don't forget about your parcels here in St. Barth. They are your birthright. It's what your father would want. Also, keep an eye on Benjamin. He is still so young."

Francois's eyes were sparkling with the thrill of adventure as he signed back, "No worries, Mama. This is my home. I will never forget it. Be happy for me because I am happy."

Catherine didn't go down to the wharf. She didn't want to see the exodus taking place. It would be too reminiscent of that long-ago voyage from Toulon. She watched Francois walk down the hill until she could see him no more. Then she turned forlornly and went back into her empty house.

At about the same time Eduard Tomas's vessel, the *Augustine,* was pulling into St. Thomas's bustling harbor, Catherine was boarding the *Louise Catherine II.*

Jonah had purchased the new vessel two years before, and it was a shiny, modern splendor with four huge, rigged masts. Marcel was in awe of it, but it was alien to Catherine because it held none on the memories of the original *Louise Catherine.*

The hardest part had been packing away their things. Catherine had spent hours crying as she stored away the life she had lived with Jonah and her children. Sorting Jonah's clothes had been pure agony. Marcel had offered to do it, but she had declined. She felt that having anyone but her put away Jonah's belongings would be sacrilegious, a sacred violation of a most consecrated trust. She had held each piece of clothing, placing it to her nose, breathing in his scent.

The second hardest task was saying good-bye, not only to St. Barth and the life she had lived, but to the people she held dear. Images of Raphael, Clara, Bella, Henri, and Emeline clouded her mind. She thought of her son, Victor. Since the day he had left, she had only received one letter from him. In it he had stated that his vessel had been commissioned to sail to America. She thought of Francois, the son who reminded her most of Jonah. She prayed he and Olivia would live long, fruitful lives in St. Thomas. She held the promise Olivia had made to write often. She couldn't think about Sarah. The chasm of pain her memory evoked was still too hurtful.

She had clung to Marie and Loretta on the wharf, not wanting to part with either of them. They were both her sisters, one by blood, the other by heart and soul.

Catherine stood on the deck alone as the *Louise Catherine II* sailed out of St. Barth's harbor. Her departure was so vastly different from her arrival all those long years ago. She turned in the direction of the helm. For a moment her heart leaped when she saw the gleaming bronzed arms and stance of the man behind the wheel, but it was only her son Marcel. She listened to Charles's booming voice giving directions to the crew, sounding so much like his father. She turned her attention back on St. Barth in time to see the fading shadows of Morne du Vitet. With tearful eyes, she placed her hand to her lips and lovingly blew a kiss to her sweet, little island home.

#

The rolling, emerald-green mountains of St. Thomas seemed endless as they sprawled across the landscape of the fourteen-mile-long island directly in front of Francois. The *Augustine* had dropped anchor in the harbor of the hub, Charlotte Amalie. Named after a Danish queen, its busy ambiance contrasted greatly with St. Barth's tranquility. Throngs of people of different ethnicities and skin colors bustled around the waterfront. Some were balancing buckets on brightly colored headdresses. Others were chatting amiably around boatloads of fish and stalls of fruits, vegetables, and other wares. They waved to the newcomers, their smiles warm and inviting, their voices resonating with various tones of Creole lilts as they bellowed boisterous "good marnings!" Enthralled, Francois and the others stood on the deck. Olivia was his ears, signing to him about the musical accents and the excited comments of their shipmates.

When they disembarked, Eduard Tomas led them eastward farther down the wharf. Offering brief descriptions of their whereabouts, he pointed out Fort Christian on their left, a bright red fort built in the

1600s to defend the harbor, and the Danish police barracks on their right.

A little farther down the street, they turned north. A black, wrought-iron sign suspended from an iron pole identified the street as Dronningens Gade. A series of twists and turns through the narrow alleyways brought them to a steep set of brick steps that seemed to go perpetually upward into the sloping hillside. Wooden houses painted pretty, pastel colors with wide galleries and lattice awnings sporadically bracketed the length of the steps. On street level, brick buildings were closely clustered. Here again Tomas pithily explained that the steps, dubbed ninety-nine steps, were built as a means of easy access to the hills above, and the buildings to the right were the offices of the Danish Colonial Council and the residence of the Danish governor. Eyeing the steps warily, the travelers listened halfheartedly to Tomas's tour-guide efforts.

When they had arrived at the very top step, Philarine whispered to Loren, "One hundred three."

"What?" her sister replied.

"The steps. Tomas said there were 99, but I counted 103."

"Phew! You were actually counting? I can hardly catch my breath."

The steps gave way to a flat surface, and they sighed with relief, only to lift their gazes and behold more sloping mountains ahead. Directly in front of them were more homes similar to the ones they had passed on the steps. A huge, stone fort flanked the area. While they took a respite from the tiresome steps, Tomas explained that the fort, also built in the 1600s, was once the home of the infamous pirate called Blackbeard.

Three Frenchmen waited at the foot of mountains, standing watch over a number of horses and wagons. Recognizing some of the newcomers, they waved excitedly, greeting each other with hugs and friendly slaps on the backs. Then they started the journey up the winding hills to the north. They climbed upward for hours, a convoy of people determined to make a better life for themselves.

As they climbed higher, the views of the glistening Caribbean Sea to the south were stunning. They could see the outlined hills of another Danish Virgin, St. Croix, in the distance.

Darkness eventually set in, and mosquitoes began to bite. There were fewer houses and denser shrubbery as the path they were traveling became more isolated. Josiah began to wonder if they all had been duped. Had he uprooted his family from their home in St. Barth only to bring them to their deaths here in the wilderness of St. Thomas? He rode to the front of the posse to confront Tomas. Some of the men followed.

"We're tired and hungry. We've been riding all day. Now we're in pitch blackness. How much farther is this place you're taking us to?"

Tomas smiled knowingly. "We're almost there, just a little farther. Food and clean lodging await you. You cannot see the beauty of your surroundings because of the night, but tomorrow you will be amazed by what you see."

Soon the trail took a downward path, eventually coming to a clearing with a series of small wooden structures. In the foreground was a larger, studier building. Tomas led them to the larger building. There they were fed and escorted to the smaller structures, each of which consisted of only one room and were all identical. The rooms were sparse, but clean. White sheets lay folded on top of cots in the corners. A kerosene lamp, a bar of soap, a towel and washcloth, a small bucket of water, and an enamel washbasin adorned the top of wooden tables in the opposite corners. Five outhouses were strategically situated a few yards away.

Tired from their journey and oblivious to the crickets making music outside, the travelers slept.

The next morning they woke to lush, green surroundings filled with heavily laden banana and plantain trees. A light rain was falling, and the mountain air smelled sweet and clean.

Tomas met with them early in the morning. He would provide meals, lodging, and a small stipend to work his farms. If it was within their means, they were free to buy land and build homes, provided they continued to work for him for one year. All things considered, it was a fairly decent proposal.

Shortly after their arrival, Francois asked Josiah for his daughter's hand, and Josiah willingly gave his blessings. Tomas loaned Josiah a wagon, and he and Agnes accompanied the young couple to the Roman Catholic Church in Charlotte Amalie. It was, in itself, a journey.

They exchanged their vows before God, Olivia's parents, three nuns, and a priest. It was the happiest day in Francois's life. Bewilderingly, this beautiful woman loved and desired only him. He had loved her all his life, and now she was his wife. He didn't have much materially to offer her yet, but he vowed to spend every day of his life working to provide for her.

The long trip back up through the mountains was filled with anticipation. Francois was impatient. He couldn't wait to finally make love to Olivia. He was going to take his time kissing every inch of her, savoring her sweetness. He felt his manhood rise hotly, and he tried to quell his thoughts, embarrassed that her parents might see his aroused state.

Later, with the cool, mountain breeze drifting into his small room, Francois experienced an indescribable rapture that his deafness could not impair. He didn't need ears or voice. His body spoke alone of the immeasurable, intense love he felt for Olivia. Together they soared in flight to a place only he could take her, and together they rode the spasms of pleasure as they spiraled back down. He lay entwined in her arms afterward feeling like the luckiest man on earth.

They lived and loved in the little room for two months. Then with the gold coins his mother had given him, Francois bought donkeys and a wagon and an acre of land overlooking the Atlantic Ocean. With Benjamin's help, he built a house and began to prepare the land for farming.

He toiled daily, irrigating the land while working full time for Tomas. The second happiest day of his life was the day he found out Olivia was pregnant.

November 30, 1917

My Dear Catherine,
It is with pleasure that I announce the birth of your grandson, Jacob Jonah Dusant. Both the child and I are

doing well, and Francois is such a doting father. At night when he thinks I am asleep, he stands in front of the cradle for long intervals. He is still afraid to hold Jacob, but he is enamored by him.

I was happy to learn in your last letter of Marcel's wedding. He is a good man who deserves a good wife. Please relay to him his brother's and my joy for him.

It is my opinion that Jacob looks just like Jonah. I promise as he grows, I will tell him all about his grandfather, his uncles, and you.

I pray this letter finds you in good health. Please give our regards to Charles as well.

I will send a portrait of Jacob as soon as I am able to have one made.

Your loving daughter-in-law,
Olivia.

Catherine read the letter from Olivia and then placed it to her lips, tears glistened her eyes. She had a grandson, her first, but he was so far away. She wished she could hold him.

She had settled comfortably into her childhood home in Marseille. Marcel had recently married and both he and Charles lived on the family's estate in Toulon. They had done their best to persuade her to move in with them, but she felt content in Marseille.

She encouraged Marcel to make annual voyages to St. Barth, and he spent months each year at La Pointe. She knew that he loved being in St. Barth, and he wanted to share his love of the island with his wife, but she was sickly, and her parents discouraged her from embarking on the long journeys.

To the contrary, Catherine could see that Charles had little interest in returning to St. Barth. She had giving him permission to oversee Ivan's fishing fleet, and with Vidal's help, he was doing an excellent job. Still, his lack of interest in their island home saddened her.

#

Life couldn't be more perfect for Francois. He spent his days toiling and his nights loving. He adored his son and rejoiced over every new phase of his life, amazed that he had helped create such a perfect little being. It had been a tremendous relief when Olivia had assured him that the boy was not deaf. Being deaf had presented him with difficulties and frustrations, particularly in his childhood. He was glad his son had not been dealt the same fate.

They had a spectacular view of the Atlantic Ocean and the neighboring islands and cays, and he longed to be out there on the sea. He was saving money to buy a boat so he and Benjamin could go fishing. Although eleven years younger, Benjamin had always been his favorite cousin, and he was happy that Benjamin had accompanied him to St. Thomas. It worked perfectly; Francois watched over Benjamin like a big brother, and Benjamin served as Francois's ears on the workplace

Before long they had a thriving vegetable garden. They planted fruit trees and adorned the yard with pretty, tropical flowers. Unlike St. Barth, the soil was rich and moist, and it seemed to Francois that overnight, everything blossomed and bloomed.

As a way of keeping the French settlers of the north connected, Eduard Tomas hosted social gatherings every other Friday evening. It was a means for sharing news about their loved ones in St. Barth and about their new community. America was actively courting Denmark to purchase the island, and with World War I in heated progress, the present political climate was on edge.

Long before the portentous war, America had aspired to purchase the Danish Virgins. They had seen the islands as a coaling station for US naval vessels. Negotiations had once gone as far as the preparation of a treaty between America and Denmark for $7.5 million in gold. Then the islands were hit by a hurricane, a tsunami, and an earthquake all in one year, and in light of the natural disasters, the treaty failed to obtain the sanction of the United State Congress.

Now because of the heightened crisis of World War I, America's interest was renewed. They had already acquired Puerto Rico. The purchase of the Danish Virgins would further ascertain the deterrence of belligerent nations gaining bases in the Caribbean. The local newspaper, *The Herald,* regularly contained articles enlightening the islanders of new developments, and Tomas faithfully bought the paper so that he could share the information.

When Francois and Olivia joined the gathering on this particularly windy January evening, they noticed right away that something was wrong. There were looks of perplexity on people's faces as they mingled and chatted in the warm glow of the lanterns. Lively music from a scratch band was playing, but no one was dancing.

Spotting Josiah and Agnes standing under a mango tree, they walked over to greet them.

"Why is everyone looking so befuddled? Is everything okay in St. Barth?" Olivia asked her father.

"It's not St. Barth," Josiah answered. "Denmark signed the treaty with America to purchase St. Thomas and the two other Danish Virgins for $25 million in gold."

"Is that bad?"

"We don't know," Josiah shrugged. "The Danes were reluctant to sell because America did not want to include citizenship and continued free trade in the transfer agreement. Tomas says the newspaper didn't specify the conditions under which they were sold, but he did mention that people are worried. I guess it's the not knowing what to expect that is troublesome."

"Well, the only thing we can do is hope for the best," Olivia replied before turning to Francois to sign to him about the news.

Two months later on March 31, 1917, Eduard Tomas and a group of French men made the journey into Charlotte Amalie to witness the official transfer ceremonies. Francois, Benjamin, and Josiah were among them.

In Charlotte Amalie, they rode east past the sprawling Grand Hotel and then south in the direction of the Danish barracks. Around every corner the American naval forces were visible. Their presence seemed out of place as they stood sentinel, contributing to the already-tense atmosphere.

The street in front of the barracks was filled with people, and they joined the growing crowd. Some were dressed in their Sunday best. Others wore their work clothes, having been given precious time off for the ceremony. Their faces were somber. Men held their hats in their hands, their suspenders gleaming in the sunlight. Women held tightly to handkerchiefs, occasionally wiping drops of sweat from their faces. They stood under the hot, tropical sun and endured the long speeches from the Danish and American officials.

When the speeches concluded, and the officials walked over to the Danish flag, a reverenced hush descended upon the crowd. The people watched as the Danish flag was lowered for the last time. They visibly flinched when the shots from the twenty-one-gun salute pierced the stark silence of the afternoon. They cried openly as the flag was folded and placed aside while the Danish band played its National Anthem. They watched somberly when the American officials exchanged places with their Danish counterparts, and the American National flag was hoisted, the unfamiliar musical notes of the American National Anthem drifting through the air. With the new flag flowing gracefully in the breeze, they walked away mumbling, "We know what we had. We don't know what we're getting."

Realizing they had just witnessed a momentous juncture in the history of their new country, the French men bowed their heads in respect as the throngs of people moved past them, and then in silence they mounted their horses and rode back to the North Side. It would be years before they received their American citizenship.

#

Careful not to wake Olivia, Francois slipped off the bed and tiptoed to get his clothes. He had been eyeing a patch of land that he wanted to clear to plant more banana, fig, and plantain trees. He planned to burn the excess bush, so he needed to start early. He paused with one foot in his pantaloon and looked at Olivia sleeping soundly. *With my whole heart and soul, I love her,* he thought.

He bent and kissed her softly. Then after checking on Jacob, he opened Benjamin's door and lightly shook him to rouse him.

Benjamin stirred, opened his eyes, and groaned. "I swear God intended to make you a rooster and then changed His mind." Looking at Francois through sleep-laden eyes, he signed, "Go ahead. I will meet you there."

It was still dark and the dew was thick when Francois stepped outside.

By early afternoon, they had cleared the patch of land and were almost finished burning the bush. Benjamin removed the handkerchief he had tied around his nose and mouth to lessen the overcoming smell of smoke and wiped it across his damp face. He was drenched with sweat and weak from exhaustion and heat. He looked around for Francois, and saw him next to the fire with an armful of bush. Benjamin walked over and touched his arm. Signing he said, "We have been working all day. The sun is really hot. Let's knock off now."

"You go," Francois signed back. "I will finish this."

"No, I will stay with you so we can finish it faster."

They were both drenched in sweat and reeking of smoke when they finally walked into the kitchen.

Olivia had just finished cooking a pot of stewed chicken. "Just wash your hands and come straight to eat while the food is hot," she signed.

"It smells really good," Benjamin said as he headed for the bucket of water and soap she had placed on the back table.

Francois kissed the top of his son's head. Straightening up, he signed, "I am filthy from the smoke. I need to clean up outside."

"Okay, but don't take too long," Olivia signed. She turned around to sign again, but he had already gone. *Oh well,* she thought, *he knows better than to take a full bath when his blood is so heated.*

Francois was in a good mood as he walked to the bathhouse in the back yard. He had accomplished everything he had set out to do today. He could envision the thick drove of banana, fig, and plantain trees that would grow in the crest of the hill they had just cleared. *Jacob will be walking by the time of harvest. I can't wait to give him a nice fat fig,* he thought as he soaped himself.

He emptied the bucket of water over his head, startled by the chillness when it splashed on his face and down his body. It was much colder than he had expected, yet it felt invigorating after the scorching heat of the sun. Reaching for the towel, he smiled. *I can go kiss my wife and hold my son now.*

As he lifted his hands to pull his shirt over his head, a searing pain traveled up his right side, and he gasped, leaning against the wooden frame. *Phew! I have to eat. Gas is attacking me.*

He finished dressing and stepped into the late-afternoon sunlight. His eyes felt funny, and he stood still for a moment to adjust to the brightness. He felt weak when he started to walk toward the house.

Francois was halfway to the kitchen door when he felt a rushing sensation in his head, and then his body went numb. He couldn't lift his hands, and his feet wouldn't move. He tried to cry out as a whirling pool of blackness enveloped him. His last conscious thought was of his wife and baby son as a tear slipped down each cheek.

"He's taking too long. He was only supposed to rinse off and come right back. Watch Jacob. I'm going to see what's keeping him."

Olivia headed out the door as Benjamin placed a steaming plate of stewed chicken on the table. When he heard her hysterical screeching, he swept up Jacob and ran toward the back of the house. He found her lying on the ground beside Francois.

Placing Jacob on the grass, Benjamin walked around to Francois's other side. He checked his pulse and listened to his heart. Then with a profound sadness, he got up and walked around to Olivia.

"Come, Olivia. Let me take you inside," he said, reaching for her shoulders.

"No!" She pushed him back so hard he stumbled, almost falling on top of Jacob.

In a quandary about what to do, Benjamin sat next to Jacob. Olivia's parents lived about a mile north. He needed to get to them, but how could he leave her in this condition? And what about the child?

He decided to try again.

"Please, Olivia. Come with me inside the house. I need to attend to Francois."

"No. He's going to wake up anytime now."

"Olivia, he's dead."

She turned tormented eyes on Benjamin. "Don't say that! Don't you dare say that, damn you!"

Trying another approach, he said, "Jacob needs you."

"I don't care! I don't need anyone but Francois. Now leave us alone!"

Resigned, Benjamin took up the little boy and started for the house to bundle him up in warm clothes. It would be cumbersome to hold the child and drive the wagon, so holding him against his chest; he began the long walk to find Josiah and Agnes.

It was dark when he finally knocked on their door. Wordlessly, he handed Jacob to Agnes. Looking at Josiah he said, "Francois is dead, and Olivia's gone crazy. I need you to come back with me."

"What happened?" Agnes cried.

"I don't know," Benjamin sadly replied.

"Why can't I bury my husband on the land he loves?" Olivia asked Eduard Tomas. He had come to pay his respects and to inform her of the proper protocol for the burial.

"Because the American government will not allow you to do so."

"So they want me to bury him in a foreign place in town, far away from me where I can't even put flowers on his grave? It's just not right!"

"I understand, Mrs. Dusant, but we cannot go against the government. I will go with you to help with the paperwork for the burial plot. We will also go to the Roman Catholic church. I will start tonight preparing matters for the morning."

"I don't want your help! I want to bury my husband on his land. Why can't you understand that?"

"Olivia, Mr. Tomas is only trying to help," Josiah interjected. "I know you are distraught, but there's no cause to be rude. We must accept God's will."

"Don't speak to me about God's will. To make me a widow and to take Jacob's father from him was His will? What kind of loving God does that?"

"Olivia, that's sacrilegious!" Josiah chided his daughter. "You must beg God's forgiveness immediately!"

"I will when I am good and ready, and it's not now!" She turned and walked out of the house, slamming the door.

"Mr. Tomas, please accept my apologies on behalf of my daughter. She is not herself."

"We must take him into town tomorrow morning. Will she be ready?"

"Yes, she will come around. It has only been hours. She is still in shock. Her mother and her sisters are preparing the body."

"Then meet me at my house tomorrow morning by seven. I am truly sorry for your family's loss, Josiah."

Sadly, Josiah nodded. "Thank you for coming. I will see you in the morning.

At first Benjamin thought he was dreaming, but the repetitious thump of a shovel persisted, penetrating the realm between sleep and wake until he sat upright in bed. Throwing the blanket off, he searched in the darkness for his shoes. Then he slipped out of his room.

The sight of Francois's body lying in the coffin that Tomas had brought earlier tonight jolted him, and he stopped in his tracks. It was surreal to see his good friend and cousin this way, the pallor of death illuminating his face in the darkness. Sorrowfully, he walked past the coffin.

He checked on Jacob first. The little boy was curled up next to Agnes. Both grandmother and grandson were sound asleep. Then backing out of the room, he felt the cold draft coming through the open backdoor.

Olivia!

CHAPTER 25

Benjamin picked up his pace. He saw Olivia in the distance of the dim light from the quarter moon, the shovel rising and descending between her hands. He sprinted across the yard, afraid to call out her name until he was close enough.

"Olivia, what are you doing?" His voice was filled with agony for her.

She stopped mid swing. "What does it look like I am doing?" Strands of her hair had come undone from the tight knot she wore. The loose wisps curled around her nape and stuck to her forehead. In the cool night air, she was sweating profusely.

She raised the shovel again and swung it to the ground, the sound echoing through the stillness as it made contact with the earth. "I am getting ready to bury my husband."

Benjamin felt like crying. He didn't know what to do or say. Finally he walked across the loose dirt and wrapped his arms tightly around her. "Olivia, you have to stop this madness. Do you understand? Stop it!"

"Let me go." She struggled. "I am going to bury him here where he belongs, near me. Let them try to stop me. Damn it, Benjamin! I am going to knock you out. I said let me go!"

"No! Not until you come to your senses. You're hurting yourself, and I won't stand by and watch you."

Olivia struggled against him until he lost his balance, and they both tumbled into the hole she had managed to dig. She turned in his arms and beat at his chest, her fists shaking his body.

"I am so angry," she cried, her fingers curling into his shirt. "How could he leave me like this? I hate him! I hate him! God, I want to hurt somebody."

"Then hurt me. Go on; keep hitting me until you feel better."

Olivia beat at Benjamin until they were both covered in tears, sweat, and dirt, and she lay exhausted, hiccupping in his arms. It was in that moment that it struck Benjamin, a most inopportune revelation. He was simultaneously racked with wonder and guilt. For it was in that moment he realized something he had already known. He was inexplicable, unfathomably in love with Olivia Dusant. He could never let her know. It would be disrespectful and derisory. He was ten years younger than she, and she was his cousin's widow. All he could do was silently vow to always protect her and Jacob.

June 1, 1917

Dear Catherine,

It is with deep sadness that I must inform you of Francois's passing. He died suddenly and unexpectedly one month ago today. He was not ailing. He was happy and robust up until the afternoon he collapsed.

I wanted to bury him here on the land near me, but the new American government declined me the courtesy. He is buried in the western sector of Charlotte Amalie. It pains me that I cannot go and sit beside him in the shadows of the afternoon. There is much I want to say to him, so daily I walk the grounds he planted, and I converse with him there.

Your son owns my heart, and he took it with him. I am bereft. Yet he left me with an indelible piece of his soul, your grandson, Jacob. Please take solace in knowing that the essence of the man we both love is alive in his son.

Always yours,
Olivia

Catherine's cries were heard only by the sparrows who had been happily chirping at the bird feeder. As if sensing her sorrow, their chirps quieted as they pecked at the grains.

She had been so happy to receive Olivia's letter that she had sat on the bench in the garden and anxiously ripped at the seal. The news of her son's death was the last thing she had expected, and it tore at her heart, bringing her to her knees in anguish. In the natural order of life, she was not supposed to outlive her children, and now she had lost three. She wailed and shook her fist; her eyes turned toward heaven and she screamed, "Why?"

September 14, 1917

My Dear Olivia,

I am still reeling from the news of your last letter. I cannot even bring myself to write the words, for in doing so, it would make what has transpired real. I'd much prefer to live in a world where my son is alive and prospering, though I know in my heart it is a fallacy.

I can imagine your agony for I know very well my own. I have enclosed herewith your passage to France. I understand from Marcel there is a vessel leaving Charlotte Amalie on the first week of the new year. Of course, Marcel can come for you himself if you cannot settle your affairs in time. He leaves for St. Barth at the beginning of the year.

I think it best for you and Jacob to come to Marseille where the family can help sustain you, and it would bring me comfort to have you both here.

I remain your loving mother-in-law,
Catherine

December 17, 1917

Dear Catherine,

Thank you for your kind offer, but I am not leaving St. Thomas. Francois loved living here. He built us a home, and he farmed his land. On this island, he realized his dream. I am firmly determined to complete what he started.

I am not alone. I have my son, my parents, my sisters, my cousins, Loren and Philarine, and I have Benjamin. Your nephew has been my strength. He continues to reside here with me and Jacob, and he diligently toils the land in honor of Francois, so you see, I am well surrounded.

Please do not be offended because I am returning the passage, and I welcome a visit from Marcel if he can make it to St. Thomas. Also, I still intend to honor my word to write often. Rest assured, Jacob will know his lineage.

I remain your faithful daughter-in-law,
Olivia

#

Josiah loved his new life on St. Thomas. He had leased a nice piece of land not far from Olivia and Francois, and he had managed to build the house of his dreams. His goal was to buy the land outright in a few years.

As he swung in the hammock on his gallery, his thriving garden and the magnificent view of the Atlantic Ocean all within view, only one dilemma perturbed him: his nieces Loren and Philarine.

In the three years they had lived on St. Thomas, he had managed to find reputable men to wed all his daughters, and he had hoped to do the same for his nieces. They were his charges, and he owed it to his brother, Paul, to see them happily married and settled. However, neither girl had turned out to be a likely candidate.

Like a pretty butterfly, Philarine flitted between suitors, her beauty enticing them until they were hopelessly in love. Then she would flutter

BLOOD AND PARCELS | 309

away to the next gullible soul, leaving a trail of broken hearts. Concerned for her reputation, Josiah had warned her she was headed for trouble. He had spoken harshly to her in hopes of her changing her ways. Instead, he had come home one afternoon to find Agnes in tears. Philarine had packed her belongings and moved in with her latest suitor.

Loren, on the other hand, showed no interest in suitors at all. Her days were spent working for Tomas, and her nights were spent at home. She kept to herself, spending little time with her sister or cousins, but she was always helpful to Agnes. She was a pretty girl who strongly resembled her mother, Loretta, and many of the eligible bachelors showed interest in her. Josiah had tried to match her with the best of them to no avail. He was baffled by her lack of enthusiasm until the day he noticed her thickening waistline and realized she was pregnant.

Felipe Girard went alone to every Friday evening gathering at Tomas's. Although he was French, he was not one of the settlers from St. Barth. To escape his rich and domineering family, he had migrated from Guadeloupe to St. Thomas to strike his own fortune.

He had married a woman from St. Barth though. She had come with Eduard Tomas on his initial voyage, and her beauty had captivated Felipe. He married her shortly after her arrival, fooled by the belief that she loved him more than his money. When they had wed, she had promised him children, and as childless years went by, she blamed him, cruelly accusing him of not being man enough to sire a child.

Turning his attention away from his loveless marriage, Felipe made his fortune in the rum trade, and his wife lived the life of leisure she had intended when marrying him.

He was lonely, yet he never considered taking a mistress. He looked forward to the Friday evening gatherings as a means of getting away from his taciturn wife. It also filled the void for the social interaction he lacked.

From the first gathering Loren had attended with her family, he had taken notice of her. Amid the throngs of people, she had stood out like an exquisite flower, and he looked for her every time. On occasions he had gotten close enough to see the brilliant blue-green hues of her eyes and smell her fragrance. He was drawn to her, and he longed to introduce himself, but his instincts warned him that he could never walk away from her unaffected.

Although she didn't have the gumption to introduce herself, Loren admired Felipe as well. With his muscular built, thick blond hair, and piercing blue eyes, he was more rugged than handsome. She studied him, calling on her gift to decipher him, but she could decode nothing. It became a habit. Her eyes searched for him as soon as she arrived, and upon seeing him, her heart raced and she felt lightheaded. She fantasized about going up to him and introducing herself. She would even start to walk in his direction, but she always stopped short—until the day those arresting blue eyes met her gaze.

"Hello," he said, reaching out to shake her hand. "I am Felipe, and you are?"

"Loren," she managed to stammer over the clamor of the scratch band.

"Do you mind walking over there where it's quieter so we can talk?"

She nodded, and walking beside her at a respectable distance, he led her to a shaded area away from the crowd.

"So tell me about yourself, Loren."

Felipe studied Loren as he listened to her speak about her family and her home back in St. Barth. There was a purity about her that mesmerized him, and the need in him grew so intensely that he instinctively reached for her. The sweet nectar of her mouth captivated him. He couldn't ever remember feeling such potent longing for a woman, and he found himself pulling her tightly against him, his hands claiming intimate privileges.

"Mother of God," he groaned, gently pushing her away. "Loren, please forgive me. I have no right."

She didn't answer. She didn't move. With his hands resting on her shoulders, he looked down at her. Those blue-green eyes stared at him. Those sweet lips, swollen from his kisses, opened and parted invitingly, the tip of her tongue enticingly peeking out to lick at her bottom lip.

"Lord, forgive me," Felipe cried, reaching for her again.

The Friday evening gatherings couldn't come fast enough for either of them. No sooner had Loren arrived than she would wander off to meet Felipe in the darkened corners. Eventually they realized they couldn't continue undetected, and wanting more from each other, clandestine meetings were planned. She would climb out the window of her uncle's house in the still of night, and he would be waiting. Together they would ride away on his horse to grassy patches in the moonlight, and there he would love her wholly.

Felipe knew it was wrong. He was a married man, and he had deflowered an innocent, young girl. He had made her his lover, knowing he could never make her his wife. In daylight, he agonized over it. By moonlight, he rejoiced in her arms. He was in love like he had never been before, and he was totally confident that his woman loved him for him, not for any material wealth he could provide her. He wanted to fall asleep in her arms and wake up beside her, and knowing that it was impossible made him want her all the more.

The day she told him she was pregnant was the happiest day in his life. He decided to confront his wife. He wanted a divorce. She could have everything. All he wanted was Loren and his child. He never expected her reaction. She cried and threatened to kill herself if he left her.

The next afternoon when he returned home from work, he found her lying on the floor with both wrists slashed. He realized she'd timed it perfectly so that he would find her before she bled to death, but her ruse had worked nonetheless. He could never live with her death on his conscience.

Josiah had no choice. Loren was his brother's daughter, but he could not harbor an unwed, pregnant woman in his house. The dishonor would fall on his entire household. Yet in good conscience, he could not put her on the streets. He pressed Loren to disclose the child's father until she relented, and then he summoned Felipe.

"You have done my niece a severe injustice, Mr. Girard. By bedding her, you have made her a scorned woman and brought shame to my house. Now she is pregnant with your child. How do you propose to rectify this?"

"I am deeply in love with Loren, Mr. Dusant. I am in the wrong, but I am not sorry. While it is true that I cannot disentangle myself from my marriage, I fully intend to take care of Loren and my child. My wife is aware of this. I will provide them with everything they need."

"Are you saying you intend to carry on your affair with my niece?" Josiah asked in vexation.

"I don't expect your approval, so I won't ask for it. Loren is the love of my life. I do not consider my love for her in the sordid contents of an affair. I will love her until the day I die, and my child will carry my name."

Felipe honored his promise to love Loren until the day he died. With his plentiful resources, he bought land and speedily built her a house not far from Josiah and Agnes. Four months after she moved in, she delivered a baby girl they named Claire, and Felipe enjoyed the pleasures of fatherhood he once thought were lost to him.

Loren was spurned in their tightly laced Catholic community, but she paid it no mind. She had Felipe and her child, and she still had the affection of her extended family. When Felipe died ten years later, his wife ascertained that Loren received none of his large estate. She even tried to take away the house and strip Claire of her father's name. However, Felipe had forethought the possibility of this occurring, and so he had deeded the house to Josiah for safekeeping. The court ruled the house lawfully belonged to Josiah, and that the little girl was entitled to her father's name, albeit nothing more of his estate.

Loren was satisfied with the results. She had the most fundamental part of Felipe, his daughter. She wanted nothing more. She never married. In time, Philarine moved in with her, and together, the two sisters raised Claire, a feisty girl with her mother's dark hair and her father's striking blue eyes.

#

"For the love of God, Olivia, what sense does it make to get so upset over a mango?" Benjamin asked, exasperated. "So the man picked a few mangos from the tree. You made such a fuss that he repeatedly apologized to you, told you he was hungry. Now please, let it go!"

"If he was hungry, then he should have asked me, not pick my mangoes like he owns them. I am going to take him to court! It will teach him not to take such liberty."

"Well, I am not taking you to town."

"I don't need you to take me. I can go by myself," Olivia replied, reaching for her hat. Then she picked up Jacob.

"Where are you going with Jacob? You can't drive the wagon and hold him too."

"Watch me," she said hotly, slamming the door.

"Stubborn-ass woman," Benjamin swore, reaching for his own hat. She was being ludicrous, but he could not let her ride with Jacob all the way to town by herself.

I hope they either lock her up or laugh her right out the jailhouse. Oh no! They'd be wiser to lock her up than to laugh at her. God help them if they laugh.

Olivia was the most obstinate woman Benjamin had ever known, and she had become even more so since the death of her husband. Yet he loved her. Everything he did was for her. He assiduously toiled the farm Francois had planted. His actions mimicked Francois's so much that Olivia begged him to slow down, fearful that the same fate awaited him. She badgered him to mingle with the eligible young ladies who eyed him at the Friday evening gatherings. His hard hours of working had resulted in strong, muscular biceps. He was short where Francois had been tall, but he was an attractive man.

Assuring Olivia he would pursue the ladies in time, Benjamin kept well the secret of his love for her. At night he lay awake in bed steps away from her, and he yearned for her. He wanted so badly to make love to her until the sweet smile he remembered returned to her face, and the sadness left her eyes. Yet he knew it was impossible. Two years had gone by, and still she wore the heavy black clothes of grief.

The day Olivia's armor finally gave way was a lovely spring Sunday afternoon. Benjamin was outside working in the yard, and having placed Jacob into his playpen, Olivia went into the kitchen to start preparing supper.

As she peeled and sliced breadfruits, she periodically checked on the little boy. He was jabbering happily to himself. She could see Benjamin through the open window. She watched as his strong arms, glistening with sweat, chopped branches off a cashew tree. She felt a tug at her stomach and blushed when she felt a long-forgotten moisture between her legs. She was overcome with guilt. Shamefully she averted her eyes, turning to check on Jacob.

"Jacob! Where are you?"

The little boy had climbed out of the playpen, and he was not in the house. Going out on the gallery, she spotted him on the far side of the yard about to yank the tail of one of the horses. Sprinting down the steps, she cried out for Benjamin.

He dropped the axe and raced across the yard just in time to yank the boy away from the horse's fierce kick. They tumbled together, Jacob fastened securely in Benjamin's arms.

"He's okay," he assured Olivia as she frantically came to a halt in front of them.

Olivia dropped to her knees. Crying, she embraced them both. Benjamin wasn't sure exactly when her lips touched his, and he didn't care if the kiss was only out of gratitude. He seized the moment. All the pent-up yearning he had been feeling went into that first kiss, and Olivia didn't pull away. He explored her mouth, letting his hands roam over the black skirt, making his way up under the fabric. He unbuttoned her blouse, eager to sip at the treasures hidden beneath, and still she offered no resistance. It was Jacob's happy gurgles as he clapped his little hands in glee that brought Benjamin back to reality. He asked her to marry him that night, and they were married the following week at the Roman Catholic Church in Charlotte Amalie.

As they lay in bed on their wedding night, Olivia's head comfortably resting in the crook of Benjamin's arm, her fingers playing with the thick mass of light, brown hair on his chest, he said, "Livy, you know I love Jacob as my own son. I want to adopt him,"

He felt Olivia's fingers stop moving, and he waited while she raised herself on one elbow to look at him. Her pretty, hazel eyes were filled with anguish when she said, "I know you love Jacob, and he loves you. In every respect you are his father, but I cannot let you adopt him. That would mean changing his last name, and he would lose his birthright. I promised Catherine I would never let that happen. In fact, you must promise me, if something happens to me, you will see to it that he obtains his share of Francois's family's estate in St. Barth. Jonah and Catherine loved those parcels." She penitently smiled. "It is also where you and I were born and where we became friends."

Benjamin felt equal spasms of jealously and guilt. Olivia was his now. He didn't want the specter of another man between them. Yet every time he thought of Francois he felt guilty for loving her so fervently. Losing her now would devastate him.

"Oh Livy, I don't want to think about something happening to you."

"You must promise me, Benjamin!"

"All right, all right, I promise."

"Good," she said, kissing him and lying back in his arms.

"But you're going to live to be a hundred so you can tell Jacob yourself all about the Dusants."

#

Marcel staunchly made his annual voyage to St. Barth, spending months at a time tending to the upkeep of the estate. As the eldest, he felt a keen sense of duty to be his family's champion, and his mother compelled him, pressing upon him the weight of protecting their estate from Clifford and Jacques.

While Catherine wrote regularly to Olivia, Marcel started writing to Jacob. The boy was sixteen now. He was old enough to understand that he had another family of his own blood. Marcel always felt sorrow when he thought of his brother, Francois. He'd died too young, never having had a chance to know his son. He was glad Olivia had married Benjamin. Benjamin was a good man, and from all appearances, he loved Jacob as his own. Still, Marcel wanted to keep in communication with Jacob. The boy was closer to him in blood than to Benjamin.

Every time Marcel returned to his beloved island home, he saw changes. Benjamin's brother, Hypolite, had remodeled Clara's boardinghouse. He had married a girl from St. Jean, and together with their two daughters, they ran a thriving business.

Marcel liked and trusted Hypolite. He was honest and forthright, much as Clara had been, and he enjoyed spending his first nights back on the island in his company.

At La Pointe he was surrounded by memories of his childhood, but so much had changed as the years unfolded. His parents' generation was gone, and among his peers only Jacques and Julie Ann lived close by. Jacques persistently offered to tend the estate in Marcel's absence, but in light of the antagonistic history between their fathers, Marcel kept Jacques at a wary distance.

By nature, Jacques was not as vindictive as his father. Yet like a knife being honed for the kill, Clifford rubbed at him until his mind was completed putrefied for revenge. Even on his deathbed, Clifford's ruthless quest to own La Pointe didn't abate.

Using his last shred of strength, he raised himself on his elbows and grasped the collars of Jacques's shirt. "Remember what you must do, Jacques," he rasped. "You must reclaim La Pointe, for me, for yourself, and for your daughter, Denise. It is your birthright. I won't rest in my grave until I know you have succeeded. Get it done! I am counting on you."

"Yes Father, I promise you we will avenge you by taking La Pointe. If I don't succeed, I will see to it that Denise does."

CHAPTER 26

The flowers in her father's garden were in full bloom as Catherine grasped the wooden railing of the gallery and painfully made her way to the little bench near the bird feeder. It was a sunny day, but she felt so cold. Even as she felt the sun's warmth touch her shoulders, she drew the ends of her robe tighter. She lifted her face heavenward, luxuriating in the rays that kissed her pale cheeks. Closing her eyes, she drew in a deep breath, letting it out slowly.

Marcel and Charles would be here soon, and she wanted these few minutes of solitude. She knew they were hurt by her actions. She was dying. She had known for some time, and she had strictly admonished her doctor into silence. Her sons had their own lives, and she hadn't wanted to burden them. Then too, she hadn't wanted them to impose on hers. They would have insisted she come to Toulon, so she had waited as long as possible to tell them.

Letting the back of the iron bench support her head, she kept her eyes closed. Other than the birds chirping, not another sound obtruded her mind. Then in the stillness she heard them, and she smiled with satisfaction.

Her father's booming laughter, her mother's soothing voice, Marie's teasing giggles, Sarah's vivacious chatter, Victor's gentle remarks, Francois's animated signing, Loretta's kindly tone, Raphael's colorful retorts, Clara's chastising yet caring reproofs, Bella's hearty chuckles, Ivan's fatherly resonance, and in the midst of them all, her beloved Jonah's passionate timbre. Had they really all existed, walked the fields of her life, or had she just imagined them all? *No.* She smiled. *They most assuredly lived and breathed, and as a result, are an indelible part of my tapestry.*

"Mama!" Charles's frantic cry scattered the birds from the feeder. "Are you okay?"

"I am fine, Charles, but you're scaring my birds yelling like that. Sit down, both of you." She made room beside her on the bench.

Her beautiful, amber eyes were the portal to her soul when she turned to look at them. She took a deep, calming breath. "There is much I need to say while I am still coherent, and I will start with my grandson, Jacob. Our blood runs through that boy's veins. He is one of us, but he is so far removed from us. I am challenging you both to continue to keep him connected to this family. Although he lives under the American flag, do not let him lose sight of us. See that he is treated fairly in his inheritance.

"Secondly, it was your grandfather, Ivan's, dream for your father to take charge of his parcels on St. Barth. Your father did so with gumption. He succeeded, and we built our lives on that island. Aside from you, his children, it was his pride and joy. See that Clifford does not succeed in his immoral attempts to take it from you.

"I have lived a full, satisfying life. I have been blessed with five children and a man who loved me beyond measure. Don't cry for me. Rejoice that I lived because you live. As much as possible, be happy, and take time to embrace the people God gives you. Life goes by too fast." Contemplatively, Catherine paused. The look of her face was a poignant mixture of wistfulness and emphasis.

"Now help me get back into the house." Gingerly she stood and steadied herself. "All the papers you need are in there, and don't think I am going anywhere with you. I spent my formative days in this house, and I will spend my last ones here too."

December 1, 1934

My dear nephew,

It is with sorrow that I must tell you of your grandmother, Catherine's passing. She died peacefully at her childhood home in Marseille. As per her wishes, we buried her beside her parents in the St. Pierre Cemetery.

She loved you deeply. She spoke your name in her last breaths.

With her passing, our family has lost its anchor. Nonetheless, I am resolute in picking up the baton. I will be leaving for St. Barth in the first week of the new year. It is my wish to make a trip to St. Thomas to see you.

Best regards on your eighteenth birthday. From your portraits you resemble your father even more as you grow older.

Please relay our love to your mother and Benjamin.

Your loving uncle,
Marcel.

Marcel never made the voyage to St. Barth that year. He developed a bad cold and cough, which led to a bout with pneumonia. He didn't make it the following year either. The bitter mistrals were harsher, and both his children were sick with fever. His wife, who had never made the voyage to St. Barth, prevailed upon him to cancel his plans.

Charles had recently married, and subsequently fathered a child. Between his new family and the fishing business, Charles declared he was too busy to make voyages to St. Barth. Marcel had noted with dismay his lax attitude, and it weighed heavily upon him, so much so that he telegraphed Hypolite, asking him to temporarily take on the responsibility of caring for La Pointe.

It didn't escape Jacques's notice that Marcel's visits were becoming fewer and farther between, and it aggravated him when he saw Hypolite's regular trips to La Pointe. He had repeatedly volunteered to tend the property. Marcel's lack of trust in him only served to cement what his father had drilled into him, that Jonah and Ivan had indeed stolen the parcels. Jacques had promised Clifford on his dying bed to extract vengeance, and now he believed he had found the way.

When another year passed and Marcel did not come to St. Barth, Jacques put his plan in motion. He penned a letter to Marcel requesting permission to farm the land at La Pointe. In it he stated how difficult it was for Hypolite, running the boardinghouse and regularly caring for La Pointe. Out of respect for Marcel, Jacques said, Hypolite would never admit his exhaustion, yet it was apparent in his features. Jacques sweetened his plea with the offer of recompense so that Marcel would benefit both from the upkeep and from the harvest. Then, knowing it would take months for the letter to arrive in France, he deceivingly wrote that he was already helping Hypolite with the upkeep.

The very next time Hypolite appeared at La Pointe, Jacques was ready. Not asking for Hypolite's consent, he took his sickle and began to clear away the weeds alongside him. A home-cooked meal from Julie Ann completed his treason.

"I know you're worn out, Hypolite," Jacques commiserated. "Two sets of hands will complete the task faster." *And noble fool that you are, you'll tell Marcel the truth when he ask if I am helping you.*

"I know it's a lot to ask, Hypolite, but although I have given Jacques permission to farm the land, I don't trust him. I need someone on the island to collect the rent and to keep receipts."

Marcel and Hypolite were seated together in what was once Clara's office. Hypolite had remodeled the space yet managed to keep its original ambiance. The big mahogany desk glowed from its recent polishing, but a new scent of lavender permeated the air. A painting of Clara and Raphael adorned the wall behind the desk. The painter had captured their essence well, and the familiar grin on Raphael's face kept arresting Marcel's gaze.

"Well, it's a lot to take on." The hesitancy in Hypolite's voice was audible. "Although Jacques has been faithful in helping me, I am not at all fond of him. He hides his true colors better than his father."

"That's exactly why I need you," Marcel replied. "While I intend to continue coming back, I cannot make these voyages yearly anymore. I am not the young man I once was."

As if on cue, a coughing spasm overtook Marcel, causing his body to convulse.

Hypolite stood in alarm. "Are you okay, Marcel? Do you need a glass of water?"

"No, no," he responded, his eyes watering as he dug into his coat for his handkerchief. "I promised my mother on her dying bed I would protect La Pointe. I was younger then. I didn't think about getting old or that Charles would have such little interest in helping me. Nonetheless, I must keep my vow. My children are not in a position to take on the task. That only leaves Francois's son, Jacob. I write to the boy regularly, and he writes back, but I get the feeling it is mainly because Olivia forces him." Clearing his throat again, he said, "Please consider accepting the caretaker duties on behalf of the family. You need not decide tonight. I will be on St. Barth for three months."

"I will do it, Marcel," Hypolite relented. "La Pointe was once my home. I have fond memories of our lives there. I will see to it that Jacques pays the rent. Not to worry. I am very good at keeping books. Now, you have just come from a long voyage. Your room is ready, so rest for a while before supper. Tomorrow before you leave for La Pointe, we will work out the details."

Those were the last three months Marcel spent on his beloved island home. Shortly after he returned to Toulon, Hypolite received a telegraph from Marcel's wife that he had died. She implored him to continue to watch over La Pointe, and so, Hypolite was charged with the task indefinitely.

#

Benjamin knew Olivia was sick, and he fervently wished it away. He had idealistically believed she would get better for two reasons: she was invincible, and he loved her too much.

With her indomitable nature Olivia fought the malady that was slowly ravishing her of her strength, defiantly rising and attacking each day with gusto, yet Benjamin helplessly watched her weaken until she could rise no more.

He had tried to get Jacob to sit beside his mother, but it was too much for Jacob. Benjamin hadn't seen him since last evening, and he had no knowledge of his whereabouts. Perhaps it was for the best. His own pain was so raw he could not bear Jacob's pain too.

"Benjamin?"

"I am right here."

"Promise me."

"Anything."

"Promise me you will see to it Jacob receives his birthright. It's what Francois would have wanted."

For an iota of a minute, Benjamin felt a jolt of jealousy. She was speaking Francois's name in her last breaths. "Yes, Livy, I promise to see that Jacob receives his birthright."

He smoothed back the damp hair from her face, his eyes filled with agony. *But I will not bury you besides Francois, so please don't ask that of me.*

#

Don't let falsely placed allegiance attack you now," Jacques's voice boomed as he spoke to Julie Ann. "You knew I was doing this. It took me months to perfect his signature. Now that we have the deed ready to be filed, it is no time to suffer a bout of conscience."

"But it's forgery! Everybody knows Jonah would never have signed that document."

"Just about everybody who knew Jonah is dead. Aside from those feeble fools in France and that young bastard in St. Thomas, who's left?

"Hypolite."

"Phew." Jacques laughed wickedly. "He's on his way out too."

For years now, Jacques had walked the land at La Pointe. He'd toiled it and tended it. With every single fruit he harvested, he thought about his father and how he had been deprived the simple pleasure, how he had been denied his rightful access to this beautiful piece of earth.

"Not anymore, Father," Jacques whispered the day he filed the fraudulent deed. "I have finally turned the wheels of justice, and I have avenged you."

After his first successful taste of depravity, Jacques turned his attention to stealing land from his neighbors, much like his father had done. In his quiet, unassuming way, he became more devious and daring than his father, and just like Clifford, he imparted his negativity to his only child, his daughter, Denise.

#

"Where are you going again?" Benjamin blocked the door to prevent Jacob from leaving.

"My whereabouts are none of your business."

"You came home drunk last night. I don't want you coming home drunk again tonight."

"Then I just won't come home. Now please move so I can pass. I am a man. You can't tell me what do to."

Benjamin looked into the green eyes of his stepson, sadly shook his head, and stepped aside. Jacob was right. Benjamin could not tell him what to do, but it hurt Benjamin each time Jacob rejected him.

Jacob was tall and built like Francois, but unlike Francois, he was laid-back and rebellious. Benjamin had tried to raise the subject of St. Barth many times, but Jacob had shrugged him off, showing no interest; so Benjamin began to despair that he would never be able to keep his promise to Olivia.

Jacob purposely slammed the door behind him. He knew he was a disappointment to Benjamin, and he was well aware that his actions were partly out of spite.

He couldn't tell for sure when the antagonistic feelings toward Benjamin had surfaced. As a boy he had adored him, but the feelings had begun even before his mother's death. He had a hunch they were the result of the letters he had started receiving from his uncle in France. Those letters had left him conflicted. He hadn't wanted to read them, much less respond to them. Yet his mother had posed no option. She had insisted that he reply to each and every letter. He had felt so guilty. His allegiance was to Benjamin, but the letters had spoken about another father and his people, a bloodline that was most assuredly his own, yet not of his heart.

Jacob was a grown man now, but still he felt penitent every time he quarreled with Benjamin. In times like these, only one person could soothe his restiveness, and he went in search of her. He knew where to look. There were only two places she frequented, the pool hall where she boasted about whooping everyone's butt or the beach where she solitarily sat on the rocks with her fishing pole.

"If you hit me with that slingshot one more time, Jacob, I swear I'll grab your balls and squeeze them."

"Yeah, well, feel free to grab away." Jacob picked up a round pebble and placed it on the sling. Smirking, he pulled back the bow and let it fly, catching Claire squarely on her left arm.

Claire put down her fishing pole and glared at him. "Jacob, I am warning you."

Jacob grinned, bending over to select another pebble. He was unprepared for Claire's swift reflexes. As he straightened, her hand grasped the full content of his crotch, and he hollered.

"There are other things you could do with it, you know."

"There's nothing else I want to do with it."

"But it's well versed in rendering pleasure."

"So you say," Claire teased back, her blue eyes dancing with mischief.

Pulling her tightly against him, Jacob tickled her until she loosened her grip.

"So when are you going to marry me?"

"I thought you weren't the marrying kind."

"I am not, but for a chance to be with you, I would gladly give up my bachelorship."

"Your father would have a conniption. It would be a scandal. I can hear it now." Pulling away from him, Claire playfully feigned, "Jacob, son of the almighty Benjamin, has selected a wife below his status. He has opted to marry Claire, the loony, bastard child of Loren."

"That's not even funny."

"But it's true, and you know it. We're good friends, Jacob. That's all we're allowed to be."

With her long, dark hair, bright blue eyes, and petite figure, Claire had grown into a beautiful woman. Having been raised by two single women, she was fiercely independent. She had inherited the gift that existed within her maternal bloodline, and like the women in her life, she was prone to dreams and intuitions. She had learned at an early age to embrace it. Born out of wedlock and raised by unmarried women, Claire was used to being spurned and talked about, so the added gossip of her gift did not faze her.

Her mother, Loren, and Olivia had remained close friends, and she and Jacob had always been buddies. In fact, Loren had once told her she had been christened in Jacob's baptismal clothes. They lived relatively close in proximity, but they were worlds apart. Jacob was accepted as part of the community. Claire lived on its outskirts.

But for Jacob, Claire was his mainstay. She was the one component in his life that never changed. With her, he could let his guard down and allow himself to be vulnerable.

In the last few years, though, his feelings for her had subtly changed. It was becoming increasingly difficult to spend time with her without needing to touch her. Not wanting to frighten her away, he tried hard to hide his feelings. She had told him many times she wasn't suited for him, but he knew the opposite was true. It was he who was not good enough for her, so he fought against the twinges of jealousy that tugged at him when he saw other men vying for her attention.

In tumult over his feelings for Claire, Jacob had already broached the subject with Benjamin. They had been sitting at the kitchen table chatting cordially. Benjamin had harvested a batch of papayas and was making thin vertical slits in the partially matured fruit to facilitate ripeness. It was seldom that they were not querulous, and Jacob had been reluctant to spoil the mood. Yet it had gnawed at him until he blurted, "Dad, I am going to marry Claire."

Benjamin's hands had stopped moving over the papayas. "You've known Claire all of your life. Where is this coming from?"

"I love her," he said simply.

"You can do better than Claire."

"Why? Because she's a bastard or because she was raised by her mother and her aunt, both of whom were never married? Which one is it, Dad?"

"Loren raised Claire well. I can't fault her for that, but Philarine"—Benjamin shook his head—"That woman is the spitting image of their aunt, Philar. You know, Philar turned out to be a gypsy, ran away from a good man to be with a vagabond from the sea. None of us could ever understand it."

"What does that have to do with my marrying Claire?"

Again deftly slicing thin slits into the papayas, Benjamin replied, "Your mother was a special woman. I never remarried because I knew I could never find anyone even close to her. You worry me a lot. She would want you happily married and settled down, and sometimes I feel like I've failed both her and you.

But Claire … I'm not sure she's right for you. You know, they're very odd women. They see and dream things, and that is not natural. I think there's a bit of gypsy in all the women in that lineage. Claire's grandmother, Loretta, used to scare the living daylights out of us. It was downright spooky how she knew things ahead of time. Think carefully about this, Jacob. Claire hasn't been raised in a proper family, and she's very freethinking. Can you handle the consequences of marrying a woman like her?"

And so, Jacob continued to tarry in seriously asking Claire for her hand until the day he realized that if he didn't act swiftly, he would lose her forever.

"Jacob, William has asked me to marry him. I am going to accept."

Jacob and Claire were playing pool, and Jacob stopped with the cue stick poised in his hands. Panic gripped him. Claire had said it so frankly that maybe he hadn't heard her correctly.

"What did you say?"

She laughed. "I guess you didn't clean the wax from your ears this morning. I said I am going to marry William."

Jacob dropped the cue stick on the pool table and walked toward Claire. "You can't do that. You can't marry that loser."

"Oh yes I can," she replied, placing her hands on her hips and looking up at him defiantly.

"No," he said firmly, gripping her shoulders, "because you're going to marry me."

"What? But your father—"

"To hell with my father. I am in love with you, and you will be no one else's wife but mine."

After Jacob passionately sealed his avowal with a kiss, Claire looked up at him impishly. "You know, Jacob, I really wasn't going to marry William. It's you I have always loved, but I finally realized that if I didn't scare the heck out of you, you would never come to your senses."

Jacob and Claire were married one month later. Benjamin stood beside Jacob and watched as Loren and Philarine proudly flanked Claire as she walked down the aisle. Automatically, his thoughts turned to Olivia.

Oh Livy, I was praying so hard for Jacob to find a wife that would make you proud, I missed the obvious choice right under my nose. You always liked Loren, and Catherine and Loretta were inseparable. How fitting then for Catherine's grandson to marry Loretta's granddaughter, and our son, he's glowing with happiness.

Benjamin glanced sideways at the tall, handsome man that was the spitting image of Francois, and he felt the stirrings of hope. *It's not too late. I promise you, Livy, as long as God gives me strength, I will find a way to fulfill my promise to you.*

PART II

CHAPTER 27

Hypolite 's firstborn daughter, Nanette, was troubled. The disclosures in her father's papers were problematical. His passing had hurt so deeply that she had delayed looking through his files. He had been sick for so long, and between running the boardinghouse and attending to him, she had been totally exhausted.

Nanette knew Hypolite had been angst-ridden over what was happening at La Pointe. He had tried his best for so long, but his sickness had eventually halted his efforts. A deep frown creased her brow as she remembered their last conversation. With a determined tremor in his voice from his urgent need to make her understand, he had told her where to find the rent books along with all the notes he had kept about Jacques's underhandedness. She had promised him she would get in contact with the Dusant descendents in France and in St. Thomas, and she was way behind on her promise.

Now Nanette's hands shook with the evidence that lay before her. Her father had kept every receipt, every pertinent scrap of paper, and he had made meticulous notes.

Jacques Dusant is a very powerful and dangerous man. How do I go about helping these people without endangering myself? She thought as she put the documents in chronological order. *The first thing I need to do is reestablish the family line, and I must find the whereabouts of the missing brother, Victor Dusant. An investigator will need to be hired to trace him.* No. She frowned. *The first thing I need to do is make contact with the rightful heirs.*

Benjamin took off his reading glasses and rested Nanette's letter on his lap. The news of what Jacques had done disturbed him greatly, and he felt responsible. The girl was only sixteen. He had hoped to wait a few more years, but now he had no choice. Jacob would have to serve as frontage, but she would be the driving force. He reached for the telephone on the corner table.

"All right already!"

The continuous shrill of the alarm clock penetrated the sound sleep Nicole Dusant was finally enjoying, and with her eyes barely open, she reached out to shut it off. She squinted to bring the clock's red numbers into focus. It was already 7:08 a.m. "Great," she grumbled. She had the last two of her senior final exams to take this morning. She had to get moving.

Stretching languorously, she staggered into the bathroom. As she pulled her hair back into a ponytail, she looked at her reflection. Pretty, hazel eyes stared back at her, and for a nanosecond, an analogous pair of eyes flashed in her psyche. It caused her hands to halt midway in pulling the elastic band through her hair. She frowned. *Who are these people, and why do they keep hounding me?*

The dreams had plagued her again.

Nicole's parents, Jacob and Claire, were teasingly badgering each other when she walked into the kitchen.

"Save it, please. I just want to eat something quickly and get out of here. Then you can go back to whatever it was you were doing."

"Morning, Nic," they both chimed in response.

Laughing, Claire stopped tickling Jacob and turned her attention to her daughter. "Your grandfather called early this morning. He asked if you could come over Sunday after church."

"Sure, what's up with him?"

"I don't know," Claire replied flippantly. "I never understood your father's loony family."

"You think they're loony? It's your side who sees and hears things that aren't really there."

"You can say that again, Nic," Jacob said. "She kept me up half the night with her wacko dreams."

Nicole looked at her mother, her expression curious. "You too, Mom? Those people wearing funny clothes bugged me all night."

"Oh Lord, deliver me from crazy women," Jacob mumbled.

"You're stuck with us. Now eat your breakfast. Your eggs are getting cold." Claire turned to Nicole, "Make sure to call your grandfather before he says I am willfully keeping you away."

"Grandpa knows no one can keep me away from him. Besides, he loads up on all my favorite snacks when he knows I'm coming."

"He spoils you rotten, that's what he does." Claire ruffled her daughter's hair.

As Nicole drove to Benjamin's house on Sunday morning, she thought of how much she genuinely liked her grandfather. Short and round in stature with incredibly clear, blue eyes, he was always happy. He was old, but he didn't complain about his aches and pains like her friends' grandparents did. With his white hair, red cheeks, and round belly, she often thought he would make a perfect Santa Claus.

"Here's my girl!" Benjamin greeted her warmly when she walked into his neat, little house. After kissing both her cheeks, he stared deeply into her eyes as if checking on her soul. He smelled of a combination of old spice cologne and fried chicken.

"You hungry? I fried up some chicken and made your favorite johnny cakes."

Without waiting for a reply, he turned in the direction of the kitchen, and she followed. His movements were oddly jittery, giving Nicole her first clue that something was bothering him.

"Are you feeling okay, Grandpa?"

"Sure thing, especially now that you're here," he said, putting two plates of food on the table.

They ate in their usual comfortable amity, with him asking how she was doing in school and genuinely listening to her responses. Then Benjamin got up and cleared the table. Nicole noticed that his hands shook when he opened a drawer and withdrew an old, brown folder. He placed it on the table and retook his seat. Then looking down at the folder, he subconsciously tabbed on it with his right thumb.

"Nicole, you know how much I love you."

"Of course, Grandpa. I love you too."

"You also know I am not your grandfather by blood. Your grandfather, Francois, died when your father was less than a year old, and your grandmother, Olivia, remarried me. He was my first cousin. She was the most beautiful, stubborn woman I have ever known, and she was the love of my life."

He cleared his throat. "I made her a promise, and up until you came to us, I wasn't sure I could keep it." In the heavy silence that followed, he sighed deeply. "Now it's more prudent than ever."

Taking an envelope from the folder, he withdrew two sheets of paper with elegantly written cursive. "Your great-great-grandfather, Ivan, used to traverse the seas exporting and importing goods to and from France. He fell in love with the unique beauty of St. Barth, and he purchased property high on a hill there in a place called La Pointe.

"In time, partly because of France's impending war with Germany and partly because his nephew, Clifford, and your great-grandfather, Jonah, were at brutal odds with each other, Ivan sent Jonah and your great-grandmother, Catherine, to build and settle on the parcels. A small group of family and close friends accompanied them. My parents, Pierre and Marie, who was also Catherine's sister, your great-grandparents, Josiah and Agnes, and your great-grandmother, Loretta, were part of that group. Loretta met your great-grandfather, Paul, on the island. Your grandfather and I were born at La Pointe.

"They worked hard to build a new life, and they were content." Benjamin took a deep breath and shook his head sadly. "Then Clifford and Roger, another ill-reputed cousin, followed them to the island, and the discord that had started in France continued.

"When Jonah died, Catherine and two of her sons returned to France. Your grandfather came to St. Thomas with Olivia and her parents. I came with them."

His fingers involuntarily played with the corners of the letter. "For years, Jonah and Catherine's eldest son, Marcel, made annual voyages from France to upkeep the estate. When he could no longer go regularly, he enlisted my brother, Hypolite, as caretaker. Hypolite did the best he could for a long time, but then he got sick."

"I don't understand, Grandpa," Nicole interrupted. "What does all this have to do with me?"

"I am getting to that. Bear with me a few more minutes."

Benjamin dolefully gestured to the letter. "I received this from Hypolite's daughter, Nanette, last week. Several years ago, Clifford's son, Jacques, prepared a spurious deed and forged Jonah's name on it. With none of the heirs present to oppose him, he has successfully filed it with the French government."

"So?" Nicole shrugged. "I still don't see what it has to do with me."

"It has everything to do with you, Nicole. These parcels are your birthright. Your ancestors fought hurricanes, droughts, and bad economic times. They braved wars and perilous seas to put down roots, and they did so with sweat and blood. They will not rest peacefully until someone in their bloodline rises to the challenge of reclaiming what rightfully belong to them."

"Are Dad and I the only ones left?" There was a tremor in Nicole's voice.

"No, you have cousins in France. Nanette sent letters to them too. She is coming here next week to meet with us. She will fill us in on the missing pieces."

"What do you want me to do, Grandpa?"

"Nothing until we speak with Nanette. Then we will set a course of action. Your father will have to sign the legal papers because you're under age, but ultimately this is going to be your fight, Nicole, and it's not going to be easy. But don't worry." Benjamin reached out and touched her cheek. "I will do all I can to help you."

Then deftly changing the subject, he said, "Now you haven't said a word to me about that prom yet. Your father told me you went shopping for your dress last weekend."

A while later, Benjamin watched her drive away until the little, red car was completely out of sight. Then he walked over to the mantle and picked up Olivia's portrait. He lovingly ran his fingers over her image.

I am keeping my word, Livy, but I am not pleased about it. She reminds me so much of you, but she's just a slip of a girl, too young to have this battle placed on her slender shoulders. We're putting her up against underhanded, powerful people.

Nanette stepped off the ramp attached to the small plane and breathed a sigh of relief. Gazing at the surrounding green hills of St. Thomas, her body began to relax. She hated flying. She didn't mind the big planes too much, but these tiny planes made her feel constricted. She had been seated so close to the other four passengers she could smell their breath, and then the man seated by her side had started an awful coughing. Turning her face toward the window, she'd closed her eyes and tried to calm her rapidly beating heart, but every little bump had increased its cadence.

Steadying herself, she walked into the terminal and started in the direction of the luggage carousel. She only had one small suitcase, but there had been no room inside the mosquito-sized plane to store it.

I am a single, middle-aged woman. Why am I muddling myself in this mêlée?

Nanette hadn't wanted to come. She'd never met her cousin, Benjamin, much less his stepson. Yet every time she tried to talk herself out of getting involved, she heard her father's beseeching voice.

Resolutely, she retrieved her suitcase and walked into the blaring, noonday sun.

"Nanette!"

She heard her name being called above the din of the taxi drivers vying for attention. Shading her eyes with her hand, she saw a shorter version of her father walking quickly toward her.

"I would recognize you anywhere. You look just like Hypolite," Benjamin said, enfolding her in his arms. Then taking her suitcase, he led her across the street to the parking area.

Nanette was taken aback as they drove through the streets of Charlotte Amalie. In contrast to the quietness of St. Barth, this island was bustling. The road they were traveling consisted of four lanes, two in either direction. It was bracketed by a busy waterfront on one side and a populated commercial district on the other.

"Thank you so much for coming," Benjamin said. "My stepson and his daughter will be joining us for dinner this evening."

"You may not want to thank me after you hear everything I have to say," she replied. "Jacques is convinced the parcels belong to him, and he has passed that conviction to his daughter, Denise. She is just as vicious as her father, and so is her husband, Xavier. They successfully filed a deed claiming that Jonah Dusant signed it. They said they have an affidavit, also signed by Jonah, acknowledging that his father, Ivan, wrongfully took ownership of the parcels although this alleged affidavit has not been duly filed alongside the deed."

Nanette looked across at Benjamin. The gravity in her voice was clearly discernable. "They are dangerous adversaries. Their misdealing has made them rich, so they have plenty of money, and people are afraid to oppose them." Looking down at her fingers, she added, "Even me."

"What are you saying?"

"I am saying that I will face their wrath when they find out I am helping you. It's a bit disconcerting because I am a single woman running a boardinghouse."

"I don't want to put you in any danger."

She touched his arm. "Don't worry. They never liked my father because of his allegiance to Marcel, so I am used to their hostility. Besides, I promised him on his deathbed to help bring about justice. It bothered him terribly that he was not able to stop the wrong being done because of his illness. I have been through his papers. He kept meticulous records, and he made his own affidavit before he died, vindicating Jonah. I have done my own research too. I have been able to reestablish the family tree and locate all the heirs with the exception of one. I am going to France next week to speak to the heirs there."

"Bless you for what you are doing."

"My father was the most honest man I knew, and seeing this injustice corrected meant everything to him. I have to do this to honor him."

"Nicole, you must take up the mantle."
"What mantle?"
"You are not alone. We are all here to brace you."
"Wait! Where are you going? You haven't answered me. Who are you? Wait!"

Nicole bolted upright in bed and squinted at the clock. It was 3:30 a.m. They had haunted her all night, drifting in and out of her dreams, faces that looked familiar; silhouettes that seemed recognizable.

"I have to talk to Mom about this," she mumbled, throwing off the covers. "This mumbo jumbo is all due to her crazy side of the family. Who are these people anyway?"

As her feet touched the floor, it hit her, and she abruptly sat back down on the bed. *Oh God! Could it be? Grandpa said they won't rest until …*

"Oh no!" she said hotly. "They're not going to drop this shitload on me! I am not interested, do you hear me?" she shouted to the empty room. "So just go back to wherever you came from and leave me alone. I don't know anything about St. Barth. I don't even know where it is. Now let me sleep for God's sake!"

"The first thing we have to do is locate the family of the missing brother, Victor, who joined the French marines when he was only sixteen. I have already taken the liberty of hiring an investigative company. As we speak, they are tracing him and periodically reporting back to me. Based on their research, he was last known to be in the state of Nevada. That was many decades ago. From there the lead is cold."

Bored, Nicole watched the older woman lean back in her chair and run her fingers through her short, dark hair, leaving the ends standing up in a funny spike. She wanted to laugh, but one look at her father and grandfather wiped any thought of humor. They were intently listening to the woman.

In her thick, French accent, she continued speaking. "I suggest you start by hiring a lawyer. Have him send Jacques Dusant a letter on behalf of Jacob. He needs to be served with an official warning from each of the heirs advising him of their intent to pursue ownership of their parcels. I should be getting a final report from the investigative company on Victor soon. I will need your financial help to pay for it, but once we have it, we will know where we stand when it comes to him. I will send you letters regularly to keep you informed of everything, including my trip to the heirs in France."

#

Nicole's admiration for her grandfather was immense. Yet she didn't share in his enthusiasm. Aside from the fragmented stories she'd heard growing up, she knew very little about her familial ties to St. Barth and much less about her ancestral bonds that extended to France.

Although he hardly ever did so, her grandfather was the only person she knew who spoke French. She was part of a culture that had become Americanized. The language and traditions of their ancestors had been watered down, and as a result, her generation had lost a vital piece of their heritage.

As her grandfather hired lawyers, and legal letters flew to and from St. Barth, Nicole matured and learned more about the zealous people whose blood flowed through her veins. Nanette faithfully reported back on her progress in long, cursive letters, and Nicole carefully read every letter. She found that Nanette was a wellspring of knowledge on the family's history, and hungrily, she questioned her, collecting nuggets of priceless information on her lineage. Nicole questioned Benjamin too, hounding him for stories of her ancestors until she felt she intimately knew Catherine, Jonah, and the others. Now she understood the origins of her intuitive sense. Its roots ran deeply in her maternal line.

At the same time the dreams intensified, enhancing an intrinsic bond, compelling Nicole to step forward and accept the mantle that had been placed at her feet. She hadn't looked for this battle. It had found her. Perhaps had she known about the decades of her life it would consume or how it would affect her future, she would have walked away.

Yet in truth she knew the choice of retreating had never been an option. She had been thrust back into her ethnicity, propelled there by forebears long gone. It was an infinite induction that would bring her full circle.

"Nic, the lawyers think it's time for you to show your presence."

Nicole watched Benjamin shuffle to the table and sit down. The tremor in his hands had become more prevalent, and his agility had significantly slowed. It saddened her to see the effects of aging slowly fleecing him of his vitality.

Yet his blue eyes still sparkled with fervor when he looked at her. "It's been a tedious and lengthy process. It has taken us years, but all the legal documents are now filed, both by us and your European cousins. Still, it hasn't dissuaded Jacques. As you know, he keeps returning our letters unopened." Benjamin shrugged. "I guess he believes that if he ignores us, we will go away."

"Mom is still not feeling well. I will have to bring Noah with me," Nicole replied, referring to her one-year-old son.

"And David. I don't want you to go there without your husband." Benjamin reached for Nicole's hand. "Nic, promise me you will be careful. St. Barth is a beautiful island with good people, and it's your heritage, but you're dealing here with bad people who won't think twice about harming you."

Nicole reassuringly rubbed Benjamin's hand. "Grandpa, you know David would tie himself to the plane if I tried to leave without him. Don't worry, everything will be fine. I will go ahead and make the reservations. The lawyers are right. It's time I finally saw St. Barth."

Two years before, Nicole had married David Michaels, an army sergeant with a winning smile and soulful brown eyes. They had met at the wedding of a mutual friend, and Nicole had intuitively known she had met her soul mate although they were complete opposites. She was well schooled and sheltered. He was outspoken and audacious.

When David had proposed, Nicole felt it was essential for him to know of her mission to reclaim her family's estate. This was her millstone. She hadn't wanted to encumber him with it, but she'd needed assurance that he would understand her purpose. She needn't have worried. David was both supportive and protective.

The tiny plane dipped and swayed. Other than the pilot and another female passenger, David, Noah, and Nicole were the only people onboard. When Nicole had climbed into the small space, she'd had second thoughts about bringing Noah, but after saying a prayer she'd forced herself to relax.

As they flew over the foaming Atlantic waters, she couldn't help but think of her ancestors and the trials they must have endured crossing the seas, not only from St. Barth to St. Thomas, but on the long journeys from France. Her destiny as an American had been decided by one of those fateful voyages.

Her thoughts were interrupted by the pilot's voice advising them to make sure their seat belts were fastened because they was descending into the airport, and her nerves went crazy again when she saw two hills sandwiching the plane and a mere strip of asphalt below them that ended abruptly with the sea.

After the pilot skillfully landed, coming to an uncomforting stop just short of the sea, they deplaned beneath the midday sun and walked from the tarmac over to the small, one-room building that served as a terminal. Nanette met them, helped them rent a car, and directed them to their hotel. She advised them to enjoy the rest of the day because tomorrow she would take them to La Pointe, and all hell would break loose.

Realizing they may never have another opportunity to explore the island anonymously, they took full advantage of the day. In the open-air jeep customary to St. Barth, they looked like ordinary tourists, and Nicole could study the island and its people unobserved. She immediately noticed the similarities to the French people of St. Thomas. So many resembled people she knew, both in character and in looks.

They explored the pristine beaches of St. Jean and Gouverneur and the unique beauty of Shell Beach, with its myriad array of shells glistening in the sand. They meandered in and out of the quaint, little shops in Gustavia. They drove to La Pointe, slipping unnoticed on to the estate. They found the ruins of Jonah and Catherine's house and took pictures in front of it. They marveled at the view her ancestors had once admired. Then as evening fell, with their baby son asleep in his stroller, they enjoyed a scrumptious dinner replete with French wine in an open-air restaurant while they laughed in amusement at the dogs lying on the floor at their owners' feet.

Early the next morning they were dressed and waiting for Nanette. The carefree mood of the day before had been replaced by apprehension.

"You ready?" David asked, touching her cheek.

"As ready as I'll ever be."

"Prepare yourselves; this is not going to be pleasant," Nanette said when she picked them up. There was a burly man in the front seat beside her.

"This is my cousin, Antoine. He's accompanying us."

Then they were on the way, driving across Gustavia to the winding hills of La Pointe.

When Nanette parked the jeep against a steep hill in front of a grocery store, she turned around in her seat to look at Nicole. "Remain calm. Do not let them rattle you into arguing. You simply want to show your presence, that's all."

Despite the burly man Nanette had brought along, Nicole could see she was nervous. "Is it okay to bring our son in there?"

"Yes, they're not stupid enough to physically attack us, but they will try to intimidate you."

Nicole's apprehension rose as they walked into the grocery store. David's hand on her back comforted her, but it did little to quell her anxiety.

The bell above the door chimed. The space inside was hot and airless. Narrow aisles overcrowded with merchandise added to the congested feeling, and the lone ceiling fan did little to alleviate it. Except for a woman and a little girl of about five quibbling over a bag of chocolates in the first aisle, the store was empty.

Nanette greeted the chubby, red-headed woman behind the register who had been so preoccupied with a magazine that she hadn't even looked up when the bell had chimed.

"Hello, Denise."

Upon seeing Nanette, the woman started yelling, rattling on in French. Nicole couldn't understand her, but she knew what she was saying wasn't pleasantries.

Two men came running from a room behind the register. Nicole knew the older man was Jacques and the younger man, a light-skinned black man with acne scars on his face, was Jacques' son-in-law, Xavier.

"What are you doing in my store, Nanette?" Jacques blurted.

"I have brought one of the Dusant heirs. Please make the acquaintance of Nicole Dusant Michaels, daughter of Jacob Dusant, granddaughter of Francois Dusant, and great-granddaughter of your father's nemesis, Jonah Dusant."

To her credit, Nanette had delivered the statement with aplomb. There had even been a bit of glee in her voice, and the shock on their faces registered the strike.

"So? Why have you brought her here?" Xavier recovered more quickly than his wife and her father.

"She's here to give you notice that she intends to reclaim her inheritance."

Jacques started laughing, and his daughter and son-in-law laughed with him. "This puny girl is going to challenge us? Let her try."

Nanette looked affronted and opened her mouth to speak.

Touching her arm, Nicole said calmly, "Let me handle this." She handed Noah to David, her eyes warning him to keep quiet.

Then she stepped in front of Nanette.

"Yes, I am challenging you. I was hoping we could settle this agreeably, but I see now that's not an option." She paused and looked at each one of them in turn. "I am not afraid of you, your money, or your wickedness. I am duly giving you notice to vacate my family's estate."

"Who the hell do you think you are?" Denise yelled. "You're not even a Dusant. You're nothing but a common bastard!"

"Oh I am a Dusant for sure, and I will prove it to you." Nicole turned to David and Nanette. "I am done here."

Denise, Jacques and Xavier watched them walk across the street. After Nanette had shifted the jeep into gear and started down the hill,

Jacques said, "That damned Nanette, she's always digging her nose into things that don't concern her. We're going to have to teach her a lesson. "Turning to Xavier, he said, "Late tonight, drive into Gustavia and flatten all four of her tires. While you're at it, key the side of the jeep too."

"It won't change the fact that she's already riled up that girl and the others in France." Xavier replied.

"You work on stopping Nanette. I will handle the girl. That dunce, Francois, wouldn't have known what to do with a woman; so your sister is right, the girl is a bastard." Jacques hawked loudly and spat into a waste basket behind the counter. "I will find out where they're staying and frighten the shit out of them tonight. Those parcels are ours. We will never let anyone take them from us."

With his plentiful contacts, it didn't take Jacques long to find out the name of Nicole and David's hotel. He grinned wickedly with the knowledge. The hotel consisted of private, single bungalows scattered all over the premises.

Jacques fought to stay awake until after midnight. He had drunk too much, and the alcohol's effect was working against him. After drinking a cup of strong, black coffee, he got into his truck and drove across the island. He parked the truck a quarter mile from the hotel and walked briskly in the darkness, the cool night air helping to sober him up.

Locating the correct bungalow, he creped quietly around it. His foot snagged on a tree stump and he stumbled. Whispering profanities, he regained his balance and waited, listening for any sounds from inside the bungalow. He could hear David's snores. Snaking against the wall, he ran his hands over the louvers near the door. The beams from a car traveling on the road below flashed against the bungalow, and cursing again, he slinked back into the darkness. When blackness reclaimed the night, he crept again to the louvers. Finding a lose one; he quietly pried at it until he successfully removed two, enough to get his hands through to the doorknob.

They were sound asleep in the darkened room. *I should kill them all now,* Jacques thought.

Stealthily he slinked over to the crib where the little boy slept on his side, his thumb in his mouth. Jacques picked up the child. As if knowing he was in danger, the boy started to cry, instantly waking his parents. Jacques pulled a knife out of his back pocket and placed it to the little boy's throat.

CHAPTER 28

David flew off the bed, Nicole right behind him.

"Take another step, and I will slice his throat."

Nicole gave a loud sob.

Jacques put the child on the ground and stepped backward, wielding the knife in front of him. "See how easy it was for me to get to you?" he said. "This was only a warning. Drop your pursuit of my parcels, or I will kill all of you." Then he backed out the door into the darkness.

Nicole rushed to pick up Noah while David hurried outside, but Jacques had disappeared into the night.

"How did it go?" Jacob asked when he picked them up at the airport the next day.

"Everything went fine, Dad," Nicole said brightly. "Now they know we mean business."

She didn't tell her father what had happened in the early hours of the morning. She would never worry him like that, but there was a new fire flaming inside of Nicole. The fact that Denise had called her a bastard had upped the ante, and what Jacques had done to make her cower had only served to intensify her determination. They didn't want a peaceful resolution, they wanted a battle, and they would get one.

Ten months later, Nicole and David were back in St. Barth. Nicole was meeting her European cousins for the first time to subdivide the estate pending the court's decision. Meeting them was a poignant moment. Although they had spent their lives on different continents, the intrinsic traits of family were immediately obvious.

The episode with Jacques still fresh on Nicole's mind, she had insisted they all stay at a hotel with rooms confined within a main building.

Sure enough, it hadn't taken long for word to spread to Jacques that they were on the island. He and Xavier followed them around, issuing threats until they retreated back to the safety of the hotel, and even then the proprietor had to call the gendarmes to remove Jacques and Xavier from his property.

"Sell it."

"No, Dad. I don't want to sell it. Those parcels are my heritage, something I can leave for my children."

Jacob looked at his daughter exasperatingly. "Those parcels will bring you trouble. That's why your cousins sold their shares."

"They sold their shares because they are so far removed from St. Barth, all the way in France. I am only forty minutes away. I am looking forward to building a second home there. Dad, you've never felt the same allegiance as I do when it comes to this."

"Nicole, those people are wicked. They will never let you live there in peace. Even your grandfather agrees with me. Sell it and buy land somewhere else if you want."

"We won the case, Dad. Those parcels are ours. I don't want just any land. I want my heritage."

The court had ruled in their favor. The deed had been successfully rescinded. Her cousins had immediately sold their shares, and their buyer had approached Nicole with a lucrative offer, but she remained adamant. Two months later they were served with a subpoena. Jacques Dusant had initiated legal charges to reclaim the parcels. Unwittingly, Nicole's determination to hold on to her birthright had unleashed the wrath of her family's nemesis, heralding an unending litany of court cases and bodily threats.

#

From the moment she felt her cell phone's vibration in her jacket, Nicole knew it was bad news. With the downward trend in mortgage interest rates, her real estate office was inundated with request for showings. She'd just finished locking the doors of the last house.

She'd missed the call. Sighing with trepidation, she looked at the caller ID. Pressing the redial button, she listened as each ring resounded in her ear and headed straight for her heart. For a moment, she thought the call would go to voice mail, but Claire answered on the final ring.

"Nicole, thank God! You need to come now."

"I am on my way."

Nicole hated hospitals. The antiseptic smell mingled with the stench of sickness made her feel queasy. The brightly colored motifs and spotlessly sterile isles contrasted in their effort to disprove the aura of death, and she swiped at the tears coming down her cheeks. Blindly rounding a corridor, she bumped into David.

He put his arms around her. "He's only waiting for you," he said softly, propelling her down the hall.

Peering into the glass panes of the door, she saw her father sitting on the lone chair in the room; her mother was rubbing his shoulders. Taking a deep breath, she pushed open the door.

"Here's my girl."

Her grandfather's blue eyes lit up against his pale skin, and he tried to raise himself off the bed to hug her.

"No, Dad, you're going to pull out your tubes." Jacob quickly got to his feet as Nicole sat gently on the edge of the bed and bent to give Benjamin the hug he so wanted.

"Come Jacob. I need a cup of tea." Claire pulled her husband to his feet. Turning to her son-in-law, she said, "You know I hate those damned elevators, so you need to come too."

With a worried glance at Nicole, who nodded her approval, David followed his in-laws out the door.

"Ah, my Nicole." Benjamin's voice was raspy. "You have brought me so much joy. But I've always felt guilty for putting the weight of your family's troubles on you. It's your grandmother's fault, you know. Never could deny that woman anything."

Drifting off, he closed his eyes. For a moment Nicole thought he had stopped breathing, and she felt like her own heart had stopped. She stole a frightening look at the heart monitor. Its squiggly lines were erratic, but they were still moving. She hated it and feared it simultaneously.

"I dreamt about her last night."

Relief, Nicole laid her head on his wheezing chest, his familiar smell comforting her.

"She was in a frenzy, cleaning the house 'cause I was coming home. I told her it didn't matter. I just want to be with her, but she wouldn't listen." He chuckled softly. "Stubborn-ass woman."

His hands were encumbered by tubes, so he couldn't move them, but she felt when he lowered his chin to rub against her hair.

"I see them, Nic. They're all here. They don't want you to lose courage. They—Livy!"

Nicole felt the instant Benjamin's heart stopped. Raising her head, she looked at his peaceful face. The smile she knew so well played at the corners of his mouth, and she knew he was in the arms of her grandmother.

In the weeks that followed Benjamin's passing, Nicole tried to immerse herself in her work. Her grandfather had been her mainstay in the ongoing court battles, and she missed his candid advice and encouragement. But mostly she missed him, and her mind remained muddled with grief.

When her interoffice line rang, she was struggling to keep her mind focused on the case she was working on. The people involved were challenging. She had shown them several houses that matched their specific requests, and they had found faults with every one. But they were repeat customers, and she was determined to keep them happy.

"Nicole, there is a Mr. Smith here waiting to see you." Her secretary, Ellen, sounded confused. "He said he has an appointment, but I don't have it on your calendar."

"Did he say what it's about?"

"He said he spoke with you last week relative to a new construction development on St. John, and you told him to come in at eleven o'clock today to continue the discussion."

"I don't remember, but that doesn't mean he didn't speak with me. Please send him in."

As Nicole placed the telephone receiver back in its cradle, the skin on her neck prickled. On guard now, she braced herself.

A man with the beginnings of a beer belly appeared in her doorway. Entering the room, he closed the door. Nicole hadn't seen him in awhile, but she instantly recognized Xavier, Denise Dusant's husband.

Calmly she stood and tried to move past him to reopen the door. "I have nothing to say to you. Please leave my office before I call security."

"I have something to say to you," he whispered menacingly, blocking her exit and backing her onto her desk. "You're a stubborn, stupid, persistent bitch. I should snap your neck right now. Accidents happen so easily." Xavier was so close, Nicole could smell his perspiration.

While he had been speaking, she had managed to reach behind her and retrieve the letter opener on her desk. Now she swiftly brought the pointy edge forward and up against his crotch. "You're not in St. Barth now. You're on American soil. This is my turf. If you ever come here or anywhere near me or my family again, I will have you deported so quickly your ass will be looking back for your head." She pressed the tip of the letter opener harder against his crotch, and he flinched. She felt when the blade punctured the cloth of his pants, and she pressed harder. "Now get out of my office before I start to scream. There are some horny men in St. Thomas's jail who would enjoy your company tonight."

The hatred in Xavier's eyes was vitriolic as he slowly stepped backward. Keeping the letter opener firmly pressed against his crotch, she reached past him and turned the door knob with her other hand.

Spit foamed at the corners of his mouth in anger. "Next time I am going to kill you." Then turning, he walked down the corridor.

David was livid when Nicole told him later that evening.
"We have to call the police."

"And tell them what? By now he's on the flight back to St. Barth. David, I didn't tell you this to upset you."

"Damn it, Nicole! You should have called me!"

"And then you would be spending time in jail. He's not worth it, and besides, his main intent was to scare me. "

"Well, I still want to beat the shit out of him."

The following Friday afternoon, Nicole let her staff go early. They had been so busy the past few weeks, working way into the evenings and on weekends, and she knew they needed a respite. She too, planned on enjoying the evening with David.

She was locking the office door when her cell phone rang. Sighing she put the phone to her ear.

"Hello, is this Nicole Michaels?" A female voice asked.

"Yes, it is. How might I help you?"

"I am so glad to reach you. My name is Samantha, but everybody calls me Sam. I don't know why; I certainly don't look like a Sam. I am all girly." The woman chuckled loudly at her own joke and then gushed on, "My husband and I are really interested in the house on Hibiscus Lane in Peterburg. We just saw the listing this morning, and we went by the house. You were there showing it to someone. I wanted to come in, but my husband said it was impolite to bust in on someone else's time. I am so sorry to call you so late on a Friday afternoon, but he's leaving on a business trip tomorrow morning, and we would really love to see it. We're available right now. Can you show it to us?"

Nicole paused. She was tired, but she didn't like turning away a potential client. Beside, the sales price for the Peterborg property was over a million dollars.

"Okay, Samatha," she replied. "How soon can you and your husband be at the house?"

The woman let out a gleeful whoop. "We can be there in half an hour."

"Make it forty-five minutes. It's almost five o'clock, and traffic will be heavy."

Nicole took the mountain route, going up through Solberg where she got caught in traffic. She looked at her watch impatiently. She hadn't expected this much traffic on this road. She liked to be at least fifteen minutes ahead of her clients. She used the time to inspect the property and open the windows and doors.

As she waited for the traffic to move, she glanced down at Charlotte Amalie's vibrant harbor, and its alluring beauty captured her gaze. St. Thomas was her home, her birth place, but she sometimes took its beauty for granted. It was in unexpected moments like these when she realized it.

The traffic finally moved, and she made it across Solberg, through Mafolie, down the winding road to Magens Bay and up the hill to Peterborg. She arrived at the house with ten minutes to spare, but she felt uneasy when she put her hand on the car door to open it.

I am spooking myself unnecessarily. That woman sounded really interested in this house, and she didn't have a French accent. So why am I freaking out?

Still, Nicole left her purse in the car and exited with only her car keys in hand. She paused, taking a moment to appreciate the view. Below her, Magens Bay glistened invitingly in the setting sun, and she promised herself that she would go for a swim this weekend.

She proceeded toward the house, and again she felt perturbed. Shaking off the feeling, she headed for the front door. As she put the key in the lock, a hand clamped tightly over her mouth.

"I warned you to stop pursuing my parcels. Now I am going to kill you."

CHAPTER 29

Nicole could feel Xavier's hot breath against her cheek as he began dragging her behind the building. His hand was covering her nostrils, making it difficult to breathe. She forced herself to remain calm, to think clearly. The car keys! They were still in her hand! With one hand, she desperately tried to undo the lid on the canister of pepper spray attached to the key chain. Relieved flooded her when she felt the lid give way. Then she aimed the canister blindly behind her. Xavier's grip instantly loosened, and she seized the chance, planting a hard back kick into his crotch. When he bent over, she tried to run, but he sprang forward, grabbing hold of her feet. Nicole fell forward, bringing him down with her. She reached for a high-heeled, black, leather shoe that had slipped off her foot, and aimed it at Xavier's face. The pointy heel caught him squarely in the left eye. Then with her car keys still in one hand, she ran to her car.

Trembling, Nicole drove back to her office and bolted the door. She knew it was an unwise move. She was alone in the office, and Xavier could have easily followed her, but she needed time alone to compose herself before going home to David. She had no intention of telling him what had happened. She knew David too well. He would immediately want to curtail her movements, and she would be damned before she allowed Denise, Xavier, and their cohorts to restrict her life. She sat at her desk willing her body to calm down, but her mind was in chaos. *Xavier knew I was at the Peterborg property earlier in the day. Dear God! That means he's been following me!*

She had to admit, tonight had been the most frightening, but there were constant threats: vehicles tailing hers, unexplained flat tires and brakes failures, dead birds and other small animals strewn in her yard and on the ground outside her car, intimidating words passed on to key people and filtered down to her, random appearances and bold stares all designed to unnerve her. They were clever, leaving no traces behind to legally accuse them

When Jacques had died, his daughter, Denise, had taken up the feud, ruthlessly determined to appeal every court case Nicole won, and the French court was allowing Denise this avenue time and time again, taking years to call each case.

But with every case Nicole won, Denise and Xavier's fury grew, and so did their crafty attacks. So many times she regretted not agreeing with her father to sell the parcels, and now it was too late. She couldn't give them away. Those parcels had become a blight, an albatross around her neck that was slowly strangling her life's blood. Yet there was no outlet, no channel from which she could escape. Nicole could only thrust forward.

#

"I don't want to see anymore damned court papers!" Nicole shrieked, frantically tearing at the documents that had just come in the mail and tossing the pieces into the garbage pail. Both her parents had died within the last year, her father just a month before, and the pain was still raw.

"Nic, you can't do that," David said patiently, taking out the torn pieces and taping them back together.

"Why?" she cried. "Daddy's dead. He died without ever seeing this resolved, and he begged me to sell the blasted parcels. I should have listened! It's a curse, David. Do you hear me? It's a curse that I was born with, and I am never going to be rid of it."

"Yes, you will. Don't lose your faith now."

"David, we're broke. We can't pay the lawyers, and we can't

re-mortgage our home anymore. Oh! I don't know why God just don't strike them down dead."

"Nicole, you're scaring the kids," David said gently, glancing in the direction of the kitchen table where four brown-haired heads bowed over their school books pretending not to listen to her outburst.

Immediately Nicole felt contrite. She was blessed with a sweet husband and loving children, but sometimes she was so consumed with the one dark cloud over her head that she failed to see the sunshine that surrounded her. None of them had ever known her without the dark cloud, yet they were her luminosity.

"Dear Lord," she said as knelt by her bed that night, "please forgive me for wishing my adversaries dead today. I didn't give them life, and I have no right to wish them death. Help me to renew my resolve to keep my heart clean from hatred, and thank you for the gift of my family."

The next day Nicole steeled herself to go through her father's files. David had packed away his clothes, but she'd wanted to sort through his papers herself. Now in the solitude of the quiet house, she sat cross legged on the floor with his cachet of papers beside her. Knowing she had to do this alone, David and the children had gone out for the afternoon.

She smiled tearfully at all the Christmas and birthday cards he'd saved. Every one of them was there, starting with the years when she could barely write up to the last one she'd given him the year before.

She sorted through a bunch of old receipts and utility bills. Then there was an array of pictures, and she lovingly held them, remembering the times when they had been taken. Toward the back end of the pile were pictures of her father in his younger years.

You were really handsome, Dad.

She frowned when a bunch of very old letters, postcards, and family portraits fell from between the pictures into her lap. She had never seen these before, and enthralled by their antiquated look, she picked them up. The envelopes were postmarked from France, and the dates on the letters and postcards were from the 1920s. The crisp, sinuous writing in English was signed by Marcel Dusant, her father's blood uncle. Memorized, she started to read.

Oh my God! It's all here! The entire family tree. All the names are written right here along with their photographs. Dad, why didn't you ever show me these? They're priceless, written in Marcel's own hand! I can't wait to show them to David!

#

"*What do you want from me?*" Nicole asked the man in her dreams, but he continued to run the knife over the scales of the large, yellow tailed fish. It lay between his open legs, which were bent at the knees. He was shoeless, sitting against the balk of a huge tree, his straw hat bent low, shading his eyes.

"*Didn't you hear me? I asked you what you wanted from me.*"

Not acknowledging her, he kept scaling the fish. Exasperated, she crouched in front of him. "*I've done everything I can do. I've fought with every resource available to me. The lawyers won't work anymore without money, so I'm done.*"

His hands stopped moving. Slowly he raised his head until she was looking into a pair of brilliant, green eyes. Dropping the knife, he raised his hands. She didn't know sign language, but she understood clearly when he signed, "*You are a Dusant. You have responsibility as a Dusant. You are not done. Go do what needs to be done.*"

"Mom, I had the weirdest dream last night," Nicole's daughter, Victoria, said as her mother placed the breakfast cereal on the table.

"Oh, what about?" Nicole replied, remembering her own dream.

"People wearing funny clothes were speaking to me."

"What did they say?"

"They told me you had a big job to do, but not to worry 'cause they're helping you."

"I had a dream last night too," her younger sister, Aimee, piped up. "A man showed me a list of names in an old-looking paper, and all our names were in it."

Oh God. Nicole groaned. *They're even stalking the girls' dreams.*

Their wraithlike visits always herald news, so it was no surprise later that day when Ellen buzzed her to announce the long-distance call. She picked up the receiver, expecting to hear a familiar voice.

"Madame Michaels, I am calling from the office of Attorney Leon Dupere. He wishes to speak with you. Please hold the line."

Nervously Nicole waited for her attorney to pick up the line.

"Aha, Nicole."

"Hello, Attorney Dupere."

"I have very good news. *La Cour de Cassation* has ruled in your favor for the second time. You've won again!"

Nicole closed her eyes and whispered a passionate prayer of thanks.

"Nicole, are you there?"

"Yes, yes, I am here. Does this mean that Denise Dusant cannot file another appeal?"

"I don't see how she can," Dupere replied. "You've won six times now in the local court, and twice now with *La Cour de Cassation*. If Denise wants to fight more, she should take it up with the court, certainly not with you. It's the court that keeps finding you in the right."

"I want to be relieved, but every time I-"

"No, this is the last time, Nicole. Denise Dusant has exhausted all her chances with the court. They will not allow her to file an appeal again."

"Thank you, Attorney Dupere. What is our next step?"

"We wait for the official court papers from France to arrive. I only know because the lawyer we hired in France to represent you called me as soon as he was notified. This is his second win for you, and of course he is elated. Um, Nicole?" Dupere cleared his throat. "I know this is a delicate subject, but he will want to be paid the second half of his fee now. Don't worry about me, I will continue to wait. However, we must pay him."

"I will get the check out to you tomorrow."

"Congratulations, Nicole. You have been a dauntless warrior all these years, and it's finished now."

"Not as dauntless as you believe, Attorney Dupere, but thank you for your faith in me. It has been a long battle for you too. God bless you."

It's finished now. The words echoed in Nicole's head as she disconnected the telephone line. She wanted with all her heart to believe them, yet she knew instinctively there was more to come.

Denise Dusant cursed when she received the news from her lawyer. She had lost her second appeal before the *Cour de Cassation*.

"The bitch has turned out to be a fighter," she muttered.

They had laughed all those years ago when Nicole had come to the grocery store and announced her plans to take back the parcels, but they had most assuredly underestimated her. She had not shriveled up in fear despite their best attempts to intimidate her.

Years ago Denise had hired a private investigator to delve into Nicole's personal affairs. She had wanted to learn about every iota of Nicole's life. She had been encouraged when the investigator had reported that Nicole was financially strapped. Surely she couldn't afford to continue to support the lawsuits relentlessly being filed against her. They, on the other hand, were wealthy. They could do this forever.

But somehow, Nicole had endured, and now Denise's lawyers were telling her that she had reached the end of her very long rope; that the court would not entertain another appeal. Worse yet, her cowardly neighbors were gaining courage because of Nicole. She was being sued left and right.

"Father must be turning over in his grave," Denise mumbled.

In a fit of anger, she knocked over the toaster. It fell with a loud clatter onto the floor, summoning Xavier from the bedroom.

"What the hell's happening in here?" he yelled.

"I'll tell you what's happening!" Denise screeched. "You're sitting your lazy ass in here while that bitch is taking my parcels. The damned court ruled in her favor again. You know how important those parcels were to my father. He asked you to protect them on his dying bed. Now do something to stop her!"

Denise gave Xavier a shove and stormed past him.

Xavier jammed his fist into the wall. He couldn't allow Nicole to gain the upper hand. Denise would be hell to live with. As it was, she was already a pain in the ass.

He opened the refrigerator, grabbed a can of beer, and popped the top. Leaning against the kitchen counter, he took a hefty swallow.

How the hell did I ever end up in the middle of this family's shit? He thought.

Admittedly, he was no saint. He was always attracted to trouble, and he had been attracted to Denise from the first day he stepped off the boat from the neighboring island of Anguilla. Her bright, red hair and mischievous spirit had captured him. Initially he had experienced uneasiness with her father, Jacques, over his race, but that was soon dispelled when Jacques realized he had gained a collaborator. Jacques had been a shrewd, old bastard, but he had entrusted Xavier with the task of keeping the parcels out of Nicole's hands. Xavier didn't care to understand all this blasted court business; that was Denise's job. In his mind though, he owned those parcels, and he had to do what was necessary to keep it that way.

Denise would never give him the credit he deserves, but he did have a plan to stop Nicole. It would involve the help of some key people, but first he would enjoy a bit more sardonic fun at Nicole's expense. Feeling better, he grinned and reached for his cell phone.

The stunningly beautiful vase of yellow roses was delivered to Nicole's office the following week. The unsigned, typewritten note simply said, "Thank you for our lovely, new home." It was an extravagant, full arrangement with at least thirty roses, and everyone in her office remarked on its beauty. Nicole made a mental note to call the flower shop to enquire about the sender, but her day was busy, and it slipped her mind.

When she walked into her office the following morning she was met with an awful stench. Everyone was holding their noses.

"The smell is coming from your office, Nicole," Ellen said. "We thought maybe a mouse might have died in there. We looked, but we found nothing."

Instantly Nicole knew. She went directly to the vase of roses. Pulling the stems out one by one, she found the culprit. Embedded in the thick bunch of stems was a decaying, black bird, its wings cruelly clipped off.

360 | T. Q. BERNIER

Below it, a typewritten note was tucked between the stems. Carefully, she extracted it.

"I am going to rip your frigging wings off once and for all."

"Oh Nicole, who would do this?" Ellen asked, visibly shaken.

"Call the flower shop; see what you can find out about the sender while I get rid of this." Nicole's voice was deadly calm.

Ellen was back in minutes, her face pale, "Nicole, they said the man who bought the roses paid in cash. He asked for a blank card, told them the roses were for a funeral, and that he would deliver them personally. Oh Nicole." Ellen wrung her hands in distress. "Who hates you that much?"

The dreaded phone call came the same afternoon. David answered on the first ring.

"Good Afternoon. I am calling from Attorney Leon Dupere's office. He would like to speak with Madame Michaels.

"My wife is at work. He can talk to me."

"Oh no, I am sorry. Attorney Dupere can only discuss the case with Madame Michaels. She is the bloodline. Please tell her to call him as soon as possible."

"Shit!" David swore as he hurriedly pressed the numbers of Nicole's cell phone.

There were seven cruise ships in the harbor, and Charlotte Amalie was teeming with cars and people. Nicole was caught in bumper-to-bumper traffic. She was returning to her office after attending a business meeting that had taken much longer than she had expected when her cell phone rang. She looked at the caller ID. It was David.

Nicole groaned. She had not called to tell him about the incident with the dead bird because she was determined not to let it rile her, but she had to admit, her nerves were rattled. David knew her so well. He would know immediately that something was wrong. She couldn't cope with his worries right now. She thought about letting the call go to voice mail, but what if something had happened to one of the kids and he needed her?

"Hello, David."

"Nicole the lawyer's office just called. After all these years, it still irritates the hell out of me that they won't give me any information because I am not the bloodline." David took a deep breath. "I don't think the news is good. You need to call them right away."

"Oh God, no, not again!" Nicole cried. "I am caught in heavy traffic on the waterfront."

"Then find a place to pull over and call them."

"That's easier said than done."

The truck in front of her moved forward, and she eased her foot off the brakes. Two young women dashed in front of her car into the busy thoroughfare inches from her bumper, causing her foot to automatically slam on the brakes again and adding to her already-frazzled nerves.

"Okay, David, I'll do my best."

Nicole switched off the cell phone and irritably threw it on the passenger seat. Tears threatening to overcome her, she flipped on her right indicator and fretfully waited her turn for the green arrow of the traffic light. Then she turned north and hooked a left westward. She pulled the car into a parking space near the Western Cemetery not far from where her grandfather, Francois, had been buried decades before. Placing her head on the steering wheel, she wept piteously. She was drained from the never-ending court cases, weary from constantly looking over her shoulders, and exhausted from trying to be brave.

She let her tears flow freely, emptying herself of the anguish, and then, refortified, she reached for her cell phone and pressed Attorney Dupere's number.

He answered the phone himself. "Nicole, I have bad news. A new case has been filed against you."

"I thought you said Denise couldn't bring any more cases against me."

"And I was right. She cannot."

"Then I don't understand."

"Denise cannot, so she convinced her cousins, Oswald and Olie Dusant, to do so."

"Roger Dusant's sons."

"Yes, When Jacques recorded the deed, he gave a third interest in the parcels to his father's business partner, Roger Dusant. Roger is now deceased, but his proposed one third interests were passed down to his sons, Oswald and Olie."

"Then how come Roger never joined Jacques and Denise in suing me?"

"I wondered about that myself, and I set out to find the answer." He paused. "You have Roger's wife, Solange, to thank for it. It appears that she was never in favor of their wrongdoings, and she dissuaded her husband from becoming involved in the lawsuits. His bowing to her wishes was double-edged though. Roger knew he had much to gain by quietly remaining in the background without ever spending a penny should Jacques and Denise succeed. Solange is now also deceased, so there is no good influence to sway her sons."

Dupere took a deep breath and then blurted, "Brace yourself. It gets worse, Nicole. They've brought criminal charges against you. This is a penal case."

"Meaning?"

"Meaning they're allegedly claiming you are a criminal. They have accused you of fraud. Basically they're saying you stole the parcels." Dupere paused. Sighing, he continued, "Nicole, you will have to stand before a judge and defend yourself, and that juncture will only be a prerequisite for the judge to determine if the charges against you have merit. Because it is a preliminary hearing, I will not be allowed in the courtroom with you. If the judge finds enough facts in your testimony and in the evidence your opponents present, the penal case will be duly filed, and the court will proceed with the fraud trial against you. That's why it will be crucial that you are prepared to handle yourself well.

"I have never stolen anything in my life." Unbidden, a loud sob escaped her.

"Nicole, this is just a move on their part to weaken and stall you. We're going to get through this."

"When does this case go before the judge?"

"I don't know. It could take up to a year."

"Another year of my life," she mumbled.

"I will go ahead and prepare the file, so we will be ready. Just know you will have to drop everything and come to St. Barth whenever the case is called. I would want you here at least a day before so I can prep you before you stand before the judge."

Dupere was silent for a moment. When he spoke again, his voice bore his sadness. "I have two more things I want to say to you. The first is that I am deeply sorry. I am an old man, and I have been a lawyer a very long time. In all my years of practice, I have never seen a case like yours. This is unprecedented. Secondly, it might be a small consolation for you to know that you are regarded as somewhat of a hero. Because of your gallantry, people have found the courage to stand up. Cases are being filed against Denise Dusant. Wrongs are being righted."

"I don't want to be anybody's hero, Attorney Dupere," Nicole replied. "I just want to finally live my life without this millstone."

Almost two years went by, and the penal preliminary hearing was delayed time and time again. Nicole recommitted her resolve not to be embittered. She forced herself to focus on the good things in her life, and there were so many, foremost of which was her expanding family. Two years had brought more grandchildren. Her present genealogy was pulsating with life, overshadowing the mantle of her forebears.

Each time the disquiet would rise within her, she reminded herself that it was beyond her scope. She had by no means capitulated. She had merely surrendered it to her God, and in so doing, she had received a measure of peace.

"Mom, don't forget to pack your swimsuit. The kids are going to want you to go on the water rides with them."

Nicole's son, Noah, pointed to the open suitcase on his mother's bed. He had come to pick up his five-year-old daughter, Allie, who was bouncing on her grandmother's bed, her two braids dancing up and down over her head with every bounce, her two missing front teeth making her grin all the more endearing.

"She already packed it, Daddy. See, it's right here." Allie pulled a blue bathing suit out of the suitcase and waved it in front of her father.

"Give me that," Nicole said, the grin on her own face matching the brilliance of her granddaughter's.

"You do know that our flight leaves at noon on Friday, right?" Noah asked, sitting on the side of the bed. "Dad told me you're planning on going to your office on Friday morning."

"Yep. That's right," Nicole replied, folding the bathing suit back into the suitcase. "Gotta go in to sign off on some files before I leave."

"Well, don't let them hold you up from getting to the airport on time."

"Not to worry. I wouldn't miss it for the world."

"Okay then. See you Friday. Come on, Allie, time to go home. We'll see Grandma and Grandpa on Friday when they go on the big plane with us."

"But I don't want to go home, Daddy. I want to stay here with Grandma." Allie stopped bouncing and folded her arms. Her pretty face transformed into a pout.

Nicole gave her son a knowing look and walked around to the other side of the bed. "Honey, the sooner you go home with your Daddy, the sooner Friday will come, and we will be on our way to Disneyworld."

"Can I sleep with you and Grandpa in your room? Just me, not the boys."

"You can sleep most nights, but we have to give your brothers a chance too, okay?"

"Just as long as I get more chances than them. Love you, Grandma." Allie gave her grandmother a big hug and took her father's hand.

"She's gonna hold you to that promise, Mom."

"Don't I know it." Nicole chuckled.

#

Nicole was teetering on a high precipice, and she knew she was in danger of falling, but she wasn't afraid. Even as the wind blew fiercely, threatening to topple her over into the abyss, she persevered, maintaining her stance on the jagged rocks.

She was so engrossed she wasn't aware of the woman standing beside her until she spoke.

"The rocks on which you stand signify your strength. The height is your faith."

Nicole turned and stared into a pair of beautiful, amber eyes. The woman's reddish-brown hair cascaded way past her slender waist and flowed melodiously around her face. Something in that face was familiar.

"Be ready, Nicole. Be ready."

"Ready for what?"

"You know."

CHAPTER 30

Nicole woke on Monday morning with a feeling of trepidation. She didn't want to hear anything about St. Barth now. She and David were accompanying their son and his family on a trip to Disneyworld on Friday.

"Maybe the dream means nothing," David told her as she poured his coffee. "You're probably just over anxious about the upcoming trip."

"I pray you're right, David, but everything inside me says differently."

She had barely stepped into her office when Ellen buzzed her. "Nicole, Attorney Leon Dupere is on the phone for you. Nicole, did you hear me? Shall I put him through?"

"Yes, yes please."

Nicole let the phone ring three times before she picked up the receiver. Attorney Dupere's excited voice bellowed in her ear, "Nicole, we just got the call. You will appear before the judge on Wednesday at eleven a.m."

"Wednesday, the day after tomorrow?"

"Yes, you need to make a reservation immediately. I would prefer you leave tonight, if possible."

"But that's insane! I have a full schedule, and I am leaving Friday on a trip with my grandchildren. No, I am not coming!"

"Nicole," Dupere said patiently, "I told you it would happen like this. You have to come. If you don't appear when you are summoned, you automatically forfeit your chance to defend yourself."

"Two years I've been waiting. Now they expect me to drop everything and come running. It's unfair!"

"I know. Don't worry about hotel reservations. I will make it for you, and I will see that you have an escort for protection."

"You didn't hear me when I said I have a trip planned for Friday? I am not coming." The anger dripped from Nicole's voice.

Disregarding her response, Dupere continued. "You will meet with the judge on Wednesday and then go straight to the airport to catch your flight. You will be back in St. Thomas by Thursday. You cannot ignore the judge's subpoena."

When Nicole hung up, she was stifling her emotions. She had a desk load of work that needed her attention. Trembling, she picked up the telephone and called David. Then putting the files back in her drawer, she locked it and reached for her purse. She needed to get to the airport to make reservations for the evening flight to St. Barth.

They flew out on Tuesday evening amid a thunderstorm because there was only one daily flight from St. Thomas to St. Barth, and the small plane was already booked for the Monday evening flight.

It was still raining when they arrived at the empty terminal in St. Barth. A stocky, muscular man resembling a wrestler and sporting a crew cut was sitting on the wooden bench against the wall. When he saw them, he stood up and came forward. Being leery of anyone they didn't know, David instinctively stepped in front of Nicole.

"Bonne nuit, Mr. et Mme. Michaels," he said in a thick, French accent. "I am Stephen. I have been sent by Attorney Leon Dupere to escort you."

"Do you have identification?" David asked.

"Oui," he said, reaching for his wallet.

David inspected the picture ID that identified him as a private detective and then nodded.

The man reached for their one piece of luggage and said, "Please follow me. For your protection, you are being housed at a private villa in St. Jean."

He drove the short distance to St. Jean and then detoured onto a dirt road off to the right side of the beach. The dark, bumpy path gave way to a paved road that led to a white structure replete with a wraparound gallery. A wooden swing suspended from the roof moved lazily in the breeze. The crickets sang loudly.

"The cupboards and the refrigerator have been stocked for your convenience," Stephen said when he opened the door and handed David the keys. "Attorney Dupere will come see you tomorrow morning. He does not advise that you make a show of your presence. Here's my number; please call me if you need anything."

When he left, Nicole dragged a heavy chair over to the door and jammed it against the doorknob. Giving David a weak smile, she said, "I am not taking any chances."

David found Nicole sitting on the gallery the next morning, a half-drank cup of tea on the small, white iron table besides her. Beyond the bounds of the gallery, the waves crashed and foamed against the sharp rocks, the repetitious, melodious sound and the smell of the sea spray permeating the morning air. He knew she had barely slept.

"The sea is so beautiful yet so formidable," she whispered as he took a seat on the opposite side of the table. She continued staring at the sea, lost in thought. Her voice was so soft when she finally spoke again that David leaned forward in the chair to hear her more clearly.

"You know, it's funny, the twists and turns of life and how just one event, one moment, can define the rest of your life. I had barely heard of this island until I was sixteen, and my grandfather dropped his bombshell on me. Now it's an ineradicable part of me. It is woven into the threads of my life, and regardless of what happens today, nothing will change that. The affinity I feel for it will never go away."

Knowing not what to say, but understanding Nicole's feelings, David continued to sit quietly beside her.

They were still sitting on the gallery when Attorney Dupere knocked on the door. The moment Nicole saw the look on his face she knew something was wrong.

"What is it?" she asked before he was even inside the room.

"Before you get upset, Nicole, please hear me out. Let's sit down."

When they were seated, he said calmly, "The judge cannot make it over from Guadeloupe today. He rescheduled your hearing for Thursday at two p.m."

"That's it. I am going home," she said, rising quickly from the sofa.

"Wait," David said, grabbing her arm. "Attorney Dupere asked you to hear him out."

"David, I am going to be on that plane Friday with my grandchildren. If I stay here, we will miss it. That's not going to happen!"

"Nicole," Dupere pleaded, "I've arranged with a private plane to fly you to St. Thomas at seven thirty on Friday morning. The flight is only forty minutes. You will have time to catch your other flight at noon. I've done all this because it is vital that you appear before the judge. You cannot afford to mess this up!"

"He's right, Nicole. We have no choice but to stay."

"And endure another day and night in anxiety," she groaned, sitting back down on the sofa.

"I've asked Stephan to hang around. Enjoy the beach, but don't stray too far. We don't want to alert Denise and Xavier or any of their cronies of your presence."

Wednesday stretched out long and excruciatingly, and the night bore on in darkness until dawn. Nicole tried to relax and enjoy the exquisite beauty of her surroundings, but try as she might, it eluded her. She knew she should sleep. She needed to be at her best tomorrow, yet she watched every hour tick by. The added day and night of waiting taxed her, and she was cognizant of her consent to its torment.

She was up and dressed early on Thursday morning. The smell of strong coffee permeated the villa.

"You know it's only seven o'clock, right?" David asked when he joined her in the kitchen.

"I can tell time, David," she replied, pouring him a cup of coffee.

"Why are you dressed so early?"

"Because we're going into Gustavia. I have already called Stephan. He will pick us up at nine o'clock. I haven't seen Nanette in decades, and I want to personally thank her for all she did to help us in the early years. It's only right."

"But Attorney Dupere doesn't want us to show ourselves."

"I am done hiding."

When Nicole looked at him, David saw the tenacity in her eyes, and he knew better than to argue.

Like a beautiful butterfly emerging from its cocoon, St. Barth had changed drastically from Nicole's first visit more than thirty years before. In her intermittent trips through the years, she had seen its evolution in progress. Now the butterfly was in full bloom. Million-dollars yachts adorned Gustavia's once-tranquil waters. Villas that looked more like mansions dotted the hills. The economy was flourishing. It had become a playground for the rich and famous, and several movie stars boasted owning homes in the exquisite "little Paris of the Caribbean."

Nicole and David blended in among the throngs of people on the narrow streets of Gustavia en route to see Nanette, the coolness of the air conditioned stores intermingling with the tropical heat against their skin as people jutted in and out the doors. Nicole couldn't help but imagine what her ancestors would think of this modern-day St. Barth. She thought of her great-great-grandfather, Ivan. He had, in truth, been a man of foresight. He had looked past its parched and desolate state and had seen the diamond beneath, for indeed there had been copious potential.

They left the busy front streets of Gustavia and started up an incline to the upper roads. They passed a huge avocado tree on the left, its branches spreading out, casting shadows on the street. A newly built house with a large gallery sat on the opposite side. Other than the two of them, the street was void of people. Ever-vigilant, David walked closely beside Nicole.

At the top of the street they turned left, passing several well-kept houses and businesses. Midway down the street, they came upon the sprawling, bright-yellow house with its white lattice trimmings. There was an air conditioned grocery store next door and an open-air bar and restaurant directly across the street. Bougainvilleas sporting deep, red flowers lined the paved walkway. A neat, white sign trimmed in yellow announced in dainty black cursive *Clara's Place*. Beneath it was a similar sign proclaiming in French and English: *Chambres Disponibles--Rooms for Rent*.

Nicole and David climbed the few steps into the gallery where mahogany rocking chairs swayed in the soft breeze. They clanged the brass bell.

"Just one minute. I'll be right with you," a musical lilt answered pleasantly from inside.

They watched through the screen door as Nanette appeared, her face registering uncertainty and then breaking out into a welcoming smile. Her short dark hair was now entirely silver, and her face reflected the almost-twenty years since Nicole had last seen her, but sincerity still gleamed brightly in her eyes.

"Oh Mon Dieu! Nicole, David!" she said, embracing them and kissing them on each cheek. "I am so very happy to see you. Please come inside."

"Nicole, keep your answers short. Don't volunteer information," Dupere advised her as he parted with her in front of the massive fort. "I cannot go up there with you, but I will be waiting here for you. You're going to do just fine."

Nicole nodded and turned to the gendarme standing sentry at the gate. He opened it and allowed David to escort her up the hill to the formidable stone structure that was once a lookout fort for invaders from the sea. Four more gendarmes stood at the top of the hill watching their progress. To Nicole they resembled giant hawks ready to pounce on her, and she silently prayed, *Dear God, stay with me. Let me not cry or lose my temper.*

When they crested the hill, the gendarme in the middle stepped forward. "Madame Dusant Michaels, please come with me. Monsieur, you will have to wait here."

Nicole followed the gendarme into the fort and down a narrow corridor to a windowless room. There was a big, mahogany desk in the middle of the room. A stout, middle-aged man, his face expressionless, sat behind it. A woman sat in the corner in front of a computer, and another woman sat in one of the two chairs situated in front of the desk.

"Bonjour, Madame Dusant Michaels, I am Magistrate Beaumont. This is Madame Gereaus. She will serve as your interpreter should you need one." He turned to the gendarme who was standing in front of the closed door. "Please swear in Madame Dusant Michaels."

When Nicole finished taking the oath, the judge asked bluntly, "Are you aware that your opponents have charged you with fraud?"

"Yes."

"Do you know the seriousness of the charge?"

"Yes."

"How do you plead?"

"Not guilty."

For a while the judge wordlessly studied her, and Nicole felt like a fly under a microscope, but she maintained her composure. Then he said, "You are not on trial today, Madame Dusant Michaels, but I want to question you to determine if the alleged charges against you have merit. I do not want to waste the court's valuable time unnecessarily. Now, please take a seat."

Nicole endured two hours of questioning, often repeating answers to the same questions asked in different formats meant to trap her. She remained poised even when the questions became harsher.

Finally the judge leaned forward on his elbows. He was close enough that Nicole could see every line on his face, which remained unreadable.

"Madame, you have maintained your answers in every question that I have asked. Still, I am not entirely convinced. You are a second-generation American. You have lived your entire life as an American. What makes you so confident that these parcels belong to your great-grandfather, Jonah Dusant?"

"Your Honor, respectfully I bring to your attention that the honorable court of which you are a member has found me in the right eight times. That alone is a testament. My opponents have exhausted the court's appeal process, so now their new claim is that I am a fraud. They allege that I am not a Dusant heir. You've asked me for further proof of my lineage. I believe I have that. May I please look inside my purse?"

The judge looked at Nicole strangely but nodded his consent.

She reached into her purse and retrieved two of Marcel Dusant's postcards, which, at the last moment before leaving home in St. Thomas, she'd slipped into her bag.

Holding the postcards in her hands, she looked at the judge. "These were written to my father from his uncle, Marcel Dusant, Jonah Dusant's son. They are postmarked from France and dated from the 1920s. On one side, there are portraits of the family, and on the other side, written in English, are the names of the family members and their circumstances as it was at that time in the 1920s. My great-uncle wrote to my father regularly back then. I have more letters, pictures, and postcards at home."

She stood and handed the judge the postcards. He was silent as he studied and read them. Then he nodded affirmatively, signaling for the gendarme to make copies. He said nothing while they waited, but from the softening of his face, Nicole could see she had made an impact.

When the gendarme returned, the judge stood. Giving the originals back to Nicole, he said, "We are finished. I will make my decision and relay it to your attorney. Have a good evening, Madame Dusant Michaels."

On wobbly legs Nicole stood. She thanked him for his time and quietly left the room. She joined David outside, and the gendarme escorted them to the bottom of the hill.

When they cleared the iron gates, Nicole turned to David. "Now I know why I found Marcel's correspondences when I did. It's mind boggling, but way before my existence, back in the 1920s, my great-uncle was writing letters to my father that God knew I would need to clear my name many decades later. David, I really feel those postcards were the crux of what I needed today."

As they walked the short distance to meet Attorney Dupere, Nicole felt a profound amity overcome her. She had done what she had set out to do, and she had done it exceedingly well. It was no longer in her hands, and again she released the burden of it. She was glad now that she had come.

"So what happens now?" David asked Attorney Dupere.

"We wait, again. These things take time and test your mettle."

Nicole laughed. "Well I must have strong mettle, because mine has been tested nine times."

When Nicole left St. Barth that Friday morning, she'd felt a deep solace. She was certain she had done well, and that she would soon receive the affirmation. As a year rolled by without any news from the court, she began to doubt herself. Had she answered the questions well enough? Had she portrayed enough confidence in herself and in her bloodline?

Even her dreams were strangely void of her ancestors, and the hollowness echoed in the empty chambers of her slumber. She had wanted them gone for so long, and now ironically she longed for them to offer her some vestige of hope, a sign to herald that something was happening.

#

"Hey, Mom." Aimee's voice sounded light and cheerful, but Nicole knew her youngest daughter well enough to decipher right away that she had something on her mind.

"Hey, you, what's up?"

"I dreamt about them last night. You remember that one dream I used to have a lot, where this guy would show me an old document with our names on it? Well, he was back in full swing last night, he and a few of the others. They harassed me half the night."

Nicole quietly listened.

"Mom? Are you there?"

"Yes, your sister called just a little before you did. She dreamt about them too."

"Well then, something is happening, Mom."

"Strange, though, that they haven't come to me."

"Sounds like you miss them."

"Yeah, I think I do."

The women were chattering too animatedly. They were speaking to each other, their hands gesticulating as rapidly as their mouths, but Nicole knew what they were discussing was noteworthy to her.

"*What is it?*" She asked, but they continued to prattle on, seemingly ignoring her.

"*Hey, I know you can hear me.*"

Abruptly the chattering stopped. Three pairs of eyes turned their gazes on her. There was an impish glint in their smiles. She knew them all. They had inhabited the realms of her dreams many times before.

As if on cue, they stepped aside to reveal a slim, well-built man. In his hand he held a scroll. As he neared Nicole, he unrolled it. The parchment was yellow with age.

His gaze was tender as he looked at her, and then he pointed to the scroll.

"*See, we are all here.*"

Nicole peered at the long list of names as he held the document up in front of her. There were two columns. At the end of the second column were her own name and the names of her children and grandchildren. With bewilderment, she looked at the man again.

He re-rolled the scroll and then handed it to her.

"*Take it, it's yours.*"

Then suddenly, they were gone.

When the call came this time, Nicole was ready. She already knew the answer.

"Nicole, are you sitting down?"

"Yes, Attorney Dupere, I am. You can go ahead and tell me congratulations."

He laughed heartily. "I will be calling you in the next couple of weeks to sign the official deed. Will I have any problem convincing you to come to St. Barth?" he teased.

"Just call. I will be there."

"I am looking forward to it."

"Attorney Dupere?"

"Yes, Nicole?"

"Words are not adequate, but thank you for not giving up on me."

The day Nicole Dusant Michaels signed the deed, rightfully claiming her inheritance was a day indelibly imprinted in her life. The mantle at last was rested.

Like molten iron, the journey had reshaped her, but for the better. She now knew the full potency of her faith and acumen. She was an American Frenchwoman, born from the loins of resilient men and women and from an indomitable bloodline.

A tiny tear slipped from the corner of her right eye, and with the knuckle of her index finger, she discreetly brushed it away. It was not a day for tears; she had shed enough of them during the course of years. She finished signing her name on the last document, but before handing the wad of papers back to Attorney Dupere, she ran her fingers reflectively over the middle word of her signature. Dusant. It was the quintessence of her being. Then poignantly she smiled and reached across the huge mahogany desk to hand them over.

"Nicole, you are owed retributions for eight cases, and much more for the alleged criminal one. We will initiate court proceedings immediately to collect on all nine cases."

"No, Attorney Dupere, we will not."

Dupere removed his glasses and peered intently at Nicole, his brown eyes quizzical.

"What are you saying? These people put you through hell. It's a matter of principal. They need to be taught a lesson."

The look on Nicole's face was a poignant mixture of finality and quietude. "In pursuing charges against them to collect on my retributions, I will be attaching them to me again, and I don't want any further attachment. This family feud has gone on long enough, and it's going to stop here, today, with me. I will not permit it to be passed down to another generation of Dusants."

"Nicole, you are making a terrible mistake."

"No I am not." There was a profound peace reflected in her voice. "I am finally free."

Smiling, she wiped the tears that quietly slipped from her eyes as the faces she knew so well from her dreams flashed before her. With emphasis, she said again, "We're finally free."

EPILOGUE

"Madame, you've been sitting in the grass here for more than an hour. Are you okay?"

Nicole looked up at the grave keeper. His heavily lined face looked down at her with concern. His clothes were wrinkled, and he looked fatigued. There was a flat, glass bottle protruding from his pocket.

Too many hours spent among the dead, she thought.

"Yes, I am fine, thank you. I will be leaving in just a bit."

"C'est bien, don't get too many Americans in here."

"How did you know I am American?"

He lifted his hat and scratched his sweaty head. "You had me puzzled for a while. You look French, but you have a distinct American way about you. Well ... I didn't mean to intrude. Take your time. Au revoir."

Nicole dusted her hands from the weeds she'd plucked around the grave. *That's me, all right, an American woman who is proud of her French, Caribbean heritage.* She lovingly ran her fingers once more over Catherine's name on the tombstone.

So, as I was saying, thank you, Catherine, for your steadfastness in insisting that my grandfather, Francois, know about his family despite the fact that he lived oceans away from you in St. Thomas. Thank you for writing to my grandmother, Olivia, and for passing that mantle to your son, Marcel. He wrote to my father for years, and those correspondences, written so long ago, fulfilled your mission of keeping your bloodline connected. I am leaving now. I am going back to my life in America, a life that's so much more gratifying because of what you and all the others have taught me about myself. I am honored that your blood courses through my veins, and I am privileged to be your great-granddaughter.

About the Author

T. Q. Bernier worked as a mortgage originator for one of the largest banks in the British and United States Virgin Islands (USVI) before she retired to pursue her writing career full-time. A native of St. Thomas, USVI, she and her three children currently live in Cary, North Carolina, with her husband, James.